Praise for Yaroslaw's Treasure

"Think Hollywood action-adventure film *Romancing the Stone*, with a dash of a young 'Indiana Jones' thrown in. Except what takes *Yaroslaw's Treasure* beyond the action, lightness, and romance into greater depths are the political issues it raises. It makes sense of them by staging a living, historical context for the modern-day contentions.

"Disputed origins and independence of Ukraine entwine with actions of the empire-addicted, KGB-controlled Russia to create a maze through which Yaroslaw quests for the treasure, a voyage as mysterious and dangerous as the deep caves of the mediaeval Ukrainian kingdom of Kyivan Rus' into which we are led.

"This spectacular expedition tumbles us into the depths of those caves. We encounter Kyiv's heroic, but realistically and humor-ously rendered, defenders during the Mongol destruction of the city in 1240. We emerge at the dawning of the Orange Revolution 764 years later, when the heroes of the twenty-first century sup-plant those of the thirteenth. From beginning to end, a journey to treasure!"

MYROSLAVA OLEKSIUK, film-maker, editor of *ePOSHTA*,
Independent Ukrainian Internet News Magazine

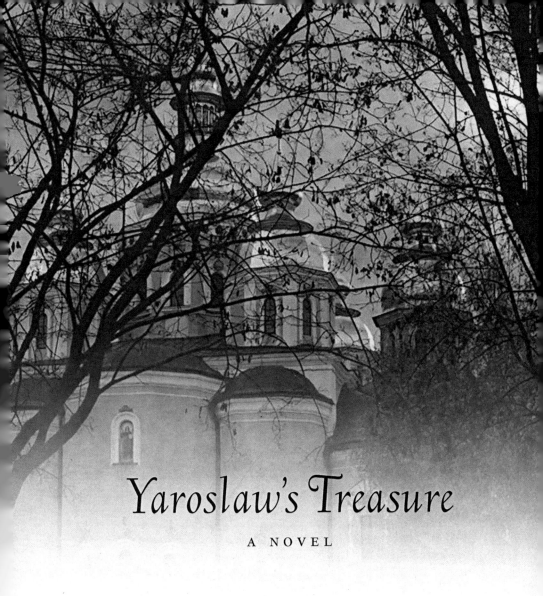

Yaroslaw's Treasure

A NOVEL

Myroslav Petriw

Blue Butterfly Books
THINK FREE, BE FREE

Blue Butterfly Book Publishing Inc.
2583 Lakeshore Boulevard West, Toronto, Ontario, Canada M8V 1G3
Tel 416-255-3930   Fax 416-252-8291   www.bluebutterflybooks.ca

Complete ordering information for Blue Butterfly titles is available at:
www.bluebutterflybooks.ca

First edition, soft cover: 2009

LIBRARY AND ARCHIVES CANADA CATALOGUING IN PUBLICATION

Petriw, Myroslav, 1950–
Yaroslaw's treasure : a novel / Myroslav Petriw.

ISBN 978-0-9784982-7-6

1. Ukraine—History—Orange Revolution, 2004—Fiction. I. Title.

PS8631.E863Y37 2009   C813'.6   C2009-901424-6

Book design and maps by Gary Long / Fox Meadow Creations
Front cover image concept by Gary Long and Myroslav Petriw
Title page photo—Mykhailivsky Monastery, Kyiv—by Myroslav Petriw

Text set in Minion

Printed and bound in Canada by Transcontinental-Métrolitho

The text paper in this book, Rolland Enviro 100 from Cascades, is EcoLogo™
and Forest Stewardship Council certified. It contains 100 per cent post-
consumer recycled fibre, was processed chlorine free, and was manufactured
using energy from biogas recovered from a municipal landfill site.

No government grants were sought nor any public subsidies
received for publication of this book. Blue Butterfly Books thanks
book buyers for their support in the marketplace.

To my wife, Luba…
and our sons,
Yaroslaw, Mark, and Adrian

Note to readers

The meaning of most Ukrainian and other non-English words used in this book are either explained in the narrative or are evident from the context. For additional background on many of these terms, please consult the Glossary which follows the main text.

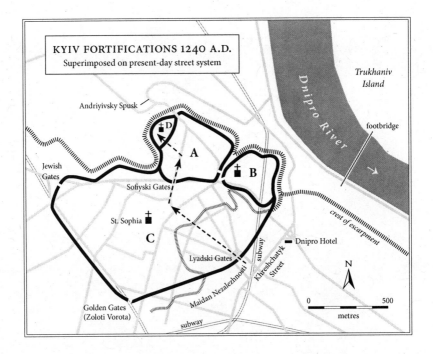

KYIV FORTIFICATIONS 1240 A.D.
Superimposed on present-day street system

Andriyivsky Spusk

Trukhaniv
Island

Dnipro River

footbridge

Jewish
Gates

Sofiyski Gates

St. Sophia

Lyadski Gates

Dnipro Hotel

crest of escarpment

Khreshchatyk Street

Maidan Nezalezhnosti

subway

Golden Gates
(Zoloti Vorota)

subway

N

0   500
metres

A **City of Volodymyr:** Old city walls that formed the citadel or dytynets in 1240.

B **City of Izyaslaw-Svyatopolk:** Walls around the Mykhailivsky Monastery. The southern portion of this area was the sector in which Ratibor's cohort was stationed.

C **City of Yaroslaw:** Newer walls surrounding the growing city, built by Yaroslaw the Wise in the early 11th century.

D **Desyatynna Church (Church of the Tithes):** Historic location of the last stand of Kyiv's defenders on December 6, 1240. Its collapse ended the battle after the 74-day siege of Kyiv.

Lyadski Gates: Location of the breach of the defences through which the Mongols broke on December 5, 1240, occupying much of the outer walls of the City of Yaroslaw that night. Today this area is the location of the Maidan Nezalezhnosti (Independence Square).

Sofiyski Gates to the citadel or dytynets through which the Mongols broke on the morning of December 6, 1240.

→ Arrows indicate the path of the Mongol breakthrough and advance through the fortifications.

Prologue

KYIV, UKRAINE

DECEMBER, 1240 A.D.

AN UNEARTHLY THUNDERCLAP and a roar like he had never heard before made Ratibor swirl about. The air itself had slammed him like an enemy shield in combat. What he now saw was beyond comprehension. The tower that had stood over the city gates, the gates themselves, the very soil of the earthenworks, and hundreds of boulders that had been bracing the gates, were lifting into the air in a cloud of smoke and fire. Ratibor saw the face of Perun, the Thunder God of old, in that fire and smoke. Staggering back, he tripped over the stoop of some building, falling through its shattered façade, landing under the protection of a snow-covered roof.

What happened next was no less diabolical. All that had flown upwards began raining down. First came the boulders, falling like giant hail among the hundred prostate figures that littered his field of view. Then came a rain of rocks, earth, logs, lumber, and men. This was followed by a shower of bloody body parts, rent shields, armour, and dirt. When such larger parts stopped falling, all he could hear was a steady hiss, as of falling rain, as torn flakes of everything, along with dirt, more dirt, and dust fell to earth. A thick cloud hovered where Kyiv's southern Lyadski Gates once stood.

For a moment, terror and incomprehension paralyzed him. But a deeply rooted sense of duty, that of a *voyevoda,* or warrior leader, overcame this paralysis. It was not courage. It was an alloy of desperation and duty. He was alive; others were dead.

"If not I, then who?" Ratibor asked himself.

He stood up and discarded the tattered remains of the fur overcoat from his chain mail hauberk. He retrieved his shield and walked directly towards the middle of the cloud of dust. He unsheathed his two-edged sword from its scabbard. An old *topir*, the Rus' battle-axe that was long out of fashion, hung behind him from his belt. As he approached, he saw that the tower of the Lyadski Gates had been converted into a pile of rubble, criss-crossed with splintered logs and lumber. It still formed a formidable obstacle to the enemy. The advantage would fall to whoever occupied this high ground first.

The former capital of the once-mighty Rus' empire had been under siege for ten weeks. The Mongols had attacked Kyiv in the early fall, just as the last of the harvest was being gathered. They arrived on the east bank of the Dnipro, covering the steppe with tents and campfires from horizon to horizon. Kyiv was the largest fortified city that Batu Khan, the leader of the Mongol Horde, had yet attempted to take. His force numbered some 200,000 men. The Khan would not countenance failure.

Ratibor's cohort was part of a force of 8,000, commanded by Tysiac'kiy Dmytro, that had been sent to the defence of Kyiv by Prince Danylo of Halych. Ratibor had come from the city of Terebovl with some 200 men. Ironically, fifty of these were *otroks*—lads too young to grow facial hair, mere apprentices of the warrior's art. The sprawling walled city of Kyiv fielded 12,000 armed men by his calculation. The peasants who had taken refuge here added some 5,000 inexperienced and poorly armed defenders. The result seemed foreordained. But Ratibor was an old hand at this bloody art. He had splintered his lance on the Liakh, the Uhr, and the Saxon. He had fought brother against brother, Rus' against Rus', whenever princelings vied for power.

The dust was settling, allowing Ratibor to see before him the sea-tide of advancing Mongol-Tatar warriors. Their cries of "Urra! Urra!" were as deafening as the thunderclap. Ratibor gained the top of the tangled barricade and raised his sword high. The rays of the setting sun lit both sword and helm with the colour of fire.

"Slava!" he shouted back.

Ratibor dared not look back to see if any survivors had followed in his steps. He examined his position. The rubble field before him was steep. The enemy would have to climb with both hands, leaving none for a weapon. If Perun was demanding sacrifice, then wagon-loads of severed limbs should be a fine offering.

Spears flew past him in poorly aimed flight. These were simply being thrown away, as the enemy could not climb while carrying them. Soon hands began grasping the splintered lumber before him. Ratibor's sword slashed into action. This was not fighting; it was lumberman's work. A dozen desperately thrown daggers bounced harmlessly off his shield and hauberk. Since the breach in the defences was as wide as thirty men, he fully expected to be outflanked. And soon there was the clang of sword on sword. But Ratibor easily turned every advantage in the height of his position into swift victory. Only now did he notice that he no longer fought alone. His flanks were well covered by Rus' warriors.

A roar of "Slava!" from behind assured him that reinforcements in the thousands would soon back him. But before him, the battlefield was slowly changing. The dead and the wounded were filling gaps and low ground while bridging obstacles in the rubble. Fresh enemy fighters now stood on higher ground. Having lost the advantage of height, Ratibor was meeting his opponents face to face. Decades of experience were paying off, but he knew he would tire. He knew this line on the barricades would turn into a great meat grinder—like a butcher extruding meat into a sausage casing. The most cruel of the two armies would be the one to prevail.

The enemy held their dead and wounded as a shield of flesh and simply pushed their way forward. By their dress and armour, Ratibor recognized the dead as Meria and Ves tribesmen of the Ryazan-Volodymyr principalities taken by the Mongols some three years earlier. Whether they were volunteers or slave-soldiers he could not know, but they were being cruelly used to break through the Rus' defence.

And so it finally happened to Ratibor. Undefeated in combat, Ratibor was finally knocked off his feet by a dead Meria tribesman pushed by dozens of Mongols. Ratibor had been on the left flank, so he rolled down the rubble pile on its east side. Bruised and exhausted, he could not move. He lay among a pile of dead Rus' warriors. His eyes were closed in pain. He did not know how long he lay there.

"Here is your helmet, *Pane Sotnyk*." It was the voice of a young *otrok*, addressing him as Lord Centurion.

"Is that you? So you're alive, Vsevolod?" mumbled Ratibor.

"Never you mind," said Vsevolod. "You have stopped the Mongols."

Ratibor looked around as he stood up, leaning on his *topir*. "I have not. The line is now a horseshoe shape. We have lost the high ground."

A flurry of Rus' arrows tore into the Mongol ranks. A storm of

Mongol arrows replied as the two forces began separating, running for cover.

"The Mongols have taken the wall," Ratibor said as they scurried for shelter under remnants of shattered buildings on the left flank.

"They have not!" protested young Vsevolod. "We will hold the wall on our sector!"

"Where is Vyshata?"

"He brought the whole cohort here to fight, *Pane Sotnyk*. Only the *otroks* are left behind."

"My God! The Mongols will move along the wall next. Our young *otroks* are all that will stand in their way. Follow me! Stay under the roofs. We must get back to our own sector."

The Rus' were fleeing towards the *dytynets,* the citadel known as the City of Volodymyr. Behind Ratibor, passage from the battlefield was blocked by accurate archery.

"Vyshata and our cohort are cut off from us," said Ratibor. "They will be ordered to fall back to the *dytynets*—if any are still alive. We are on our own."

The sun had set and it was only the patches of untrampled snow that provided reflected light to navigate by. But the dark of night also blunted the aim of enemy arrows. On their way they met one other Rus' warrior. A fresh wound scarred his face from the corner of his eye to his chin. His upper lip was peeled back, revealing shattered teeth and bone. He did not speak, and silently joined the pair. Avoiding arrows, they flitted from post to wall through a thicket of shattered wooden buildings. They finally reached the scriptorium building that had served as their quarters for the last months.

"Holy Mother of God!" screamed the monk, Nestor, when he saw Ratibor. He stood in the doorway holding a cross before him as if to repel a vampire.

"It is I," Ratibor said, then realized that he was totally covered in blood and looked more like demon than man. "Have you never seen the blood of battle before?"

Looking like a blood-spattered devil himself, Vsevolod announced to the gathering *otroks*, "I have brought our *Sotnyk* back. All will be well."

A dozen *otroks* came running down the ladder from the battlements to greet their commander.

"St. Nicholas will come early tonight," said Ratibor. "If you boys could open that crate that is standing by the wall, you will find new bows. I had ordered them from our craftsmen."

Ratibor had barely finished before some fifty boys ran to the far wall of the scriptorium.

"And there are quivers in the sack on the second floor by the big stone," added Ratibor. "But keep quiet, the enemy does not sleep yet."

The *otroks* received new, scaled-down bows to fit the thousands of Mongol arrows that they had been collecting. The quivers, too, were sized for those shorter arrows.

"*Panove*," Ratibor addressed the boys, "take all the arrows you can carry and climb to the battlement. Vsevolod, you are their leader. Use all that I have taught you about formations. I will join you soon."

When the boys were gone, Ratibor called for his *dzhura*, Kyrylo. The boy brought a tub of water and a towel, then offered cold roasted pork on a dagger to both Ratibor and the scarred stranger. The scar-faced warrior, clearly in great pain, refused all food.

Nestor, the monk, frowned at the commander's menu. "*Pane Sotnyk*, those boys can get killed!"

"Look here, dear Nestor," said Ratibor, scrubbing dried blood off his face and hands, "do you see that city there? Tomorrow, it will be burning. Tomorrow, women and infants, children and soldiers, Christians and Jews, will be dying together. And, living or dead, everyone will look as I look right now, covered in gore. That fate won't escape any of us. I merely gave those boys a chance for glory."

Ratibor wiped his face with the wash towel. He was beginning to look human again. He hungrily attacked his meal.

"Then I must finally tell you my secret," said Nestor.

"I almost forgot your promise, but I hold you to it."

"Below this building is an entrance to a cave. It is that cave that is the actual Great Library of Yaroslaw the Wise. Only I and one other monk know of its entrance. We bring books up for copying in the scriptorium, and take our scribes' best work down for safekeeping. Today, we write up here where the light is better. But I'm told the earliest chroniclers actually wrote day and night in the cave."

Ratibor stopped chewing on his meaty bone. "And so then, what is the Pysaniy Kamin, the Written Rock that stands above us?"

"It is there to seal the entrance to the Great Library. This is how we were to protect the wisdom of the centuries if the city ever fell or was put to the torch."

"And how many times was it employed?"

"Never successfully," said Nestor. "In the year 6677 by the chroniclers' count, when Mstyslaw, son of Andriy Boholubskiy of Suzdal, razed this city, the ihumen did not have the strength to move the wedges that hold the rock. Many books were lost but it was God's will that the fires did not burn through the floor."

"And you think that you have the strength?"

"With God's will."

"With rope," said Ratibor. He turned to where his page was drawing a cup of mead for his master. "Kyrylo, find me a goodly length of strong rope." He took the offering of strong drink. "Mind the arrows if you go outside."

"I know where such materials are stored, *Pane Sotnyk*," replied the young *dzhura* as he scurried away.

"One more question, my dear monk," continued Ratibor. "When the great rock drops, do you intend to be above it or below?"

"I do think, above," said Nestor, feigning courage. "Death would be swifter."

"So, there is no passage out of the Great Library except for the one under our floor?"

"There is also a great door in the Library," said Nestor slowly. "It bars entry of unclean spirits and demons. It must never be opened."

Ratibor downed the last of the contents of the cup as he mused aloud, "I have seen the great demon. Nought could surpass what I witnessed today."

"Ratibor!" cried Vsevolod from above. "They come!"

Ratibor stood to arm himself. "I thank the unclean devils for allowing me to sup before battle," he said; then, raising his voice so that Vsevolod could hear on the battlement above, he called, "Bid them prepare, for I go on them!"

Ratibor observed that Vsevolod had prepared his formation cleverly. Here, where the newer battlements of the City of Yaroslaw met those of the older City of Izyaslaw-Svyatopolk, they formed an acute "V." Vsevolod had placed archers in three rows of four facing along the Yaroslaw wall as it sloped down towards the now missing Lyadski Gates. Ten paces behind these, he stationed twelve more in the same manner. On the old battlements of the City of Izyaslaw-Svyatopolk, he placed two rows of twelve archers behind the parapets, facing across to the new battlements which were lower and thus fully exposed.

The Mongols had been facing tough resistance from defenders on the wall, who had fought to the last man. But now, in the dark, they were moving quickly along the battlement in massed formation like a black tide towards Ratibor's sector.

"Vsevolod," said Ratibor, "the enemy is well within range."

"Ready!" commanded the leader of the *otroks.*

"Row one shoot! ... Down!" began Vsevolod.

"Row two shoot! ... Down!"

"Row three shoot! ... All stand!"

"Row one shoot! ... Down!"

"Row two shoot! ... Down!"

This process had deadly effect. By the time each archer had shot but twice, the young *otroks* had killed and wounded as many as Ratibor had at the Lyadski Gates. Now the archers on the old battlements began shooting into the rear of the Mongol formation, creating an obstacle of dead and wounded. Vsevolod ordered the second group of twelve archers to replace the first. This gave the first group time to rest and refill their quivers. The mass of Mongol-Tatars had stopped advancing, and a half dozen ran back in panicked retreat. To Ratibor's amazement, these few were cut down by their own rearguard. The cruelty of Mongol tactics was beyond his comprehension.

"This battle is over," announced Ratibor. "You have covered yourself in glory. Now I expect they will bring up their own archers. Move to the ladders. I want the rear group of twelve down and into the scriptorium now. If they shoot arrows, I will order the rest of you down."

A hundred arrows whistled through the sky towards Ratibor's sector.

"Down the ladders now!" ordered Ratibor. He used his shield to cover the *otroks'* retreat.

"What now?" asked Vsevolod.

"They are disengaging for the night. We hold the high ground and it is dark—so their shots aren't effective."

"So what do we do?"

"Go mind the boys below. Bid them sleep. But station a half dozen *otroks* on the old wall as sentries."

The Mongols ignored Ratibor's isolated pocket of defenders. They too were resting and preparing for the next day's assault. Several hundred Mongols were pressed to the job of clearing a mountain of bodies and smoothing the path through the gap where the Lyadski Gates once stood. The ground had to be level to be able to bring the *porok* trebuchet catapults inside the outer walls of Kyiv.

Ratibor woke to a sound like thunder. He climbed up a ladder to the old battlements. He faced the sun as it rose from behind the snow-covered steppes on the left bank of the Dnipro River. Its light glinted on the white prairie and outlined Kyiv's ramparts in gold. Ratibor doffed his pointed helmet, and slipped off the leather hood that shielded his head and neck from the savage cold. The scalp-lock on his clean-shaven head whipped in the wind, as did the drooping tips of his bushy moustache. Both were snowy-white, except for the dark bit at the tip of the *oseledet*s scalp-lock, serving to remind Ratibor of long-faded youth. He wore these in the forgotten style of Rus' war-riors of old, harkening back to the days of Sviatoslaw the Conqueror. A gust blew frigid crystals off the wooden battlements. Eyes closed to the sting of sun and wind, Ratibor silently asked the Sun God, Dazhboh, for his blessing. As it was for many others in his cohort, the worship of the dead foreign gods of Christianity was only for show. In times of real need, they turned to the gods of old.

The sound of thunder had come from the Zoloti Vorota behind him. There was fire and smoke by the Golden Gate.

"What was that?" asked Vsevolod, shaking from more than just the cold. He was one of those on sentry duty.

"That's the demonic thunder that they used to make the Lyadski Gates fly."

"I count four *poroks* inside the outer wall," Vsevolod said matter-of-factly, trying his best to mask the terror that the sight before him created.

"They are closer to the walls of the City of Volodymyr than they need to be," said Ratibor. "They are there to draw the last of Rus' arrows."

The noise of a hundred thousand Mongol-Tatars shouting "Urra!" thundered and echoed between the walls of the city. The area between the outer wall and the *dytynets* was filling with a hundred thousand men. The *poroks* cast their huge boulders but could not be heard over the din. Flaming arrows streaked over the walls of the City of Volodymyr. Flaming arrows also streaked towards Ratibor's sector. Almost unnoticed was the advance of the battering ram against the Sofiyski Gates of the citadel.

"Sentries back down inside!" commanded Ratibor.

Ratibor was the last to descend, his courage but a mask, put on to comfort those in his charge. The terror was palpable among the young *otroks.*

"Where is Nestor?" asked Ratibor. There was no answer. Terror had deafened all that were close enough to hear above the roar of the enemy.

"Where is Nestor?" Ratibor bellowed.

"The monk is gone!" said Vsevolod, quaking in fear of both the enemy and his angry commander. "I beg your forgiveness."

"Never mind, I think I know."

Ratibor examined the room. The second floor ended at a balustrade within the building itself. It was supported by massive log columns. The Pysaniy Kamin, the Rock with two centuries of graffiti on it, stood on a pedestal on that second floor, at a short ramp that was directed at the balustrade. It became clear to Ratibor. When freed from its wedge-shaped chocks, the gigantic boulder would roll down the ramp, break through the balustrade, and drop to the first floor at a spot right here. He walked to the spot just below the balustrade and examined the floor. There was an inconspicuous knothole in one plank.

"Kyrylo!" Ratibor shouted for his *dzhura* over the din outside. "Did you get the rope?"

"Yes *Pane*. Here there is lots of rope, and of different sizes."

"Thank you, son. Now how about a short stick or a dowel."

"Here."

There were fires all around. One could barely see outside for the smoke and flames. The roof was beginning to burn. Ratibor fished through Kyrylo's treasures. He tied a short rope around a dowel. He pushed the dowel all the way through the knothole. It acted as a toggle. Ratibor pulled up on the rope and a section of floor lifted with surprising ease. He ran up the stair to the second floor carrying the rest of the ropes. The wedge-shaped chocks that immobilized the boulder were cast iron. They had dug into the wood just enough so that they could not be easily removed. The chocks had rings at their ends. Ratibor tied a rope between the two rings. He then looped his longest rope around this connecting rope, and tied one end to the rail of the balustrade. The other end he let dangle over the balustrade. It almost reached the floor. This system, he figured, would give him two-to-one mechanical advantage. He ran back down the stair.

"There are Mongols outside!" cried Vsevolod, unable to hide his panic. "They carry torches. Soon they will be in here."

"Guard the doorway with our scar-faced friend," commanded Ratibor, making sure the stranger heard. "We start the evacuation now. Kyrylo, my faithful *dzhura*, you will be the first."

Ratibor gathered all the *otroks* around the rope sticking out of the floor. He pulled on it and lifted the hinged section of floor. "*Panove*, there is a ladder down here, and a cave where all the books are stored," he said. "Go down and you will live a day longer. Stay here and you will die within the hour. You have already covered yourselves in glory. There is no more glory to be had by staying here. I will be the last down this ladder."

The process of moving four dozen young men down one ladder took a long time. Burning sections of the roof crashed down on tables stacked with painstakingly written manuscripts. It was this fire that had kept the Mongol-Tatars from investigating the building, but Ratibor knew that soon his sword and *topir* would find work again. The scar-faced warrior waited by the door with sword and dagger. Young Vsevolod covered the entryway with his bow.

"Guests are coming," announced Ratibor from his vantage by a window. "Four of them."

Ratibor glanced at Vsevolod, who was positioned directly in line with the door. What happened next took seconds. As the door opened, Vsevolod's arrow killed one, and a veritable windmill of sword and battle-axe dispatched the others even before the scar-faced warrior could assist. The last of the *otroks* were crowding by the trap door.

"We have exhausted the element of surprise," said Ratibor, kicking the door closed. "Here come the rest."

The door crashed open and a flurry of arrows whistled in. Vsevolod loosed one of his own just as he was struck in the chest. A half-dozen Mongols rushed the doorway. Ratibor engaged two, the scar-faced one challenged a pair himself, but two more ran straight for the wounded Vsevolod, swords in hand. The curved Mongol swords made swift work. In two strokes, Vsevolod was dispatched, cleft, and beheaded.

Ratibor buried his *topir* in one and speared his sword into the other. He whirled to face Vsevolod's attackers, crashing his sword through the shoulder of one just as his scar-faced companion sliced into the helmet of the other.

"Farewell, brave Vsevolod!" cried Ratibor, tears bursting through to wash the blood-spatter down his face. "To the ladder!"

The scar-faced one scampered down the ladder. Ratibor seized the rope dangling from the balustrade and jumped into the open shaft after him. Nothing happened. Ratibor found himself hanging above the opening. The Written Rock did not budge.

Ratibor swung to the floor and ran for the stair that led to the second level. Without sealing the entrance, they would be no safer below ground than above. Another squad of Mongols tore into the building, and Ratibor found himself engaged with the lot of them. A Tatar leapt in through a window, rolling upright to his feet just to Ratibor's right. Off flew the fur-trimmed Tatar hat.

"*Zdorov, Pane Sotnyk!*" greeted the voice of Vyshata, Ratibor's *desyatnyk.*

"Hail, Vyshata!" yelled Ratibor as he ran up the stair.

"The city has fallen. It's a melee out there," Vyshata reported. "Here, let me hold them off."

A Mongol followed Ratibor up the staircase, who was in turn chased by Vyshata. A dozen more chased Vyshata. Ratibor dove headfirst over the balustrade, grabbing the rope on the way over. Not to be outdone, the Mongol did likewise. Seeing a dozen pursuers, Vyshata threw his sword at them, and placing a dagger in his teeth, dove for the hanging rope himself.

The weight of three men on the rope was more than the chocks could bear. As the chocks slipped free, the three men dropped into the hole, snapping to a stop when the slack was taken up. They grabbed for the ladder.

There was a great rumble and the Pysaniy Kamin began to roll.

Part I

VANCOUVER, CANADA
August 2002

YAROSLAW HELD THE TILLER in his right hand while tensioning the mainsheet with his left. Heeling to starboard, the sailboat seemed to come alive. Releasing his grip on the main, Yaroslaw switched hands and turned to tilt the outboard motor out of the water. Astern, the boat's wake painted a smooth ribbon on the water. To port, low hills were interspersed with buildings and trees. To starboard, a forested peninsula jutted into the wide bay against a backdrop of more distant mountains. The sloop rocked as it broke across some waves, a forgotten wake reflected off a stony beach. Yarko returned his attention to matters of sailing. Reducing his pull on the tiller, he pointed the boat more sharply into the wind. Instantly the boat heeled even more and picked up another knot of speed against the splashing of salty foam.

"I see your seamanship has improved," said Yarko's father, Mirko, as he quickly hardened the starboard jib sheet to match the new heading. "You're learning fast."

"The world is for the young, Dad," said Yarko with his wry smile, "and you're getting a bit old for this."

Mirko raised his eyebrows at his son's remark and cuffed him affectionately on the head. Despite their teasing of each other, father and son were close. Mirko was also proud of his son. At twenty years old, Yarko had turned into quite a good-looking young man. He wasn't tall, but his broad shoulders spoke of many a late hour in the gym. He had finished his third year of university and had been accepted into medical school. This caused his mother no end of joy, although Yarko himself was not looking forward to the long nights of study.

Such thoughts were on everyone's mind as the family enjoyed their last cruise of the summer. The Vancouver sun still shone warmly, but gone was the mid-summer heat wave of early August.

"I smell a hint of fall in the air," said Luba, Yarko's mom, as she climbed from the cabin to join the men on deck. She had been resting below while Yarko and Mirko were busy on deck. She had waited until the sails were raised, the motor silenced, the fenders put away, the docking lines coiled and hung below, and a steady northwest course set. When this chaos of a dozen tasks on deck calmed down, Luba left the cabin to enjoy the warmth of the sun and the scenery of the Pacific coast. Her chestnut-brown hair was flecked with bronze and gold. Dark eyes sparkled from under her bangs as she stretched her legs in search of that last chance for a tan. She looked more like Yarko's older sister than his mother.

"Less than two weeks to go before school," she added with a hint of satisfaction well understood by all mothers. "Then I'll finally have some rest."

From the darkness of the cabin a voice protested this ominous forecast. Mark, Yarko's eighteen-year-old brother, climbed out of the cabin's opening, his mouth still bearing the reddish evidence of a feast of barbecue chips.

"You look like a clown," teased Yarko, with a sarcasm that was sure to elicit a response.

"And you're an asshole," came the predictable response. "I'll kick your ass in the water."

Mark always had the last word. Although younger, he was taller and no less muscled, so this was no empty threat. But Yarko ignored Mark's challenge. There would be no crisis, as the brothers loved each other in a way only brothers can.

The sailboat was called *Tryzub*, Ukrainian for trident, the heraldic symbol of the Ukrainian coat of arms. A blue-and-yellow flag fluttered on the starboard shroud. In this way, Yarko's father maintained the memory of a country he had actually never seen. It was August 24, 2002—the eleventh anniversary of the proclamation of Ukrainian independence. The trip was the family's way of celebrating.

The *Tryzub* sailed past anchored freighters, tacking twice before finally aligning her course with the evergreen shores of the Sunshine Coast. The metropolis of Greater Vancouver, with a population of nearly two million, lay but a few miles behind, but the steep pine-covered shore of Bowen Island off the starboard bow betrayed no sign of mankind's presence at this distance. That was the remarkable nature of this place. Despite its growing population, Vancouver had not scarred the primordial beauty of its surroundings. The rugged shorelines were covered in evergreen forest. Distant peaks glistened white against the azure sky. The Georgia Strait, which divides Vancouver Island from the mainland of British Columbia, provided sheltered waters for small craft to explore its various islands. Setting a course northward, Yarko had the westerly wind on his port beam.

The *Tryzub* held this comfortable course all day, until the setting sun threatened to slip behind the mountains of Vancouver Island.

Deprived of its energy source, the wind died to a whisper. For a brief moment, the orange sun to port scattered a path of fiery flecks on the waters leading towards distant Schooner Cove on Vancouver Island. Yarko squinted, scanning for other watercraft, or the barges and log booms that were a constant hazard in these waters. None could be seen. Before them rose the dark mass of Lemberg Point on South Thormanby Island. Yarko knew, from countless lessons in Ukrainian history, that Lemberg was the Austrian name for the Ukrainian city Lviv, the City of Lions. Yarko's grandparents had emigrated from Lviv during the Second World War.

The boat's destination was a bay just to the west of Lemberg Point. Mirko dropped the leg of the outboard back into the water and started the motor. Yarko now steered a westerly course while his dad busied himself lowering the sails. Mark went below to find a jacket. It was getting chilly.

"Could I go to Europe, Dad?" Yarko asked. He was dreaming of the beaches of the French Riviera, the limitless autobahns of Germany, and the vestiges of imperial splendour in Vienna. "Not now, I mean, like, next year. Next summer. I can make enough money to cover both school and the trip."

His father thought for a moment before answering, casting a long glance at the shoreline. "I understand. I think I just might agree to that. You're certainly at that age when you need to explore the world, to spread your wings. However, you should also go to Ukraine, for at least a week."

"Damn it, Dad! I don't want to go to Ukraine. There's nothing there for me. And my Ukrainian isn't all that good. I'd rather go to Austria, then to Germany or France."

"Not quite true, Yarko. There is a reason for you to go. For one, by going there you'll improve your Ukrainian." After a long pause, he continued. "Just go to Lviv, where our family comes from. You'll love it there."

"How's that going to be fun? Damn it, Dad, it's like going for a full week of fucking Ukrainian school right after finishing my semester." Yarko was boiling over from all the subtle pressure a young Ukrainian feels all his life. Learn the language, sing the songs, read the books, find a Ukrainian girl, and so on. He could find no room for Ukraine in his fantasy vacation. He was sensing that his father would try to bargain with him. That unsubtle pressure was likely to last to the next summer.

Mirko rose to the bait. "Watch your language, Yarko." Then he stopped. There's no room for argument on a small sailing craft.

Behind another tree-covered point of land was the entrance to a narrow bay. The sun had set and dark shadows already hid the details of the shore as they entered the bay. Mark had the task of dropping the anchor off the bow. Yarko revved the motor in reverse to set the anchor. The bow swung around to point at the spot where the anchor had found grip. The boat stopped. Yarko shut off the outboard, then walked forward to check the anchor line. Dark grey clouds, outlined in purple and pink, covered the western sky. Mark dropped through the cabin opening to join his mother below decks. Luba had set about cooking a warm meal on the alcohol stove. Yarko and his dad stayed on deck, hanging fenders and rechecking the anchor to ensure that it held secure and that the boat was not drifting.

"Dinner is served," Luba called.

"Coming," Yarko replied as he walked back to the cockpit. He followed his father through the opening and down the two steps to the cabin. Chopped-up sausages in pasta with sauce with shredded cheese tasted like a gourmet meal after a day of sailing.

"Mom," Yarko began after taking a gulp of pop, "I was telling Dad that I plan to go to Europe next summer—you know, Germany, Austria, maybe France."

"Sounds nice," said Luba. "Are you sure you'll be able to afford it?"

"No problem. I'll have enough. It's not that bad if one buys the Eurorail pass."

"That sounds wonderful."

"But Dad wants me to visit Ukraine." Yarko knew exactly where to look for an ally.

"No way!" exclaimed Luba. "What for? It's way too dangerous. They are killing reporters and politicians all the time. No way. I'm not going to spend sleepless nights worrying about you."

"Come on," said Mirko. "You're overreacting. It's nowhere near that bad. And what's more, Yarko is not a politician or reporter."

"So they'll rob him and leave him naked in the street like they did to what's-his-name."

"Sounds like a helluva way to meet girls..." Mirko grumbled to himself, fully realizing that he was already outvoted and outgunned, and all further arguments would be futile.

Yarko was stuffing his face with more pasta and sausages, knowing that he wouldn't need to add anything more to the discussion. He did not participate very much in further dinner conversation. The subject matter had been changed to the scenery and experiences of the day's sailing. A day of sun and wind had taken a lot out of them, so the family crawled into their sleeping bags quite early.

But Yarko couldn't sleep. He stepped out on deck. His mind was a hive of conflicting thoughts and feelings. He needed to be alone. He stood by the mast and watched as clouds alternately covered and uncovered the moon. He stood there feeling waves of anger and guilt. He was still angered by memories of the force-feeding of Ukrainian school, Ukrainian soccer, Ukrainian boy scouts, and Ukrainian church. He had resented taking language courses, which earned him no credits, and being subtly pressured to find himself a Ukrainian girl. Hell, how do you go about doing that in Vancouver?

These feelings of anger and resentment were gradually replaced by something else. It was a physical pain in his gut. It was the feeling of guilt. He felt guilty for rejecting his Ukrainian upbringing. He could see no real use for it in his life here on the west coast of Canada. And yet all those stories of heroic battles, the stories of struggles amid the deprivation suffered by direct members of his family—they somehow demanded similar achievements from him personally. Nobody actually said this to him. It was just the legacy of growing up ethnic. And every day that he shirked this undefined obligation only added to the guilt that he now felt.

A warm hand touched his shoulder.

"Crazy, this business of being Ukrainian," said his father. "There once was this homeland that you couldn't live in. Within the span of one generation, the city of Lviv was ruled by…" He paused to ensure he got the order right. "…Austrians, Ukrainians, Poles, Russians, Germans, and then Russians again. The poet Taras Shevchenko lived most of his life exiled outside of Ukraine." Mirko was speaking of the Ukrainian equivalent of Robbie Burns. "He was in Russia when he wrote the poem titled 'To the Dead, To the Living, To the Yet Unborn,' which defined better than anything written before or since, that four-dimensional concept of a nation."

This was exactly the reason why Yarko was feeling that guilty pain deep in his gut.

"'Study, my brothers, Think and Read. And study foreign things, But do not reject your own, for he who rejects his mother is shunned by all,'" his father quoted from the poem, adding acid to that ulcer in Yarko's gut.

"It's not easy, son," his father added. "It just seems to be the price all Ukrainians pay. Here, hang on to this. I was going to read it. But heck, I've read it before. It's *The Kobzar*, the collection of Shevchenko's poetry." Mirko squeezed a hardcover book into Yarko's hands. "This one belonged to my father; although I guess it must have been my grandmother who brought it from Ukraine. The darn thing has to be over seventy years old."

Thankfully, Mirko left without adding any further to Yarko's turmoil. Yarko felt the boat rock slightly as his father stepped down the ladder to the cabin. Unconsciously, he squeezed the book in his hand. Again he was alone on the deck.

Yarko stood leaning against the mast for a long time. The moon slipped out from behind the clouds and momentarily lit the waters with a thousand sparks. Yarko's spirits brightened for that moment. The shoreline that had been wrapped in black now revealed a wet tangle of roots, driftwood, and rocks. The tide was rising, and so the shore seemed different and farther away than it had been just an hour before. Yarko looked around to reassure himself that the anchor was still holding. But then a thick black cloud covered the moon. The cramp in Yarko's gut returned. The stars that had been peeking from between these clouds winked out one by one. The night turned to solid blackness. The horizon that had still been recognizable far beyond the entrance to the cove disappeared into equal blackness above and below. Yarko could no longer tell where the sea ended and the sky began. He felt dizzy for a moment. He glanced down at the fibreglass deck of the boat to regain his balance as he grabbed at the shrouds for support. The slight movement of the boat on the incoming tide caused the anchor line to silently slice the surface of the sea, stirring a wake of yellow-green phosphorescence where it entered the water just off the port bow.

The cramp in Yarko's gut gradually eased and he felt well enough to make his way back to the cockpit. A single white anchor light, as required by boating regulations, shone on a pole affixed to the transom. He sat down and leaned against the railing.

He looked at the tattered book. It spoke of its own rough history. There must be as many stories on the cover as inside it, he thought.

He knew exactly why his dad had dug this relic up from the bottom of an old hat box. His dad's uncle had passed away that summer. Since Yarko's grandfather had died many decades ago, that left Yarko's father as the oldest surviving member of the family. The living links with the family's past had been severed. That was the reason that this ragged *Kobzar* was again seeing the light of day.

The white vessel-at-anchor lamp threw just enough light that Yarko could leaf through the book. He had no intention of reading it just now, but about two-thirds of the way through he found a makeshift place marker. Yarko looked at it closely. It was a very old, yellowed envelope. The front of it had a purplish stamp cancelled with a smudged imprint. The words read "80 Groschen, Generalgouvernement," and a small swastika could still be made out on the stamp. The return address clearly read "19 Koronska, Lemberg, Distrikt Galizien, Generalgouvernement."

The envelope was addressed in German and Yarko couldn't make out the cursive writing well enough to read it. He looked inside and pulled out a small, carefully folded letter, written on what seemed like tissue paper. Yarko began deciphering the script.

April 24, 1944

Dearest Slavko,

I hope you are well. It's hard to wish you a Happy Birthday in these circumstances. I'm sure you already know that Father died on March 29. It was not possible for any of us to attend the funeral. I don't think we will ever learn exactly where he is buried. Fortunately the rest of the family is staying healthy. We supplement what foodstuffs we can buy with preserves from last year. This supply has almost run out. But that no longer matters.

The front lines are near Brody. We can hear the artillery every night. Pidzamche station has been bombed. Ours is the only house on the street that does not have cracked windows. The situation is such that we have decided to leave home and seek safety in the West. Mother and grandmother will be working in the Zeisswerke factory in Jena near Leipzig. Can you believe it? They will both be Ostarbeiters. But I don't think I can work in a city. The green forest is much more to my liking.

The Gestapo has come around searching again. I think they like our house too much. Dyzio has come to visit, so he will help with the packing. I know how much you worry about it but I have managed to keep your ancient treasure well protected. Unfortunately, it is much too cumbersome to take along with us and too precious to risk getting destroyed. There are many papers and things that we must also leave behind. We can only take what we can wear or carry in our hands. Mother is packaging all these family heirlooms along with yours. Tomorrow, with Dyzio's help, we will bury them in that place by the coal furnace in the basement. Mother doesn't think we will ever see Lviv again. The Nimci are kaput. She says it will be our children or grandchildren that will eventually find what we are hiding. God willing.

Mother will write you from Jena. Keep healthy and safe
Take care
Koko

Yarko was not wearing a sweater, so he was shivering in the chilly air of the night. In his hands was a letter to Yarko's late grandfather, from the youngest of his two brothers. It was written as the family was preparing to leave the country that they had so loved. Yarko could pick out one of the code words. He knew that the reference to green forest meant that Koko intended to join the Ukrainian underground, the UPA. This letter was, in fact, Koko's last contact with his oldest brother. Koko was to disappear shortly after that. He would have no contact with any of his family until after he returned to Ukraine from the Siberian Gulag in the 1970s.

But what intrigued Yarko most was the reference in the letter to his grandfather's precious ancient treasure. He had no idea what it could be. He had never been told of any such family treasure, yet now he sat holding the key to it in his hands. His restless brain began to dream of treasures far beyond anything that could be logically gleaned from the letter. A fantasy about treasure-hunting adventures was already playing in his mind. A side trip to Ukraine during next year's vacation was starting to look a lot more interesting.

After quietly committing himself to actually making this trip to Ukraine, he found that those conflicting feelings of anger, resentment, and guilt that he had felt but an hour before were receding. Mixed with the developing excitement about the prospect of a visit to Ukraine was a sense of anxiety, trepidation, and foreboding. Yarko knew well that the Ukraine of President Leonid Kuchma was no Disneyland.

Part II

LVIV, UKRAINE

July–August 2003

1

THE SOUND LEVEL of the airliner's engines had dropped by a decibel or two. Yarko opened his eyes. In his sleep, his mind had tuned into the constant rush of the powerful turbofans. The slight change in their sound was enough to wake him. He looked at his watch. Almost nine hours flying the great circle route from Canada. We'll be starting the descent soon, he thought. Another hour and I'll be in Lviv.

Yarko had a window seat on the left side of the plane. Through the window he could see a bright horizon lit by the rising sun's rays. The land below was covered in dark forests, but from time to time he caught the silver reflection of light from the surface of some stream or pond. Just ahead, a large river spread among the trees and stretched far towards that glowing eastern horizon. Yarko closed his eyes.

"Polissia," he muttered, through sleepy semi-consciousness, answering a question that his sleepy reason had yet to form. This was the great marshland on the borders of Ukraine and Belarus. Into his still fuzzy mind came a torrent of fragmented thoughts. He remembered a history lesson taught years ago, and the name of an ancient city, Iskorosten'. This was the walled city that some 1,100 years ago Princess Olha had burned to the ground in revenge for the murder of her husband, Prince Ihor. Yarko was looking in its direction, at the modern town that had been built on the ancient fort's ruins. Squinting in the blinding light of the rising sun, Yarko thought he could see the glowing embers of the wooden fortifications of that city.

He remembered other conversations with his dad.

"Today, Ukraine is in a state of creeping revolution," his father had said. "Without strife or bloodshed, and seemingly without conflict, this country had suddenly slipped from being a colony of the Russian Empire to national independence. As a result, this has become a land with no right or wrong. There are no truths or lies there. There are no demons and no angels. It is, in fact, a country in a state of moral anarchy. And it is this very ambivalence that is most dangerous—it is as a ship with no compass. Veterans of the Soviet Red Army are still heroes. Those who fought to conquer Finland for their masters in Muscovy are heroes. Those who invaded Afghanistan for this foreign empire are still heroes. But those who fought in the Ukrainian underground, the UPA, against German, Russian, Pole, and Communist Czechs alike have become heroes too—at least in the west of Ukraine—along with those who fought tooth and nail against them. And, as can be expected, they all claim to deserve a pension.

"The Ukrainian language is the state language, but Russian is still the unofficial 'official language.' The president himself had to learn Ukrainian soon after he was elected. His father died in the defence of Stalin's empire somewhere near Leningrad, thus his loyalties have forever been to a foreign state. Both sheep and wolves live in the same flock..."

It's like *Alice in Wonderland*, thought Yarko. "Everything is not quite as it seems."

Yarko's mother was dead set against this trip. She had once visited Ukraine, on a school trip in the seventies. But these were more dangerous times now. There had been many a long family discussion before she reluctantly agreed to let Yarko go. His father, of course, had been all for the trip—wishing to send Yarko on this journey to satisfy some patriotic fantasy. But Yarko agreed to it for the promise of adventure—for the adrenaline rush of a treasure hunt.

Adventure, that is all, thought Yarko as he continued his airborne snooze. He could picture himself now, racing through the streets of Lviv, hunting for treasure. He had dismantled and packed his favourite mountain bike for this trip, thinking it would provide him with an easy way of getting around. Shimano in the land of Sturmey-Archer—the thought made him smile. He could already picture himself riding the narrow trails far below in that forest that stretched eastward on both sides of the Prypyat River.

This reverie was interrupted by the heavily accented voice of the plane's captain speaking English, the international language of air transport.

"On ze eastern horizon, some hundred and fifty kilometres from us, lies ancient town of Chornobyl'. In April 1986, an accident and fire in Block Two of ze Chornobyl' nuclear power station resulted in ze largest peacetime release of radioactive contamination..."

Yarko did not hear the rest of the captain's words. His thoughts and attention were again focused on that eastern horizon. He remembered the prophetic words of the nineteenth-century bard, Taras Shevchenko: "*In flames, and plundered they will wake her.*"

Somehow as he returned to a deeper sleep his mind unconsciously formed the words "Flaming Vengeance."

In his mind, he could again see the red embers and wind-whipped flames of the burning fortifications of Iskorosten'. He could see dark figures of warriors with swords and shields, their faces blackened by soot, as they battled desperately in this fiery hell. He could even smell the smoke of this imagined conflagration. Spontaneously, he whispered the phrase, "It smells of history."

And truly, the soils of Ukraine were soaked in the scents of ancient memories of mankind. The relics and traces of ages past had long been destroyed by countless wars. This distant past was crushed and plowed deep into the depths of its fertile land. Artifacts of the early ancestors had been plundered and scattered to the four corners of the earth. Their blood had long since soaked into the soil of this land, which drowned all their traces in an endless black sea.

But the depths of this fertile soil gave birth to generation after generation of peoples. Wave after wave, they spread to all parts of Europe and Asia. This was the prehistoric homeland of the Indo-European language group. It was the land of the master potters of the Trypillian culture that had built cities of multi-level homes some two millennia before the Egyptians even dreamt of pyramids.

It was also the land of those who had first tamed the horse. For countless generations of steppe dwellers, a horse was to the endless plains what a boat is to the sea. It was the means to conquer the otherwise unconquerable vastness of the steppes. And so the waves of peoples spread farther still. The mysterious Tocharians of the Chinese hinterlands; the Hittites with their chariots on the borders of biblical Egypt; Greeks and Latins; Celts and Germans; Balts and Slavs: all spread from these lands. It was the land of the Cimmerians, of Conan the Barbarian comic book tales. It was home for centuries to the warlike Scythians who defeated King Darius, fascinated Herodotus, and battled the great Phillip of Macedon. It was a land known by many names: the biblical land of Gomer, the Scythia of the *Histories*, the Sarmatia of the Romans.

It was more recently known as the historic Rus', an empire that brought Christianity and the written Church Slavonic language to the Finnish tribes of the future Muscovy. Much later, an expanding Muscovy appropriated Rus', in its Greek form, as its own name, in order to lay claim to the storied past of Rus'. The people of the Rus' nation began to favour their word for country, Ukrayina, as the new name of their land and, eventually, as the name of their nation.

The constant throughout millennia had been the land and the people who worked it. But the recent manifestation of the Muscovite Empire, the Soviet Union, was to change even that. In a planned famine-genocide known as the Holodomor, it eliminated some seven million Ukrainians. Millions more were deported to Siberia, or ground to dust as cannon fodder in the great battles of the Second World War. Now only the land remained constant. Yet it still breathed with the scent of its ancient past.

Yarko woke with a start as his head flopped onto his right shoulder. His eyes opened wide when he glanced through the window. Gone was the forested terra firma. All he saw was sky. The plane had banked sharply to the right and was beginning its descent. Soon the clear sky was replaced by the grey fog of cloud as droplets streaked horizontally on the outside of the glass. Minutes later, through wisps of the grey fog, he made out individual trees, bushes, buildings, and roadways. The wet ground rose to meet them as Yarko readied for the inevitable impact of landing. He braced his feet on the floor, tightened his stomach muscles, and gripped the armrests more tightly, trying not to let any of this anxiety show on his face.

It was raining. This reminded him of his Vancouver home, where

such drizzly rain continued for weeks. The plane seemed to taxi forever on its way to the gate.

Yarko was remembering the various pieces of advice he had been
given, as well as the strange mission that he had chosen for himself.
Fresh worries crowded into his head. Treasure hunting in the basement of someone's home now seemed like a totally ridiculous idea. In
any case, he'd need help. But how would he find a friend who would
agree to such a task? Who could he trust in this land where wolves
lived among the sheep in the same flock? The current police force
was composed of many of the same communists who had served
previous masters. The streets were filled with thieves of every stripe.
For an American dollar or two they would perform any service, or
they could simply kill you. Maybe in a church he could find some
honest people, but certainly not of the kind who would agree to the
risky adventure that he had in mind. This could certainly be some
adventure.

Yarko reviewed the details of the challenge. He needed to locate
a certain house. He had to enter its basement. And by some old furnace or stove he had to dig up a treasure that had been buried there
a half-century ago. Then he had to get whatever the treasure was to a
safe place. Somehow, he would have to do this under the nose of the
very people who would be living in that home today. It was unlikely
anyone would agree to this challenge without demanding a piece of
the action.

He still didn't know what this family treasure could be. His father
had explained to him that his grandparents were teachers. Long
before the war they also had a little bookstore. Nobody got rich in
that kind of business. So the family treasure could consist of nothing but photographs, documents, perhaps a little jewellery—things
that could not be safely taken with them, but could also not be left
behind. And then there was his grandfather's precious ancient find
mentioned in the letter. In his imagination, Yarko was Ali Baba, and

as for the forty thieves, they certainly would never be hard to find in the streets of Lviv. "Both sheep and wolves," he mumbled under his breath. "I'm sure we'll have wolves in sheep's clothing. Those I'll have to watch out for."

Pushing these thoughts from his mind, Yarko looked about him to find the last of the passengers slowly filing up the aisle to the exit at the front of the plane. He snapped to his feet and grabbed his knapsack from the overhead storage bin. He caught up to the last passengers as they filed through the exit door. Leaving the plane, he heard a fragment of the conversation of the captain and his crew. He couldn't understand a word of the Russian they were speaking. The badge on their tunics showed a yellow trident lying on its side, looking like a falcon in flight

Yarko climbed down the stairway and onto the wet tarmac, bracing himself against the cold wind and rain as he hurried towards the doorway of a grey, colourless building. Only then did he notice that on both sides of him stood soldiers wearing the green uniforms of Ukraine's border troops. Neither their uniforms nor their comical oversized officers' caps had changed since the days of Gorbachev. For Yarko, these hats and uniforms symbolized the bloodthirsty Empire that was no more. Yet here, in a free and independent Ukraine, its troops still wore the hideous dress of their former masters.

Without realizing it, Yarko broke a sarcastic smile at the thought of the very incongruity of it all. A nearby trooper smiled back with such a bright smile of welcome that now Yarko felt totally embarrassed. Well and truly red-faced, he quickly entered the building.

Now that, he thought to himself as the doors closed behind him, that was surely a sheep in wolf's clothing!

And again that crooked sarcastic smile creased his face as he hurried to the baggage collection area. The passengers were packed into a small area, waiting for any sign that their baggage would be arriving. The wait became a little uncomfortable for Yarko. Something was surely not right. Yet the locals seemed quite content to wait patiently for what seemed like an eternity.

Patience is a virtue, thought Yarko, but this country no longer has time for such patience. The world is passing it by, he knew. In fact, the world seemed quite prepared to forget about Ukraine completely.

Yarko knew that in seven days he would be leaving this flock of sheep and taking the train through Hungary to Austria. He was bored already. After several more minutes of waiting, he saw airport staff carrying the baggage, one suitcase at a time, to the waiting room. It was after watching nearly everybody's luggage get carried in that he finally spotted his suitcase, then his duffel bag, and finally his dismantled mountain bike wrapped in a dozen layers of cellophane.

Knapsack on one shoulder, duffel bag on the other, his bike under his right arm, and dragging the suitcase with his left, he felt like a biblical donkey as he made his way through to customs.

To his surprise, he cleared customs with ease, answering the official's questions in a mixture of both English and Ukrainian. His next task was organizing some inexpensive transport to the Hotel Ukrayina, near the centre of Lviv. Taxi pimps, opportunists who brokered taxi transport, jumped him, offering him a ride in a choice of ancient Skoda or dilapidated Lada for a mere $40—American dollars, of course. Almost tempted to accept, he thought better of it after learning that bus fare was under a dollar. The buses were tall Mercedes vans called *marshrootka*, from the French term *marche-route*. Two hryvnias, or about fifty cents, was the going price, but the driver balked at Yarko's extra luggage. Prepared for such eventualities, Yarko slipped his chauffeur five dollars to assist with his load. This was more than enough to secure enthusiastic assistance. Yarko didn't realize it at the time, but the tip amounted to a half-day's pay for the driver.

"Hotel Ukrayina, if you please," said Yarko in studied Ukrainian.

"I'll stop right in front of it."

Sitting comfortably in the marshrootka, Yarko complimented himself on his newfound ability to negotiate in this foreign land. The wad of American dollars in his pocket appeared to be an effective social lubricant for getting over those rough spots. The rain was still falling, so the view through the van's window fell short of that promised in travel brochures. Pot-holed roads and grey concrete apartment buildings looked even more sombre when streaked with wet stains in the rain. Metal surfaces that had been painted over a dozen times still bled rust. Military trucks repainted in garish colours appeared to have been recently pressed into performing civilian duties. The automotive landscape in this part of the country appeared, for the most part, to be a throwback to the seventies. There were very few recognizable models. He recognized Ladas and the old four-wheel-drive Nevas—once known as Cossaks in Canada—but it would take him a few days to learn to spot Ukrainian Tavrias, Russian Volgas, Czech Skodas, and the Korean Daewoos that populated the roads. Yarko closed his eyes and caught another snooze.

The driver woke him as the marshrootka pulled in front of the Hotel Ukrayina. Again Yarko found himself outside in the rain, burdened like a mule, looking at a yellowish four-storey building that clearly had seen better times. Run-down areas of Vancouver also had hotels such as these; only there, they'd be surrounded by drunks and addicts. Here the sidewalk was empty. On the street level of this building was a store, the Smerichka, or Fir Tree. The store window display was sparse. The room windows above displayed the occasional crack, and one was boarded up. It attracted attention like a black eye on a passer-by's face. Yarko shivered both from the cold rain and the thought of actually staying in this building. He entered the lobby and after paying by credit card, was directed to the second floor.

The second-floor hallway was presided over by a seriously overweight middle-aged matron at a desk station by the elevator. She babbled something in Russian about his passport. Yarko had been warned about the leftover Soviet practice of holding passports hostage, and absolutely refused to comply. After several minutes of argument, where he learned to use English as a trump card, he registered himself in her book and went to his room.

There was no water in his washroom. Instead of a refreshing stream, the taps issued an ominous hiss. There was no point contacting the front desk. Yarko had been warned that Lviv, having been founded as a fortress on high ground, was located on a divide; as a result, water supply was a constant problem. Yarko knew that in an hour or two, certainly by the next day, the water would be turned back on.

To cheer himself, he busied himself assembling his bike. He had no doubt that an aluminum-framed, fully suspended, twenty-four-speed mountain bike was just what he would need to explore his grandparents' hometown. Designed for forest trails and mountain slopes, such bikes were also ideal for traversing city landscapes. In Vancouver, they had long become the favourite of its business-area couriers. Such couriers delivered packages from one office building to another, traversing parks, sidewalks, roads, alleys, and entryway stairs with unequalled ease. Judging from the state of Lviv's roads, bringing a mountain bike here was a stroke of genius.

As Yarko studied a map, kneeling on the floor and using his bed as a table, he was pleasantly surprised to feel the warm touch of sunlight on his shoulder. Even the limited view from his window now seemed to promise him a tour more akin to that displayed in travel brochures. Lviv was a city founded in the thirteenth century as a bulwark against Mongol intrusion. Like other parts of Ukraine, it had been ruled by various empires; however, it was the Austrian period that left the most beautiful architectural legacy. Often compared to Prague, it certainly matched it in beauty, but fortunately it still had some way to go before matching it in price.

Yarko changed into his shorts and his bicycle jersey. He threw a knapsack over one shoulder, while lifting the bike by the frame with his free arm.

"*Idu na Vy*," he said, quoting the warlike challenge of tenth-century Prince Svyatoslav the Conqueror. "I go (to war) on you!" was the news feared most by the foes of Rus'. Now Lviv was about to meet its bike-mounted match, thought Yarko. But the first order of business would be a coffee, and a nice light snack.

Across from the hotel, at the beginning of a very wide boulevard, stood a monument. A bronze figure, long covered in a green patina, with some equally green winged creature descending upon it, occupied the very end of this grassy boulevard. It was the memorial to the Polish writer Adam Mieckewicz. Next to this monument stood a structure that must have been a fountain, but this being Lviv, it was silent. Rather than spraying water, the fountain, having been wetted by the rain, was surrounded in a haze of evaporating moisture.

Riding north along the Prospekt Svobody, or Liberty Boulevard, Yarko stopped at a cobble-stoned square. His attention had been captured by another monument, much smaller than the previous, yet much more accessible. Atop a rock pedestal was a black-metal, cylindrical cartoonish head of a moustachioed kozak with a long scalp-lock hanging before his left ear. On a level below it was an equally cartoonish cannon or mortar next to a pile of cannonballs. The sign on the rock had the name "Ivan" above a horseshoe. This was the monument to a kozak warrior by the name of Ivan Pidkova, or, translated into English, Johnny Horseshoe. Yarko smiled as he thought of this literal translation.

Ukrainians knew that their kozaks were the fierce frontiersmen of the steppes, living as free men on the no-man's land beyond the reach of three empires. It was centuries later that the Russian Empire would draft such frontiersmen into serving as the dreaded shock troops of the empire, known today as cossacks.

Yarko placed his hand on this rock and looked into this kozak's fiercely huge eyes, which gazed out from under a furrowed brow. He felt a renewed energy flowing into him. There was courage, pride, and a sheer ferocity that revitalized Yarko's spirits. He forgot about his hunger. Mounting his bike, he turned eastward towards the Rynok, the historical market square.

The Rynok was a square of cobblestone streets walled in by buildings on the outside, with the historic city hall and its tower, the Ratush, inside. The tower was topped by the waving blue-and-yellow flag of independent Ukraine. This view gave him particular satisfaction, because it matched photographs of events on November 1, 1918, when Ukrainians seized their opportunity to declare an independent Western Ukrainian Republic as the Austro-Hungarian Empire collapsed. The view had been no different on June 30, 1941, when Ukrainians caught Hitler by surprise by declaring independence in a land freshly cleared of Bolshevik rule. These had been the short flashes of freedom that kept those embers of national independence glowing throughout the last century.

Closing his eyes, Yarko could see crowds of people singing and shouting, and he imagined the staccato crack of gunfire that always seemed to signal the end of such revelry. The history of the century-long liberation struggle was now speaking directly to him. Gunfire echoed from the walls of the buildings, and the acrid smell of cordite and gunpowder penetrated his nostrils.

As he opened his eyes, he found another smell penetrating his nostrils, but this was the smell of coffee, not gunsmoke. Turning around, he realized that he was standing mere steps from one of Lviv's cafés, the Café Pid Levom, or, literally, the Café Under the Lion. Above him he saw the gargoyle of the lion that this café was under. He chained his bike to a lamp-post and entered the café.

It was lunchtime, and the café was full. He found the very last vacant table and sat down, his back to the wall, and his backpack beside him to discourage anyone from joining him and engaging him in conversation. Yarko preferred to keep to himself just now, and any attempt to exercise his Ukrainian language skills would simply be too painful. He ordered coffee and two sweet rolls, and made himself comfortable. The background music was some pop song. Yarko listened to the words: "…all week I walk and live among the lions, no wonder they call this city Lviv." This song about the city of lions, along with the sweetness of the honey-glazed roll, momentarily rekindled that rush of energy that he had felt at the monument to Ivan Pidkova.

He enjoyed a good view of the patrons from this location, so he took advantage of it to satisfy his talents in applied anthropology. He eyed the young waitress who just now was serving coffee on the opposite side of the room. She had short brown hair, a confident smile, and a mischievous twinkle in her eyes. She was slender, but far from frail—hers was more of an athletic, or more accurately, a gymnastic build. Smallish breasts, and long legs under dark nylon completed this look. Her rear-end must have been just a bit fuller than her seamstress had expected. As a result, her black tunic tended to lift a touch as she bent to serve another coffee. A dark strip of shadow on her thighs confirmed that she wore stockings, not pantyhose. The shimmer of dark nylon smoothly accented the muscled contours of her legs. This view held Yarko's attention like a beacon in this turbulent sea of people.

A shiver ran down his spine when he realized that she had caught his gaze and was calmly looking back at him. Taken aback, he briefly lowered his eyes to check something in his coffee. When he looked up, the young waitress was gone. In embarrassment, he wiped a crumb of white honey glazing from the corner of his lips. Frustrated, he decided to continue with his anthropological studies. Momentarily a new beacon caught his eye in this sea of lunchtime patrons.

Yarko, like all young men, had an extremely well developed sixth

sense that allowed him to instantly home in on any attractive example of the opposite sex. Far to his left sat a long-haired blonde, a
beauty quite worthy of his attention. Long wavy blonde hair framed
the smooth skin of her face, accenting her blue eyes and pouty lips.
Batting her long eyelashes, she was flirting with a middle-aged man
sitting across from her. But Yarko's attention was drawn lower, to full
breasts trying to tear through a sleeveless sweater that was somewhat
too tight and somewhat too short. Lower still he could see a strip
of bare midriff, then a short red skirt supported by a black belt that
hung low on her hips. The blonde and her friend got up and headed
for the exit. Yarko had a brief opportunity to examine her legs and
rounded rear-end, which rocked with every step as she walked by.

Damn, thought Yarko, now I've lost them both. Saddened by this
turn of events, he lowered his gaze and went back to studying his
map of the city. He was looking for the old suburb of Zamarstyniv.
There he would have to search for Koronska, the street where his
grandparents had lived. With every wave of history that had changed
the rulers of this land, the street names were changed too, so the like-
lihood of finding a Polish-era name in this time of Ukrainian independence seemed slim. He had been studying the map with some
degree of frustration when he heard a pleasant female voice.

"Are you visiting Lviv for the first time?" It was Ukrainian with a
somewhat softened accent. It expressed a genuine friendly interest.
Yarko lowered his map. He saw before him a navel and the tanned
skin of bared midriff, and below, the black belt and red skirt. Yarko
held his breath as he slowly raised his eyes to take in the skimpy
knitwear, then the rounded contours of firm breasts that mercilessly
stretched the white yarn. Finally, he met the friendly gaze of the
young lady with wavy blonde hair. He stared back much too long
before attempting a reply.

"No ... but, but yes, yes ... it's, it's my first time."

"Are you alone?"

"Alone," he replied, then decided to add, "but what happened to your friend?" before realizing too late that he had given away the fact that he had been admiring her previously.

"That? That was my uncle. A little presumptuous of you, isn't it?" Keeping Yarko off balance, she continued, "My name is Dzvinka."

"And I, I am Yarko," he stuttered. "Yaroslaw," he added as if by way of explanation.

"American or Canadian? I hear a bit of an accent."

"Canadian. But my grandparents came from here."

"First time?" asked Dzvinka breathily, leaning just a little closer as she seated herself across from Yarko.

"Here you mean?" he replied, a little flustered, not sure where to look.

"Is this your first time in Ukraine?" Dzvinka clarified while adjusting her sweater.

Yarko refocused on her eyes. "First time in Ukraine."

"It can be very confusing without a tour guide. You'd have no idea where to look."

"But it also gives me more freedom." Yarko had to force his eyes not to stray below the neckline. "And I hate *nahliadachi*." He used the word for overseers, not knowing the Ukrainian word for chaperones.

"So have you planned everything out for the day? And do you know what you're doing tonight?"

"No plans for tonight. I wouldn't have the greenest idea where to go," answered Yarko in idiomatic Ukrainian.

"Okay, Yarko Yaroslaw," she teased, "this evening, you could come to the club called Vezha. We'll have nice music, dancing, some drinks. Here, let me show you on the map."

As she spoke, she bent low over the table to study the map. A pair of rounded breasts swung before Yarko's eyes from above the décolletage of the knitted sweater. He could see where tanned skin met delicate whiteness. The rest was just barely shielded from his gaze by the happily overburdened yarn of her knitwear. Yarko held his breath. He swallowed hard despite his suddenly dry throat.

"Let me see, here's the Stryisky Park so the Vezha nightclub is here," Dzvinka said. "A bit lower. Can you see, Yarko? Right here."

As Dzvinka turned slightly to look at Yarko, the resulting jiggle repeated her invitation in a more direct manner. "See you later, about ten o'clock," she said, surprising Yarko with her barely accented English. She turned, rotating on spiked heels, and exited the café. Yarko rose to follow her, but a pressing tightness in his shorts made modesty the better part of valour.

2

THE SUN HUNG LOW ON THE HORIZON. Yarko stepped off the Number 3 streetcar at the Stryisky Park stop. It was past 10 p.m. The long shadows that filled the park and the entranceways to the buildings gave the city a mood of romantic mystery. Several young couples had exited at the same time and headed straight for the park. Yarko followed them.

The central entrance to the park was framed in a tall, delicate, columned gateway with five arched entranceways. Dark green leaves of birch trees surrounded the meandering cobblestone walkways of the park. Yarko had read about it in the tourist brochure. Created in the 1880s as a set piece for an imperial exposition in 1894, it was filled with rare and exotic plants and trees. It included artificial ruins of a fictitious castle, and an orangarium—a tropical arboretum. It was the site of one of Europe's first electric tramways. The swans that inhabited its ponds to this day served as a romantic reminder of past imperial splendour. Several minutes of strolling brought Yarko to the Vezha nightclub.

On entering the club, Yarko was stunned by a wall of sound and coloured strobes that attacked his senses. The dance floor was filled with silhouettes of lithe writhing bodies against a backdrop of flashing purple. It was hot. The women seemed to cope with this by wearing as little as possible. The men coped by avoiding excessive movement while dousing their thirst in beer and *horilka*.

"Yarko!" rang a familiar voice from across the room.

Yarko spotted Dzvinka leaning against the far wall. She was wearing a dark red dress with a single strap on her left shoulder. It was cut to reveal more than it covered in tightly fitted elegance. She was nursing a martini in a long-stemmed glass. Yarko made his way to her, pushing past drink-laden tables. To cope with the ambient noise, Dzvinka limited her greeting to a peck on his cheek as she motioned him to sit at a nearby table. Yarko ordered beer from a passing waitress. He did not know the local brands and the noise level did not allow for much explanation. He motioned "yes" with his head at each suggestion and ended up drinking a Lvivske Strong. He would later learn that in this heat, a 1715 would have been a more refreshing choice.

Dzvinka dragged him off to dance. It didn't seem to matter what music was playing. Familiar Western tunes were mixed with the local material. A songstress by the name of Vika gave a raunchy rendition of "*Boolochka z makom*"—Poppy Seed Buns—and "Hot Dog," a song describing delights far from the culinary variety. Yarko thought of this as fusion rock. Ukrainian words were grafted to sixties or seventies Western music. It appeared as if Ukrainian artists were fast-tracking through a half-century of Western musical rhythms and styles in an attempt to catch up on everything they missed while cloistered behind the Iron Curtain.

Yarko spent the evening chatting in English. He found it so much easier, and Dzvinka obviously had had much practice. She rarely had to search for words. The beer was followed by the "normal" serving of four ounces of ice-cold *horilka*—firewater of the Hetman brand. Yarko was having a genuinely good time.

It was well past midnight when they left to wander the dark foot-paths of Stryisky Park back to the streetcar stop.

On the streetcar, once the flow of conversation dropped off to a dribble; Dzvinka cuddled closer and, taking him by surprise, suddenly pressed her lips to Yarko's. This was a language that needed no translation. Yarko replied by wrapping his arms around her and, as her lips parted, he savoured her sweetness. He explored the coolness of her back with his right while working his left to her breast. The streetcar bell rang as it slowed for the stop at Mieckewicz Square.

"This is your stop," said Dzvinka, liberating her lips from Yarko's. "But I still have a way to go. Tomorrow for lunch at the Pid Levom?"

It seemed that the moment Yarko felt he was in control, Dzvinka would redraw her boundaries and again take the upper hand. They said their goodbyes, and promised to meet at Pid Levom for coffee. Yarko stepped off the streetcar. It was drizzling lightly. He stood by the obelisk watching for a long time until he no longer heard the screeching of steel wheels on the wet rails, and the red tail lights of the streetcar had disappeared in the mist.

Yarko slept for a long time. He awoke just before noon. The shower, which actually worked, was cool and refreshing. It was Saturday morning. A sunny day. Yarko grabbed his knapsack and rushed to the café on his mountain bike. Dzvinka was waiting for him. The place was half-empty, so it was much easier to talk freely. He knew that he was going to need a helper if he were to find his grandparents' house. He wondered whether Dzvinka could be the answer. Carefully he began by explaining how his grandparents used to live in the suburb called Zamarstyniv.

"I would like to find the old place," he said. "It's on Koronska Street. I've already found it and marked it on the map. Luckily it still has the same name as when my grandparents lived there."

"I have a bicycle with me too," said Dzvinka. "We can ride there together. And coming back, we can take a trail to the top of the Vysokiy Zamok." Vysokiy Zamok, or High Castle, she explained, was the name of the hill that overlooked the city. "From there, we can see the whole city. It will be fun. If we're lucky we can catch the sunset."

Such a proposition was hard to refuse. Dzvinka got up first to get her bike while Yarko felt around for his wallet. This gave him a chance to appraise Dzvinka and her latest outfit. She was dressed in the shortest of shorts and, again, in that undersized white sleeveless sweater. I should definitely let her lead, thought Yarko as he paid the cashier. The view promised to be quite remarkable.

They rode along Krakivska Street for about half a kilometre, then it seemed that the road changed names to Bohdan Khmelnycky and then to Zamarstynivska. The name changes reminded him of his native Vancouver where the same roadway could have several names.

"Seems it's a lot easier to nail a new name to a post than to build a new road," joked Yarko.

Dzvinka laughed. "Or repave the old one. But you will rarely find a post with a street name. It is far cheaper to attach the street name to the wall of a corner building instead."

Yarko was riding beside Dzvinka but just a little behind, giving him a great view. Her shorts revealed as much as they concealed, and whenever she bent over the handlebars, her sleeveless sweater hung loosely enough to expose milky flashes of her breasts. Yarko was missing much of the historic scenery of this part of town. Centuries-old buildings and churches went unnoticed. He almost missed crossing the railway tracks, and a gentle turn to the right also went unnoticed. Only as Dzvinka slowed near an abandoned factory did Yarko return to full consciousness. Old stone houses were in a uniform state of disrepair. A short side street was marked by a sequence of yellow puddles rather than any semblance of pavement.

"I think this is it," said Dzvinka, catching her breath.

Yarko could just make out worn black lettering on a white board on the side of a corner house. "Koro …" was all that was legible. "Yes, this should be the street," he said. "The house number was 19. At least that's what it was before the war."

He walked his bike between puddles while scanning for house numbers. The smell of flowering vegetables came wafting on a slight breeze. Bordered by crumbled stone, brick, and rubbish was a garden of some size along one side of the street. Neat rows of onions, carrots, and cabbage brought a hint of order to this scene of dilapidation. In the silence, a quiet hum of busy insects could be heard. Bees and butterflies flitted from flower to flower.

Across from this garden was a large house that caught Yarko's eye. He remembered the description of the house in family legend as being a fortress, a veritable bunker. Flaking stucco revealed stone and brickwork underneath. This house was as close to a two-storey cube of stucco-encased masonry as could be imagined. On one corner a signboard read "19 Koronska." This had to be it.

"Family legend had it that as my great-grandfather, a school principal, was building his house, the neighbours jokingly accused him of building a bunker," explained Yarko. "But then later, during the war, when the nearby railway station was carpet-bombed, no home escaped damage. Only the principal's bunker stood without so much as a cracked window pane."

Yes, this was the family bunker. Standing silently before it, he again felt that inflow of energy, that bravado that he first felt at the monument to Ivan Pidkova, the kozak warrior named Johnny Horseshoe. Much like the hero of the movie *Taras Bulba,* Ivan had fought the Turk but was betrayed by the Pole. His blackened bronze visage today marked the spot where his Polish allies beheaded him. Yarko knew the story.

Although feeling this renewed strength, he also felt, deep within him, a strange uneasiness. Something twisted his gut, as a shiver ran down his spine. Not all is as it seems here in Wonderland, some voice was whispering. Maybe it was the thought of having to break into this house that was bothering him. He could not form a plan, yet he felt unready to share his thoughts with Dzvinka. She had been standing behind him, not daring to interrupt his silent contemplation. Only when he moved did Dzvinka dare to speak.

"Today there will be three or four families living in this building, not just one as before," she said. Her voice had a slight accusatory tone, Yarko felt. She sounded like a lecturing Intourist guide, more appropriate to this land some decades ago.

Yarko did not reply. He was more than prepared to argue the merits of private ownership. The pitfalls of government ownership were in full display before him. He just didn't want to go there at this time.

"If you're hungry, I brought a *butterbrod*," she said, trying to change the subject. "A sandwich, if you prefer the English word." She could feel that Yarko was not in a chatty mood just now. Her bicycle had a pair of travel bags with snap pockets. She opened one and gave Yarko a rye bread sandwich with Krakivska sausage. Yarko silently handed her his water bottle in return. His thoughts were still far away, as he unconsciously chewed on his bread. He looked the building over from all sides. He could feel that there was something here that was dear to him.

Dzvinka interrupted the silence again. "Come on. Let's go to the Vysokiy Zamok. It's getting late."

In order to focus his distracted attention and convince him to follow her, she lifted her arms as if to clear her hair from the nape of her neck, and, simultaneously, stretch her tired muscles. This motion revealed even more of her breasts through the arm openings of the sleeveless sweater. Her belly button narrowed between twin strips of muscle and her shorts slipped even lower off her hips.

"Let's go, then," agreed Yarko. "You lead."

The Vysokiy Zamok was on the route home. They had ridden around it to the west on the way here. Now they would ride around its east side. They crossed under a railway bridge and then turned up a switchback road heading to the hill's peak. The last part of the climb was along a walking path that led to the top. The mountain was crowned by an artificial conical hill with a spiralling path leading to its top. Dzvinka rode straight past this hill and past the remains of old battlements to a small clearing surrounded by dense bushes and trees. Barely visible through this vegetation was a tall radio tower behind them. Tired and panting, the two lay happily in the grass. Dzvinka propped her head up on Yarko's knapsack. She could just see the end of a roll of American dollars showing from under a flap.

"I see you've brought some hard currency," she commented. "Be careful with that kind of amount around this town."

"Don't worry. It's just a few bucks for the road. The rest is much better hidden."

Lying on her back, Dzvinka lifted herself on her elbows to keep her hair off the grass. To stretch her muscles, she bent one knee to the point that her heel just touched her buttocks. Yarko checked out her tanned legs. The sweaty wrinkles of her shorts failed to conceal her panties, whose delicate lace seemed a strange selection for bike riding. Dzvinka closed her legs to shield herself from Yarko's gaze, and smiled back at him coquettishly. Yarko couldn't hold back and pressed his lips passionately to hers. Dzvinka embraced him, and while gripping his thigh between hers, she smartly rolled him under her. She laughed at his surprise at this deft manoeuvre.

"Wait here," she whispered. "I'll be right back."

Yarko watched breathless as she crawled on her knees to her bike and reached into her other travel bag pocket. Multicoloured clouds of this romantic Lviv evening were playing with the last of the sun's rays.

"You know, Dzvinka," he said, staring at the slivers of white lace exposed with every movement of her thighs, "I'm going to need your help. I have this interesting task. There is some kind of treasure in that house we were looking at. It's something my grandparents left behind during the war before abandoning their home. I have no idea what it is, but somehow I'm going to try to find it."

Dzvinka closed the pocket of the travel bag and turned to answer. "Sure, I can help you. It will be an adventure," she said, crawling back on all fours with her top sweater button now having surrendered to the strain. "We can put a plan together right now! So where is this treasure hidden? And what will we need to get it out? You don't look like much of a treasure hunter, so you'll definitely need my help." In her excitement, she mixed Russian words with her Ukrainian.

She lay down on her back beside Yarko. Gently taking his hand into hers, she slipped it under her sweater.

Suddenly, from behind the trees, the sound of several loud voices shattered the quiet seclusion.

"Blyaa; it's the militsya," Dzvinka whispered hoarsely, mixing Russian expletives with her Ukrainian. "They are looking for us. Let's scram! Damned *menty*! May they…" She jumped on her bike.

Feeling totally confused, Yarko followed suit. Then instinct and reflexes took over. "Down this way," he shouted. "Westward towards the setting sun. They won't see us. The sun's rays will be in their eyes and the shadows will be long."

He said all this while gathering speed down the slope. Twisting between trees and bushes, he made sure they couldn't be followed. All this was a natural reaction, for as with most young men, this certainly wasn't his first time evading cops.

In just a couple of minutes they found themselves out of the park on Smerekova Street. It was only then that he could soberly review what had just happened. Why did they have to flee from the cops? Yarko could not understand.

"I didn't think that was a 'no trespassing' zone," said Yarko when they stopped at a traffic light. "I thought it was just a regular park, a public place."

"Not in the exact place that we were," said Dzvinka, having switched to accented English. "There was a radio tower; we aren't allowed there. You understand; we could have been terrorists or something. It is military installation, you know. I take you there on purpose because nobody go there. There is many bushes, trees. Is quiet—understand? We would have been there alone. And now look what happened." Dzvinka blushed and lowered her long eyelashes, shielding tears.

Yarko asked no more questions. And yet he still couldn't understand the adventure that had just happened on Vysokiy Zamok. There weren't any No Trespassing signs, no warning signs in any language. Why run from the police? Were the voices actually those of police? The terrorist threat angle didn't feel right either. He had seen the radio tower. They were far from it. There certainly were a lot of things that he didn't understand about this strange country. Or maybe it was just Dzvinka that he didn't understand.

After this wild escape, all remnants of a romantic mood had evaporated. They rode home in silence. It was getting dark. He said his goodbyes on Krakivska Street, promising to meet again at Pid Levom, the same as today. He rode to his hotel alone.

Early the next morning, just as the sun was rising, Yarko was awakened by the ringing of his telephone.

"*Shliak by trafyv*"—may one have a stroke—he swore, using the old Lviv expression still favoured by many in the Ukrainian diaspora.

He lifted the receiver and looked at his watch. It was six in the morning. It was Dzvinka waking her sleepy friend.

"Listen, Yarko," she babbled excitedly, "do you know what day this is?"

"Sunday. So what?" he answered, annoyed at this early wake-up call.

"And do you know that on Sunday people go to church?"

"Gee, I had no idea! I'm so glad that you woke me at six in the fucking morning to inform me of this. Otherwise I would have slept for hours without this bit of deep wisdom." Yarko was definitely not a morning person.

"You're funny, Yarchyk," said Dzvinka. "Listen, if we get lucky, then the people who live in that house on Koronska will all go to church for Liturgy. The building will be empty. Then we'll go in and check it out. We'll figure out where your treasure is hidden. Now get dressed. I'll be there in half an hour. We have to get there in time to see when the occupants leave for church. Can't you figure anything out for yourself, Yarko?"

Yarko was irritated both by the early wake-up and by the fact that Dzvinka had thought things through for him. "Thanks for spending all night doing the thinking for us both, but tell me, if the door is locked, how will we get in? Maybe, since it's Sunday, the Holy Ghost will let us in."

"Don't worry. I've got a friend who opens doors without a key," she explained with a giggle. "He'll lend me his tools. It's high quality equipment—German, you know. So don't worry, I'll handle the door. And you just hurry up and don't think too much. Leave that to me. Now put your pants on because you're probably standing there in nothing but your *gachi*. Half an hour—no longer. Bye-bye."

"Bye," said Yarko. God, how he hated it when women ordered him around.

He was standing by the phone in his *gachi*.

There was no water in the washroom.

Forty minutes later he was on his bike riding along Krakivska, following Dzvinka. She had totally changed her appearance from the day before. Her clothing was now much more workmanlike and practical: navy jeans, a loose black sweater with sleeves, and a black cap that somehow managed to hide most of her hair, which had been tightly wound in a French roll. She could now pass for a boy.

Without yesterday's anatomical distractions, and little traffic to worry about on this Sunday morning, Yarko was able to study the details of the route to Zamarstyniv much better. Every church and every building hid a morsel of history behind its façade. Street names spoke of specific pages of this history, but only to those who already possessed its knowledge. The street named Detko reminded Yarko that the mid-fourteenth-century warlord of that name was the last Ukrainian ruler in this city until the sporadic flashes of independence in the twentieth century. Foreign rule had left its mark on the street names, the architecture, and the ethnic makeup of Lviv. The horrors of the Second World War and the horrors of Bolshevik rule had changed that ethnic makeup once again. The Jewish and Polish components were but shadows of their former glory. Their emptied residences had been filled by the Russian invaders.

It was truly remarkable, then, that over time the historical Ukrainian character of Lviv had gained the upper hand, transforming it into the Piedmont of Ukrainian rebirth. Equally remarkable was that the essential spirit which had been characteristic of a Lviviak a century ago had infused itself into today's mostly non-native inhabitants. This spirit, this attitude, this cachet, was an odd mix of the soul of a philosopher, the taste of an aesthete, the class of an aristocrat, and the street smarts of a pickpocket. A Lviviak had edge. It was quite understandable that the writers Leopold von Sacher-Masoch and Ivan Franko, as well as economist Ludwig von Mises, all came from Lviv.

Dzvinka, however, did not strike Yarko as a Lviviak. She had not been sufficiently infused in Lviv's spirit. A Lviviak was subtle. Dzvinka was brash. He realized that he had been seduced into telling her everything about himself and his family, while she had revealed absolutely nothing. Now, while riding these streets, he found himself planning the recovery of the treasure very much on his own. He was feeling very uneasy about the fact that he had brought her into his scheme.

Having crossed Tatarska Street and a set of railway tracks, he followed Dzvinka as she turned to the right into a dilapidated section of town. The houses here bore the scars of a half-century of neglect, and yards were strewn with garbage. Far beyond them, against the background of the tree-covered High Castle Hill, stood two window-less structures, one painted a garish pink, the other an equally garish lime green. Judging by their position in relationship to the railway tracks that ran a block or two behind the houses, these structures appeared to be storage silos of some sort.

Dzvinka turned left onto the unpaved Koronska Street. Yarko followed her. Yellow pools of rainwater marked the deeper portions of the ruts in the hard-packed soil. Dzvinka stopped, resting her bike against the remnants of a wrought-iron fence. Yarko did likewise.

There were just a few houses on this side street. Between some of them were empty squares of scarred land, looking like missing teeth in the haggard smile of some old babushka. Amongst traces of pre-war foundations and piles of broken bricks someone had attempted to plant a vegetable garden. He had not paid much attention to it yesterday. Today, he noted with satisfaction that a raspberry bush clinging to the remains of a stone foundation wall would provide cover for them and a place to keep their bikes while they watched for the residents of the old family bunker.

They hid their bikes behind this wall and waited. Dzvinka's deduction proved right. First one, then another, and finally a third family left the dwelling. A father, mother and a son; a father, mother, and a daughter; then the parents and grandparent of a pair of young girls exited the house walking single file. The well-pressed suits, tidy fashionable dresses, and flashes of polished leather shoes belied the humble appearance of the home that they had just left. Yarko and Dzvinka waited another minute or two.

"Maybe we should check any mail in their garbage to figure out if any more families live there," Yarko suggested.

Dzvinka ignored him. She leaped up and skipped across the road to the door of the house. By the time Yarko caught up with her, the door was open. Inside, on the left a well-worn staircase led down, turned right, and ended in a short hallway with two doors. They descended quickly. Yarko imagined how his grandfather must have run down these same steps a thousand times.

"Which door?" asked Dzvinka.

Yarko thought a moment to remember on which side he had seen the chimney. "On the left," he said confidently.

They entered a dark and dank room. To one side stood a large stove made of tile and cast iron, which had once served as the coal-fired furnace that heated the home. A sloping pony wall of brick would at one time have hidden a mountain of coal behind it. A bricked-over rectangle replaced the narrow window through which this fuel would have been delivered. Naked joists ran overhead. The brick walls of this furnace room rose as high as the joists, thus serving as internal supports of the home. In front of the stove, well hidden under a layer of dust, was a large rectangular concrete plate that had been sunk into the floor. Kneeling on the ground, Yarko began poking the seam of the plate's edges with his finger.

Dzvinka shone a flashlight. "So the treasure is under this plate?"

"Either under this plate or under the stove itself. In either case, we'd have to start by digging here under the plate."

Yarko took out his hotel key and ran the point of it around the edge of this plate. He wondered how on earth anyone could ever raise it. Dzvinka handed him a knife. Yarko briefly admired what was clearly an old Soviet bayonet. Apart from the serial number stamped on the polished twenty-centimetre blade, it was otherwise unremarkable. He dug the tip of it into the seam of the plate. By his estimate, the plate was at least eight centimetres thick. With a surface of at least a square metre, it had to weigh a quarter of a ton. Yarko tried to imagine how he was going to lift this weight.

"Look here, Yarko." Dzvinka shone her light on a spot of slightly lighter grey in the middle of the plate.

Yarko poked at this spot with the knife. It appeared to be plaster. This plaster plug flaked away, revealing a round hole wide enough for Yarko to fit three fingers in. Oddly, the hole appeared to be threaded. Clearly something had been screwed in there to allow the plate to be handled. Yarko took Dzvinka's flashlight and began searching around the furnace room.

"Hey, we've been here for ages," exclaimed Dzvinka. "Let me pop outside to check if anyone's around."

"Okay," was Yarko's laconic reply, although he shuddered when he remembered where he was, and how long he had been there.

Yarko ran the beam of the flashlight along the top of the walls of this room. Since the brick wall ended at the joists, there were gaps in between the joists above the wall. These were too high to inspect with his light. Yarko left the flashlight on the ground. He jumped up and grabbed the top of the wall with his left hand, and poked between the joists with the bayonet in his right. That way he could check two gaps with each jump. Repeating this a half-dozen times, he suddenly felt something heavy and metallic with his knife. He reached for it with the blade and flicked it out. The steel object clanged loudly as it hit the ground. At that moment Yarko heard Dzvinka's footsteps rapidly descending the stairs. He swiftly grabbed the object and squeezed it into his pocket.

"What fell?" asked Dzvinka excitedly.

"Nothing. Just your damned knife."

"Haven't you finished yet?"

"Give me a few more minutes, please. We'll leave in five."

Dzvinka walked back up the staircase.

Yarko carefully checked out what he had found. It was a large steel ring fitted through a very fat stubby bolt with a square-cut thread. Yarko tried threading the bolt into the hole in the plate. It fit perfectly! This was how the plate was handled! He slipped this ring back into his pocket. He heard Dzvinka's quiet steps behind him.

Cholera, he thought, swearing in the native Lviviak jargon. She's poking around too much. Looks like she's seen it. Without even turning around, he began to sheepishly excuse himself. "Dzvinka, I was going to show you—"

Bang! A gunshot rang from just outside the house. *Bang!* Another one. Instinctively, Yarko dropped to the ground. I'm still alive, he thought. Nothing hurts. He rolled over to check Dzvinka. She was still standing, pale as a ghost, frozen in fear. They could hear voices outside.

"I left the outside door open," she whispered. "There's something going on there."

After a long moment, they worked up the courage to sneak upstairs and look through the crack of the slightly opened door. Two policemen were arresting two other men. They shoved them into their police car and drove off. A second car, a powder-blue Lada, was parked on the street. No one else was around. It was apparently the property of the arrested men. Dzvinka stepped outside and headed towards the car. She motioned for Yarko to follow. Yarko closed the house door and followed Dzvinka, who was already standing beside the blue car. Suddenly she bent down to pick something up.

"What luck! They've dropped their car keys! Let's take the car."

"But—" Yarko began to object.

"Who's going to report it stolen? If those two are arrested they are not likely to miss it today. And after that, how likely are these characters to report to the cops that their car was stolen? Hurry! We can put our bikes into the trunk."

Things were happening too fast for Yarko. Dzvinka was already sprinting across the street to where their bikes were hidden. Yarko started to follow, but she was halfway back wheeling both by the time he got only a few steps. They stuffed the bikes, or what would fit of them—the rear wheels and frames—into the trunk. Yarko thought it odd to see in there a pair of muddied shovels—fresh wet mud of a distinctively yellow hue.

Dzvinka drove fast. At the Mieckewicz square, she let Yarko out, along with his mountain bike, in front of the hotel Ukrayina.

"I'll pick you up at six," she said. "And in the meantime you'd better get washed. You look like shit, Yarko."

Yarko watched as the powder-blue Lada sped around the corner, Dzvinka's bike sliding from one side of the open trunk to the other. He caught his reflection in a storefront window. His face was smeared black, as were his hands and clothes.

Damn lucky if the water supply is turned on, he thought, realizing he looked somewhat worse than his Sunday best. He noted that the fountain near the Mieczkiewicz monument was happily spraying its rainbow-hued shower.

Now that bodes well for the water supply, he decided.

3

IT WAS 10 A.M. Yarko took a quick bath in a tub full of cool water. At least he had water. He decided right then that he should fill the tub whenever there was water available. He filled the sink too. Changing into clean clothes, he threw the morning's dirty laundry into the tub to soak.

Through the opened window he could hear something he was not used to hearing in Vancouver. Church bells from all corners of the city were summoning the faithful to Liturgy. He remembered that this was Sunday. His mind had been full of fragmented thoughts and ideas. An hour's calm at a church service seemed to be a good place to get his head together. He needed to digest the events of the last twenty-four hours, and to develop a plan of action for the remainder of the week. He stuffed the iron ring into a pocket of his cargo shorts, and walked his mountain bike down the hall to the elevator. The ring was the key to his mission, he thought. Something was telling him not to leave it in his hotel room.

He rode along Hnatiuk Street to the boulevard of The November Uprising, a street named after the declaration of independence of November 1, 1918. This led him straight to Saint George's Cathedral. An imposing architectural masterpiece of the baroque-rococo style, it was almost impossible to describe: it embodied the intricate beauty of a Fabergé egg applied to the cruciform shape of a Byzantine-rite Catholic cathedral. Yarko took a few minutes to admire its beauty. Seemingly for the first time since arriving in Lviv, he was actually being a tourist. He chained his bike to a black wrought-iron fence that surrounded the property. Knowing he was late for the church service, he sheepishly climbed the steps to the platform in front of the imposing bronze-plated doors. These had been wedged open to allow the summer breeze to mix with the incense-laden atmosphere inside. To his further surprise, the church was actually packed. Despite this being the second or third church service of the day, it was a standing-room-only event. Yarko worked his way to a comfortable corner, and leaning against a wall he began scanning the countless icons on the walls. An older priest, with thinning white hair and equally white bushy eyebrows, was reciting the Divine Liturgy.

Yarko didn't pay much attention to the Liturgy. He was using this time to run a mental inventory of everything that he would need for his treasure quest. At least shovels wouldn't be hard to find. The trunk of the blue Lada contained two of them. He would also need a block-and-tackle setup, including at least fifteen metres of thick rope. That would give him the leverage, he thought, to lift the floor-plate by himself. But would he be able to carry the treasure up the stairs? How could he transport it on his bike? Any way he looked at it, he would still need Dzvinka's stolen blue Lada, but the thought of working with her bothered him.

There were things that simply weren't adding up. The flight from the police on High Castle Hill made no sense. Today's incident with the two criminals being arrested was an even stranger coincidence. What would such crooks be looking for in that slum? Why would they be carrying shovels? Certainly not for pilfering cabbages and onions from some poor slob's garden, he thought, as another of his sarcastic smiles creased his face. Even the bit about finding car keys on the ground beside the Lada seemed somehow way too fortunate. The echo of the gunshots still reverberated in his ears. Things just didn't add up—or perhaps more accurately, they were adding up too easily.

These thoughts played and replayed in his head while he leaned on the wall in the corner of the church. The mass had finished and it was the general flow of the hundreds of faithful towards the exit that finally snapped him back to reality. He found himself exiting the church among the very last of these. He was in no hurry, so he stood on the steps and admired the view around him. He could see a hotel called Arena; he scanned the buildings of the Ivan Franko Lviv University. Parks and grassy boulevards were interspersed with steep and narrow cobblestone streets, centuries-old buildings, and historic monuments. He was finally enjoying the beauty of this city. He could spend a month here and not just the handful of days that he had left. Instead, he was chasing some ancient family treasure.

At this very moment, a friendly hand touched him on the shoulder. Yarko turned to see a young priest. With dark, stylishly trimmed hair, a closely cropped beard, and a youthful face, the man before him didn't seem to fit the image of a priest. Tall, but far from willowy, he had the build of an athlete, not of some monk.

"You don't look like you're from around here. First time in Lviv?" asked the priest.

"Yes, Father, I'm from Canada," replied Yarko.

"Here for a vacation?"

"You could say that."

"You seem to have some worries, son," said the priest. "If you find that you need some help, some advice, don't be afraid to come to me. My name is Onufriy—Father Onufriy if you prefer. Here's my phone number. Call me any time." He squeezed Yarko's hand as he handed him his business card. It was a simple card—just a cross and a phone number.

"I'm Yaroslaw. Thank you, Father. Who knows, I just might find that I need your help some day." Yarko tried to feign calm that was far from a reflection of his emotional state. But he was not one to ask for help. Getting Dzvinka involved, he figured, would be the last of that kind of mistake. Yarko left the steps of the cathedral, and, unchaining his mountain bike, headed in a direction away from his old Hotel Ukrayina.

Unseen by Yarko, the young priest flipped open a cellphone,

clicked a single key, and spoke at length while watching the mountain bike shrink away in the distance before finally disappearing into a side street.

Yarko wanted to explore the city. On a mountain bike he could ignore the map. The Ratush could be seen from most of the old city and served as a beacon that could always lead him home. He passed the monument to Ivan Franko as well as the majestic classical Ivan Franko Theatre that together with Saint George's had come to symbolize the very best architecture that this city had to offer. He ate at the Lviv Restaurant on the street named for the 700th anniversary of Lviv. Re-energized by this lively bike ride through history, he returned to his hotel.

He had water! And hot water at that! Yarko stripped to his boxer shorts and started doing his laundry in the bathtub.

4

YARKO SPLASHED AWAY IN HIS BATHTUB. For the first time since his arrival he could actually take a hot bath. He just couldn't let such an opportunity slip by. He took great pleasure in this chance for relaxation. He had hung his clean laundry on a rope above his head. Pants, shorts, underwear, and shirts formed a wrinkled fringe above his tub. He sank his head under the surface and blew bubbles as he relaxed every tired muscle in his body. When he lifted his head above the surface, he heard knocking at his hotel-room door. He ignored it. Then he heard Dzvinka's voice from the hall.

"Are you there, Yarchyk? Open up. Let me in."

Yarko didn't reply, but stood up in the bathtub and tried drying himself with an undersized hotel towel. He heard Dzvinka call him a second time. He searched for a dry piece of clothing. He had none. Everything had been freshly washed. He put on the first thing he laid his hands on, a wet pair of white boxer shorts, and opened the washroom door. Stepping out, he was stunned to see that Dzvinka was already in his room. She had her back to him and was bent over in search of something by her purse beside his bed. On his bed lay the bolt and ring.

"What the …" began Yarko in surprise.

Dzvinka jumped, no less surprised by Yarko's presence. "But, but, I had no idea you were here! Boy, did you scare me," she stammered. "I decided to open the door myself to wait for you to return …Wow! Are you ever wet, my friend!"

She examined him hungrily. Her gaze flowed down slowly over his wet body. From his towel-tussled hair, it followed the drips running down to his lips still wide-open in surprise, down rivulets curving over a well-muscled chest, then down that dark strip of hair that separated his abdominals before disappearing beneath the translucent white of wet boxer shorts, and finally dripping to the rock carvings of legs, well streaked with wet black hairs. Slowly raising her eyes, she lapped up this view in reverse order.

While Yarko stood motionless, she stepped forward and pressed her lips to his, wrapping her arms around his body. She held this kiss for a long time. One arm explored his back and the other pressed his hips tightly to hers. Stepping back, she undid button after button down the front of her white dress that now clung to her body in diaphanous wetness. The dress split apart. Underneath there was nothing but the briefest of lace panties. Her nipples had hardened to the touch of his wet skin. Dzvinka stepped away to sit on the edge of the bed with her back to Yarko. The dress slid down her back from under her blonde hair. She hooked both thumbs under her panties and bending forward slipped them down in one smooth motion to the floor beside the bed.

She sat up straight and began to turn towards him. Her right hand held a gun. "My gun. My treasure," she said, and then finished in ironic Russian, "*Zdrastvuy.*"

At that moment, the door to the room burst open to reveal a uniformed figure holding a pistol with both hands.

"Stop! Militsya!" the man commanded.

As if in a slow-motion movie, Yarko watched as Dzvinka, without so much as a flinch, pointed the gun at the stranger.

Ba-bang! Yarko heard the explosive reply. He saw a simultaneous muzzle-flash from both guns. The thunder of the shots echoing off the walls slammed his ears. The stranger in uniform remained standing with both hands outstretched and the gun barrel now safely pointed upwards. Yarko saw the Dzvinka's right arm drop lamely and heard the dull thud of her gun hitting the carpet. Her body slid off the bed, leaving only her head resting on it. Unseeing eyes stared at the ceiling. Her legs, bent at the knees, were awkwardly spread.

Yarko opened his mouth, but no sound would come out. The man in uniform calmly re-holstered his weapon, then straightened himself as he looked at Yarko. "You're lucky, my son ... she was going to kill you. We've been tracking her for quite some time. We've had the task of carrying her completed works down from the High Castle Hill three times now. That's her favourite killing place. You would have been her fourth. I'm amazed that she didn't kill you there last night. We would have arrived too late to help. She's a bloody criminal and a killer to boot," he explained in a matter-of-fact tone. "She was scum ... KGB!"

Yarko began to shake uncontrollably. He was suddenly very cold. His soggy underwear and wet hair just made it worse. "But the KGB doesn't exist any more!" he said, mustering the desperate courage to actually argue with the gunman.

"Not true, my son. The KGB in Belorus still exists without so much as a name change. And they continue to serve Moscow as before. The Muscovite and Ukrainian KGB-sty continue to exist too, except under different names. Whether in the police, in the military, in the SBU—or in one mafia or another—they remain at their posts ready to serve the One and Indivisible Russian Empire. Even under Ukraine's blue-and-yellow flags, with tridents on their caps, this scum awaits orders from their former masters in Moscow. You just won't believe it.

"For example, this departed one. She's an officer of the Belorussian KGB, and a servant of Moscow. She makes a living off violent crime, as well as contract killings. I'll bet she found some American currency on you. You're probably carrying quite the wad, aren't you?" The uniformed stranger spoke in a calm, almost deadpan voice.

Yarko was still shivering, though his mind had started to function again. "Then explain how could a Lviv city cop manage to track down a pro like her?" He could see that behind the cop, high up in the crown moulding of the wall, there was a freshly splintered hole. Apparently the bullet from Dzvinka's pistol had whistled past the cop's left ear and lodged in the wall. Yarko had been feeling ever since the morning that Dzvinka was somewhat less than angelic, but he had never expected this kind of threat at her hands.

"The Lviv police never knew anything about her," the stranger said. "They still don't know, and they probably aren't going to know … So don't judge me by my uniform. Although I look like a cop—and although I am, in fact, a cop—damn it, how should I explain it to you?" For the first time the stranger was struggling for words. "I just don't know if you're smart, or just another dumb Canadian …"

"I understand," Yarko said, still shaking feverishly. The stranger's intimate interest in the KGB meant only one thing to him. "You're in an underground organization, aren't you? Don't worry, mum's the word." He stepped towards the stranger, offering his trembling hand. "I am Yaroslaw … Yarko."

As he did this, he had a closer look at the dead temptress. Blood trickled downward in a dark stream from between her breasts. It stopped at the level of her navel, where it had formed a horizontal stripe in a crease of skin, before continuing down to where it flooded the golden-haired triangle in sticky red. Her ankles were still entangled in a wisp of white lace.

A violent cramp twisted Yarko's gut. His mouth opened, but the only sound was guttural choking. Bent in half, he retreated to the washroom. Falling to his knees and shaking feverishly, he embraced that hated stainless steel bowl, noisily surrendering to it some of the finest of the Lviv Restaurant's culinary art.

"And I'm Vlodko," replied the uniformed stranger with deadpan cool while Yarko still crouched in the bathroom. "Pleased to make your acquaintance. Stay there—stay there Yarko, don't worry. We'll clean things up.

"In answer to your question, though: Yes, I am a member of an organization. Such things are needed now. It's even more dangerous for Ukrainians today than before 1991—that is before independence. Presidential candidate Chornovil was killed in 1999. The Internet reporter Georgiy Gongadze was killed in 2000. The head of the National Bank was blown up by a car bomb in '98. The secretary of the Rukh organization, Boychyshyn, disappeared back in '94 and his body is yet to be found. The singer Ihor Bilozir was beaten to death just last year—right here in Lviv. Some are killed in staged automobile accidents, some are blown up, others are poisoned, but most are simply gunned down. Do you think the police, or the SBU—that's the state security organization—or Berkut or any other state security apparatus even give a damn? They're the ones doing it! Damn them all. They live off Ukrainian taxes, but continue to serve Moscow..."

Vlodko continued his diatribe, but Yarko wasn't listening. He didn't need to hear any more of that long list of victims. He knew that historically the countries of the West had proven to be no safer for

Ukrainian leaders. Stefan Bandera had been assassinated in Munich, Yevhen Konovalets in Rotterdam, and Symon Petliura in Paris. He did not need to hear justification for why a clandestine organization was needed. What he needed right now was for that painful cramp in his bowels to go away.

In a while he was able to get up off his knees. The face in the mirror dripped with beads of cold sweat. The taps in the sink hissed their disobedience, so the tepid bath water had to do. He felt very cold. Still wiping his face in a towel, he stepped out of the washroom. All signs of the shooting were gone. There was no body. There was no blood on the carpet, just an innocent wet spot. The only remaining reminder was the splintered hole in the crown moulding. Vlodko was sitting at the table, finishing smoking a remarkably stinky cigarette. Yarko fished around in his backpack and pulled out a carton of Craven A's.

"Here, Vlodko, have some of these. They are no less unhealthy, but at least they don't stink so bad ... Myself, I don't smoke. I brought these along just in case, you know—for bribes ..." Quickly, he added, "But for you Vlodko, they are a gift."

Vlodko laughed. He opened the carton and lit one of the Canadian cigarettes. He offered one to Yarko. Yarko hesitated for a moment, then accepted the smoke. He understood that few people here could hope to reach an age where they would actually have reason to worry about lung cancer. He now felt very much a Ukrainian. He lit up and inhaled. His shakes were gone. He looked at Vlodko, and Vlodko looked back at him. Vlodko broke the silence first.

"So what were you doing this morning on Koronska Street? We saw your bike there. We caught a couple of KGB-sty there from the same gang as your dearly departed Dzvinka. She must have been there with you. Her bike was next to yours. We arrested those two characters for carrying illegal weapons. They had plenty of them. Enough for a small war. I have a feeling that they were preparing a nasty surprise for you … We came back a half-hour later looking for their car, but it was gone, and so were your bikes …"

Yarko remained silent.

"Never you mind. But let me leave you with a little piece of advice," continued Vlodko. "If you're having some kind of trouble, or if you're ever in need of somewhat more reliable company, then show up at the Café Pid Levom and order two coffees at once. Understand? Two coffees at the same time. For now, I've got to run. Lots of work, you know … Take care, my son."

Yarko silently motioned his farewell. He was now all alone in his hotel room. He glanced at the hole in the wall. He looked down at his bed. On the bedspread lay his rusty bolt and ring. Beside it, lay the set of keys to the blue Lada. Vlodko must have left him this gift on purpose. How thoughtful of him!

Yarko felt the onset of the shakes again. It was only now that he realized that all this time he had been wearing nothing but his soggy boxer short underwear. He removed them and slipped naked into bed. His teeth still chattered as he continued to stare at the splintered hole in the wall. Somewhere, deep in that hole, was a bullet with his name on it.

5

THE MORNING SUN was pouring through the window when Yarko opened his eyes. He lay in bed for a long time. He was realizing that his adventure vacation was no longer just a game. There was one dead body already, and if not for Vlodko, the corpse could have been his. On the other hand, he now had keys to a stolen car, although he still had to find where Dzvinka had parked it. The emptiness in his stomach would not allow him to stay in bed any longer. He was hungry. Remembering Vlodko's words, he decided that another visit to the Café Pid Levom was in order. But first he would complete a brief search for the Lada, and only then grab breakfast at the café.

It was 10 a.m. when he walked into the Café Pid Levom. He was spinning the car keys on his finger feeling quite smug about finding his trophy car so soon. The morning clientele had already abandoned this aromatic haunt, and it was still far from the lunchtime rush. The café was empty. Yarko ordered two coffees to start from the man behind the counter. He helped himself to a menu and made himself comfortable at a table. A moment later a young waitress emerged carrying a tray with his coffees. He recognized her immediately. This was the same slender brunette that he had spotted the first time he came here. She was the one who had disappeared when he took his eyes off her. This time he decided not to lose sight of her, so he skewered her with a steady gaze. Now it was the young waitress who lowered her gaze.

"Would you like some company with your two coffees?" she asked. "You certainly can't drink both of them at once."

"Please. Have a seat. I happened to have ordered one just for you," fibbed Yarko, "and I could certainly use some company for breakfast. As you can see, I'm here all alone. I'm visiting from Canada—from Vancouver."

"I know all about you, Yarko. Vlodko told me everything."

This time it was Yarko who had to lower his gaze to his coffee cup. What had Vlodko told her? Did she know about Dzvinka? Did she know about last night? Should he risk telling her, or simply shut up?

"Why do you look so worried?" she asked. "Are you embarrassed that Zvenyslava Mykytivna Polikarpova, better known as Dzvinka, tried to seduce you? You're certainly not the first—merely the last, thank God. She already killed a pair of tourists just like you on High Castle Hill. They found the victims naked. Each had been shot three times. Investigators say that the first shot was from below—through the gut into the heart. The other shots were in the head—one under the chin and the other in the eye. Soft tissue wounds, all of them. See, she carries a small-calibre pistol. A 5.45-mm, if I'm not mistaken.

"She'd rob her victims on the spot, and then she would take their hotel keys and clean out all the valuables from their rooms. The thing we don't understand is how come you're the first not to lose his pants along with his sorry ass on that hill. Now, don't be shy. You can tell me the whole story. Oh, by the way, my name is Ksenia. Vlodko is my older brother."

There was a long silence as Yarko absorbed all that Ksenia had told him. Finally Yarko was able to compose a reply. "Yeah, I might have told Dzvinka something that would have changed her plans."

"Well, what was it that you said? Because whatever it was, it certainly saved your life—if not your honour," Ksenia said with a hint of sarcasm.

"I assure you that both my life and my honour remain intact," Yarko fired back, "and whatever it was that I said to Dzvinka—maybe I will tell you and maybe I won't." He realized that his words were but a childish attempt to regain the upper hand in the conversation. He needed to change the subject. "Vlodko told me that she murdered three victims on High Castle Hill. You are telling me about only two. So who was the third?"

"Ah, the third—now that was a political matter. More accurately, he was actually the first victim on the hill. He was a journalist, a newspaper reporter. A patriot. He used to write things that Moscow and Kyiv, which seem almost the same today, didn't like very much. First he was beaten by some thugs. These were not our native Lviv *batiars*—these were, shall we say, imported hoods. But this journalist did not stop writing his exposés.

"They say that he was on the trail of the kidnapping and possible murder of the Rukh Party secretary in Kyiv. As you know, Rukh was the movement that fought for Ukrainian independence, and triggered the break-up of the Soviet Union. They say that somehow this reporter had come across the missing man's wallet, here in Lviv! That meant that the foul play now had a Lviv connection. He informed the Lviv police about his find. And the next day, Vlodko found the reporter's body on High Castle Hill. The killer had shot him from behind. The bullets were a match to those that killed Dzvinka's later victims—that's why we think it was her. But that is still not the end of your temptress's story. She may have had a fourth victim. Vlodko tells me that about eight or nine years ago Dzvinka was sent to Toronto, to Canada. While she happened to be there, there was a shooting death of a Ukrainian store owner. He was shot at night, just after closing, in his own store. Somebody needed him dead very badly to go to all that trouble."

After all these unpleasant stories the two fell silent. They sipped their coffees and looked at each other. Ksenia had the delicate features of a young girl, but her eyes, from time to time, revealed a certain hard-edged fierceness. Like a reef under the water's surface, there was a hard core under that pretty exterior. Looking at her renewed that same feeling in him that he had first felt at the Ivan Pidkova monument. Cast iron and rock had forged that spirit in him then, and something equally tough was renewing it here. He could not put a name to the feeling: confidence, pride, courage, maybe bravado. That feeling felt good. It was his fourth day in the city of lions.

He continued to examine the beauty before him. Her hair was the colour of roasted chestnuts, cut short and parted just off-centre. Dark eyes. Thin black eyebrows. A delicate nose that was just a little turned up at the tip. Full moist lips that temptingly parted to uncover a row of pearly white teeth. She was dressed in a simple waitress uniform—a white high-neck blouse with a short black necktie, and a short black skirt with a white apron sewn onto its front. Black stockings accented in silky sheen every athletic curve and hollow of her legs. No wonder he had stared at her that first day. Ksenia's eyes were looking him over too, scanning his face as if searching for something. Yarko held his breath. Something squeezed hard in his chest. He wanted to get to know this girl.

"Is there some place that we could go after you finish your shift?" began Yarko awkwardly, realizing the weakness of his position as a tourist in proposing a date. "I don't know Lviv that well so you will have to help me here."

"Well, there is always the Lviv Opera House," teased Ksenia, "if you remembered to pack your tuxedo."

"Uh, no. Sorry, no tuxedo."

"I didn't think so. I hear your fashion tastes run more along the line of wet underwear." Ksenia broke out in girlish giggles.

"So your brother did tell you everything," said Yarko, feeling somewhat like a bug on a pin.

"Maybe instead you can come to our place, to Mom's for dinner. Vlodko will be there. I know he'd love to talk to you. I'm finished work at six."

"I'd be delighted," replied Yarko, not quite truthfully. "I'll meet you here."

"Now aren't you going to order breakfast with all that coffee?" asked Ksenia, staying in control of the conversation.

"What's the special? Ham and eggs, I believe?"

"Ham and eggs it is."

"Make it two," added Yarko. "You look hungry."

Yarko eyed Ksenia as she walked to the kitchen. Definitely, the seamstress had miscalculated by a couple of centimetres.

He was happy to share breakfast with Ksenia. He figured this would be as close to a one-on-one date as he would have today. Ksenia ate quickly. The lunchtime clientele were beginning to arrive. Yarko left a generous tip and stepped out into the noontime Lviv sunshine.

Re-energized by all this, he rode off to explore the city on his bike. He explored Stryisky Park; he rode by the historic Lychakiv Cemetery, the Lviv University, and the recently remodelled Lviv Train Station. He saw the Powder Tower on Pidvalna Street, the Uspenska Church, the Armenian Church, Holy Friday's Church, the church of the Boyims, the church of the Carmelite nuns, as well as the monastery of Bernardine monks. All of these were centuries-old architectural treasures. At the monastery, he became a sensation to the locals by riding his bike down one staircase into an underground walkway and then up the staircase on the other side. Mountain biking had yet to catch on in Ukraine.

When he finally returned to the Mieckewicz monument, he noted with great satisfaction that the fountain was spraying a glorious fan of rainbow-jewelled drops. That meant that he'd have water in his hotel room. He was glad for the chance to get thoroughly refreshed before visiting with Ksenia's family.

At 6 p.m., Yarko met Ksenia at her café and drove her in the twice-misappropriated Lada to her home. Ksenia's mother, Mrs. Olya, had prepared a simple meal. The family was sitting around the table, Vlodko by a wall beneath a big trident. Yarko located himself across from him. Ksenia sat by the window, and Mrs. Olya was closest to the kitchen. The meal consisted of sausages, carrots, and mashed potatoes in mushroom gravy. There was much to talk about at the table.

Yarko found out that Vlodko and Ksenia were both born far from Ukraine. "So where exactly did you live?" he asked.

"We lived in a town called Stolbovaya, by the Korkodon River in Siberia," said Ksenia. "That's in Kolyma, one of the most desolate regions of the infamous Gulag Archipelago."

"The Soviets had arrested me for my Ukrainian nationalist views," Mrs. Olya explained. "You know, the standard charge of anti-Soviet slander. That was good for fifteen years in the labour camps in Siberia.

Then after the fifteen years, if you were still alive, you remained in internal exile. In other words, you could live anywhere in the USSR except you could not return to the Ukrainian SSR."

"Why was that?" asked Yarko. "Were they afraid you would join some underground organization?"

"Not necessarily," said Mrs. Olya. "It was one of the tools of ethnic engineering. Ukrainians were scattered throughout Siberia or Kazakhstan. Today, Siberia is populated by the Russian-speaking grandchildren of the very people that had fought so desperately for an independent Ukraine."

There was a minute of silence as each of them digested their thoughts.

"I met their father in Stolbovaya. He had been a UPA partisan—a fighter in the underground. He served two successive fifteen-year sentences in the camps. We got married. Ksenia doesn't remember him. She was a baby when he died. Vlodko was six, so he still remembers a little."

"I still remember," said Vlodko. "I remember his stories about battling the NKVD."

"And then came glasnost," Mrs. Olya continued, "followed by the Chornobyl' disaster. After that, we could move back to the Ukrainian SSR. I joined Rukh."

"I remember holding hands," Vlodko added. "We were forming a human chain from one end of Ukraine to the other."

"And around the world," said Yarko. "We formed a chain in our Ukrainian school on that day."

Again there was silence. Vlodko and Yarko looked at each other, realizing that they had touched each other, indirectly, some thirteen years earlier. That day, as young kids, they joined hands in a struggle that even today was still far from complete.

Silently Vlodko poured three large shots of cold *horilka*.

"To the Dead," said Ksenia, quoting from Taras Shevchenko, "to the Living, to the yet Unborn Countrymen of Mine, In Ukraine and Beyond Ukraine—My Friendly Epistle."

Better than anything before or since, those words described the very concept of a nation.

They drank a silent toast to a Ukraine in the pangs of its rebirth.

Dinner was finished. It was late in the evening. Mrs. Olya left the room carrying the last of the dirty dishes. She claimed that she needed her rest and stood no chance of keeping up with the young folk. Vlodko winked and himself disappeared into the kitchen. He came back with three bottles of Lvivske 1715 beer as well as a second litre of *horilka*. He turned his seat around, and sat leaning forward on the seat back with his legs spread as if astride a horse. He had poured fresh four-ounce shots of *horilka* and offered one each to Yarko and Ksenia. It was quite dark in the room, with the only light coming from a naked bulb that hung above the table. He had accidentally swung the lamp while pouring the drinks, so now it cast strangely moving shadows onto the walls of the room.

Having taken up the stance of a KGB interrogator, he began in a formal voice, "So, Yaroslaw, can you tell us what you were doing yesterday, so early in the morning, on Koronska Street?"

"How do you know I was on Koronska?"

Ksenia leapt up, feigning wounded honour, and scolded her brother. "So, who do you think you are, a Muscovite KGB-ist, that you think you can interrogate this innocent-as-the-driven-snow tourist? I'll be damned if you treat my guests that way! Now turn your chair around before you split your only decent pair of trousers."

Both Vlodko and Ksenia exploded in laughter. But before Yarko could recover from his own confusion, there was a flicker of mischief in Ksenia's eye. "Drink up. So why were you on Koronska Street? Vat ver you doink zere?" she inquired, feigning a foreign accent. Then, checking with her brother, she asked, "So where is Koronska?"

"It's a short little street in Zamarstyniv," said Vlodko, downing his drink.

"I was looking for my grandparents' house," said Yarko, belting down the four ounces of alcohol.

"Then why do I recognize the street's name?" Ksenia asked her brother. "Was I ever there?"

"No, it happens to be the street that Mykhaylo Boychyshyn's wallet was found on. You've heard me talk about it."

Ksenia turned back to Yarko. "So did you find it?"

"Find what?" Yarko was confused.

"Your grandparents' house."

"Yes."

Vlodko refilled the glasses. "And did you and Dzvinka go inside?" he asked.

"Yes we did."

"Why? What's inside?" asked Ksenia.

"It's a secret." Yarko was weighing the pros and cons of sharing it with Ksenia and Vlodko.

Vlodko lit up a Craven A.

"You know how Mom doesn't like smoke in the house," scolded Ksenia.

"This is different." Vlodko offered Yarko a smoke.

"Thanks," said Yarko, accepting his own gift back. It bought him time to think.

"Whatever it was, it attracted some unsavoury characters," continued Vlodko, taking a long drag, "Anyway, I guess it's your business."

"It is and it isn't," said Yarko, trying to think things through. "You saved my life, I think."

"That I did," Vlodko agreed. "But then that's my job, so no thanks are needed."

"Do you always go by the book?"

"No. And you know I don't. We cleaned up the primary crime

scene, did we not? And you don't know it, but I created an alternative scene of Dzvinka's death. So I guess that's not quite by the book, is it?"

Yarko saw his chance to momentarily reverse roles. "And you are in an organization?"

"We are," Vlodko said, making it clear that Ksenia was involved too. "We need to be."

"Why?"

"Our parents and grandparents fought for a free independent Ukraine, and now we have it, except the independence is a sham, the freedom is a sham, the government is a sham, the law is a sham, and the police are a sham. It is worse than before independence. Before independence, government had lost its authority. For a while the people actually had the upper hand. Today, the very same sons-of-bitches are back in power, back in authority, but now, it is based on a mandate of sham independence and staged democracy. They manipulate both to stay in power."

"And your secret organization will change all that?"

"Today we can, at best, keep their excesses in check."

"So you won't betray me," said Yarko jokingly.

"No," said Ksenia. She looked seriously at Yarko. "And you won't betray us?"

"No."

Yarko explained everything.

"So according to the letter," he told them, going into all the details, "this treasure is either right under the furnace or under the plate in the floor in front of the furnace. Now, this plate appears to be concrete, so it's heavy. There's a threaded hole in it. I found a bolt and ring assembly that screws right in. Now all we'll need is a block and tackle to lift it up."

"You sure you're not going to find a bag of cat poo there?" teased Ksenia.

"Who knows? But it probably includes important family archives and stuff."

"Even a deed to the property would be pretty important," Vlodko remarked. "In any case, I'm sure you are wondering how you can dig it up while three families are still living there."

"That's the dilemma. And I'm in Lviv for only a couple more days. I've got a train ticket to Vienna."

"Let us work on that for you," said Vlodko. "But right now you are going to bed. Too much of this *horilka* has evaporated for anyone to be driving back to a hotel. Yarko, you're sleeping in my bed."

It was now Tuesday, or, by Yarko's count, day five out of seven. He awoke long after sunrise. Both Vlodko and Ksenia had left for work. Thanking Mrs. Olya for her hospitality, Yarko drove off in the Lada.

He was late for coffee at the café. The place was packed with the lunchtime crowd. He did penance for his laziness by having to stand in line for a seat. When he finally sat down he ordered two coffees and two poppy seed rolls. Ksenia brought him one coffee only.

"One should be enough for you. I'll be real busy for a couple of hours at least. But two poppy seed rolls, that you can have. As the old Ukrainian saying goes, Eat it you fool—it's with poppy. Now pay attention, my sleepy prince, there's a *gryps* from Vlodko under the cup." *Gryps* was Lviviak slang for a secret note. "And don't you dare start staring at strange women just because I'll be busy in the kitchen, my dear Romeo. 'Cause next time, we're not going to save your honour or your sorry arse again!"

Under the coffee cup was a tightly folded note. With some difficulty Yarko made out the tiny print.

The 2 crooks were released this morning. Hide the Lada far from the hotel. Meet at 3 p.m. by Ivan Pidkova to talk.

Yarko stuffed the note in his pants, left a five-dollar American bill on the table, and departed. There was little time. He drove to his hotel and brought down his bike. If he were to hide the car far from here, he'd need the bike to make it back for his 3 p.m. appointment. When he opened the Lada's trunk to put his bike in, he noticed more than just dirty shovels. He saw block and tackle with plenty of thick rope, a crow bar, and two large flashlights on top of the dirty shovels.

"That *suka*," he said to himself, using the Ukrainian word for bitch. "She had everything prepared!" All she still needed, he thought, was the bolt and ring. So that was all that she had come to his hotel room for. Once she had the ring—the customary three gunshots and it would have been all over. The question remained: What were the two KGB-sty crooks doing on Koronska? And what were they digging for, and where?

Yarko drove off to find a safe place to park. Somewhere by the train station, on Kulparkivska Street, he found an ideal spot. He rode the bike all the way back to the Ivan Pidkova monument. Vlodko was already there, waiting. Yarko greeted him.

"*Servus*, Vlodko," said Yarko, greeting Vlodko in the Lviv vernacular. The Latin *servus* was used in the sense of "your humble servant."

Vlodko skipped the pleasantries. "Where did you leave the car?"

"On Kulparkivska, in a guarded parking lot."

"Not bad. Unless one of the guards is mafia or KGB. But for now that is good. Do you have all the equipment that you are going to need?"

"In fact, yes I do!" Yarko said proudly. "Turns out our Zvenyslava got everything ready and put it in the trunk. She's got block and tackle, flashlights, and a crowbar. That's in addition to the two shovels that were already there."

"Okay. Now pay attention. On Koronska, in that house of yours, there are three families. Altogether eleven people live there. In each family there are school kids. I just finished talking with my sister.

Here's her plan. We'll find some excuse to give everyone in that home complimentary tickets to the classic drama *The Dniester Mermaid*. That should empty the house for over three hours. It's a wonderful play for both children and adults alike. Ksenia knows an actress that stars in that play. She may be able to organize some pretence. Listen, Yarko, would you have a hundred American? That would be for the tickets."

"I've got the money in the hotel."

"Okay, five o'clock in that bookstore, The Book Building, across from your hotel. Go to the history section. That's where you'll pass me the money in an envelope. I'll pick up a book and put it back. You pick up that same book and slip in your envelope and then you get lost. I can't have anyone seeing me taking anything that looks like a bribe. We've known for a while that we have an informant on the force. Otherwise, that journalist reporter would still be alive. Five o'clock at the bookstore, don't forget. And at six you're to see Ksenia at the Rynok Market Square." Vlodko then turned and left without so much as a goodbye.

Yarko rode his mountain bike back to the hotel. The fountain by the Mieckewicz monument stood silent. From a distance, the winged muse above Mieckewicz's head looked like a bat-winged demon descending onto the head of a victim. There were few buyers at the Smerichka store, and even fewer goods. Such was Ukraine. Yarko entered the hotel dragging his bike with him. He had plenty of hidden currency. There was a hundred sewn into his duffel bag. There was an even larger roll inside the frame of his bike. Yarko counted out ten-dollar bills, ten of them, slipped them into a hotel stationery envelope, and headed back out. He wanted to get to the bookstore early so he could do some shopping.

He found it quite baffling that the bookstore, here in the capital of Western Ukraine, where most residents speak Ukrainian, was packed full of Russian-language literature. He saw clearly the results of Russia's policy of ethnocide, the killing of a nation. The Russians had just about succeeded. There was anger in Yarko's eyes. Again he could see the flames, the burning city, the bloody warriors around Iskorosten'.

"Flaming Vengeance," he heard himself whisper involuntarily.

"What were you saying?" It was Vlodko's voice from behind Yarko's back.

"Nothing. I'm just wondering how come the store is full of Russian-language books."

"Don't worry, Yarko. There's almost no one in this store. People aren't buying this stuff anyway. They can't afford such luxury."

"Then tell me, would you expect Moscow to have such a quantity of Chinese books, or would St. Petersburg have so many in Ukrainian?"

"You're right, of course," said Vlodko. "Here, Russian books are cheaper than in Moscow. Russian first editions actually appear first in Ukraine. They sure know what they're doing, these sons of bitches!"

Vlodko stood quietly turning the leaves of some Russian history book. He allowed the echoes of their heated conversation to die down. He placed the book on the shelf and walked to another aisle. Yarko picked that book up and slipped in the envelope. Without even looking around he left the store. He needed to find Ksenia.

He walked briskly towards the Rynok Market Square. It was quitting time. Streams of pedestrians flowed from every street and alley around this central square. A couple of American dollars bought him the finest bunch flowers from a street vendor. He brought this bouquet with him to the Café Pid Levom.

Ksenia was surprised by this unexpected gift. She quickly took the bouquet back to the kitchen. Meanwhile, Yarko found himself a table. He ordered the obligatory coffee along with a full meal. The clientele thinned out, and Ksenia finally found the chance to talk with Yarko.

"Hurry and get your Lada. I'll wait for you in the lobby of your hotel. That's where I'll fill you in on how we aim to present all those complimentary tickets for the *Dniester Mermaid* play. We have a plan. And we'll get help with it from my friend Roxy, an actress in that play," she said excitedly.

"Give me a chance to finish eating. I'm starving."

"Okay, but hurry. We have to complete everything before nightfall, and it's now almost six. Let me give you a quick run-down of the scheme … Roxy will have an accident. Some drunk in a blue Lada— that's your role, Yarko—will hit her as she's riding her bicycle along Koronska, and knock her down. Hit and run, you understand? The children playing outside will see it happen and the parents will call the police. The duty officer after five is one of ours, from the organization. Of course, Vlodko will be the one to rush to Koronska Street to drive Roxy to the hospital. Roxy will want to thank all these good folk, and of course a packet of tickets will be duly delivered to them the next morning. Now hurry, its past six o'clock. We're out of here."

They left the café. Ksenia held her bouquet. Yarko received a gift in a large envelope from Vlodko. It was a new set of licence plates. The change in numbers would buy him some time. The two of them had to rush to complete their little play act on Koronska Street before dusk.

6

YARKO CROUCHED BEHIND A KALYNA BUSH in the corner of the vegetable garden someone had planted across the street from his old family home. Without any bikes to stash, this spot was much better for observing the house. Ksenia was beside him. It was Wednesday— day six of the Ukrainian leg of Yarko's European vacation. Yesterday evening's little drama had played itself out on the street before them with brilliant success. The residents of this house were truly grateful for the tickets to the play. By Ksenia's calculations, the three families were due to leave right about now. It was evening. The western horizon was aflame in shades of pink purple and grey. Behind them, the eastern sky was dark. The easterly wind was a sure forecast of rain.

Between their hiding spot and the road were a dozen neat rows of vegetables. This summer's harvest looked quite plentiful. Yarko and Ksenia were playing a game of "name that veggie," just to pass the time. The young lady was definitely ahead on points. The one incongruity in this garden was a linear pile of freshly dug dirt a dozen metres to Yarko's right. It was quite late in the season for planting, and Yarko couldn't imagine any vegetable that needed to be planted that deep. Ksenia convinced him that they must have been planting fruit trees, although the season was all wrong for that too.

Their whispered discussion was cut short by children's laughter. Sure enough, the residents were leaving on their way to the play. They carried folded umbrellas anticipating rain. Yarko counted as they walked by. "... nine, ten, eleven—that's all of them," he whispered.

Once the residents disappeared around the corner, Vlodko walked down the street wearing his policeman's raincoat. His timing was perfect, because just at this moment large drops of summer rain began smacking the dry dirt of the vegetable plot. Vlodko's role in this endeavour was to open the door, then stand guard outside. The raincoat would definitely be needed. Yarko and Ksenia picked up all their tools and stepped gingerly between the neatly hoed rows of vegetables. Yarko glanced at the piles of dirt that he had been looking at before, and noted that the rain was spotting the grey soil with a definite yellow hue. It dawned on him that the yellow mud matched the colour of the mud on the shovels in the Lada. Curiosity overcame him. He voiced his suspicions to Ksenia, adding, "Let me take a look."

"So what if it is, we've got work to do. And the rain is starting to come down in buckets. You'll get soaked."

"Give me a minute. It'll take Vlodko that long to open the door anyway."

Without waiting for a reply he hopped from row to row until he reached the pile of wet yellow soil. Behind it he saw what appeared to be a fragment of a ditch. It was a trench some two metres long, and over a metre deep. A yellow puddle was already forming in its bottom. Fruit trees be damned, he thought. This was a grave! It all suddenly came together for him. The two KGB-sty crooks who dug this grave had meant it for him! He was to have been killed in the basement and then buried quickly in this nearby grave. That would have given Dzvinka and her gang a free hand to retrieve the treasure themselves. He felt a shudder rush up his spine. Vlodko and his mysterious underground organization had saved his life not once, but twice last Sunday. If not for Vlodko, Yarko would have been pushing up, if not quite daisies, then certainly onions and cabbages. Yarko ran, leaving big water-filled footprints in the soil, catching up with Ksenia and Vlodko at the house.

Vlodko had just opened the door and Yarko was happy to get in out of the rain. "Hey, Vlodko," he shouted over the noise of the rain. "Just to the right of where we were hiding, there's a pile of dirt. Behind that pile is an open grave. I think that one may have been meant for me. I think they were going to kill me here and dispose of my body there across the road."

Vlodko was quiet for a moment. His mind was racing. His thoughts were already far beyond Yarko's description of a possible grave. "Cholera! That's brilliant! A grave under the vegetable plot! A rectangle of disturbed dirt would raise no suspicion. Give me one of your shovels, Yarko. Only one of you two is going to be digging at any one time anyway, so one shovel will suffice. Now go play in the basement. I'm going to do a little farming of my own—just to see what else may be planted here."

Not really understanding what Vlodko was talking about, Yarko dutifully surrendered his shovel, then followed Ksenia down the basement stairs.

Everything in the furnace room was as he had left it. Dzvinka's Soviet bayonet lay on the ground right where he had forgotten it. Yarko threaded the bolt with the ring into the hole in the floor plate. There was a fat joist in the ceiling directly above it. Yarko hung the block and tackle from the joist and fastened the lower block to the ring. The weight of both Yarko and Ksenia was just enough to suspend the plate above the floor. Both Yarko and Ksenia ended up on their knees, nose to nose. Yarko looked into her eyes. Ksenia coyly turned away. "Okay Hercules," she teased, "now swing this darn thing aside and let it drop."

The noise of the plate coming down on the floor echoed throughout the empty house. The space that the plate had been covering was filled with a hard-packed mixture of clay and sand. Yarko started digging first. When the hole was deep enough for his legs to disappear in it, he handed the shovel to Ksenia. "Your turn," he said. "I'm exhausted. From here we dig forward under the stove."

As luck would have it, after only the third or fourth shovelful, Ksenia hit something solid. Digging with hands and shovel they finally liberated the "treasure chest."

The chest proved to be a wooden suitcase of average size. It had been carefully wrapped in wax paper, and all gaps in this packaging were sealed with candle wax. The family treasure was theirs. Yarko checked his watch and began refilling the hole. When finished, they swung the plate back in place, removed the bolt and ring, and headed back up the basement stairs. Since there was no easy handhold on the package, it took the two of them to manoeuvre it up the steps. They parked it by the door, and Ksenia ran back down to get all their equipment along with her knapsack. The rain had stopped. The blue Lada stood conveniently right next to the house. Vlodko, all covered in mud, was standing guard beside it. A navy blue police car, also a Lada, stood by. Vlodko helped Yarko wrestle the package into the trunk, then both cars headed off to Vlodko and Ksenia's apartment.

Mrs. Olya had prepared a working dinner of sandwiches accompanied by a choice of buttermilk, tea, or cherry juice—a daily staple, the equivalent of orange juice in Canada or the USA.

The package was placed on the table with a certain amount of formality, much like a huge birthday cake. Yarko inserted the blade of Dzvinka's Soviet bayonet into the wax paper and slit it all the way around the package. He saw the irony in the fact that his grandparents had buried it and left their home to escape the approach of the very army that was armed with this weapon.

"If you're planning to be a surgeon you may as well practise on paper," joked Ksenia. "It's much safer for all concerned. Just careful that you don't cut yourself."

Yarko ignored this comment and carefully removed this outer covering. There was a label on the outside of the wooden box. It was a handwritten note:

For my children, grandchildren, and great grandchildren, I leave this souvenir. I.P.

Something squeezed Yarko's throat, pushing tears to his eyes. He couldn't stop the flood. He silently buried his face in a towel. Yarko was named for the grandfather he never knew, but this was the first time he felt this cross-generational family link so directly. The initials were his great-grandmother's. The room was silent. Recovering his composure, Yarko wiped his tears on his forearm and returned to the task at hand. With great care he flipped open the two latches and slowly opened the lid of the wooden suitcase.

Any fantasies that he might have had about golden riches were dashed immediately. All that he saw were carefully wrapped packages of various shapes and sizes. He opened a small package first. In it were three pocket watches, some wedding bands, brooches, and religious medals. A second, larger package, contained documents, report cards, and receipts. The third package was irregularly shaped and surprisingly heavy. Under the wax paper wrapping was a second wrapping of white cloth. Inside the cloth wrapping Yarko felt the unmistakable shape of a gun. When Yarko finished unwrapping it, Vlodko let out a long, low whistle. As the local expert in such matters, Vlodko picked it up, holding it by the cloth wrap, like a piece of evidence.

"Ay-ay-ay," he exclaimed. "I see that your grandpa had a political bent... What an interesting gun! It looks American. Yes it is. It's a Smith and Wesson. In those times it would have been a rather rare item in Ukraine." Vlodko sniffed it, and looked it over some more. "Certainly, this piece had been used for something. It smells of history. Two rounds have been fired. There are six left. Interesting."

Vlodko then gave the gun back to Yarko.

"I see that in your peaceful city one can certainly find good use for such a toy," said Yarko.

"You Canadians are all cowboys," joked Vlodko. "Now be careful. A weapon that old may misfire. I certainly wouldn't rely on such old cartridges."

Yarko took his bayonet and continued to slit open the paper wrapping of various packages. He found an old photo album, some books, and more documents. He left the largest package until the end. Finally he carefully slit open the wax paper wrapping on this last package and slowly revealed the contents. This was a very large, old, and heavy book. The cover was made of leather. Yarko lifted the cover and saw that it was not like any book that he was used to. This book was written by hand, as was done before the invention of the printing press. The pages of the book weren't paper, either, but parchment.

"Now this, my dear Vlodko," said Yarko, standing for dramatic effect, "now this truly smells of history."

Vlodko, Ksenia, and Mrs. Olya were already standing, possibly as a reflexive reaction to the surprise discovery, or as a gesture of respect for the majesty of what they were seeing. There was no doubt that Yarko's find was extremely significant, but its details were fated to remain a mystery a while longer. Old Church Slavonic is a language that few can read today.

The long period of silence was finally broken by Ksenia. "If you don't mind some advice, we need Father Onufriy. He'll be able to read such a Bible. Let's bring the book to him."

Yarko's eyebrows went up. "Father Onufriy? Is that the priest from Saint George's? Young guy, black hair, close-trimmed beard."

"Sounds like the one—but where on earth do you know him from?"

"I met him Sunday after church." Yarko fished in his pockets. "I have his card here somewhere. He even told me to call him if I get in any trouble."

"He's one of our boys," explained Vlodko. "He's also from the organization. I think you really should visit him at Saint George's early in the morning. But I'll have to leave you there alone. Me and my boys have to go to Zamarstyniv to finish the job I started today. You know, if those two KGB-sty that I arrested had actually killed you and buried you among the onions and cabbages last Sunday, you would have had company in that clay mud. There is definitely another body buried there! We'll be digging the place up tomorrow. Couldn't do it today because it was too late to get our boys together. The organization has to stay on top of this one. We can't let this get swept under the rug. It's sure to be a political matter. Our one lead in the Mykhaylo Boychyshyn disappearance case was the wallet found on that very street. So now I'm just putting two and two together. This is one dead body that won't lose its head. Not like that of Georgiy Gongadze."

Vlodko was referring to the September disappearance and apparent murder in 2000 of Internet journalist Georgiy Gongadze, whose headless body was found by police many weeks later in a park outside Kyiv.

"And you behave yourself in church, Yarko," warned Vlodko. "Our dear Father Onufriy is a former kick boxing champion. He could give you a lesson that would have very little to do with catechism.

"Ksenia, you will go to work tomorrow as always. But now we'll all go to sleep. It's getting late. Yarko, you've got my bed again. Except please keep that revolver under the bed, not under your pillow. I don't want you accidentally shooting off any important parts of your anatomy."

Yarko gladly accepted Vlodko's offer of a bed. This home was one place where he felt safe.

He lay for a long time without even trying to close his eyes. He couldn't sleep. The smell of antiquity lingered in his nose. It truly was the smell of history. He finally closed his eyes and slept. In his dreams, he saw a hellish battle, a vast flaming city, burning crossbeams falling to the ground in showers of embers, raining dark figures of warriors locked in mortal combat, their bloody swords dripping pitch. Somehow he knew that the burning city was Lviv, not Iskorosten'.

"Flaming vengeance," he whispered in his sleep.

7

EARLY ON THURSDAY MORNING, Yarko and Vlodko drove to the Cathedral of Saint George. Father Onufriy was already waiting for them at the top of the steps to the platform in front of the entrance. Clearly, Vlodko had called to inform him of the task at hand. Yarko admired Vlodko's capable, intelligent, yet cold-blooded nature. Again all things were prepared and in control. After letting Yarko out with his suitcase next to the church, Vlodko met up with a second police car and the two vehicles sped off in the direction of Zamarstyniv.

Yarko found himself standing on stone steps that led past a wrought-iron fence and a gate that opened to a square before the church. From here a set of steps led to the platform before the doors to the majestic edifice itself. Father Onufriy stood on this last set of steps apparently for the sole purpose of watching this young man struggle uphill with his oversize wooden burden. Yarko had expected an offer of help with the awkward load. All the weight was at one end of the suitcase, making it a real test of one's wrist as well as biceps and shoulder. Yarko was thinking of something sarcastic to say, but the young priest opened the conversation.

"Glory to Jesus Christ. Welcome, my son. Do you remember me telling you to call me if get into any kind of mess? And lo and behold, you have finally come to me! It was on that same Sunday that I told Vlodko to keep an eye on a crazy Canadian with his wild bicycle. I had a feeling that something evil had a hold on you. As it turns out, Vlodko was familiar with your bike already. Anyway, if I'm not mistaken, it was that same day that Vlodko had to save you from the amorous advances of our infamous Dzvinka—eternal be her memory… And now getting down to business, Vlodko tells me you are bringing me quite the gift." Father Onufriy was keeping Yarko as off balance in the conversation as he was in the process of climbing the steps with the suitcase. Yarko was now holding the handle with both hands as he negotiated one step at a time.

"Glory forever, Father." Yarko's words were laden with full dose of sarcasm. But he softened his tone to bring peace to the verbal duel. "So it was you who sent me my guardian angel? Well, for that I am certainly in your debt. I had no time to find you a gift, but I'll be glad to share something that will interest you."

"As it turns out, there is no need to thank me," Father Onufriy said modestly. "Vlodko tells me that Ksenia also informed him that our dear Dzvinka had found herself a new victim. We just didn't know where to find you. So on Sunday when I told Vlodko which way you were headed, he was able to pin a tail on you again and he tracked you to your hotel. Then it was just a matter of waiting for Dzvinka to arrive. The rest, as they say, is history … But let's not talk here on the steps." Father Onufriy motioned Yarko to the cathedral.

Yarko climbed the final steps. He was glad that Vlodko ordered him not to take the gun. The extra weight tugging at his pants would not have helped at all. He had also left his stolen blue Lada behind. Ksenia had promised to visit him at the church after lunch and to bring the car with her.

Yarko and the priest entered the church through the large, ornate, bronze-covered doors. Once inside, they turned left down a set of stairs that led to the basement of the structure. Yarko carried the suitcase, barely keeping up to Father Onufriy. They walked down a long corridor. On both sides were doors to individual monk's cells. They entered into one such small room. Father Onufriy turned on the light and sat behind a small table. Yarko wrestled his burden onto it. He opened the suitcase, withdrew the book, and placed it in front of the priest.

Father Onufriy pulled out a notebook and opened it beside the book. He took a pencil and placed it in his teeth; only then did he open the book. He read silently for a long time. From time to time he returned to the first pages. After a half-hour of silence he raised his head and drilled his eyes into Yarko's. Yarko felt a shiver run down his spine.

"Do you know what you have here?" the priest asked.

Yarko felt sheepish, like an accused before a judge. "Not the slightest idea."

"This may be the greatest historical find of the twentieth century in Ukraine. At first I thought it was fifteenth century, but no, this was written in the first half of the thirteenth century. That's over 750 years ago. And it is not a Bible. It is a chronicle—a history. What's more, the author, or possibly the co-author, was in the army of Prince Danylo. He was in his princely court. What is even more interesting is that he describes the defence of Kyiv against the Mongol Horde of Batu Khan. It's as if he were an actual participant in the battle. History records that Prince Danylo of Halych sent his warlord Dmytro to defend Kyiv. It just may be that the author was part of this warlord's retinue. There's reading here for a week or two. There are a lot of interesting facts."

"Well, what sort of things did you read, Father?"

"I'm not sure. It is hard to read, but here, for example, it appears that the Mongols had help from the tribes of Ves and Merya of the Suzdalian Princedom to the north, which the Khan had conquered three years prior. I guess that has some logic. Having plundered Kyiv once in 1169, it stands to reason that the katsaps would do it again."

The word "katsap" was derogatory slang, referring to the Muscovites, somewhat equivalent to "Russki" in English. It translates roughly as "the goat-bearded ones."

Father Onufriy continued. "It is also interesting, that to break through fortifications the Mongols used something that's referred to here as thunder and fire. I can't be completely sure what that refers to, but just think about it, Yarko, having never seen it before, how would you have described an explosion of gunpowder? This may be the first recorded case of the military use of explosives. Anyway, no more questions, let me continue reading."

The priest read very slowly, often writing in his notebook. Yarko grew bored. He watched the pages of the book get turned slowly one after another. Father Onufriy's ascetic studiousness gave the impression of a mediaeval monk. The cell they were in only reinforced that impression. The walls were windowless and bare except for a black cross hanging on the wall behind the hunched figure of the priest. These walls were once white, but they were now very much yellowed by a half-century of neglect. In places, the paint was cracked and peeling, hanging down in curlicues at the ceiling. The furnishings were equally ascetic—a table, a chair, a bed with no sign of a mattress, and a black wooden trunk. Yarko had the dubious pleasure of observing every square inch of this undersized room for over two hours.

Sitting silently all this time, he had noticed a sliver of white showing among the tan-coloured parchment pages of the book. At first this sliver was almost imperceptible, but after every turn of a page, it became more and more obvious. Yarko didn't give it much thought. This white marker became simply a measure of the progress the priest was making. Yarko checked his watch from time to time and calculated how many more hours of such reading it would take to reach this white marker. Yarko was very aware of the time. He was booked on the 9 p.m. train that would take him through Hungary to Vienna, Austria. It would take him two hours to pack, including the time to dismantle the bike into a more portable package. He was regretting the fact that items such as the gun and the book could not be taken across borders without risking confiscation.

And so, page after page, this mysterious sliver of white was clearly revealing itself to be white paper. In his state of boredom the significance of modern paper in an ancient book did not sink into his brain. Finally, he realized that he was looking at notepaper that had no place in a mediaeval text. It was a place marker much like the letter in the old Kobzar.

"Father, here among the pages of the book is a white sheet of notepaper!"

It proved to be a sheet of lined paper. On it was some neat and tiny handwriting in blue ink, as well as a sketch of some sort. There were some numbers and calculations. Father Onufriy and Yarko examined it carefully. Together they read some underlined words that served as a title for these notes: *The Library of Yaroslaw the Wise*.

They breathed in simultaneously as if the legendary prince himself had appeared to them in person. They held their breath in anticipation of what might follow. They continued to read the note.

> *The Library was not lost at the time of the destruction of Kyiv by the Mongols of Batu Khan, because the main repository of books was underground in a natural cave in the limestone bedrock of Kyiv. The Tartars only destroyed the building that stood above the entrance to the underground passage to the cave. This building was for the reading and transcription of books, but the storage itself was underground. Per the data given by the author of this book the location of this entrance would be east of the church of Saint Sophia, in the area of the Mykhailivsky monastery.*

Both Yarko and Father Onufriy were stunned. They stood motionless, each coming to his own realization of what they had just read. Yarko, who after three hours of boredom had been more than ready to take the train to Austria, was now calculating how he could manage to stay. He didn't want to leave either the book or the city of Lviv and his new friends in Ukraine. He sensed that he was witnessing something unbelievably important for both Ukraine and Europe. Whatever it was, it was beginning right here.

Father Onufriy had an even deeper understanding of the implications of the new challenge that had appeared before them. "Did you know, Yarko, that at the time of Prince Yaroslaw the Wise, Kyiv was the second-largest city in Europe, not counting Byzantium. Yaroslaw's Library is said by some to have contained over 1,000 handwritten tomes. This was second only to Byzantium. At the time that Western Europe was experiencing the Dark Ages, Kyiv was a centre of learning, and a centre of trade with all corners of the Earth. Imagine: Byzantium, Bulgaria, and Arabia to the south, Scandinavia to the north, Khozaria, Persia, India, and China to the east, and to the west there was Poland, Saxony, France, and England. And the land of Rus' stood on the crossroads! We know the chronicler Nestor had much older historical sources to work from when he wrote *The Tale of Bygone Years* in the twelfth century. But all this ancient material disappeared along with the Library after the fall of Kyiv in 1240 to the Mongol Horde. My head gets dizzy just imagining what we could find there."

The priest's words were marked with sadness, even trepidation, the reason for which was not quite clear to Yarko. The explanation did not take long to come.

"For three and a half centuries," Onufriy continued, "Ukrainians were at war with Muscovy. We fought not only for freedom and independence, but we even had to fight for our history. As you know, almost all nations of this world have had to fight for their freedom at one time or other. Many also had to fight for their very existence. But for a nation to have to fight for its history, even for its historic name—now that is something quite unique in this world. It was just our luck of the draw. Instead of making enemies of Germans, French, English, Arabs, or Chinese, it was our luck to have Muscovites for enemies. For them it was not enough to seize lands and exterminate aboriginal populations. They had to take the history, the glory, and even the name of those they conquered."

"Okay, but Ukraine is independent today," said Yarko, "so in the end, haven't we won?"

"Independent, my arse," said Onufriy, revealing a somewhat less than ascetic side. "Ukraine has been selling off its independence piecemeal for a decade. We gave the Muscovites our 4,000 tactical nuclear missiles. We leased them Sevastopol as a naval base. We sold them our uranium mines. If I were to step outside and merely whisper that we found the Library of Yaroslaw, by this evening, a planeload of Muscovite specialists would arrive in Kyiv. By morning they'd have the whole thing packed up and flown to Saint Petersburg for study. By noon the next day, selected items would accidentally be lost in a fire. And by nightfall some famous historian would have prepared a seminar about the achievements of the great Russian nation and the recently discovered treasures of its history."

Yarko looked sceptical.

"I'm not kidding," said Onufriy. "If I were to whisper this in our dear president's ear, he'd have the historic treasure sold to the Muscovites for the price of two days supply of natural gas to Kharkiv. And the proceeds would be in his brother-in-law's bank account within a week."

"So why would the Russians want to re-take Ukraine again? If they're getting everything they want already, what's the big deal?"

"To answer that, one has to answer another question first: What is the Muscovite nation? And no, it is not Churchill's riddle inside an enigma." Onufriy was pointedly using the historical name of the Russian Federation. "At the end of the first millennium, they were Finno-Ugric tribes which were conquered by the Rus', our forefathers, the Slavic-speaking people who lived in the lands around Kyiv. The Rus' brought Orthodox Christianity, culture, and a written Slavic language to those tribes. The written language, usually known as Church Slavonic, quite logically became the basis of the language of state, church, culture, and trade in those areas, although their native Finnish language was not eradicated for hundreds of years. The Muscovite language is what eventually developed from this mix, which even includes some Mongolian. They are no more Slavic or Rus'-ian than Romanians can be Romans.

"Those northern lands, having become an independent princedom in the twelfth century, were known by many names, including Suzdal and Muscovy. The name Rus', on the other hand, historically was applied strictly to the Slavic people in what is Ukraine today.

"After its destruction by the Mongols in 1240, Kyiv ceased to exist—at least as a political centre. Remnants of the Rus' state survived in the west of Ukraine as the Halych-Volyn princedom for another hundred years. After that, it ended up being incorporated into Lithuania and then into the Lithuanian-Polish Commonwealth. Meanwhile, Muscovy was able to grow and expand on the carcass of a decaying Mongol Empire. This expansion was more like a creeping coup d'état, a change of the ruling class in the empire, not an actual reconquest. In the eighteenth century, when they finally gained control of Kyiv and much of today's Ukraine, the state of Muscovy was renamed using the Greek version of the name Rus', namely Rossia.

"Prior to that, there was no confusion between Rus'-Ukraine in the south and Muscovy in the north. Due to this resulting confusion—and I'm talking barely a century ago—the Rus', or Rusyny, began calling themselves Ukrainians simply to differentiate themselves from the Muscovites-Rossiany."

"And the conclusion is?" prompted Yarko, who had heard this thousand-year history a dozen times before.

"The conclusion is that without Kyiv and Rus'-Ukraine within their borders, the very name Rossia becomes a lie. The existence of an independent Ukraine destroys their national myth," explained Onufriy. "It challenges the lie at the heart of the Russian mentality. Then Rossia, the empire, must revert to Muscovy, the nation-state."

"I don't get it," said Yarko. "Are you saying Russia needs to re-incorporate Ukraine or even risk war simply because of some national myth? Are you saying some poor slob in Chelyabinsk would even give a shit?"

Yarko had forgotten that he was talking to a priest, and this last outburst left him a little red faced.

"It works on many levels, Yarko," said Father Onufriy, smiling at Yarko's embarrassment. "Intellectuals, writers, and a few politicians may, in fact, relate to a national myth. A much larger layer of citizenry sees war as an opportunity for profiteering, and plunder. Another group truly enjoys the killing. Then there's the great mass of poor slobs, as you put it, who can't think for themselves, and are presented with no alternative. Just think of the Germans in the Second World War. National Myth. War Profiteering. Bloodlust. And the great bunch of your poor slobs who were given no alternative. Stalin's Muscovites were no different. And now there's your Americans in Iraq."

"I'm from Canada. They are not my Americans."

"Whatever... There seem to be machines set up to eliminate criticism of the state, to eliminate any alternatives. They killed Starovoytova in St. Petersburg. I'm betting that Mazepa-Politkovskaya will be the next journalist to die. It seems to be a universal phenomenon. I read that in England, just yesterday, someone bumped off a Dr. David Kelly. He was a vocal critic of the whole Weapons of Mass Destruction in Iraq fiction. Suicide they called it. Of course it was. And then there's Ukraine."

"I know, I know," Yarko interrupted. "The murders of singer Bilozir, presidential candidate Chornovil, journalist Gongadze, and so on. You guys need a revolution."

There was silence for a minute or two.

"So now what?" asked Yarko. "What's the plan? Would it not be better to bury what we found, just like my grandparents did? "

Father Onufriy sighed. "That may not be possible. I don't think that this genie fits back inside the bottle. To me it looks like we'll have to repeat in Kyiv what we just pulled off in Lviv—except on a much larger scale of course. Under the very nose of our dear president, and of the whole of Parliament, and the SBU security service, along with the Berkut interior troops and a few hundred Muscovite spies and agents—and even under the very feet of two million residents—we're actually going to find and dig up the real treasure. And we'll manage to do it in secret."

"Treasure?" said Yarko. "Yes, I guess it would be a treasure. Yaroslaw's Treasure!"

"Your treasure or the prince's?" teased Onufriy. "Anyway, just imagine the things we might find!"

"So how the hell do we go about organizing such an operation? And how do we do it secretly at that?"

"It will take a year or more. We'll have to create an organization operating both here and in the diaspora. A secret organization. We'll need funding, at least a few million American."

Yarko was sceptical. In a land where $200 was a monthly salary, this priest was talking about millions. Somehow the image of a priest and an international clandestine organization seemed totally incongruous. Yarko said nothing, but his crooked sarcastic smile gave away his thoughts.

"Don't laugh, Yarko, it's been done before. The church has worked clandestinely for decades, and the organization too. Although you can still see the old Communist Party apparatchiks pulling the strings of power every day, what you can't see so readily is the second set of strings being pulled by us from below. We've got our people everywhere too. But none of that matters now, because it is way past lunchtime and I'm starved. We'll grab a bite, and then I must get back to this book to recalculate the measurements. Your grandfather made some estimations to locate the cave, but I'll have to make calculations of my own. There are maps of the layout of the original city on the Web. It's actually easier to calculate this now than a half-century ago. But for now, lets go and eat."

They walked along the corridors under the church to the opposite side of the building. The lunchroom was as ascetic as the rest of the rooms. One difference was that here they had the company of four other priests or monks. The other difference was the presence of a radio that stood on a shelf, quietly playing some boring music. The food consisted of a couple of fat slices of bread and a mug of watery tea. There were slices of lard that everyone happily slapped on the bread in place butter. Yarko begged off. Nobody talked much. Yarko and Father Onufriy sat across from each other. Both were lost in thought. Yarko found it chilly in the church basement, so he was quite happy to warm himself with the tea.

The music on the radio was interrupted by a news flash:

"Today in Zamarstyniv, the Lviv city militsya discovered the decomposed body of a man in a shallow grave. Investigators report that they have reasons to believe that this may be the body of the head of the secretariat of the Rukh Organization, Mykhaylo Boychyshyn... Mr. Boychyshyn disappeared in 1994 from the Rukh office in Kyiv under mysterious circumstances... In Kyiv the Ministry of the Interior has not made any official comment. The minister himself has not been available. We are anticipating a press conference at the Ministry at five o'clock. Here in Lviv, the chief of police..."

Yarko could not hear the rest of the report because the cafeteria was suddenly abuzz with excitement. The four priests who had sat there in silence suddenly all had something to say. Yarko glanced knowingly at Father Onufriy. "Well done, Vlodko!" he whispered.

Onufriy whispered back, leaning conspiratorially towards Yarko. "Just listen to that idiot of a city police chief bragging on the radio. That jerk couldn't find his di—er, keys in his pocket, never mind a buried body. But that's fine. It's good that there is no mention of

Vlodko on the radio. We need to stay anonymous. And actually, if I've understood Vlodko right, you deserve some credit for all this too. Thank God your personal grave has remained empty so far. Now keep it that way, my friend. I hate doing funerals… Actually, weddings are more my style."

Yarko didn't miss the wink at the end of Onufriy's comment. He found himself turning red again. So far he hadn't really thought about romance. He knew that he felt comfortable and happy when he was with Ksenia. It was as if he had known her for years. He realized that without her he might actually feel a certain emptiness. Unfortunately, Yarko had a train to catch that night.

This chain of thought was interrupted by the appearance of Ksenia herself in the church basement lunchroom. Her sudden arrival confused Yarko and added to the excess blood-flow to his face. He had forgotten that she had promised to come and bring the blue Lada after lunch. Ksenia appeared quite agitated and out of breath as she came through the doorway.

"Have you heard the news?" she asked

"Yes, we heard, we were just listening to the report on the radio," said Onufriy.

"But I mean have you actually seen the city? People are leaving work and are filling the streets! Offices are emptying. The streets are filling. They say there's going to be a press conference by the Ratush tower of the city hall. But there's a crowd forming here around the Saint George's Cathedral also. There's going to be a demonstration bigger than anything we've seen!"

"Or more likely a riot," grumbled Onufriy. He had the maturity to foresee that there can be very little difference between a spontaneous demonstration and a riotous mob. There was a significant percentage of Russian-speaking inhabitants in Lviv. They could easily become the target of unfocused anger. It was up to him. He was the right person in the right place to try to maintain order.

"Father Peter, run to the Metropolitan," Onufriy ordered, taking charge of the group of priests. "Tell him about all the news—tell him everything. In half an hour we hold a prayer service outside, in the square before the church. After that we head up a slow, orderly procession towards the Rynok square to the Ratush. Today the Church must take charge and lead, or else the mob will trample us. We can't be late. I'll be in front of the church in ten minutes."

Then he whispered to Ksenia and Yarko, "We need to run back to the cell, Yarko. And you too, Ksenia. We need to stash the book in a safe place. Now!"

They ran down the corridor, almost mowing down an old priest who was heading in the opposite direction. He was quite bald, with mere tufts of white hair above his ears, a scraggly white beard on his chin, and bushy white eyebrows.

"Father Ivan," said Onufriy. "I don't have time to explain, but there will be a Moleben prayer outside in ten minutes. Go tell the sisters, we need everyone there."

Entering his cell, Onufriy quickly wrapped the book and put it back in the wooden suitcase. In his haste he did not notice that something had been disturbed. He grabbed the suitcase and headed out across the hallway. Two steps to the right, he opened the door to a dark room on the opposite side and flicked on the light. The ancient brown Bakelite light switch was screwed directly to the wall in the hallway outside the room. The blinding yellow light from the naked bulb in the fixture inside revealed the strangest of rooms. This was an old disused coal locker. On the wall opposite the light, a dusty mountain of coal rose to the very ceiling. Jutting from the corner formed by the wall and ceiling was an old galvanized sheet metal chute that once guided fresh loads of black fuel delivered through an opening on the outside. Along the walls stood some disused rusty grates and bars along with several burlap-covered rectangles that may have been icons.

Yarko watched carefully to see where his suitcase would be hidden. Father Onufriy reached into the thick layer of dust on the floor and lifted a steel plate that covered a compartment not much larger than the suitcase. He lowered the suitcase and slowly placed the steel plate back down. A small cloud of black coal dust hovered above the place where the case and the plate had disappeared. With two catlike steps the priest was back out in the hallway. He took off his shoes and wiped the black dust footprint with his sock.

"I've got to change anyway," was his laconic comment as he disappeared back into his cell.

Moments later he emerged wearing a gold-trimmed chasuble, the cape-like robe of Byzantine-rite priests. They hurried down the hall and up the stairs to the foyer before the bronze portals. Opening these doors, they were met by quite a sight. It seemed that the buildings of the whole city had disgorged their occupants. They filled the streets and alleys and every square foot of parkland or lawn with a multi-hued flow of humanity. Lviv, the Piedmont of the reborn Ukrainian nation, was about to give a piece of its mind to a regime composed of crooks and profiteers for whom the retention of power was everything. For them, an independent Ukraine was only a means to protect their turf from their kin to the north and to extract international respect where none was deserved. Today, the discovery of the remains of one of the victims of the machinery that kept the crooks in power was a fit occasion for the people to have their say.

The grassy hill on which the cathedral stood was covered with people. The handful of clergy stood on the steps before the church and began the solemn Gregorian chant of a prayer. Yarko understood that this was a calculated exercise to calm and refocus the crowd. He understood what Father Onufriy had feared. A crowd of a hundred thousand, never mind an angry crowd of one hundred thousand, was a guarantee of violence. Yarko thought of his scheduled train trip that evening. With secret satisfaction he concluded that with the whole city on foot and with abandoned cars everywhere, there was no realistic hope to make the station on time. Yarko smiled; he didn't want to miss this event for anything.

"Yarko, by nightfall this crowd will be a mob. Our mob mind you, but still a mob," Ksenia said.

"Father Onufriy and his band of clerics will have their jobs cut out for them."

"Then let's skip these prayers and follow the crowds to the Rynok. That's where the action is bound to be." As they turned and pushed their way through the crowd, Ksenia looked around with a puzzled look in her eyes.

"What's wrong?" asked Yarko.

"The car, the blue Lada, it's missing. I parked it right here."

"It couldn't have gone far with these crowds. In any case, it looks like its rightful owners may be back in operation."

The two of them joined the broad stream of humanity that filled the roadway from sidewalk to sidewalk and flowed eastward towards the market square. Abandoned cars were like rocks in a mountain stream, briefly parting the flow but barely slowing it at all. Flags had begun to appear. The national blue-and-yellow flag was matched by an equal number of red-over-black flags. The latter was the battle flag of the Organization of Ukrainian Nationalists, whose guerrilla army, the UPA, had once battled Nazi and Soviet alike. The colour of blood over black earth warned any invader of the price that would have to be paid for every metre of Ukraine's soil.

At one intersection, a wrinkled old lady had strategically stationed her cart and was doing great business selling miniature flags. Yarko bought two. He kept the blue-and-yellow one for himself and gave the black-and-red one to Ksenia. It was impossible to converse over the din of the crowd, but Ksenia's mischievous smile spoke reams about the understanding that this gesture signalled.

With a kilometre still to go, the flow of the crowd slowed to a crawl. Ksenia motioned to go to the right. Yarko understood that in the end it might prove easier to get to his hotel than to try for the epicentre of the political activity. The roar emanating from the area of the Market Square was briefly matched by that of two storm-grey aircraft. Ksenia and Yarko watched as a pair of multi-engined Antonovs banked sharply as they turned for their final approach. Then the roar of the crowd drowned out the aircraft.

"That's our visitors from Kyiv," explained Ksenia. "It's a military transport. It's either SBU, the state security service, or the old OMON Interior troops, except now they are called Berkut, the Golden Eagle. Instead of coming to help with the Boychyshyn murder investigation, they have come to battle the crowd."

"What do you mean?"

"One plane is more than enough to carry a forensic team. Two planes means there's a regiment of assault troops—sent to bust heads."

"You mean Ukrainian-style crowd control?" chuckled Yarko. He knew no reply would be needed.

By now the sound level of the crowd was beyond description. It was a noise matched perhaps by Niagara Falls or an inbound tornado.

"To the hotel," Ksenia commanded. "I can't do any more here. I'll report to my contact just in case. I just hope Vlodko made it to the Ratush. Us two will have to watch the action on TV."

Moving against the flow of people, they were close enough to distinguish the Mieckewicz monument and the fountain, which was happily spraying water. What they could not see, far behind them, was the long procession of the faithful, led by both Orthodox and Catholic clergy, that snaked through the crowds along the Street of the November Uprising, steadily approaching the Rynok Market Square. They also missed the column of green canvas-covered trucks that was just now turning from Tershakivska Street onto Pekarska.

8

A RAY OF BRIGHT SUNSHINE crept slowly across his face. Yarko was sleeping on the floor. Ksenia slept on the bed covered by only a sheet. The television in the corner silently winked in multi-hued light, like the giant unseeing eye of a cyclops. The drapes had been drawn and now hid the bright blue of the sky. A sliver of sunlight broke through the tiniest of gaps and slowly crept along the floor like the hand of a giant clock. The sun stood high in the sky.

Yarko awoke. He scanned the room. His head was still buzzing from the previous day's events. He remembered the scenes from the live TV newscast that they had watched until late into the night.

Closing his eyes, he again saw the images of the crowd before the Ratush tower. Over the constant din, he had barely been able to make out the words of the speakers on the podium, who stood shielded by a curtain of blue-and-yellow flags. He could sense again the agitation of the crowd. He remembered holding his breath as he watched the advance of the Berkut Interior troops in their black-blue-white speckled urban camouflage and black helmets with visors, pushing their black shields through the crowd, pressing for the podium. He heard again the crowd's roar of "Shame, OMON, Shame." OMON, he knew, was the Soviet-era acronym for these despised troops. These chants had been followed by an even louder "Ge-shta-po, Ge-shta-po." Then followed the words of a song popularized by a perestroika-era rock-group: "Return the language—an order not a request…" Yarko knew that these troops were likely Russian-speaking, and in this town, before this crowd, that was enough for them to become the focus of every sort of anger.

He remembered watching breathlessly as unarmed young men in white T-shirts, from the Tryzub youth organization, blocked any further progress of the troops just as they had pushed through to the podium. This made the troops a stationary target for rocks and bottles as well as the more traditional vegetables and eggs. A few dozen Lviv city cops carrying automatic weapons then took the stage and faced the black shield turtle that had been formed by the Interior troops. Finally, the Interior troops began a slow retreat. Then the crowd began the chant of the political movement known as "Ukraine without Kuchma" (President Kuchma). This movement was a nationwide reaction to the murder of the Internet journalist Georgiy Gongadze. Shouts of "Kuchma het; Kuchma het" (Kuchma out, Kuchma out) accompanied the slow retreat of the armed machine that was dedicated to keeping the powerful in power, and the country's people in check.

Yarko remembered how the arrival of the religious procession finally brought a degree of calm and order to the crowd. The noise level dropped off to the point that individual speeches could be heard. The speeches were followed by songs born out of previous struggles for national independence. The tension that had threatened to erupt into violence or vandalism had changed to a more festive mood. A religious anthem sung by a hundred thousand voices under the twinkling stars of a clear night sky was a fitting finale to this tumultuous day. "Oh One Great God" was a hymn Yarko had sung many times around Plast boy scout campfires. Hearing it echoing off downtown Lviv buildings, sung by tens of thousands in the dark of night, was an experience that had been simply majestic.

Lying on his back on the hotel-room floor, Yarko opened his eyes again and turned his head towards the TV. A muted news commentator was unusually animated in his delivery. Yarko rose and turned up the volume. The commentator was just completing the story about last night's events. This was followed by a brief commercial in Russian for some kind of vitamin supplement. When the news came back on, Yarko could not help but notice that the newscaster's Ukrainian had become much more understandable than it had been on previous days. It seemed that after the previous day's events the newscaster had taken the time to prepare his material with additional attention to its grammar and language.

Yarko had observed that it was usual for Ukrainians to throw in Russian words, or to use Russian phrases, or use Russian sentence structure when speaking Ukrainian. The result was a kind of pidgin-Ukrainian that became even less understandable when the speaker attempted to throw in English words. The strange complication with English words is that most Ukrainians learn them indirectly from their Russian neighbours. The Russian language has no "H" sound, so when borrowing English words the "H" gets replaced by either a "G" or a guttural "Kh". To add to the confusion, the Russian symbol for "G" is the Ukrainian symbol for "H". The Ukrainian language, on the other hand, has all three sounds, and a symbol for each. One would think this should make adoption of English words into Ukrainian quite easy. But not so. By relying on the Russians as their informational middleman, most Ukrainians are sure that movies are made in Khollywood. They are convinced that Wayne Hretsky plays Khockey. They are quite surprised to learn that Bill Hates is not on the board of directors at Microsoft, and that Al Whore is not the name of the presidential candidate who had lost to George Bush.

Yarko was listening carefully to the broadcast.

"...the head of security at the Lviv airport has confirmed that one of the two aircraft is not preparing to leave. Troop transport trucks are encamped around the plane and appear to be preparing for a lengthy stay.

"The events of the past night in Lviv have impacted the political arena in the country's capital. The Presidential Information Agency reports that President Kuchma has postponed his long-awaited visit to Moscow. The reasons given were the current cabinet crisis and the unusual events in Western Ukraine. The Agency reports that the president has scheduled a press conference for 4 p.m. This channel will be

reporting from the presidential press conference live, beginning at four. There are unconfirmed rumours that the Minister of the Interior, Yuriy Smirnov, who had been in Moscow in conjunction with plans for the presidential visit, has submitted his resignation citing reasons of health. Moscow sources report that he has been admitted to a local hospital. The Presidential Information Agency says that there are no grounds for the previous reports of additional resignations being submitted by certain other cabinet ministers...

"In Moscow today, General Gusov has denied rumours that planes of the Russian Federation have resumed bombing the approaches to the city of Grozny, saying that life in Grozny is peaceful and that the program of the pacification of Chechnya has been crowned with the brilliant success of Russian military forces.

"And closer to home, the Sixth and the Ninth Army of the Russian Federation is continuing its joint manoeuvres on the territory of the Belorussian Republic..."

Yarko turned the TV off. He could hear water splashing in the washroom. It seems that Ksenia had out-manoeuvred Yarko, occupying this strategic position while he was still watching the news.

"Yarchyk, lets go to Saint George's. You take your bicycle and I'll manage by streetcar...So how did you like our OMON Interior troops? They're a remnant of the old Evil Empire, you know. They were trained to hate Ukrainians. Some years ago they beat the shit out of us in Kyiv by the church of St. Sophia. It was during the funeral of Patriarch Volodymyr. I was there. They tried the same yesterday. But when Mykhaylo Boychyshyn disappeared the bastards didn't lift a finger. Absurdity, wouldn't you agree? Our taxes pay for these servants of the Muscovite Empire just so they can continue to oppress us. That was the whole point of the crowd's anger yesterday. We are actually paying the salaries of our enemies. Not only these OMON-Berkut guys. We pay to maintain statues of Lenin; we pay for Muscovite schools, Muscovite newspapers, Muscovite TV and radio. Absurdity.

The Communist Party is still legal, but the Ukrainian youth organization Tryzub is not. Simply absurdity."

The sounds of a toothbrush and running water interrupted this bathroom monologue.

Riding the bike, Yarko beat Ksenia to the cathedral by over an hour. He locked the bike to an iron railing well hidden by bushes, and ran up the stairs and through the bronze portals to the church. Father Onufriy shared some bread and tea with Yarko, and led him to his cell. Onufriy brought the suitcase with the book and continued his research. It was only after Father Onufriy had pored over several pages that Ksenia finally announced her arrival with a knock on the cell door. Yarko let her in.

It was clear that Ksenia had gone home to change. She was now wearing a pale yellow sleeveless dress with a row of golden buttons from top to bottom. It was a simple dress. Its beauty lay in its ability to reveal every movement of the lithe body underneath.

"The author was an architect or a builder as well as a soldier," said Onufriy as he looked again at the book. "He describes buildings in great detail. Now here is the key. As we know from history, most defenders of Kyiv were at the Desyatynna Church, which collapsed killing them all. Dmytro, as we know, gets captured. But the writer, along with a cohort of soldiers, avoids the final slaughter by escaping underground, under the burning library. A shaft in the bedrock leads to the main repository of books—in a large underground room. The author says he collapsed the entrance, sealing it. It's funny that historians always believed that the library was attached to the church of St. Sophia. Turns out that it was a separate building right by the city walls. Here was the entrance to a cavern complex that was also an escape route, but only for those few that knew about it. This entrance was a vertical shaft with stairs or a ladder of some sort.

Below it was the library... and then some other tunnel that led who knows where. You know, that also explains why so few books fell into Mongol hands."

"So you know where the great library is?" asked Yarko.

"Close, real close. Your grandfather did a good job with his estimate. Right now we're about forty metres apart. That's close given that he would not have had the kind of archaeological data that I accessed on the Internet this morning."

"I don't see a computer here," said Ksenia.

"You know Father Ivan, don't you? He let me use his while he was at vespers," explained Onufriy. "I used his printer too. The archaeological map's scale is different from the street map's, but if you know where to find the reference points it's just simple trigonometry."

"A sine from heaven," said Yarko in English.

Onufriy continued reading. His face was a complex of emotions. There were tears in his eyes. Rather than let a tear stain the book he closed it and wiped his face in his sleeve.

"My God. You know, the history of Rus'-Ukraine lives. Although buried alive for centuries. It still lives!" Onufriy's voice was hoarse with emotion.

In an effort to recover himself, Onufriy stood up and walked to the door of the cell and then back to the desk, stretching his tired body. "I'm really stiff," he said. "What time is it?"

It was five in the afternoon. As well as being tired from sitting, they were all starving. They had eaten no lunch and barely any breakfast. Yarko was the first to propose the obvious.

"Lets hit a restaurant before the supper hour to miss the rush. I saw one near here yesterday. Here, Father, let me take the book and suitcase. I know where it goes. Just give me the key. You guys go ahead. I'll catch up."

Ksenia and Father Onufriy headed down the hall to the stairs that would lead them up to the church portal. Yarko carried the suitcase to the old coal locker. He placed it in its hiding spot, swearing at himself for getting his hands dirty. He locked the door and chased after his friends, who had already disappeared outside. Leaping several steps at a time he climbed the stairs and swung open the cathedral's doors on the run.

The very moment that he hit the doors he heard the unmistakable sound of automatic weapon fire. Outside was a hellish scene. Two men were running down the steps, dragging Ksenia between them. Rolling down these steps was the blood-spattered black-clothed figure of Father Onufriy. Right before him on the entry platform lay the unconscious figure of another stranger. Parked just down the road was the light blue Lada; a black one stood just behind it.

Distracted from the scene before him by a movement to his right, Yarko saw that his momentum had carried him right between two other men, both of them clothed in grey. They were holding short-barrelled automatic weapons. The barrels swung towards him. For a brief moment the two hesitated. They would have been firing directly at each other. They then turned their weapons around to strike him with the stocks, but by then Yarko had thrown himself back through the closing portal. He heard the weapons discharge behind him, the bullets ringing on the bronze facing of the door.

A savage terror squeezed Yarko's gut as he scurried back down the stairs and down the hall, back to the room where he had just hidden the book. He opened the door with the key just as he heard footsteps running down the stairs. As he closed the door and locked it, he heard the intruders discharge the remainder of their clips in his direction.

"Blyaa… motherfucker!" he heard as the shooters hammered on the door.

The room was pitch black except for the sliver of light that glowed faintly under its thick wooden door. Yarko was trembling from the rush of excess adrenaline. Life was so dear to him. He realized that it was now being measured in seconds. Every additional second was a victory stolen from those men in grey. He counted two handfuls of such tiny victories already. His mind had hit replay: Surprise at the portal—tick. Guns pointed at each other—tick. Clubbing with gunstock—tick. Doors swing to outside only—tick, tick tick. Key in hand—tick.

Wham! wham! came the sound of the men slamming the door. The darkness in the room seemed a guarantee of another one-second victory. He heard footsteps as additional strangers joined those slamming the door. Yarko thought he made out at least four different voices.

"Damn, the goddam light bulb," he thought, and took a backhanded swing at the bulb jutting out of the wall, smashing its glass.

Wham! wham! came more impacts of bodies on the door.

He desperately wanted to become invisible, to become a ghost in the darkness, so that he could just melt through the walls and run. He began scrambling up the mountain of coal to be as far from the door as possible.

Wham! wham!

He lost his footing and slid down the pile. This momentarily raised a cloudlet of coal dust, making even the sliver of light under the door disappear.

Wham! wham!

"I can hide in a cloud of black dust!" he muttered to himself, seeing the means to gain another one-second victory.

He grabbed for the burlap-covered icon that had stood by the wall. Fanning all parts of this little room, he raised a cloud of old coal dust so thick, so solid, he could feel it choking him. His eyes were closed tight.

Wham! Crack! The door jamb was giving way.

Yarko scrambled blindly up the mountain of coal again, grabbing at the metal chute near its top.

Crack! The door opened.

"Blyaa ... I can't see a fucking thing. Hit the bloody light switch!"

A hand reached out to that Bakelite blister of a switch and flicked it. Electrical current heated the filament of the broken light bulb to white hot, and ignited the coal dust that hung as a solid anthracite cloud in the coal locker. The resulting explosion ripped the door off its hinges and blew out the internal wall, spraying bricks into the hallway.

The shockwave hit Yarko like a giant fist and flung him up the disused coal chute. His back slammed against a rusty plate that covered the long-forgotten opening to the outside. Decades ago it had been plastered over with a thin skin of cement on the sidewalk outside. This concrete eggshell shattered as the plate flew into the air. A rag doll form of a young man flopped over the edge of the hole. Yarko was outside the cathedral, lying on the walkway that surrounded the structure. His legs dangled in a rectangular hole that was emitting a column of black smoke backlit by an unearthly yellow light.

9

YARKO REGAINED CONSCIOUSNESS. An overwhelming buzzing sound filled his head. The pain in his temples pulsed in time to some huge internal bell. The pain then flowed down his backbone to his shoulders. A grey fog had dimmed his sight. His nostrils burned with the acrid smell of smoke. He coughed. Through this grey fog he could see that his legs were hanging inside a rectangular opening from which shone the bright yellow light of a raging inferno. Again he imagined the dark shapes of fighting warriors against the background of the burning walled city of Iskorosten'.

"Flaming Vengeance," said his raspy voice.

The soles of his shoes, dangling just above the flames, were beginning to burn his feet. It took a while for this new pain to overcome the existing pain in his head. When it finally did, Yarko screamed and jumped to his feet. Milliseconds later an explosion of flame blew a yellow torch skyward from the opening, temporarily clearing the smoke. It was only then that Yarko realized that he was actually outside the cathedral walls. Before him, partly hidden by bush and trees, stood his bicycle. Beside the bike knelt some young lad, mouth wide open, staring at Yarko.

Yarko began to understand what had just happened, mentally piecing together the dramatic events of the past few minutes. He visualized what all this must have looked like to a bystander. The very flames of hell bursting from the ground, ejecting a coal-black figure in a column of smoke right beside a cathedral, would certainly not be something that one sees every day. The very thought of this made Yarko crack an ear-to-ear smile, flashing white teeth on a background of black.

Seeing this, the young lad whispered "Matko Bozka" in pious Polish, crossed himself with his left, and took off as fast as his feet could carry him. Yarko limped to his bicycle. He saw that the lock had been picked. It lay open on the grass.

"Bastard!" Yarko yelled after him, but he could not hear his own voice.

It was only then that his battered brain remembered what he had witnessed in front of the church.

"Ksenia!" he shrieked in emotional pain. "Where are you?"

The buzzing in his head wouldn't quit.

He scanned the surrounding streets. From the vantage point of this hill he had a panoramic view. He wiped his tears with his blackened hands. He heard, as if in a dream, the near-silent siren of a fire engine as it sped along the Street of the November Uprising. Just in front of the fire engine Yarko saw a light blue Lada turn left onto

University Street. The black Lada that was following it in the curb lane tried the same manoeuvre but brushed the fire engine. It recovered from the resultant spin and continued on University at high speed.

In mere seconds Yarko's mountain bike was flying across the University Park, along Slovackiy to Stefanyk Street. Yarko rode like a madman, between cars, across sidewalks, dodging pedestrians, but by the time he reached Martovych Street he had well and truly lost his quarry. He stopped in the middle of an intersection, oblivious to the traffic around him. He could not hear the honking of horns. He seemed to stand there for an eternity, like one of the many monuments in this city, looking up and down both streets. It was hopeless. At that point he noticed that a police car had stopped beside him. The officer was very interested in this totally black traffic obstruction. Through the open driver's window Yarko recognized Vlodko's face mouthing a steam of words that he could barely hear.

"I recognized the bike. There isn't another one like it in Lviv. Is that really you, Yarko? What on earth happened?"

Scarcely hearing his own voice, Yarko tried to explain things as briefly as possible. "No time for details. Some assholes seized Ksenia and drove off with her. They have the light blue Lada and a black one too. They shot Father Onufriy on the steps of the church. There was an explosion under the church. They are some ten minutes ahead of us, but I lost them. They headed east. The black Lada would be damaged on the left side. It collided with a fire engine. Can you hear me? They got Ksenia."

"They kidnapped Ksenia? Bastards! Let me help you throw the bike in the trunk, then get in quick"

Next thing Yarko knew he was in the car and they were making a U-turn with lights and siren on. Vlodko was moving his lips while holding the microphone. Straining, Yarko could just make out the words over the wail of the siren and the buzzing in his head.

"...Check. Ambulance already at Saint George's. Now block off the east end of Zelena and Lychakivska. Might as well block off Staroznesenska and Plastova. We're looking for a light blue Lada and a black Lada with damage to the left side of the car. Consider the suspects armed and dangerous. They have a female hostage. Careful..." Vlodko's voice choked with rage. "It's my sister."

Yarko observed how the road traffic parted before them like the Red Sea before Moses. Vlodko was flying.

Unable to hold a conversation, Yarko was trying to think this turn of events through. The reason for such a well-organized kidnapping had to be the book. How anyone could have found out about it and its significance was beyond him. Yarko suspected that the kidnappers had to be associated with the grey military transport plane that the TV reporter said stayed behind at the Lviv airport. But how? Yarko let his mind drift as he watched the city flash by.

An hour of chasing around the streets of Lviv yielded no result. The only useful thing was that Vlodko was receiving constant updates on the situation around Saint George's Cathedral. The fire had been put out quickly. It had been localized to one basement room. Among the ruins of the interior wall in the church they had found four burnt skeletons. The two unconscious persons from the steps in front of the church had been taken to the nearest hospital.

The evening sun hung low in the sky when Vlodko drove Yarko to the Hotel Ukrayina. Yarko had to get washed. During the final stages of the search, Yarko had noted with relief that the constant buzz in his ears, which sounded as if he were standing inside a waterfall, was decreasing. Yarko thanked his good fortune that he actually had water in the washroom. He bathed and got dressed. He put on a black short-sleeved shirt and khaki-green cargo shorts. As he was leaving his hotel room he noticed a white envelope under the door. He hurriedly shoved it under his shirt and rushed out.

Vlodko was already waiting. Yarko got in the police car, noting with some relief that his bike was still sticking out of the trunk. Vlodko drove off briskly. "Way to go, son," he said. "You managed to rub out four of them. And with no weapons on you to boot. That just won't do. Now open the glovebox and pull out your Smith and Wesson revolver. You've earned it ... Better still, take Dzvinka's little PSM that's next to it. It has six rounds left in the magazine and one in the chamber. We know that gun works."

"I'll take both," said Yarko.

"Cowboy!"

Yarko carefully examined the small gun. A lightweight pocket pistol, the 5.45-mm PSM was an ideal concealed weapon.

"Such pistols used to be standard issue for KGB special ops," explained Vlodko. "The PSM doesn't have the firepower, of say, my Ukrainian-made 9.25-mm Fort, but it is a lot easier to stuff in your pocket. Oh! I almost forgot. You've also earned some supper. Food's in the back. Now let me fill you in. While I was organizing some chow at a restaurant on Pekarska, I found out a few things from the shop owner. He remembers seeing a light blue Lada being followed by a black one with damage on the left side. They flew by at high speed, but the shopkeeper thought nothing of it, figuring the black car to be police of some sort. However, our police roadblocks report seeing nothing. That means our friends are somewhere nearby."

Vlodko made a turn onto Pekarska, and then continued his thought process. "We have them trapped. Also, the fact that the roadblocks didn't see anything says that they either have someone on the inside, or that they monitor police radio."

"So where are they? They couldn't have disappeared underground."

"Now there's a thought! Not quite underground, but inside our search area we do have the Lychakiv Cemetery. Plenty of quiet hidden places there. We better check there now. It's already getting dark."

With a pair of well-timed turns, Vlodko cut through the traffic and entered the cemetery. "Most of the paths here are too narrow for a car, so I'll block the entrance. From here we go on foot."

"Or by bike," said Yarko. "I can ride ahead and check a larger territory in a shorter time than you can on foot."

"Okay. Except be careful. It is getting dark. I need not remind you, those bastards are armed—and they do have my sister. So that means no heroics—got it? If you see anything, hurry back and get me. Oh, and remember, your old Smith and Wesson may misfire, and you're short two rounds. And remember also, that little PSM won't stop anybody with just one hit."

"Got it. And no heroics."

Ukraine, despite independence, was still far from the land of their parents' dreams.

As Yarko stepped out of the car he suddenly remembered the envelope he had shoved under his shirt. He pulled it out and handed it to Vlodko. "I almost forgot. This was under my door."

Vlodko scanned the note quickly. "It's in Russian. Those Muscovites want to trade Ksenia for your treasure in the suitcase. How can those bastards know about it? My God! Anyway, we can't do that. We don't trade in human lives. And Lord knows what's left of the book. There was a fire in that room."

"I think there's nothing left," said Yarko. "Between fire damage and water damage… No way out for us except to fight them."

"Yeah, our history is full of such situations. Anyway, good luck on your reconnaissance. Just remember, no heroics."

"No heroics," repeated Yarko. He pushed the PSM deep into his shorts pocket and shoved the big Smith and Wesson revolver under his belt behind his back. Vlodko had already pulled out the mountain bike and was straightening the handlebars. Yarko kicked his leg over the seat and headed off into the darkening twilight.

10

YARKO RODE AMONG THE LENGTHENING SHADOWS of the cemetery. This was not a cemetery like any he had ever seen in Canada. This was indeed a very old burial ground. Many monuments marked graves from centuries earlier. Some above-ground mausoleums broadcast more than a century of neglect. Tree roots had lifted monuments and crosses so that now they jutted out of the ground at crazy angles, like some surrealist painting done in black and grey. This was truly a necropolis: a city of the dead.

A deep-rooted anger again welled up inside him, reawakening that feeling of bravado that he had first felt at the statue of Ivan Pidkova. The buzzing and roaring in his ears was now gone. His mind was clear. He was riding a zigzag course through a forest of crosses, monuments, and mausoleums that competed for space with ancient oaks whose gnarled limbs reached out for Yarko's face. The long, late-evening shadows inked a black web over the white of weathered marble. No Hollywood movie could match this sight. Under other circumstances Yarko would have turned and headed back, but his adrenaline-fuelled fury made him oblivious to all but his goal. Somewhere in this city of death was Ksenia.

He must have ridden almost half an hour when he stopped to rest on a narrow trail. He was shaking from both the evening chill and the physical exertion of riding. He straightened his back. He felt the pressing discomfort of the cold steel of the revolver against his lower back. The weight of the PSM was tugging at his right pant-leg. He stuck his hand in that pocket and fingered the safety.

This was nightfall. The eastern horizon was black with clouds. It was at this moment when day turns to night that Yarko felt an absolute quiet. The echoes of the city did not reach here. The birds and animals of the day had long fallen silent, but the denizens of the night

had yet to awake. Yarko looked around, checking the darkening contours of bushes and gravestones. Through the black tangle of trees
on some distant hill stood a black cross, silhouetted against the navy
sky to the west. The smell of mosses, fungi, and grasses floated in on
a cool mist from among the old graves.

"It smells of history," he whispered despite himself.

At that moment he heard a distant sound, like someone groaning.
This sound was echoing somewhere on the left, or northern, side of
the trail, behind a jumble of bushes and trees. Yarko silently lowered his mountain bike to the grass. Pulling the Smith and Wesson
out from behind his back, he crept in the direction of the sound. In
the darkness, white marble gravestones faded in and out among the
trees like ghosts of the dead. The night fog parted momentarily and
Yarko clearly heard swearing in Russian. From behind some bushes
he spotted a large monument. A low brick pony wall surrounded the
grave plot. Stone columns rose from the corners, topped by some
twisted wrought-iron decoration.

Tied to the decorations on the top of these columns were the out-
spread arms of a young woman. Her ankles were lashed to the columns themselves. Her wet hair covered her face and a dirty yellow
dress stuck to her scratched and bruised body. Ksenia!

Beside her stood two men. One, dressed in black, was slapping
her face while the other, a tall blond-haired man dressed in grey,
hissed something in her ear. Ksenia was not reacting. Her head was
hanging helplessly.

Yarko saw a knife in the hands of the one that had been hissing
something in her ear. He remembered Vlodko's words, "No heroics,"
but he saw no alternative. The situation dictated his actions. Yarko
kneeled behind a bush, and using both hands to hold it, aimed the
big revolver at the blond man with the knife. This man was methodi-
cally hooking the blade under each golden button on Ksenia's dress,
and flicking them off one after another. The dress opened like the

skin of a banana. At this moment the moon emerged from behind a
cloud, lighting the white bra and panties on Ksenia's trembling body.
Bracing the gun with his left arm, Yarko adjusted his aim. The blond
man slit the front of the brassiere, baring white breasts to the moonlight. He then slipped the blade under the side of her panties. Yarko
had no opportunity to shoot now as the man stood directly between
him and Ksenia. A shot from the revolver would penetrate them
both.

"*Stoy!*" Yarko heard the Russian word for "stop" behind his back,
and felt the cold steel of a pistol pressed to the back of his head.

"Hand over the gun, you motherfucker!" commanded the Russian
voice behind Yarko's head.

He had no choice. He had to obey. Strangely, he felt no fear.
Again the situation was dictating his actions. Yarko slowly handed
the revolver back with his left hand. He could feel the pressure of
the stranger's knee under his left shoulder. He saw the reflection of
moonlight off a black boot to his right. In front of him, screened
by the figure of the blond man, he saw a wisp of white cloth fall to
the ground. Yarko slowly slipped his right hand into his pocket and
flicked the safety on his PSM.

"What's up, Sasha?" shouted the blond man. He turned to face
Yarko, momentarily unscreening Ksenia.

Yarko instinctively recognized this moment of inattention. It provided the only hope that he had. He threw his whole body backwards
between the booted stranger's legs while simultaneously withdraw-
ing his PSM, aiming it upwards.

Bang! The stranger fired first, but too late. Yarko was already lying
between his legs and firing upwards, one shot and then another.
Bang! Bang! The first bullet drilled through the stranger's guts and
into his heart. The second hit under his jaw, smashing his palate, and
ricocheted into his brain behind the orbit of his left eye.

Still lying in the same position, Yarko fired at the blond man. *Bang,*

bang, bang! He kept squeezing off shots until his target tripped and fell backwards. The blond man's companion, the one dressed in black, had unshouldered his Kalashnikov but didn't shoot. The figure of the dead man in shiny boots was still standing, while Yarko was lying hidden beneath. Yarko aimed at the black figure and fired again. At that moment, the corpse of the man in shiny black boots collapsed in a heap on top of Yarko. Now the figure in black sent a volley in Yarko's direction. From under the corpse Yarko fired again. *Bang!* Click. His PSM was empty. The man in black fired two more volleys at Yarko. The bullets smacked into the corpse, drenching Yarko in blood. Then the automatic weapon stopped firing. It too was empty. Yarko rolled the shredded corpse off himself and found his Smith and Wesson on the ground nearby. By this time the man in black had shielded himself behind Ksenia's tortured figure and was busily inserting a second magazine.

"Lousy position, time for a tactical retreat," muttered Yarko to himself as he bent in half and scampered like a rat between bushes and gravestones. The man in black inserted his second magazine and fired wildly in the dark in Yarko's general direction. Ricochets whistled among the marble stones and shattered branches in the trees. But Yarko was no longer there.

The situation had changed. First Blood! Yarko thought, remembering Stalone's classic flick. He had tasted human blood—quite literally at that, as he had been thoroughly sprayed with the blood of the man in the shiny boots. The smell of fresh blood and gunsmoke blended with the dark smells of the cemetery and the mist of the night. Some primordial warrior instinct was reborn in him. For a moment he again imagined before his eyes the flames of Iskorosten' and the black figures of warriors fighting on its ramparts.

"Flaming Vengeance!" announced his voice quite unconsciously. A desperate courage was reborn in his heart. It was now multiplied tenfold. He was the hunter now, not the quarry.

He stalked the man in black by making a wide clockwise circle. The moon disappeared again behind threatening clouds. Hiding behind gravestones, he steadily made his way to his target. He recalled the old family war stories of hunting Soviet tanks with nothing but hand-held panzerfausts or panzerschrecks, or destroying them with nothing but hand grenades. Today Yarko could live up to the standard set by these legends, by prevailing in this uneven battle, and against the same enemy.

Yarko crawled towards the man in black from behind him and to his right. The man was still standing behind Ksenia. Yarko had to crawl to a position that allowed him a clear shot without endangering Ksenia. Not quite trusting the old revolver and equally ancient cartridges, Yarko decided to aim high for a head shot. The distance closed—thirty metres, fifteen metres, ten. He masked his position well, lying low by a gravestone. Propped up on his elbows, he braced the revolver, aiming it by his target's right ear. He took a deep breath, then slowly exhaled half, and pressed the trigger.

Blam! The large-calibre revolver thundered and jumped in his hands. Where a moment ago there was a head, he saw the sudden bloom of blood and brains. The legs of the man in black turned to rubber, dropping him to his knees, and then he fell forward, his face digging into the dirt.

Yarko stood up. He breathed in deeply. The buttons of his black shirt were ripped, and the cloth hung on his chest like twin bloody rags. Again the moon slipped out from behind the clouds and illuminated the necropolis in an other-worldly light. He saw the bloody head of his victim. Farther away, about fifteen metres in front of Ksenia, he saw a viciously shredded pile of rags and meat. It was once the armed stranger in shiny black boots. Just to the left of Ksenia lay a knife. But the blond man in the grey suit was nowhere to be seen.

"Cholera! He's still alive! But where is he?" Yarko thought.

The guttural wheezing of Ksenia's breathing sent Yarko hurrying to her side. The yellow dress that hung behind her was splattered with blood, brains, and shards of skull. He took the knife and began cutting her legs free. Her breathing was laboured. When she had still possessed the strength to stand, she could breathe normally, but when her legs collapsed, her crucified arms restricted her breathing to small gulps of air. Freeing her legs, Yarko lifted Ksenia upright. He held her in his arms as she panted to catch her breath. She turned her head and searched Yarko's face with her lips. She felt no embarrassment that in this embrace she had pressed her naked breasts to his chest. She desperately wanted to squeeze him, but her arms were still tied.

Bang! Twee! A gunshot and a ricochet whistled past Yarko's ear. Realizing the danger that he posed to Ksenia, Yarko quickly scampered away, far to the right. He heard two more shots while running and saw a muzzle flash to his left. He dove behind a headstone. Lying there, he stared at the spot where he had seen the flash. Sure enough, some fifty metres in front he could see a moving shadow.

In the dark before him was nothing but open space with no cover between him and the moving shadow. He could not move closer. "Too far," he thought. "At this distance—only in cowboy movies. But what the heck." Yarko braced his revolver against a rock and fired.

Blam! The revolver jumped in his hands.

Bang! Bang! Two shots in reply.

"A bit too low, I figure," Yarko thought. He aimed again. The blond man, not knowing where Yarko's shot had come from, had failed to find proper cover. Half his body was exposed.

Blam! Yarko fired, wounding his opponent in the thigh.

Bang, bang, bang! The blond man returned fire in Yarko's general direction, then, dragging his injured leg, tried to find better cover. Yarko had had enough of this. He aimed, breathed in, breathed out.

Blam!

Again he aimed, breathed in, breathed out.

Blam!

And again he aimed, breathed in, breathed out.

Blam!

That was enough. The first shot shattered the blond man's arm. It dangled like a broken doll's. The second shot hit somewhere that caused the button of the grey jacket to fly off. The third scored in a way that a large dark spot appeared on the blond man's white shirt.

The revolver felt warm in Yarko's hand. He stood up from behind the headstone. The smell of gunsmoke burned his nostrils. He slowly walked towards Ksenia with the measured pace of a victor. Ksenia was still slouched with her arms spread wide, tied to the tops of the columns. Her rib cage was being pulled apart as her small breasts jerked with every laboured breath. Her abdominal muscles trembled from the strain. Below, in the light of the merciless moon, the dark silky triangle glistened with sweat. Yarko picked the knife up from where he had dropped it and freed Ksenia's limbs. She fell into his arms as if cut from the gallows. A black cloud covered the moon and a sudden rustle accompanied the downpour of cleansing rain.

"What the cholera?" gasped the breathless voice of Vlodko in the dark. "Where the devil have you been? I've been hearing gunfire all over the place. What were you thinking? This is Lviv, not the fucking Crimea! Goddam! How many corpses have you got here? Didn't I warn you not to play the hero, Yarko?"

The insistent pressure of wet lips parted Yarko's, adding sweetness to the taste of sweat and tears. A pair of young breasts pressed their cool softness against Yarko's chest. Yarko closed his eyes, and slipped to the ground from her embrace. His left arm was dripping blood. His own.

Yarko awoke in a clean white room. An excruciating pain stabbed at his left arm. Every breath caused additional pain in his back. Hanging before his eyes was a clear bag with some kind of liquid, and a bundle of tubes and wires disappeared somewhere under his bedsheet.

I'm in a hospital, concluded Yarko. He didn't dare move because of the pain.

A bullet in the arm, a bruised back, a pain in the back of my skull, glass cuts on my right hand, scorched face and eyebrows…Did I miss anything? Yarko silently recounted every wound and injury that he had accumulated the previous day. From somewhere beside him he heard Vlodko's voice.

"How are you, young man? You've been sleeping here way too long, my dear Sleeping Beauty. Right now it's nighttime—again. To be exact, it's Saturday night. You've been out like a light for twenty-four hours. I was just about to start to seriously worry about you. In fact, I was afraid that my sister would have to give up on you and find herself a somewhat livelier boyfriend."

Yarko could only smile and blink in response. The pain didn't allow him to so much as raise his head.

"We'll have to get you some morphine. I see that you are in some serious pain, you poor bugger," continued Vlodko. "Now, just before we get you more drugs, let me tell you all about a few things. First of all, Ksenia is okay, although she's bruised all over. The only real problem is that she seems to have fallen for some damned cripple who won't get up out of bed. She sat beside you all goddam day. Only now did she leave to get something to eat. Cholera—the damned nurses have to keep wiping her saliva off your face. She has attached herself to you like a leech." Vlodko had returned to his habitual strain of caustic humour.

"Next—our saintly Father Onufriy doesn't seem to want to leave this sinful world quite yet. Although, dammit, the poor bastard almost drowned in his own blood. However, if you could, my dear quadriplegic, if you could actually turn around, you would see that our Onufriy is occupying the bed next to you, keeping you company with some groaning of his own. Anyway, turns out our holy one broke one bastard's neck before getting drilled full of holes. But his biggest beef is that, in one day, you've wasted more of the enemy than he has during his entire life! Seriously, seven of them. Count 'em. You fried four in the Cathedral of Saint George, then gunned down three in the cemetery ... Christ! You're a bloody genius, Yarko. Either way, each of them had only a short trip from where he lay to reach the Almighty."

Yarko heard a quiet giggle from the neighbouring bed. Father Onufriy also enjoyed Vlodko's brand of humour. But today he was finding it hard to speak with all the holes in his lungs, so there were no comments from him.

A nurse walked in holding a large needle in her hand. For some reason, as in most of the world's hospitals, the head nurse's appearance and character were more appropriate for a concentration camp commander than an angel of mercy. No doubt the inevitable result of limited budgets, Yarko thought. Not wasting any time, she stabbed Yarko where the sun don't shine, and then left the room without saying a word.

"And the third important matter," continued Vlodko, hardly missing a beat, "is that your treasure—your book—is undamaged. The book is now with the Metropolitan of the church. The plans for operations in Kyiv are already being worked on ... And the fourth matter is that we've had to extend your visa for a week. You can forget your plans about travelling in the Alps. The last train to Vienna this week left some six hours ago. And I'm sure they won't let you out of this hospital for another two or three days anyway. And as for Ksenia, I'm afraid she won't want to return you your freedom for a somewhat longer period of time."

Ksenia was standing in the doorway, blushing like a schoolgirl—which was good, because it drew attention away from her black eye, her bruised cheek, the bandage on her jaw, and a pair of extremely puffy lips. Her chestnut-coloured bangs hid more bruises on her fore-head, but the tight cut of her red dress could never hide the sculpted shape of her femininity.

Vlodko smiled and headed for the door. "I'm going to leave you two love-birds alone. And I better cover up old Onufriy, head and all. 'Cause if he could see what's going to be going on in the bed beside him he'd surely have a stroke!"

Laughing, Vlodko actually did cover up Father Onufriy. As he passed by his sister, he jokingly turned out the light and closed the door behind him.

Part III

KYIV, UKRAINE
JUNE 2004–MARCH 2005

1

UKRAINE'S CAPITAL CITY WAS STILL ASLEEP. On the wide palette of the sky above, one by one the stars winked out. On the eastern horizon, a bright band of grey-blue forecast another cloudless summer day. Yarko stood on the corner of a very wide crossroads with a floral circle at the hub of its roundabout. The streets were empty. From time to time a lonely car would negotiate the roundabout and continue on its way. The first rays of the rising sun lit the very tops of the chestnut trees with bright green flames. The birds of the parkland on the western shores of the Dnipro River awoke, greeting Kyiv's citizens with a medley of twitters and song. The cold metal arc of a Soviet-era monument caught Yarko's eye, looking like a huge unfinished McDonald's sign. For some reason it reminded him of the words of Taras Shevchenko's "Epistle": "*Break your chains and water your freedom with the enemy's evil blood ...*"

No, thought Yarko, these chains are yet to be broken. And blood has yet to water anything around here.

His tie squeezed uncomfortably around his neck. The cool morning breeze ruffled his carefully combed hair. Unconsciously, Yarko buttoned his suit jacket against the morning's chill. In his left hand was a shiny metal briefcase. He had all the appearance of a proper businessman.

It was now a year since his first visit to this country. A year had passed since the tumultuous events in Lviv. He had returned to his home in Vancouver, back to the daily grind of university lectures and tutorials. But in addition to this schoolwork, he had acquired some new assignments. He had travelled to the major cities of Canada and the USA. He had visited Toronto, Edmonton, New York City, and Chicago. In each city, he was the guest speaker at secretive meetings, conferences, discussions, and conversations. He had visited private homes of millionaires as well as the halls of various cultural centres or national homes. He had conversed with bishops, scientists, historians, and businessmen among the widely scattered Ukrainian diaspora. An organization was being created. Funds were being collected. This organization was quilted from select elements of both the Orthodox and Catholic churches, the League of Ukrainians, Plast and CYM youth organizations, and the various foundations of the Ukrainian diaspora. The Scholarly Association of Taras Shevchenko, known best by its Ukrainian acronym, NTSh, became the coordinating body of what was in essence an archaeological project. Simultaneously, in Ukraine, a similar organization was being created incorporating both religious and patriotic organizations. Yarko's role had been that of a speaker—simply put, his role was propaganda. He had to encourage the carefully selected individuals to participate directly or to financially sponsor the project. The organization of the operation unfolded under the code name Slava, a word that translates roughly as "fame and glory."

After the end of the school year, the organization had sent Yarko to Ukraine, to Kyiv, its capital. The plans for the archaeological dig were being put in motion.

It was almost six in the morning. Most of the stars had disappeared. A ghostly gibbous moon hung over the western horizon in a gap between grey silhouettes of distant buildings. Traffic was beginning to pick up. Yarko checked his watch. He looked up and down the streets. At every intersection that he could see, stood a businessman with a briefcase much like his. Others, spaced some 200 metres apart, stood between the intersections. A large black Russian-built Chaika limousine sailed past his position, turning left towards the Dnipro Hotel. In the accepted Kyiv manner it drove onto the wide sidewalk, stopping a short distance from the hotel entrance. The car looked like a rejected 1960s Detroit styling exercise, but in fact, would have been only a few years old.

Yarko watched as an apparently high-ranking cleric in a black chasuble exited the car, assisted by two of lesser rank, as well as by the chauffeur. This was the Ukrainian Greek-Catholic bishop arriving early for the day's proceedings of the Conference for Unification of the Churches, which had already been in progress for three days. Yarko placed his briefcase flat on the ground and pulled out a package of Canadian Craven A's. Shielding his lighter from the wind, he lit his cigarette. From the corner of his eye, he noted that every businessman with a briefcase had done likewise. Yarko placed his foot on the briefcase and bent over to retie his shoe.

At that moment, a violent explosion obliterated the Chaika limousine. The three-ton behemoth lifted a few metres in the air as its doors and hood blew clear. The black giant smacked back down in a shower of broken glass. Smoke and flame enveloped the interior. A tire rolled and bounced down the road past Yarko. The hood, which had flown like a sheet of paper high in the air, came down with a loud clang some forty metres from the wreckage of the car.

Yarko waited a moment, and then picked up his briefcase and calmly walked past the location of the incident. He entered an underground passage that also serves as an entrance to the Kyiv subway system, or "Metro," and disappeared from the street. The other "businessmen" with briefcases, who had stood like Yarko at various locations, also dispersed underground. For a long time there was silence along this section of Khreshchatyk Street. The birds ceased their singing. The only sound was the crackling and hissing of flames in the wreckage of the Chaika. No other cars, nor any pedestrians, could be seen. Here and there the lights in the windows of the Dnipro Hotel winked out, betraying the fact that some curious spectators were casually watching the spectacle below as if this were a daily occurrence in the capital of the Ukrainian state. Finally, in the distance, the wail of sirens broke the silence of the morning.

There were already several dozen people in the subway station. Yarko heard snippets of conversations in Russian. This was now the tenth day that Yarko was in Kyiv. He was no longer surprised that here, in the very capital of an ostensibly independent Ukraine, the conversational language was still Russian. A foreigner could not recognize whether Kyiv was the capital of the Ukrainian state or merely a regional centre of a Russian colony. In fact, it had all the appearance of an occupied city. All signs and banners were in Ukrainian. All official pronouncements were made in Ukrainian. But the language of daily discourse for most residents of Kyiv was Russian. It was as if a Ukrainian government had occupied a foreign Russian city. But even those officials who made pronouncements in Ukrainian would themselves turn around and continue their private discourse in Russian. The habits of centuries under the colonial regime of the northern neighbour had certainly left its mark. Yarko did not like this city. Neither the clear blue skies nor the warm late-June sunshine could reawaken in Yarko the kind of feelings that he had experienced in Lviv. Often he felt quite depressed walking the deep passages of the

Metro, or while travelling on the crowded subway cars filled with people speaking a language he did not understand. It was a depression that bred a quiet rage that furrowed his brow as he sat in the subway car.

Yarko got off at the University station. Several other young men exited at the same time. All wore the suits and ties of businessmen and all carried metal briefcases. They kept apart from each other and did not speak. Yarko entered a large building in the middle of green parkland. He walked along a long corridor and down a set of stairs. He knocked on the first door to his right. One sharp knock.

A young man carefully opened the door. An AK-74 hung from his shoulder. His finger nervously rubbed the trigger.

"Mark! Boy, did they ever find you a strange job!" exclaimed Yarko as he hugged his brother. "When the hell did you get here? And how come you get all this ferocious weaponry? You're taking archaeology in school, not bloody guerilla warfare!"

"Hey, didn't you see *Indiana Jones*?" Mark retorted. "See, today archaeologists can get into firefights just like cowboys did in the movies."

"Well, to me you seem to be just a bit too nervous to handle a toy like that. Heck, you might actually shoot someone!"

"Well, hell! You killed seven Russkis last year, so don't you think it just may be my turn to shoot some. Just let some KGB-ist show his face here."

Yarko laughed at his younger brother's bravado. "You fool, you didn't even ask for my password. What if I were a KGB agent?"

"*Ratatatat*, then I would drop you right here... But anyway, Yar, how's it supposed to go now? Slava!"

"Yaroslava!" Yarko responded with the required code word. He walked past his brother into the room.

After Yarko, more men in business suits arrived—singly, one after the other.

"Slava."

"Yaroslava."

"Slava."

"Yaroslava."

"Slava."

"Yaroslava," pronounced a half-dozen young men checking into the university computer lab.

In the laboratory, a lot of people seemed to be just milling about. A couple of armed guards hung around the only entrance door. Three scientists stood by the mainframe computer, and in the corner, under a ventilation fan, sat an older-looking professorial type puffing on his pipe. Individual white hairs failed to cover his balding head. His white dangling kozak-style whiskers swung gently with every puff of aromatic tobacco smoke. Professor Verbytsky was scanning a plaster model of downtown Kyiv and seemed to be anxiously waiting results of the mainframe's calculations.

Several young "businessmen," including Yarko, opened their briefcases. Inside each was a laptop and a jumble of electronics bearing the Hewlett-Packard label. With a few tickles of the mousepad, each laptop began spitting out a disk. These disks were handed one by one to the computer technician, who dutifully fed them to the appropriate drive attached to the mainframe computer. Due to a shortage of chairs, Yarko and most of the young men sat on the floor. Only Professor Verbytsky remained standing, watching a blank computer screen.

"May cholera take you! When the devil are we going to see the map of the cave? This is taking way too long," he said nervously. He seemed like an expectant father in a waiting room.

"Then why the devil did you decide that you needed seismological testing in the heart of Kyiv anyway?" asked one of the computer programmers. "And secret seismological testing at that! Did you think it would be easy to set off a secret explosion in the heart of the capital city of any other country? Well I for one would have said it was impossible. And then your crazy Canadian friend comes up with the idea of blowing up a fucking limo! So now you have it, one more variable offset by some redundant data. Well that takes time. It takes X more iterations, then a best fit … Oh hell, just be patient."

Yarko turned beet red. His colleagues were all looking at him. Yarko had been involved with Operation Slava all year and he was certain that his academic marks had suffered as a result. However, he often had a chance to offer some input into the project's plans. The exploding limo was his idea. And now it was about to bear fruit.

"You're right," said Yarko. "In any other capital such a plan wouldn't work. But in Ukraine, where cars get blown up every week, and where officials get shot in the streets—hell, in Ukraine, setting off a downtown explosion was a no-brainer."

"Quiet children! We have something on the screen," interrupted the professor.

And truly, on the black screen of the mainframe, some red lines were congealing into the form of a quadrilateral. To the right of this quadrilateral extended a thin line like a rat's tail. Professor Verbytsky stared at the screen for a long time. He then walked back to his plaster model of downtown Kyiv.

"The cave is there," he began, "close, but not quite in the place that Father Onufriy had predicted. However, it just might be easier to gain access, not to the cave itself, but to that underground passageway leading to it. That's what this thin line happens to be." The professor pointed to the "rat's tail" on the computer screen. "What's even more important, the cave is straight. It is four sided and has a flat, horizontal floor. In other words this cave, this underground chamber, is an artificial creation and not some natural hollow in Kyiv's limestone bedrock. We have, in fact, found the Library!"

The head computer programmer ran his fingers over a keyboard like Mozart playing a concerto on a piano. First the image was rotated, then the scale of the image shrunk. As a result there appeared a wide red band on the extreme left of the screen. The faces of all those watching turned to frowns.

The silence was broken by Yarko. "I know what that is! That's the subway, or as all you Frenchmen here call it, the Metro. Probably the very one that I rode in this morning."

The professor nodded. "You're right, it's the subway. But not the route you were on this monrng. This particular one would be the line to the Obolon suburbs."

"But cholera, that was sure close," exclaimed another. "Do you guys realize that when they were building the subway—another fifty metres to the right and they would have found Prince Yaroslaw's Library. Just fifty metres and they would have shipped our history off to Leningrad."

"And burned it like *Slovo O Polku Ihorya*," added someone else, citing the twelfth-century epic poem, the original of which was lost to fire in St. Petersburg.

Yarko recalled the Memory Hole of George Orwell's *1984*. The Memory Hole was a concept perfected by the Russian Empire over the centuries. It was George Orwell who wrote, "Who controls the past controls the future. Who controls the present controls the past." The Empire knew this well. Yarko now understood, more clearly than ever, the significance of Operation Slava.

"Okay, enough fooling around, children," scolded Professor Verbytsky. "Tomorrow we start serious work on the project. As for this evening, I invite you all to my room for beers. Fourth floor of the Dnipro Hotel—Room 401. We'll check the evening news. I'd like to hear what the militsya is saying about our little explosion. There's been nothing on TV as yet."

Having been given a half-day off, Yarko and Mark decided to do some shopping and to get to know more of the city. On the sixth floor of the hotel, Vlodko was finalizing security arrangements for the priests and bishops who were attending the Conference for Unification of the Churches.

2

YARKO FOUND THAT HE HAD BEEN VOLUNTEERED to continue in his role as propagandist for the project. People whose skills or financial assistance would be required for the undertaking were carefully selected and screened by the organization. Once it was certain that the candidates were politically reliable, it was Yarko's role to act as the closer. He talked about the book found the previous year in Lviv, and how it revealed the secret of the actual location of the underground chamber of the Library of Prince Yaroslaw the Wise. Of course he never disclosed this location. At this point there was no need to know. Yarko's presentations were intended to gain either personal commitment or financial assistance from these people.

It was this last part, the financial assistance, that had proved the most difficult, since those with the means to donate had, in most cases, already made commitments for political contributions. Ukraine was in the preliminary stages of a presidential election campaign. The current president, Leonid Kuchma, constitutionally prevented from serving a third term, was being replaced. It appeared that there was a credible chance for the first real political choice in this country.

The July sun shone brightly. Tired and discouraged by the previous evening's meeting with businessmen, who had donated much smaller amounts than expected, Yarko had consciously decided to sleep in.

Now he found himself quite alone in the hotel's restaurant, sipping on a coffee while his order of eggs and sausage was being prepared. He was pleasantly surprised when he saw Vlodko walk in.

"*Servus*, Vlodko!"

"*Servus*, Yarko!" Vlodko pulled up a chair and joined Yarko at the table.

"Listen, Vlodko. This election business is getting in our way. And what's with the sudden surge in orange ribbons in the streets today? I saw them from my window this morning. There were always a few hanging around, but dammit, they must have multiplied overnight."

"That's because today, July 4, Victor Yushchenko is expected to formally announce his run at the presidency. Orange is his campaign colour."

"Everyone knew he was running. You mean he hadn't made his formal announcement yet?"

"I guess not. There's a political rally in the Spivoche Pole, the Singing Field, this afternoon. No doubt he will announce during the rally. I too have the day off, so I can drive you there. I'm going to check it all out myself."

A waitress delivered an oversized plate of scrambled eggs and sausages. Yarko's thoughts wandered to the memory of another waitress a year ago. Their romance had been frustrated because he had to leave, but the feelings did not end for Yarko. He could only hope that Ksenia shared his hunger.

With a twitch of the spare fork, Vlodko indicated his desire to share Yarko's meal. Struggling with his first mouthful of eggs, Yarko nodded approval. He swallowed and asked, "So are you saying that Yushchenko is in the organization?"

Vlodko chomped down on a fatty sausage. "No, he's not," he said, "although he's a decent enough guy. Like most Ukrainians, he just hasn't got his head around what being Ukrainian means. His father fought in the Red Army against the Nazis, and in fact the guy was captured and spent time in Auschwitz. Yushchenko thinks that his father fought for Ukraine. In fact, he fought and suffered for an imperial regime that had liquidated over seven million Ukrainians in the man-made famine, the Holodomor. That famine happened just eight years before the war started. So his father fought on the side of those who had just perpetrated a genocide of his nation. For any father's son, the implications of that would be just too ugly to bear. It becomes too painful to judge, so one suspends judgement. Hell, he's a decent enough guy though, but he's still President Kuchma's creation."

"What? What do you mean Kuchma's creation?" Yarko was shocked that the great democratic hope in the next presidential election might, in fact, be a fraud. "I thought that the other Victor, you know, the dumbed-down Tony Soprano with hair—oh what's his name?—Yanukovich—was Kuchma's puppet."

"They're both unwitting players in a game where the devil Kuchma is pulling all the strings," said Vlodko. "Although I'm sure that neither one knows it yet. For them, I'm sure they think the contest is real. But don't get me wrong, the emotions that you will see and feel during the rally on the Singing Field are very real. The people are fighting for democracy. They are fighting for a government of the people, by the people ... And oh, by the way, today is American Independence Day."

"Are these just smart-ass opinions of yours or what?" Yarko was feeling genuinely hurt that the orange euphoria he was beginning to feel was being somehow betrayed.

"In the end they are all still politicians, and human. But it's not just my opinion. The organization has its sources. In fact our highest-placed source, a member known as Saint George, witnessed the laying of the plans."

"You mean Saint Yuriy, don't you, Vlodko?" Yuriy was the proper Ukrainian version.

"No, the code name is Saint George. Not the Ukrainian, Yuriy, but the English name, George. Of course we usually call him simply The Saint. And this Saint George has slain even more dragons than you, Yarko." There was a hint of annoyance in Vlodko's reply.

"Could I ever meet him?" Too late, Yarko realized how childish the question sounded.

"You never know, but his face was on TV some three weeks ago— just about the time you arrived in Ukraine. This guy was in the news." Vlodko's voice tailed off, indicating that it was not good news.

Both turned their attention to clearing the plate. Yarko was excited at the thought of joining the political rally. Young people were in the vanguard of the orange movement. Orange, being Yushchenko's party's colour, was beginning to symbolize something a lot bigger. As he thought about all the young people that he would meet, Yarko found his thoughts turning to Ksenia. He hadn't seen her since a year ago in Lviv.

"And when is Ksenia coming to Kyiv?" he asked.

"She is real busy, but she'll join us next month. I don't know where she gets the energy. She's in the organization, she's working for Yushchenko's party, Our Ukraine, and she's also active in PORA… and when she arrives in Kyiv I'm having her work in security for the Conference for Unification of the Churches."

"Still looking for the mole in the Ukrainian Greek-Catholic Church are you?" Yarko gave Vlodko a knowing wink.

"Cholera—you've been around us too long. I guess I'll have to consider you a member of the organization too. You're starting to think like one of us."

The two of then got up from the table.

"So who runs PORA?" asked Yarko. He pushed a wad of Ukrainian hryvnias under the edge of the plate. Vlodko mentally calculated the generous size of the tip and raised his eyebrows.

"What, Vlodko? Its only four bucks in total."

"pora has no leadership," said Vlodko. "It's an organization created by young activists to ensure that the elections are fair. They have no president and no executive. Their communication is by Internet and cell phone. They have a website, and that's it. In fact, when I think of it, they're structured exactly like the Internet. It's a network of young people united by the idea of democratic elections."

"Wow, is that ever unique, and so absolutely modern!" exclaimed Yarko as they left the hotel and began walking up the street to where Vlodko's car was parked.

"Modern, yes. But not unique. Our organization is structured the same way. In fact, we did it first. The organization is united by the idea that the Ukrainian nation will not be destroyed; we won't allow it to happen in this so-called independent Ukrainian state."

"Dammit, doesn't your organization have a fancy name, or at least a bunch of initials?" Yarko was annoyed by how difficult it was to talk about something with no name.

"Nope. Just organization—with a small 'o.'" They reached Vlodko's Lviv militsya Lada and climbed in. "By the way, Yarko, did you not once tell me that you sailed yachts?"

"Not yachts, just sailboats."

The conversation fell silent as they drove through Kyiv's streets. Yarko had a lot of information he had to mull over.

The political rally was unlike anything that Yarko had experienced. Tens of thousands of people, all waving orange, or wearing orange or holding something orange, made this the biggest party that Yarko had ever been to. People had come from all centres of Ukraine. Young and old stood side by side. There were rock bands, there were politicians, there was food, and there were young ladies in the skimpiest of summer clothes. If it was ever possible to have a clean-cut, idealistic, drug-free Woodstock, then this was it. The bands sang in Ukrainian, the girls in skimpy shorts spoke Ukrainian, and the candidate for president pronounced his party's platform in Ukrainian. He enumerated a long list of misdeeds by the authoritarian oligarchy that was the current Ukrainian government of Leonid Kuchma.

"*Our country stands on the edge between the past and the future. The time has come to change our lives for the better. The whole country demands it: from Lviv to Luhansk, from Chernihiv to the Crimea...*" said Yushchenko. "*Today, the national resources only fill the pockets of the oligarch clans; access to social benefits has become not the right of all but the privilege of the chosen—and this is the fault of today's criminal regime. Today a citizen is not free in his own country; he is powerless before the arbitrariness of bureaucrats, tax collectors, police, and the public prosecutor.*"

"Yush-chen-ko," chanted the crowd, interrupting the speech.

"*Today,*" continued Yushchenko, "*today they are dividing this nation into easterners and westerners, they are dividing it by language, history and faith. In actuality, there is only one conflict in this country: that between the state and the people. To steer this country in the right direction we need unity...*"

"Yush-chen-ko, Yush-chen-ko."

"*I have a program for Ukraine, a plan that will let us implement the plan, and I have the team that is capable of delivering it. In a year, this will become a different country. We will build a country where there will be work for the hands and minds of all, no one would have to leave its borders to seek his fortune.*"

"Yush-chen-ko, Yush-chen-ko."

"*I will win this election, and it will be a victory for us all! I believe in Ukraine, I know my responsibility. Together we will win!*"

"Yush-chen-ko, Yush-chen-ko, Yush-chen-ko!"

And when Yushchenko said that he was submitting his candidacy to the Central Election Committee that day and he pronounced the words, "*I am going for the presidency,*" the roar of the crowd was deafening.

What struck Yarko most was that the people were happy. They were laughing. They were unafraid. The state police had been pushed to the sidelines. They were the only ones showing bafflement and fear. Yarko now realized that freedom had a taste, freedom had a colour, freedom had a sound—and that freedom was joy. Yarko understood that most of all, freedom knows no fear. Those momentary feelings of courage and bravado that he had felt from time to time a year ago in Lviv came rushing back.

It was a happy exhaustion that he felt when he returned with Vlodko to his hotel. The ever-cynical Vlodko had to have felt it too. But there was no conversation.

As they parted ways in a hotel hallway, Yarko challenged, "*Slava Ukrayini,*" or Glory to Ukraine.

Vlodko made the required reply, a firm, "*Heroyam Slava,*" or Hail the Heroes.

3

ACTUAL WORK IN THE SUB-BASEMENT of the Hotel Dnipro began the day after Victor Yushchenko confirmed his candidacy for the presidency at the Singing Field rally. The preparation of the project infrastructure, however, had begun many months earlier.

The personnel manager of the hotel was a member of the organization. Over the previous six months he had been able to place key people on the hotel's staff.

The Conference for Unification of the Churches had been created as a cover for the tunnelling operations of the Slava operation, although the negotiations themselves were for real. The three leaders of Ukrainian churches were all well informed of the operation, and they assisted at every step. Only the Orthodox Church of the Moscow Patriarchate had been left out. That church had been subordinate to the Soviet KGB in the past, and continued to serve the interests of Muscovy today. It was Putin's tool for political control in Moscow's "near abroad."

The organizers of the conference had rented not only the hotel's meeting hall and a dozen rooms on the fourth, fifth, and sixth floors, but had also established access to the sub-basement of the building. It was from there that miners would bore a tunnel under Khreshchatyk Street.

The control panel of the one elevator that had access to the sub-basement was quietly replaced one night by a specially modified version. Gone was the button indicating sub-basement. Instead, the panel was programmed to respond to certain simultaneous sequences of buttons. One sequence locked it in secure express mode; a second sent the elevator to the now "non-existent" sub-basement, which housed the normal support equipment of a hotel. Stairwell access to the sub-basement was locked out, and the entrance door was re-labelled with the ubiquitous *Attention, Authorized Personnel Only* sign. Legitimate access to the sub-basement and its equipment was limited to the recently hired electrical and maintenance specialists. It was crucial that there be no accidental visitations in the next few months.

The foundation wall in the sub-basement was breached at the north-east corner of the hotel, and a new room was excavated outside of it to provide for equipment storage and as the base of tunnelling operations. The breach was closed by a pair of large soundproof steel doors. A sign—*Attention, No Entry, Authorized City Personnel Only*—further legitimized this subtle modification. In this external underground room was the entrance to the tunnel, which would be bored to intersect with the "rat's tail" underground passage to the library, as had been identified through the seismic tests. This modified plan, using the newly discovered passage, cut over a hundred metres of boring distance from the original concept.

The tunnelling operation was expected to generate nearly two hundred cubic metres of high-quality limestone gravel. This material needed to be disposed of continuously, but discreetly, during the boring operation. Quite remarkably, the hotel suddenly had plans for some revised landscaping at the back of the property, which would require large amounts of gravel.

Yarko was quite impressed at how the widely scattered resources of the organization had been enlisted in support of the Slava operation. On the day after the evening news reported that the Donbas coal-mining region was hit by another coal miners' strike over unpaid wages, nine skilled miners from Donetsk checked into the Dnipro Hotel. Their arrival was followed by the arrival of a sophisticated piece of tunnelling equipment, a laser-guided rock-boring machine that could bore a one-metre-diameter tunnel with a deviation of less than one centimetre in a hundred metres. Electrical power for the tunnelling operations was easily "borrowed" from the city since the sub-basement had access to the hotel's power supply as well as its backup generators.

By the end of August 2004, the tunnelling operations room had taken on the appearance of a proper command centre, with lighting, refrigerator, microwave, phone hook-up and a computer terminal, plus high-voltage electrical supply for the boring equipment. The tunnel itself was to head almost due north at a slight down-slope through solid limestone bedrock. It was carefully aimed to intersect the "rat's tail" underground passage. A bundle of cables and wires disappeared into the round opening of the tunnel to provide power for the boring machine as well as lighting and hard-wire telephone access. A cable-and-pulley system allowed a wheeled "belly wagon" to be pulled into and out of the tunnel along guide rails. Gravity allowed it to roll quite freely into the tunnel, but hauling it back out manually when loaded with gravel was another matter. A motorized version was already in the works for when the length of the tunnel made the manual process too tedious.

The work was scheduled in three shifts to provide for round-the-clock operation seven days a week. Each shift consisted of two miners and three young assistants. Two of the assistants would fill burlap bags with the gravel that came out of the tunnel, and transport them to the elevator. The third assistant would serve as armed security, patrolling the sub-basement and the elevator entrance. The organization had provided a very remarkable arsenal for guarding and defending the project. There was a good selection of handguns and automatic weapons, as well as various other items of absolutely first-rate combat equipment. All this was kept in one of the storage rooms across from the elevator doors.

From time to time, one of the archaeologists or other scientists would visit the tunnelling operations room. In the early going this was done more as a courtesy than an operational necessity. They would sometimes sift through the gravel, but any fossilized dinosaur bones would have been crushed beyond recognition by the boring equipment. Occasionally one of the Orthodox archbishops or the Catholic metropolitan would also pay the lads a visit. Invariably they would signal their arrival to the miners in the tunnel by sending sandwiches and a bottle of sacramental wine, or a couple of bottles of beer down the tunnel shaft on the belly wagon. This was a form of Holy Communion most appreciated by the miners.

4

It was well into August before the actual tunnelling operations started. Yarko and Mark found themselves performing the miner's assistant role. It took twelve such assistants to keep the work going round the clock. The plan was for each assistant to bag gravel two days and do sentry duty one day and have every fourth day off. Each assistant's schedule was staggered to ensure that work could go on seven days a week. The luck of the draw was such that Yarko and his brother, Mark, almost never had the same day off. On the other hand, when they were working at least they would be working on the same time shift.

It was Yarko's luck to have to work the very first two days in a row as the gravel-bagger. This was back-breaking work. The offsetting benefit of this unhappy draw was that the third day, which Yarko would have off, would be August 24—Ukrainian Independence Day. Vlodko had promised a surprise for him that day. A condition of this promise was that Yarko had to meet Vlodko at 7:00 a.m. in the hotel restaurant for breakfast.

Yarko walked into the hotel restaurant a few minutes after seven. Vlodko had already ordered breakfast. On the corner table where he sat was a bowl of scrambled eggs, and another filled with sausages. Beside the mandatory carafe of coffee stood two large tumblers of cherry juice.

"You're late," said Vlodko by way of welcome.

"Tired." Yarko was still stiff from eight hours of moving gravel.

"Eat fast. Then I want you to go to your room, get dressed in shorts and a T-shirt, and pack your knapsack with a light jacket, a cap, swimming trunks, and a towel. This is your day for some recreation."

"How about I just sleep?"

"I'm taking you to Trukhaniv Island. It's time for some sand, sun, swimming, and who knows, maybe even some sailing."

As he dug into his breakfast, Yarko comforted himself with the thought of sleeping on a beach. Egged on by Vlodko, he ate fast. This breakfast was no longer a meal but a refuelling stop.

"Meet me in the lobby," Vlodko commanded as Yarko headed for the elevator.

A few minutes later, Yarko was back, looking somewhat like a boy scout.

"There's nowhere to park, so we'll walk there," Vlodko said as Yarko got off the elevator.

"Not quite what I wanted to hear." There would be no rest for his aching muscles.

Trukhaniv Island is a large island in the Dnipro River, formed at the confluence of the Desna River, and extending south for several kilometres to well past Khreshchatyk Street. Kyiv stands on the high west bank of the Dnipro, so any trip to the river involves a long, steep descent through a wooded park. After a half-hour hike, the two found themselves crossing the Dnipro on a long footbridge leading to the island itself. Vlodko walked briskly. Yarko couldn't quite understand why the rush if this was to be a day of rest and recreation. Once on the island, Vlodko led Yarko quite purposefully along a path across the grassy flats.

"Do we have an appointment, or something?" asked Yarko.

"Well, in fact, *you* do. See the marina up ahead? Well, Yarko, you are going sailing."

"What do you mean me? Aren't you coming along?"

"Naw, I'm too much of a landlubber for that. But don't worry, you won't be alone. In fact, you're going to be crew. See the man rigging the sails on that little sloop? That is The Saint. You are his crew for today."

Blinded by the sun in the eastern sky, Yarko couldn't see, but he certainly heard the wink in Vlodko's voice. When they got closer, Yarko was able to take a good look at the man coiling a halyard and hanging it on a cleat on the mast. He was tall and well muscled for a man over fifty. He had a military bearing. He wore white shorts and no shirt. On his head a rumpled army forage cap shielded his eyes from the sun. His face was handsome, although slightly too round to make the list of Hollywood hunks. This stranger looked at them, clearly recognizing Vlodko. Yarko noted that the roundness of the face and welcoming smile were just enough to soften and offset the strict military manner of the man.

"Vlodko!" came the cheery welcome.

"Yuriy!"

"Didn't you say he was George, not Yuriy?" Yarko asked as they approached the boat.

"Name and code-name, Yarko," said Vlodko. "Two different things. We usually refer to him as The Saint anyway."

Yuriy studied Yarko. "So is this the young man, Vlodko?"

"Yes, General, this is Yaroslaw—Yarko," Vlodko said in a tone that echoed military formality.

Yuriy laughed. "One of your tunnel rats? Now why would this limestone Swiss-cheese under Kyiv need another hole. I always thought the Metro subway was more than enough."

"Not just one of the rats, General, but the very Rat who started it all. I'm sure you remember last year's events in Lviv."

Yuriy laughed again. "Of course I remember! So this is the Yaroslaw, grandson of Yaroslaw who discovered the Library of Yaroslaw the Wise." He turned Yarko. "Well, Yarko, I think we're almost related. You do know that Prince Yaroslaw's Christian name was Yuriy, don't you?"

"Yes, I knew that," said Yarko, still somewhat overwhelmed by The Saint.

"Dammit, I haven't been on the water yet this year, and the summer is almost over," complained Yuriy as he stepped ashore. "I either couldn't find time or couldn't find crew. I'm a bit old to single-hand this sloop. Of course now that they relieved me of my job, finding the time will no longer be the main problem...Well, Yarko, how would you like to join the Yurko and Yarko sailing club?" Yuriy used the diminutive form of his name. He gave Yarko a great big bear hug.

"If I could get off gravel duty, we could do this every day."

"You're not getting off that easy," said Vlodko. "Anyway, I have to go. I'm sure you can find your own way back to the hotel when you're done, Yarko."

"Get aboard, Yarko," said Yuriy, "but first undo the bowline, loop it around the bollard, and just hold it until I say. I'll take the helm."

This sailboat was considerably smaller than the one Yarko sailed back home. Below decks there was just enough room for one person to curl up out of the sun beside the ropes, bailing bucket, and life jackets. The boat was long and slender with very little freeboard, much like a giant kayak with a mast. There was no sign of a centre-board trunk. Yarko figured it must have a fixed keel with considerable ballast. There was no motor either, so close-quarter docking and undocking manoeuvres would require some sailing skill or strong paddling arms.

"Yarko, you hold the bow while I raise the jib," ordered Yuriy. "Then when I say let go, you let go while I pull in the jib-sheet to set us on a starboard tack." Yarko was surprised to hear Yuriy giving his orders in perfect English.

The undocking procedure went without a hitch and the boat sailed under headsail alone down a long inlet before clearing the southern tip of Trukhaniv Island. The wind blew from the west. Yuriy steered to starboard, holding the bow to the wind while Yarko raised the main. Yuriy then let the bow fall off a few degrees while he hardened the main. Yarko hardened the jib. The craft picked up speed and heeled sharply to port. Yarko and his new friend braced themselves on the starboard gunwale, hooking their feet under straps that ran lengthwise along the bottom of the cockpit. Yarko looked back at Yuriy. Yuriy's round face was beaming with joy. A series of synchronized movements and they had the vessel carving through the water at some six knots.

Yuriy raised his voice above the background din of the waves and wind. "Ready about!"

"Aye, ready."

"Helm's a-lea!" Yuriy pushed the tiller to the opposite side. Yarko responded by snapping the port jib-sheet out of its cleat, while maintaining tension by hand. As the wind hit the port side of the jib, helping turn the boat to starboard, Yarko released the port jib-sheet, and working hand over hand, hardened the starboard one. In those few seconds the boat snapped from a southwest to a northwest heading up the middle of the river channel and paralleling Kyiv's shore. Both sailors now leaned over the port gunwale to decrease the angle of heel and thus increase the area of sail exposed to the wind. Yuriy had his eyes glued to the red and green strips of ribbon flying from the luff of the jib. He responded to minute changes in wind direction with tiny corrections of the tiller. Yarko saw an image of his father at the helm.

Yuriy broke the silence. "I'm heading upstream on purpose, Yarko. That way if the wind dies we can drift back to where we came from. Of course we'd have to paddle the rest of the way up that inlet in the island to our dock."

"That's what I figured," said Yarko. "Lucky that the current is slow or we really couldn't do any of this."

They sailed upstream for a couple of hours. It was high noon when the wind seemed to die off. Although water still flowed past the hull, the landmarks on the distant western shore no longer moved. The sails were set for a beam reach. In this weak wind there was no heeling, so both sailors sat on opposite sides of the cockpit collecting the warmth of the sun's rays. Yarko had time to recount the wild adventures of his previous year's visit to Lviv.

"Someday I'd love to visit the west coast of Canada," said Yuriy. "I hear its beautiful there."

"The best sailing in the world, I'd say. And the politics are not quite as crazy as those in Ukraine."

Yuiry smiled. "Maybe not."

"I was really impressed with Victor Yushchenko," Yarko continued, "but Vlodko tells me not to get my hopes up. He says that you feel he is the current president's puppet."

"Puppet is too strong a word. But maybe an actor on a stage, performing a play to President Kuchma's libretto. It is a very strange play at that. But Kuchma is the director who picked all the players."

"What do you mean? And how do you know?"

"Let me tell you a fairy tale," began Yuriy. "It happened not too long ago, in a land, er, not too far away. It was wintertime. There must have been a half-metre of snow on the ground. The curtain opens to a setting in an office inside the Presidential Administration Building. President Kuchma had been scheming about staying in power for an additional term. The Constitution does not allow that sort of thing. But if one can get the Constitutional Court to declare the first term in office not to count, maybe because the Constitution was adopted part way through that first term, then one can certainly try. Unfortunately, Kuchma's popularity ratings were so low that even the dirty tricks in his bag of election manoeuvres wasn't going to deliver a win. In addition, Kuchma was tired. His second term was no fun at all. Shunned by the West because of the Georgiy Gongadze murder, he was also being pushed around by a new group of advisors. He was being brought closer and closer to Putin's solar system of client states. His own business clan was losing its grip on the country and the competition from Donetsk was gaining economic power."

"Wasn't he the most hated man in Ukraine?" Yarko interjected.

"Yes he was. Whether he deserved it or not is another matter. Anyway, on this wintry day, Kuchma began hatching a new scheme. He no longer wanted the presidency, or at least he no longer wanted to fight another presidential election campaign. Now he wanted two things: protection of his personal fortune; and revenge on all of his enemies—both political and business enemies. There was only one man in his cabinet he could share his thoughts with. That was the minister of defence, Yevhen Marchuk. And Yevhen was the slickest schemer of all. He was the former head of the Ukrainian KGB back when the USSR still existed. But during the last presidential election he repackaged himself as the nationalists' great white hope. He could be everything to everyone. Once the number one stool pigeon, he had now become a breeder of stool pigeons."

"We're not making any headway," noted Yarko, returning his attention to sailing. "We may as well start drifting home. What's the current's speed in the Dnipro?"

"Around here? Less than two knots. So without any wind, it will be dark before we dock. Aye aye, let's turn around."

The boat fell off on a run to starboard. Then they jibed the mainsail across to drift down current on a starboard tack.

"So anyway," continued Yuriy, "Kuchma wanted to discuss ideas with Marchuk, but he suspected that every office of the Presidential Administration Building was bugged. So he calls Marchuk in, and they decide to take an evening drive in the snow—in a borrowed police car. See, Kuchma was convinced that all of the official cars were bugged too. So they call the car park below the building and talk to some poor cop. They go down and borrow the poor bugger's unmarked car, an ugly dark blue Daewoo. As luck would have it, the copper is in the organization. Hell, he's one of my friend Fedora's recruits from six years earlier. Our smart lad leaves his MP3 player on Record and stuffs it in a discarded lunchbag in the back seat."

Yuriy almost choked on his snickers. He coughed and continued.

"So the minister of defence drives the president around for a whole hour in the dark, and the next day the organization has a recording of every fucking word they said! ... And that actually happened two days in a row. So sit back and listen. Let me tell you the whole fairytale."

5

MINISTER OF DEFENCE General Yevhen Marchuk slammed the door of the dark blue Daewoo and turned the ignition key. "At least it's front-wheel drive. I'd hate to get us stuck in the snow tonight," he joked.

"Get us stuck and I'll bust you to fucking private, Yevhen Kyrylovych," said Commander in Chief, President Kuchma, not sounding amused at all. The stress of the last three years was showing. "So what did you pay that poor cop to borrow his car?"

"I gave him two hundred hryvnias for his troubles."

"Generous, but no matter."

"So which way, Leonid Danylovich?" asked Marchuk.

"Oh, any direction that avoids traffic and keeps us out of deep snow," said Kuchma.

Yevhen Marchuk made a couple of lefts and headed south on Lesia Ukrayinka Boulevard. There was silence for a few minutes.

"Fucking glad we're out of the recording studio," said Kuchma.

"What do you mean?" Marchuk was genuinely baffled.

"You know, that goddam Presidential Administration Building. Everybody is recording everyone in there. Hell, I can stop going to the proctologist now. If I ever really need to know what's up my arse, we'll just ask the Kremlin for the latest film. That son-of-a-whore Putin knows every time I fart. Shit, I bet my haemorrhoids have their own website! And if the Russian FSB and our own SBU aren't record-ing me, then the CIA probably is. Why don't we just burn that build-ing?"

Marchuk tried to soothe his boss. "Leonid Danylovich, I told you that my boys checked that place over with a fine-toothed comb. It's as clean as a teardrop in there. Nothing left. We cleaned out every listening device, every pinhole camera—everything."

"Oh, that makes me feel so much better. And how do I know, Yevhen Kyrylovych, that you aren't working for your idiot prime minister or for your old friends in the KGB?"

"If you believed that for a minute, you wouldn't be talking to me right now."

"I'm talking to you by default. All the good people have left me," complained Kuchma.

"Now tell the truth, Leonid Danylovich. You fired all your good people and hired scum. I'm the last that you didn't fire." Marchuk sounded much like a scolding mother.

"Fuck you. You know I was forced to fire the good guys and forced to hire the scum. But I still know the difference. And then there's Medvedchuk. He orders me around like a dog. Sit, stand, roll over, beg. Hell, if he's not FSB then I don't know who is."

"He's FSB," confirmed Marchuk. "So I see you never did get over the Gongadze-Melnychenko affair."

"No, and I never will—incompetents, fucking incompetents. So I bitched about that two-bit jerk of a journalist—hell, he couldn't even get a by-line in a real newspaper—and surprise, surprise, the bloody Russian FSB has got me on tape. Then someone wastes the poor bugger and cuts off his head. Talk about a set-up! Next thing you know, the whole country thinks I did it! Hell, it wouldn't be bad if it were just the whole country. It's the whole fucking world that thinks I go around ordering the death of two-bit Internet journalists. Do you remember that NATO meeting right after the Melnychenko tapes were publicized? They went and changed the fucking alphabet just to make sure I didn't sit beside George Bush. Hell, they changed the English United States to some French États-Unis just so Ukraine and United States didn't sit side by side. Talk about embarrassment! Cholera! You'd think I had the plague. And that Bush. Now that's a piece of work. I wonder who's pulling his strings?"

"I'm sure you didn't make me your chauffeur for a day just so that you could rant about that," said Marchuk.

"No, I didn't, Yevhen Kyrylovych. In here we can talk in private without someone listening." Kuchma sighed. "I've decided that I won't run for president next year. No matter what the Constitutional Court decides, I'm not running."

"Oh come, Leonid, you're the smartest of the foxes. You even out-foxed that sly old silver fox, Krawchuk. And you walked away from all of the candidates in the last election, including me."

"No, don't bullshit me. If Chornovil hadn't been killed by that Kamaz tractor-trailer, he would have got me."

"Unfortunate accident, that one," said Marchuk.

"I said no bullshit," snapped Kuchma. "He got rubbed out. Erased. I asked some political adviser for advice on how to campaign against Vyacheslav Chornovil and a week later the poor bastard is dead. I'm surprised that the motherfucker Melnychenko hasn't got that bit on tape too. No, I'm campaigning no more. If I could stay president without an election campaign then I would. Otherwise I'm out."

"So you want the election cancelled?"

"Or declared null and void—that will be easier. But never mind. There is something that I would like even more, even if I do step down from this post and someone else becomes president. And don't get yourself all excited. You personally won't ever make it as president. You've already cashed in all your chips."

"Such confidence," sneered Marchuk. "And here I look up to you like a father. But go ahead tell me what you really need."

"Go fuck yourself, Genia!" Kuchma used the diminutive of Yevhen. "There's no fun in this presidency business. And no profit. Those Donetsk bastards are taking everything."

Yevhen Marchuk waited in silence while driving for two more blocks in the snow.

Kuchma restarted the conversation. "But I will tell you what I want most of all. What it is that will make me truly happy at last."

"Well, tell me. I have to turn right here. Soon we'll be out of town."

"Revenge ... What I want is revenge ... and easy on the autobahn in the fucking snow. I know you're a KGB-trained driver, but you're still no Michael Schumacher ... I want revenge on every fucker that ever crossed me. I'll give you a simple list. Here it is. I want you to screw the Donetsk crime bosses, er, I mean the Donetsk business oligarchs. And I want you to screw Putin so bad that he won't be able to sit for a year. Up the arse, I tell you, all the way to your elbow up his arse. Hell, please don't tell me whether old Krawchuk squirrelled away any tactical warheads on cruise missiles—but if he did, then you can shoot one up Colonel Putin's arse and detonate it in Red Square. I never want to crawl to that skeleton-faced bastard on my knees again. He laughs behind my back. The cunt. Never again."

"Is that it?" asked Marchuk. "Is that your deepest wish?"

"It is, and I'm serious." Kuchma fixed Marchuk with his beady eyes. "Now turn left on Science Prospect and get me home to Koncha-Zaspa. Now if you could also get one of your Kamaz drivers to do in that bitch Yulia Volodymyrivna—for that I'll be eternally grateful."

"Are you serious? The Donetsk Gang, Putin, and Tymoshenko. You want them all rubbed out?"

"Don't be so fucking literal, Genia. I want them to be, how should I put it, embarrassed, defeated, tricked, fooled, dismantled. They need to know that in the end they got a lot better than they gave. When they are ashamed to look at their own face in the mirror, then I will have won."

"So you are serious," said Marchuk like a schoolboy taking down his homework assignment. "And what about Ukraine?"

"Let me coin a phrase: What's good for Leonid Kuchma is good for dear Ukraine. Am I not right? And one more thing: Let's go for a drive like this tomorrow. You can tell me all about your plan then. I have confidence in you."

"Seriously. You want me to mess with the Donetsk Gang, Putin, and Tymoshenko."

"Exactly," said Kuchma, "and produce the plan tomorrow night."

The MP3 recorded the sound of the door slamming.

One day later Leonid Danylovich Kuchma and Yevhen Kyrylovych Marchuk again borrowed the same unmarked police car. An MP3 player, set to Record, was in the same paper lunchbag. It had freshly charged batteries.

"I missed you today, Yevhen Kyrylovych," sneered Leonid Kuchma. "Called in sick for the meeting of the Cabinet, did you? Don't you respect your prime minister? Or do you have something on him that keeps him off your back?"

"I have what I must have. And I have some ideas that we need to discuss."

"Go on, you have your president's ear," said Kuchma, feigning formality.

"Well, Mr. President," Marchuk began formally, "you remember the lessons of political technology in a democracy?"

"I do." Kuchma smiled. "I think I wrote the book."

"Exactly, Leonid Danylovich. Lesson One: You win the horse race where you own all the horses. Lesson Two: You win big when you own both horses in the race and can make sure the right horse loses. Lesson Three: You disqualify or cripple all horses that do not belong to you. Lesson Four: You win if you can make sure the last competing horse is crippled."

"Go on," encouraged Kuchma.

"There is more. You win biggest if you can get all your enemies to bet on the losing horse."

There was a long moment of silence punctuated by the *wop-wop-wop* of wiper blades on snow.

"I hate to say it, you old goat-herd," said Kuchma, "but now you are starting to make sense."

"Thank you. So the basic outline of the plan would be as follows: You get the horserace down to two horses. You get all your enemies to bet on one of the two. You make sure that's the one that loses. Now if you play it right, you get your revenge, and Ukraine gets a much needed victory to boot."

"So how do you play this out? How do you con your enemies to back a loser?" asked Kuchma.

"Ah yes, it is a con game for sure, and the way to send the rats over the cliff is in fact to lead them there yourself. What I mean is that you personally must be seen backing this same losing horse and doing everything to make it look like the fix is in—for the losing horse. This will take courage on your part. Remember the end of the story of Samson and Delilah. Samson suckered all his enemies under one roof then pulled the edifice down on himself as well as his opponents."

"Ouch," said Kuchma. "So you are asking me, dear Yevhen Kyrylovych, to sucker everybody I despise to back my presidential candidate, and in the last minute to have the bugger lose."

"You got it."

"And it took you all day to figure this out?"

"No, I also got some of the details of Project Samson worked out."

"Project Samson, eh? I sure hope so, because I can't see how you will ever get Yulia Volodymyrivna under the same roof with Putin and the Donetsk Gang, and certainly never under the same roof with me."

"Tymoshenko is Stage Two. She'll actually help make our Stage One work, but then we'll build a separate edifice for the lady and collapse it on her."

"So who are the horses?" asked Kuchma.

"We must think this through carefully, and I want to hear your ideas, but for a start I think the losing horse could be Victor Fedorovich Yanukovich, the Donetsk Gang puppet who is playing at prime minister today."

"So you have some compromat on Victor Fedorovich?" Kuchma was quickly getting the hang of this game. Compromat was the slang term for compromising material for purposes of political blackmail.

"Yanukovich is an ex-con."

Kuchma let out a long whistle. "An ex-con for president! Whew! You've done your homework, Genia. And who is your knight in shining armour?"

"That's harder. It can't be Tymoshenko because she's the planned victim for Stage Two. I thought of Kinakh, but he has zero charisma and can't act for beans. Yuriy Kirpa won't oppose Yanukovich. Young Taras Chornovil maybe? He'll have the mantle of his late father."

"No," said Kuchma. There was a shiver in his voice.

"Yekhanurov," suggested Marchuk.

"Maybe, but not my first choice. Again, no charisma, just like Kinakh, and he won't resonate among the nationalists of Western Ukraine. I think if we are to set up a battle with the Donetsk Gang from the east on one side, then the nationalists from the west are their natural enemies. The knight in shining armour candidate has to satisfy the Halychany."

"Should I try to resurrect Bandera," joked Marchuk, naming the wartime leader of the Organization of Ukrainian Nationalists.

"No. And his grandson is too young," said Kuchma in a deadpan voice.

"Tarasiuk, the foreign minister?"

"Maybe. But I'm afraid he may have too much backbone. When I pull this edifice down about my ears, I expect to be able to wriggle my way out of the rubble. With Tarasiuk as president that may not be possible. Same applies to old Lukyanenko. That guy with a sabre in his hand would scare me to death."

"So let's get this straight," said Marchuk. "You prefer no backbone, but an electable face with the language skills to thrill our Ukrainian Ukrainians. And you told me before that I personally have no chance. That leaves whom? It's Kostenko or Yushchenko. Kostenko could never garner the votes, and has no experience governing. So is it Yushchenko?"

"We've had a Leonid against Leonid election before. So are you proposing a Victor versus Victor battle this time?" Kuchma chuckled. "Well for sure the backbone is flexible enough for my purposes, he's Hollywood-handsome, his Ukrainian is impeccable—but he's just a bloody banker with presidential ambitions. Can you package and sell him?"

"We'll get American help. They can package him as the second Messiah. He'll need huge financing, and it can't come from the current regime. Also the Americans can't be seen sending financial support. So who else hates Putin as badly as you say you do, Leonid Danylovich?"

"Boris Abramovich," answered the president.

"Who?"

"Berezovsky. The Russian tycoon."

"Okay…Now for the stage directions, just before I drop you off at home. From now on, you are that asshole's Yanukovich's biggest fan. Build up his confidence. Flatter the pig. Same goes for Putin. You are his long lost brother. You are ready to sell him Crimea for a bag of glass beads. And the Donetsk Gang, offer to sell them every steel mill, every coalmine or shipyard that their heart desires. Make them deals that they can't refuse. And once Yanukovich is running, we'll set him up with the wackiest Russian political technologists. We'll dream up the most blatant forms of election rigging to impress his backers while simultaneously alienating the honest voters. We'll stage manage the greatest show on the planet."

"And what about Yulia Tymoshenko?" asked Kuchma.

"If spineless Yushchenko is the knight in shining armour, then Yulia better be his horse or he might fold on us like a house of cards," laughed Marchuk, mercilessly mixing metaphors. "We certainly need her in the beginning. But there's enough history between those two that it will be simple to provoke Stage Two of the plan. In any case, we'll put some of your people in Yushchenko's camp. We will need strings on that puppet too, to make sure he doesn't run out of control after he wins the presidency."

"Exactly. And what if somebody gets original ideas?" asked Kuchma, knowing well that an operation like this never goes according to plan.

"We have wild cards. First of all there is Yulia Tymoshenko, the original political storm trooper."

"Not a Princess Leia?" joked the president.

The defence minister smiled. "You wish. More like the Iron Lady with looks. Another wild card is the militsya. Another is Parliament, all bought and paid for. Then there is the Supreme Court, also firmly in your back pocket. Then there are the diplomats of Western foreign governments. There is Kwasniewski, the Polish president. Finally, the very last wild card is the electorate—the Ukrainian people."

"If you say so. So you'll be the hidden puppet-master pulling all these fucking strings," mused the president. "Are you sure, Yevhen Kyrylovych, that you can pull them effectively when you are standing so close to Samson under the edifice?"

"When that time comes, you may have to cut your puppet-master loose. Fire me, give me a head start, and then order my arrest. Instant credibility."

"Good night, Macchiavelli," said President Kuchma as Yevhen Marchuk let him out in front of the gated mansion in Koncha-Zaspa.

"Good night my dear Samson."

6

AFTER THE TWO DAYS OF CARRYING GRAVEL, the work schedule called for one shift of sentry duty. This was easy work. All Yarko had to do is carry an AK-74 on a strap and walk around in the sub-basement. His schedule had shifted from daytime to the graveyard shift, which assured a total absence of traffic at the elevators. The lads doing gravel duty would move a pallet of gravel sacks via the elevator shortly after beginning their shift, then again some four hours later. The rest of the time they worked behind the twin doors to the tunnelling ops room. This made night-time sentry duty lonely indeed. Yarko was very glad that he had company at the beginning of his shift. The lead miner, whose job was overall planning and supervision, had decided to stay for the beginning of this late night shift. Yarko had met Sergei before, but had never actually talked to him.

"Good evening, Sergei," greeted Yarko, knowing full well that the clock had already slipped into morning.

"Good evening," Sergei responded in Russian, not showing any great enthusiasm for the time of day. He opened the weapons closet and selected a short-barrelled Kalashnikov. "I'll join you on sentry duty for a while."

Smart choice, thought Yarko, since the alternative was gravel duty behind closed doors. He noticed that Sergei was remarkably comfortable carrying that automatic weapon. Yarko thought this would be a good opening gambit to strike up a conversation.

"Listen, Sergei, you look like you were born carrying that grease gun. Don't tell me you guys use lead to mine coal in Donbas."

"Nyet, we don't." Sergei spoke now in mixed Ukrainian. "This here trade I learned in the Red Army. They draft me very young. I serve in Afghanistan. I flew helicopters. No, I didn't actually fly them—I flew in them. I was a gunner. I had the machine gun."

There was a long pause. Yarko couldn't think of anything to say.

Sergei broke the silence. "Nowhere to hide it. I am second Taras Shevchenko. They press me in army. They send me to foreign country. They ask me in this foreign desert to shoot children for the Party and the Fatherland. But those fucking kids would shoot back at us. The older ones got Stingers. They shoot down helicopters very well. They got me twice. Always as we were coming back to land. They would hide near the base. We would return low on fuel. What could we do? We fired flares and dropped as fast as we could to beat the Stingers. Damned helicopter engineers. The turbines exhausted at the sides. That's just what the devils with the Stingers needed. One time they got us just as we landed. Right in the engine. Everything was on fire. I was the only one to survive… The others were cooked. I still remember the smell. Burning kerosene and roasted flesh… That's how it was."

Sergei didn't want to talk any more. Yarko understood. Some veterans returned from war with scarred bodies, others carried their scars on their souls. All were casualties.

The doors to the tunnelling ops room opened. Mark and his partner muscled a loaded dolly over the stoop and pushed it towards the elevator door. Sergei joined them in the elevator. Clearly he wanted to check out the disposal procedures at the back of the hotel.

"Good night, Yarko," said Sergei in perfect Ukrainian. "I go sleep after this." He seemed happier having told his story.

Several minutes later Mark and his partner came back and pushed the empty cart to the tunnelling ops room. The doors closed, and Yarko again was all alone. He regretted that he hadn't brought a book.

An hour later Yarko heard the familiar sound of the elevator dropping past the first basement on its way to the sub-basement. No one was scheduled to come by at this time of night. Yarko swung the AK-74 that hung off his shoulder "response right" to cover the elevator door. He happened to be several metres down the hall, so he couldn't see any intruder until they actually stepped out of the elevator. He made a mental note that a pair of large convex mirrors opposite these doors and at one at the end of the hall would improve security. The elevator doors opened. Out poked the unmistakable underslung barrel of an AK-74. It was followed by a tanned leg in a black high heel pump.

"Ksenia?" Yarko blurted, though his mind had yet to confirm it.

Out stepped a beauty in a short, tight-fitting black dress. Yarko barely recognized her. Her smooth, sun-tanned legs stepped one before the other, rocking her hips as she walked towards him. With each step her thigh parted the split on the left of her dress. Her chestnut brown hair was pulled back into a high ponytail tied with a red-and-black ribbon. This veritable waterfall of long hair swung in rhythm to her walk. Dark eyes from under coquettish bangs drilled through to Yarko's soul. Moist lips parted to flash pearly white.

"Wow, Ksenia, you've changed!" Yarko exclaimed, again realizing too late that he wasn't sounding very suave. He was complimenting the unexpected length of her hair.

"Changed? I haven't changed, Yarchyk. I've just let my hair grow." She crushed him in a passionate embrace and latched onto his lips with her own. She pressed her breasts to his chest and squeezed her thigh in between his. Ksenia needed to steal back from an uncaring fate that which had been denied her last year.

A tickle of saliva ran down to his chin. Yarko was powerless against this female advance. The initiative was fully in the hands of Ksenia. He wanted to say something witty to regain some equilibrium, but he couldn't. Still, as a man, he felt he had to convert this rout into a counterattack. He wrapped his arms around her and squeezed her even tighter to his chest. His tongue probed past her lips and teeth. He felt a hardening against the pressure of her leg. His hand travelled lightly down the hollow of her back and over the muscled mound of her behind to the cool smoothness of the back of her thigh. He slowly slipped his hand upward under her dress. It was uninterrupted in its travel over silky skin. Reading his mind, Ksenia whispered, "I'm not wearing any."

She took Yarko's other hand and slipped it beneath the unzipped front of her dress.

The initiative was now very much in the hands of the woman. Yarko had no will to resist. Without releasing her lips from his, Ksenia backed him step by step into the open door of an equipment room. Yarko tripped and fell. Ksenia fell on top of him as both weapons clanged to the ground. She wrapped her arms and legs around him, creating a woven wreath of young bodies in the heat of a late summer night.

7

It was some three weeks since his passionate reunion with Ksenia. Yarko found that his rotating shifts left very little opportunity for romance. He rarely had a chance to see the sights of the city. The constant regime of hard work in the sub-basement left him too tired for tourist pleasures even on his days off. Whenever he did have the opportunity to explore Kyiv, he knew he could not enjoy it if he had to experience it alone. The intense work regimen did have its benefits, such as an increased upper body strength. But the monotony of the work routine was becoming a difficult challenge. Yarko coped by daydreaming. And no matter how he tried to steer his reveries, his thoughts would always return to Ksenia.

His was much more than a desire to possess again every inch of her youthful beauty. Ksenia was filling a much deeper void in his heart. He had felt that void all year while he lived in Canada. He did not ever want to spend such a year without her again. He felt incomplete without her. Knowing that she was now living here in the same hotel as him, but unreachable all the same, made the pain that much greater.

Meanwhile, Ksenia spent her daylight hours dressed as a nun, patrolling two floors of the hotel as well as the meeting room of the Conference for Unification of the Churches. This meant that even when Yarko saw her during the day, he dared not flirt or show recognition, as that would threaten Ksenia's cover. It was the second week of September before Yarko, Mark, and Ksenia could arrange a day off all at the same time. They met for breakfast in the hotel restaurant.

"Good morning, Yarchyk," Ksenia greeted him sweetly, using the diminutive as he walked in.

"Good morning. What's new?"

"Not much, except that Yushchenko seems to have disappeared."

Yarko was a little annoyed that Ksenia had suddenly refocused on her work while he was expecting a morning kiss.

"What do you mean, disappeared?" Yarko was also annoyed that Ukraine's bitter politics had displaced the anticipated sweet touch of her lips.

"He hasn't been seen in public for three days," Ksenia explained.

"Officially we've been told to tell the public that he's resting, but none of our Nasha Ukrayina Party people seem to know. Chervonenko, his security chief, is gone too. The only one doing any campaigning for the orange side is Yulia Tymoshenko, bless her egotistical soul."

"Then I guess my news is nowhere near as important," said Yarko.

"No, go ahead," encouraged Ksenia.

"Well, you know how PORA wants more international observers to ensure fair elections? Looks like my father is coming next month. He arrives October 26, five days before the election. Maybe the Ukrainian diaspora from around the world has finally responded."

"We'll be needing them," said Ksenia. "This presidential race is getting close. Two months ago Yanukovich had barely twelve percent of the decided vote. Today he's breathing on Yushchenko's tail. It's almost a dead heat. He's not beyond using dirty tricks to win."

Yarko spotted new patrons entering the restaurant. "I see Mark has come in with Sergei. Let me introduce them."

After the usual round of introductions, the four sat to breakfast.

"Ksenia tells me that Yushchenko has disappeared," said Yarko.

"Disappeared? How?" asked Mark.

They were interrupted by a waitress who came to take their order. No one was in the mood for culinary intricacies. "Four specials," ordered Sergei in Russian.

"For about three days," began Ksenia, "nobody that I can talk to in his campaign organization has seen him. Appearances had to be cancelled. There is confusion in his election headquarters. The only fact I have is that Chervonenko, his security specialist, is gone too."

"So where was he seen last?" asked Sergei.

"Somewhere between Chernihiv and Kyiv. He had appearances scheduled in Kyiv."

"Doesn't sound good at all," said Yarko. "Chernihiv is near the border with Russia, and Kyiv is full of agents and criminals and mobsters of every sort."

There were several minutes of silence. The waitress brought the plates of scrambled eggs and sausage. Everyone dug in, but their thoughts were far from the meal before them.

Sergei broke the silence. "Look, there's nothing we can do about any of this at the moment. I suggest something to take our minds off things—a little sightseeing maybe? I don't know about you guys, but I haven't visited St. Sophia's yet."

Yarko and Mark hadn't either.

"Then it's decided," said Ksenia. "We'll go to St. Sophia's. I haven't been there since the funeral of Patriarch Volodymyr. So, we can walk there uphill, or if we take the Metro subway we can start our sightseeing from the Zoloti Vorota first."

"The Metro sounds good to me," said Mark. "I can use the chance to sit and rest. My last shift was hauling gravel. We actually ran three wagonloads up the elevator last night. The landscaping is all done and the extra bags are piling up."

"I noticed that too," said Sergei. "We'll have to slow the digging and work on tunnel infrastructure in the meantime. We need to change the creeper to the electric-powered version. We also need to install two more lights and extend the phone line to the end of the tunnel. I have arranged for a truck to come every day at six in the morning and haul the gravel away. We'll need the late-night shift to help load the truck at that time. I'll be posting instructions tonight."

Yarko noticed that Sergei's Ukrainian had improved since the last time they talked.

The four finished breakfast and walked out to Khreshchatyk Street. A crew of three old ladies with brooms were sweeping the sidewalk, or trying to. The wide sidewalk also served as parking for a collection of bmws, Mercedes, Audis, and Porsches that made run-of-the-mill Opels, Fords, and Skodas look decidedly second-hand.

"Cholera," muttered Sergei. "Back in Donetsk half the roads have crumbled to goat-paths. A twelve-year-old Tavria is a treasure of a car. There is no money and no work, and yet look at this. They polish these sidewalks daily. And look at the cars. Kyiv looks like a city of millionaires. Hey, Yarko, do you have cars like these in Canada?"

"Only a few. Most of the cars I see littering the sidewalks here, I can only see at car shows at home."

"Bastards! And our people go hungry."

"And Ukrainians in Canada ship containers of goods as care packages to Ukraine."

"Don't complain, Sergei," said Ksenia. "Most of these cars belong to your very own Donetsk millionaires. They moved into Kyiv when Yanukovich became prime minister. And look at all of your Donetsk boys in black leather jackets. Those are the bodyguards for the cars, and their owners. They are also their muscle in business matters."

"I hope Yushchenko wins and throws the bums in jail."

"It's your Donetsk voters who elected them into Parliament," Ksenia teased. "As you know, by Ukrainian law, a Member of Parliament is untouchable. He is above the law and immune from prosecution. That is why every big-time criminal tries to get elected to Parliament. He can either buy his way onto a party list or run in a riding. The first way is preferred because there is no electioneering involved—just a big donation to Yanukovich's Party of Regions. For any big-time gangster that is money well spent."

Access to the subway was from the underground pedestrian walkways under the busy street. In these walkways were the actual entrances to the subway escalators that dropped even deeper underground. This day, however, the subway entrance was barricaded, and a helmeted work crew was busy moving boxes and equipment.

Mark groaned. "Dammit, we can't get to the subway from here."

"Let's forget the subway and walk," said Ksenia. "It's not really all that far."

"Look at these guys," said Yarko. "They've got to be the most efficient city workers I've ever seen. They're actually breaking a sweat!"

"Nothing wrong with the subway but they are working on it anyway," Sergei complained. "What will they do? Gold plate the tracks here in Kyiv, while Donbas lives in poverty?"

"Well, Lviv lives in poverty too," said Ksenia. "People travel to Italy or Spain to find work."

Yarko remained silent and watched the repair crew at work. The crew leader, a man of advanced age with thinning white hair and bushy white eyebrows, snapped orders in Russian, and his men obeyed with military precision. There was something familiar about him.

Sergei wasn't finished criticizing Kyiv. "This whole city is a fake," he said in perfect Ukrainian with a hint of a Lviv dialect. "It's a fraud. It's all a masquerade—all the façades of the buildings, the BMWs, the Bentleys. Listen how the people all speak Russian but all the signs are in Ukrainian; it's a masquerade; it's a bloody Potemkin village."

Yarko smiled at Sergei's comments without replying. He was glad he wasn't the only one who felt this way about Kyiv. He also smiled at Sergei's newfound Ukrainian language skills. Sergei must have been hanging out with Vlodko and his Lviviak friends.

After walking along Khreshchatyk a short distance they turned and crossed a large open square. Along the edges of the square were open-air shops that sold everything from trinkets and Soviet-era medals, to folk art and Ukrainian literature. An arch with an angel on top was the centrepiece of the square.

"This is Maidan Nezalezhnosti, the Independence Square," Ksenia said. Trying to brighten the decidedly grouchy mood of both Sergei and Yarko, she added, "And don't forget that somewhere deep in this bedrock beats the eternal heart of Ukraine. Somewhere down there is the Library of Prince Yaroslaw."

"Forever and ever, amen," said Sergei.

Yarko saw an opportunity to pull his leg. "I didn't think you were that religious. Don't tell me you go to church."

"I want you to know that I do. Or at least I've begun. To the Ortho-dox church."

"Which one?"

"The Autocephalous, the independent Ukrainian one."

"You're gutsy, Seryozha," said Ksenia, using the Russian diminu-tive of Sergei, knowing well how difficult that choice would be in Donetsk.

"I'm not Seryozha," corrected Sergei. "I'm Ukrainian, so I'm Ser-hiy."

Another ten minutes walk, northward, brought them to the high ground of this city. Just ahead was where the oldest walled fortifica-tions of the citadel had stood a millennium ago. Soon they reached another open square with a golden domed church at both ends of it.

"To the left is St. Sophia," said Ksenia, playing tourist guide. She led them to an entrance gate in the wall around the complex. Admis-sion was one hryvnia, or about a quarter dollar.

Yarko muttered something about the state barricading the his-toric church from the people of Ukraine. Built by Prince Yaroslaw the Wise in 1036, this church was now a museum. Yarko hated walls.

They walked into the church. Yarko was not religious, but the enormous mosaic of the Virgin Mary over the central nave of the church seemed to speak to him. This was a different Virgin Mary, a St. Mary with a very masculine face. There was no sadness nor even tenderness in her eyes, as would usually be depicted in icons. This face radiated a strength belying its sex. But Yarko also saw a shadow of disgust in those eyes, like that of a mother scolding her children. Get up off your knees, she seemed to say. Be a nation at last. Yarko wondered whether all those young people who were volunteering for the Yushchenko presidential campaign, and who had bedecked the capital of Ukraine in orange flags and ribbons, were in fact the vanguard of a movement that could finally raise this nation off its knees. This happy thought was clouded by the realization that the presidential candidate was a puppet selected for this task thanks to his weakness, not his strength.

Ksenia woke him from his contemplations. "Yarko, we're going."

"Where to now?"

"Well, first to the statue of Bohdan Khmelnytsky, then to the Holodomor Monument."

The Bohdan Khmelnytsky statue occupied a central position in the square. Bohdan, the leader of the seventeenth-century rebellion against the Polish overlords, sat astride a horse, pointing his mace in a north-easterly direction. Erected at the time of the Soviet regime, the gesture with the mace was interpreted by Russians as meaning "There are your friends." Ukrainians tended to view it as meaning "There is the enemy."

"On to Moscow," said Yarko, pointing to the statue.

Serhiy shook his head. "No such luck. He died before he could gather his forces."

"You didn't learn that in any Donbas school!" Ksenia said.

"Nope. My grandmother taught me."

Yarko found himself staring at a soldier standing by the statue. He was wearing the green uniform, unchanged since Soviet times, of the Border troops. For some reason an expression came to him, something about sheep and wolves. But before he could try to understand the reason for this thought, he saw Ksenia walk up to this soldier and say something to him. The soldier put on his hat and walked across the square.

"That was Petro," explained Ksenia. "He too is in the organization. I told him not to shepherd us quite so closely. In fact, Yarko, he's your guardian angel for those times when you leave the hotel complex. You won't always see him, but he'll be there."

Yarko opened his mouth to say something in protest, but realized the necessity of such arrangements. He felt somewhat embarrassed. Again he had a feeling of déjà vu. For some reason this guardian angel seemed familiar to him.

"Next we visit the Holodomor Monument," said Ksenia.

"She must be a Lviviak," said Serhiy. "They love being in charge. Everyone's a general."

"She is," whispered Yarko to Serhiy with a wink, "and, yes, she loves being on top."

At the opposite end of the square from St. Sophia was another church, with a simple white cruciform monument in front of it.

"And this is the only memorial to the Holodomor in Ukraine. This white cross and the tableau behind it were funded by our American Ukrainians. It's a shame that in their own land, Ukrainians honour neither their heroes nor the victims who died at the hands of the enemy." Ksenia provided this running commentary as they approached the church of Saint Andrew.

The information on the tableau was in both English and Ukrainian. Serhiy stood in front of the Ukrainian side reading every word. "My grandfather and two of his children died that year," he explained. "Only my grandmother and my father survived the man-made famine of 1933. When you see the Donbas and the rest of Eastern Ukraine voting for Yanukovich this year, the reason for that goes back to the ethnic cleansing of the area in 1933."

Serhiy was in a pensive mood for the rest of their walking tour. Yarko understood even better now why Serhiy seemed to have a personal stake in all that was going on in Kyiv.

The foursome turned north and soon found themselves headed down a steep cobble-stoned street lined on both sides with artisans' booths. This was the Andriyivsky Spusk. Ksenia appeared to delight in chatting with all the merchants and artists. The men trailed behind and were satisfied to simply admire the artworks and trinkets offered for sale.

"Hey!" Ksenia cried suddenly, hurrying back to the men. "I've just heard that Yushchenko has been poisoned!"

No confirmation was necessary. The entire street had become a hive of activity. Merchants were closing their booths. The public was rushing away in all directions, no longer interested in leisurely shopping. There was a general buzz. It was clear that everyone wanted to catch the news on Channel 5—the only station that broadcast news that had not been previously massaged and approved by the authorities. It was billing itself as the Channel of Honest News, and was constantly in conflict with President Kuchma, his cronies, and his heir-apparent for the presidency, Victor Yanukovich. The words "Channel 5" could be heard over and over as the rumour of the poisoning spread over the whole area.

No discussion was necessary. Yarko, Ksenia, Mark, and Serhiy turned and headed as fast as they could back up the steep broken-up sidewalk to get back to the Hotel Dnipro.

8

YARKO WAS IN THE SUITE in the Dnipro Hotel usually occupied by Professor Verbytsky. The room was filled with over a dozen key members of Operation Slava. Among them he recognized the bearded face of Father Onufriy. Yarko hadn't seen him since his hospital stay in Lviv well over a year ago. The young priest appeared to be fully recovered.

"Glory to Jesus Christ," Yarko addressed him in the traditional formal manner. "How's you're health, Father."

"Glory forever, my health is just fine. Boy, it's good to see you, Yarko. Got tired of your studies, did you? If you've come looking for more KGB-sty to chase, you've certainly come to the right city."

The two embraced like the long-lost friends that they were.

"You're right about getting sick of school, Father," said Yarko. "Things are so much more interesting around here. Although, as usual, I always seem to find myself digging a hole in this country ... So what brings you to Kyiv, Father?"

"I arrived yesterday. I'm doing a series of lectures at the university. In fact, I just finished my first one a few hours ago. It's all about the formation of Orthodox Brotherhoods in the sixteenth century. You're more than welcome to attend. Of course, I'm also the Church Slavonic resource for Operation Slava, for when you tunnel rats finally finish digging your hole."

"Quiet everyone," interrupted Professor Verbytsky. "A special edition of Channel 5 News is coming on."

The news announcer was introducing Oleksander Zinchenko, the chief of staff for the Yushchenko election campaign, whose press conference was about to be rebroadcast.

"So why does that news announcer always wear a red shirt and suspenders?" asked Yarko.

"Quiet, Yarko," said Vlodko. He lowered his voice. "That is Mykola Veresen. That happens to be his trademark. Rather un-Soviet, wouldn't you say?"

"*Today we have sufficient basis to announce that there has been an assassination attempt on Victor Yushchenko*," began Mr. Zinchenko's press conference. "*This has been a poisoning, but not a common poisoning. It is not even a strong poisoning. I speak of a process whereby there was a risk to the life of Victor Yushchenko. There is a sufficient basis to declare this to be an attempt on the life of the candidate to the presidency of Ukraine. We have information from the Rudolfinerhaus Clinic in Austria where Mr. Yushchenko is being treated.*"

There was a general buzz among those present watching the TV. Mr. Zinchenko continued. "*The diagnosis is acute pancreatitis in the presence of multiple secondary complications. I could list them all, but this is a complicated matter for medical personnel. In the words of doctors that I spoke with, if left untreated for just a few more hours, this condition would have had a probability of lethality of eighty percent."*

The news commentator in the red shirt summarized the press conference. *"...The diagnosis is acute pancreatitis with multiple complications likely caused by an intentional poisoning. This is a similar medical diagnosis to that for the late Mr. Oleksenko, who as you recall recently died of unknown causes. The prognosis for Mr. Yushchenko is that he will be able to resume his campaigning in just a few days. Left untreated, Mr. Yushchenko's condition would have left him physically, mentally, and emotionally incapable of ever performing the duties of a president.*

"This is just the last of a long series of political assassinations that began a decade ago with the disappearance of Mykhaylo Boychyshyn, and included the death of the presidential candidate Vyacheslav Chornovil in a car accident some four years ago during the last presidential campaign. The mysterious videotape of a member of Ukraine's SBU describing the plan for Chornovil's murder seems to have disappeared and that particular case is no longer being actively pursued. As you may recall, the body of Mykhaylo Boychyshyn was discovered over a year ago buried in a garden patch in Lviv. That discovery resulted in a night of mass demonstrations and was followed next day by the death of several members of various Special Services in two separate incidents."

Vlodko motioned Yarko to a vacant corner of the room. "The poisoning is an unpredicted complication," he said. "Definitely not part of Operation Samson as it had been described to me. The operation may have fallen off the rails, or else outside forces are involved. We may need you to visit The Saint to get a revised political evaluation. The weather is holding up, so are you up for another sailing adventure?"

"I certainly am. Can I go tomorrow?"

"Too early for anything reliable, and in any case you have three days of work coming up. Let's set up the sailing trip for four days from now. Now let's get back to watching the news."

"Okay, program's over, let's check the Pluses," announced Serhiy, referring to Channel 1 + 1, one of the pro-Yanukovich TV stations. "I'd like to hear what they have to say."

The TV flickered to another channel just in time for them to watch the end of a broadcast with a female news commentator reading. "*...President Kuchma forwarded the deepest sympathies of the Ukrainian people to President Putin of Russia in connection with the tragic finale to the terrorist standoff in Beslan.*

"*Earlier today, Prime Minister Victor Yanukovich announced that the Sixty-first Anniversary of the Liberation of the City of Kyiv by the Red Army is being moved up to October 27. The city will be celebrating with a parade of veterans and a show of military equipment from the Great Patriotic War. The prime minister added that the Russian president, Vladimir Vladimirovich Putin, is expected to accept the invitation to visit Ukraine's capital for this celebration. In anticipation of this event, the city will begin erecting grandstands along the Khreshchatyk in just a few weeks.*

"*To summarize, the absence of presidential candidate Victor Yushchenko from Ukraine and the interruption of his campaign has been explained as a need for medical treatment outside the country for an undisclosed chronic medical condition.*"

"Scum," said Ksenia, commenting on the misleading spin being given to the Yushchenko story. "And that's the only version of the story that is being fed to the eastern part of the country."

"Looks like a *temnyk* has already been prepared and distributed," said Father Onufriy, commenting on the ongoing practice of the Kuchma government to supply the media with *temnyk* guidelines on which stories to emphasize, which to downplay, and the correct spin to give each story.

"No, I don't think so," said Vlodko. "They would not have had time. I think what we have is Channel 1+1 anticipating the appropriate spin while downplaying the story until firm instructions are received. Notice how they are playing to patriots by emphasising that Yushchenko left Ukraine to seek medical treatment. That implies an insult to his country. Also note that the condition has been described as chronic, showing Yushchenko as possibly being medically unfit for office. Of course there is no mention of any poisoning, and I expect that in the future, all claims of poisoning will be ridiculed. These guys have become entirely predictable. It's going to be hard for the truth to break through all the background noise of guided disinformation."

"And that bastard Putin will be in Kyiv just four days before the first round of presidential elections," said Professor Verbytsky.

This seemed to be the trigger for a conversational free-for-all in the room. The noise level increased and the TV was now totally ignored, with everyone in the room trying to explain his latest conspiracy theory to everyone else. Yarko felt it was best for him to head to his own hotel room to catch some sleep. He waived goodbye to Ksenia, but she was totally absorbed in explaining "temnyks" to Serhiy. Having come from the Donbas, he had no idea that alternative views of the news could even be shown on TV.

9

YARKO JOGGED ALONE DOWN THE PATH to the marina on Trukhaniv Island. He was pleased that the summer's warmth had continued well into the first month of fall. Ahead he saw Yuriy—The Saint—standing on the bow of one of the sailboats, cranking a turnbuckle to tension the forestay.

"Should be breezy today," Yuriy said in greeting. "We'll want to tighten the leach of the main."

"No reef in the main, Mister Yuriy?"

Yuriy smiled. "Naw, the Dnipro is still warm." He raised the main and let it luff in the wind while he pulled on the halyard for the jib.

Yarko pulled on a life preserver. "The docking lines are mine. I'll be the human knot."

"Stay aft, Yarko, and take the tiller. You'll be the helmsman today."

"Aye, captain. Same plan as last time? Head north until the wind dies, then drift down-current to the marina."

"Should do. Although I expect wind all day."

The day's sailing proved to be a physical workout for both. Carrying a touch more sail than advisable for the windy conditions resulted in a hefty heel angle despite both sailors hiking well over the windward gunwale. It was clear that Yuriy craved this workout. Yarko had no need for additional exercise, but loved the feel of possibly the last of the sun's hot summer rays. It was the brief commands and even briefer responses in the language of sail that cemented a bond between the two. It was well past noon before the conditions were calm enough for Yarko to initiate a real conversation. His opening was less than subtle.

"So what do you know about Yushchenko's poisoning?"

Yuriy laughed. "You and every spy agency in the world is asking that question. I expected Vlodko to send someone my way. I'm truly glad that he chose you."

"Thank you. I enjoyed our last conversation about Operation Samson. When all this craziness blows over, I'm inviting you to Canada to enjoy our West Coast sailing."

"Thanks, I know you say it's the best, but things are getting truly difficult here. They will get even more difficult for Operation Slava too. A few months ago, when I was still in the Cabinet, I was going to buy the Hotel Dnipro in the name of our ministry's employee pension fund. That was my way to clear the road for Operation Slava. Now I'm no longer in the government, but a sale of the hotel is still going through. To the wrong kind of buyers. In a month or two you guys may have some real problems with the wrong characters owning the building, if you know what I'm saying. These guys are the real Russian Mafia. Now, with the right government in place, maybe you guys could go public. Who knows? But until then, you are facing a big risk. The sale is planned for November. Right now, I am going to try to handle that problem for you guys myself."

"I'll pass that information on to Vlodko," said Yarko, "but how about the Yushchenko poisoning?" He was impatient to get at the juicy political story.

"Yes, I still have contacts with my boys in the Special Services. That in itself is scary, for I am now outside the command structure. Part of the SBU, the security service of Ukraine, is still loyal to Russia. Part is loyal to the concept of an independent Ukraine. Some are simply trying to make a public service career for themselves, but others have made it an integral part of their own criminal operations. As you can imagine, orders do not get passed down. Other orders get disobeyed, and still others are countermanded. I have to be careful to make sure that I get the real truth. This place is awash in disinformation. What I am doing is morally right—but it is quite illegal."

"I understand," said Yarko, encouraging Yuriy.

"So enough bullshit, let me cut to the chase. As you know, part of Marchuk's Project Samson was to get Yanukovich to hire some crazies from Russia. Of course, Marchuk planned to leak this fact at just the right time as an additional form of compromat to ensure Yanukovich's defeat. This relates to the poisoning. One of the crazies is Gleb Pavlovsky, a past advisor to Putin. Gleb dreams up this poisoning plan and gets other crazies from Russia's FSB to help out. It is what is usually referred to as a rogue operation. Or possibly the crazies in the FSB dreamt it up and sold the plan to Gleb. Either way, I cannot answer whether the chicken came first or the egg.

"Anyway, the FSB has been developing some very interesting poisons. The one used on Yushchenko is a specially prepared fast-acting form of Dioxin. I gave the Rudolfinerhaus Clinic an anonymous tip about this two days ago. The normal progression of Dioxin poisoning is very slow, and there is very little medical history on it, so even a top medical expert could never have figured it out in time. The question that I can't answer today is whether Gleb's operation had Putin's blessing or not.

"Don't get me wrong, he certainly had Putin's blessing to work for Yanukovich. The question is whether this particular plan had Putin's blessing or even the blessing of the head of the FSB, which I guess is the same thing. Now Pavlovsky wouldn't know Dioxin from cow's milk, so the details of the idea definitely had to have been dreamt up by someone in the FSB Special Ops department. That is why I prefer to think the idea did not originate with Gleb, but was sold to him. Maybe it was someone he worked with before, while helping to clear the path for Putin's own election.

"Honestly, I don't think that Yanukovich knows about it. He is just a puppet. The big concern today is that this puppet has successfully attracted a billion dollars in help from Putin. The puppet is definitely taking on a life of its own."

"Something like a very large Pinnocchio," commented Yarko.

"Exactly." Yuriy broke into a smile for the first time since his monologue began. "With a magic fairy in Moscow and puppet-master Gepetto-Marchuk asleep in Kyiv. Anyway, the polls are showing a close race—about forty per cent to forty-two per cent, with the usual three per cent error either way. So Yanukovich's Russian advisors are now shooting for an outright win in the first round of elections. They see the magic 'fifty per cent plus one' within reach.

"I do expect that puppet-master Marchuk will start desperately yanking on this puppet's strings to make Yanukovich discredit himself. This is also the time when various bits of compromat will be leaked to the press or to the Yushchenko camp. The universally hated Kuchma will cooperate by being seen unfairly helping Yanukovich. The 'administrative resource' will be blatantly supporting Yanukovich. Such things will be caught on film. The hope is that these violations will elicit an opposing reaction from the electorate. The presidential *temnyks* will become ridiculously one-sided and then the detailed facts of the government's pressure tactics on the press will be leaked. That's how such things get done. But quite seriously, Marchuk has got to get going to slam the brakes on the Yanukovich campaign. It may have gotten out of his control already."

"And what about the Putin visit to Kyiv?" asked Yarko.

"Another Gleb Pavlovsky initiative. But this one should backfire. If by that time there is an undercurrent of opinion that the Russians poisoned Yushchenko, then the visit will be seen as more blatant meddling in Ukrainian politics. It should then elicit a strong opposing reaction."

"How do we ensure that such an opinion exists by that time?"

"Excellent question, my friend. That just might be a job for my remaining rank-and-file friends in the SBU, and the last independent TV channel in the country." Yuriy was clearly plotting something. "Under the circumstances, Yarko, would you find it hard to believe that rank-and-file Security Service agents would be reporting directly to the press rather than to their treacherous superiors?"

"Channel 5?"

"Channel 5 … and my young colleague Vladimir."

There was silence as the two busied themselves with a jibing manoeuvre. It was time to head back.

"And what if Yushchenko dies?" asked Yarko.

"He better not. If he does, the country will erupt in violence. And

Yulia Tymoshenko would be just the one to stoke the fires. Kuchma would call off the election, leaving himself in power for another year. But then he would find himself at war with Tymoshenko, with blood literally flowing in the streets. He would then be most certainly pushed into the open arms of Vladimir Putin. So much for Operation Samson. The West would make lots of noises but would not interfere. Yes. That would be the scariest scenario of all."

Again there was silence. The boat was now heading south along the shores of Trukhaniv Island, back from whence they had come. Sailing again demanded the full attention of both Yarko and The Saint.

10

IT WAS THE MIDDLE OF OCTOBER. Ever since Yushchenko's poisoning, a general malaise seemed to have affected Operation Slava. Funds were running short. A third of the mining crew was sent home to the Donbas region, and the work schedule reduced to two shifts. Serhiy was now himself taking regular work shifts in the tunnel. The Conference for Unification of the Churches was coming to an end. The sunny Kyiv skies had turned grey. Yarko hadn't seen Ksenia in weeks.

Yarko was working guard duty for the night shift. Mark was working the same shift, but being on gravel duty, he had to spend most of his time on the other side of the double steel doors. Serhiy was deep inside the tunnel manning the boring machine. Breaking the strict security rules, Yarko had invited Ksenia to drop in on the tunnelling operations that night after she completed her conference security duties.

Yarko was pacing the sub-basement with the ever-present AK-74 slung over his shoulder when he heard the unmistakable sound of the elevator passing the first basement level on its way down to the sub-basement. By force of habit, Yarko's hand found the pistol grip of the automatic weapon and swung it "response right" using the shoulder strap to steady it. The elevator door opened and out stepped a nun in the traditional dark blue garb.

"Ksenia?" Yarko was still not quite used to seeing her in the guise of the Order of Sisters Servants of Mary Immaculate.

"It's me." Ksenia dropped the shawl and freed her hair from the pins that had held it in check. She shook her head to liberate every last strand.

Yarko released his weapon. He wrapped his arms around Ksenia and planted his lips firmly on hers. Ksenia's slender figure seemed lost in the folds of the religious disguise. Yarko's eyes scanned for the door to the equipment room as his arm swept behind her knees to lift her up like baby. Moaning in protest, Ksenia became a kicking confusion of stockings, garters, nun's habit, and thighs.

"Not now," she breathed, breaking free of his lips, "and not in this."

Yarko's lips were sliding down the side of her neck, his tongue flicking a taste at its base.

"Please," Ksenia panted in feeble protest.

Yarko felt a tremor under the navy folds that promised an end to further resistance. Holding her in his arms he braced his back against a wall and slid down to sit cross-legged. His legs wrapped around Ksenia's hips. He was holding her legs high, having placed his right hand under her habit just above the top of her stocking. Protecting her exposed thighs from his gaze, Ksenia pulled Yarko's face down onto hers. Her long kiss did nothing to stop the quivering that betrayed her feelings long before her words did.

"I love you," she whispered, her voice hoarse with emotion.

"Yarko, Help!" Mark's voice suddenly echoed from down the hall. "Something happened. Help! The tunnel! I think it collapsed!"

"Okay. Okay. I'm coming." Yarko looked at Ksenia. His mind was in that confused state on the edge of passion that precluded clear thought. Ksenia's eyes were screaming "don't leave," but she managed to whisper, "Go. What are you waiting for—we have to help!"

Yarko went first. Ksenia limped behind him trying to adjust her shoes on the run. The double steel doors in the north wall of the sub-basement were opened. Mark was standing at the door, cordless receiver in hand, yelling in English into the speaker. Mark's gravel-duty partner stood by looking even more confused than Mark. A grey cloud of dust hung in the circular opening in the limestone wall of the tunnelling operations room.

"What happened, Mark?" cried Yarko, hoping in vain for a logical reply.

Ksenia caught up to the guys in the ops room. She calmly took the receiver from Mark's hand and spoke into it in clear Ukrainian.

"Can you hear me? Allo, allo, this is Ksenia. Is everything okay? What happened? Can you hear me?"

Anxious to hear any sounds from the tunnel, Yarko pushed the speaker button on the telephone's base station. There was no sound. It appeared that even if Mark may have once had a connection, there was nothing at the other end now.

"Hey, if their lights are out, maybe they simply can't find the hand-set," Yarko suggested.

"It's still extension one, isn't it, Mark?" asked Ksenia. "I'll hang up and dial nine plus one to get their phone to ring again."

Ksenia dialled again. The speaker phone broadcast the ring tone ring after ring after ring. Finally there was a click at the other end and the sound of coughing.

Yarko smiled. "Dead men don't cough!"

"Allo, allo, this is Ksenia. Is everything all right? What happened?"

After a series of hacking coughs, a voice could finally be heard. "We found the passage. We found the passage. We tunnelled right under it. Now the ceiling collapsed on us and we can see it."

Yarko turned towards the tunnel just in time to see Mark's shoes disappear into the opening.

There was only one shuttle, so everyone else had to wait its return.

"I hope he took a dust mask," said Ksenia.

"And a camera," added Yarko.

"Hey! If we are all standing around in the tunnel ops room, then who's standing guard in the hall by the elevator?" To emphasise her security reminder, Ksenia winked and teasingly hiked up her ankle-length habit, revealing a holstered PSM at the top of her right stocking. This did nothing to alleviate Mark's partner's state of total confusion.

"Breach of security protocol, my arse." Yarko eyed the silky flash of thigh. "That pistol sure looks like my favourite little gun from last year. I would thank you to give it back to me later tonight." Yarko turned and headed past the steel doors towards the elevator, hoping the promise of this night would yet be fulfilled.

Mark had never ridden the shuttle to the end of the tunnel. He had taken short rides when the tunnel was some twenty metres long and the dolly was worked by rope and pulley. He now remembered that the 200-metre mark in the boring operation had been passed weeks ago. His flashlight could stab about four metres through the cloud of fine dust before him. The tunnel opening behind him had become a dime-sized white disk fading in the dust. Mark, lying on his stomach on a metal tray on wheels, was being whisked into the darkness by an electric motor that spun a pulley underneath. The tunnel was carved into solid bedrock and was barely a metre wide. Mark felt the darkness pressing around him. He closed his eyes. He suppressed a scream. Being the only trained archaeologist present, he had felt obliged to be the first through the tunnel when it was completed. Now that he was deep in the tunnel, he wished that he had demonstrated somewhat less professional pride. Only when he heard voices ahead of him did he dare to open his eyes.

Mark found himself stopped before a mound of broken rock. Above him, in the diffuse light of a distant bulb, dangled a pair of feet from the opening in the tunnel roof. A disembodied voice echoed down. "How are you, Mark? How do you like our tunnel?"

Mark was temporarily disoriented. "So where the hell are you?"

"Here, shine your light up here." It was Serhiy's voice from somewhere in the passage that intersected the tunnel at nearly ninety degrees just above Mark's head.

"If the broken rocks are in your way, pass them up to us, we have plenty of room here," came another disembodied voice that Mark now recognized as that of Victor, the other miner.

Mark cleared the loose rocks and lifted himself up into the ancient passage.

Serhiy, covered in grey dust, was grinning. "So how do you like it? In the time it took you to get here we added another four metres of extension cord to put a light bulb up here."

Mark looked around. The passage sloped to the left towards the actual Library of Yaroslaw the Wise. The air was chilly and had a peculiar smell. It seemed to be harder for him to breathe. The single light bulb threw fantastic shadows along the walls of the passage. Mark took his camera and took pictures of the two miners.

"Not a digital?" asked Victor, the second miner.

"No, I forgot my digital in my hotel room. I was taking some pictures of Kyiv last week. This camera is the one that was lying around the ops room. It's not mine. I'm sure glad it has film."

"Well?" asked Sergei, guessing what was on Mark's mind.

"Well, I guess we may as well wander along the passage and see what we can see," said Mark. "But first let me phone the ops room to tell them everything is okay."

Stabbing the darkness ahead with their flashlights, the three began the hike towards the lost Library. The passage had a roughly quadrilateral cross section. Mark decided that this was a natural crevice that had been enlarged and enhanced by man. The width averaged three metres. The height varied from three to five metres, but generally it was higher than it was wide. The floor had been smoothed in places and finished with flat rocks in others. Stalactites and stalagmites materialized out of the dark, acting more as markers than actual obstacles. Several minutes into the hike, Mark spotted something on the ground ahead. They came upon the rusted remains of a pointed helmet and the brittle leather of what appeared to be a quiver.

"Leave these things where they are for now," Mark instructed. "For now all I take is pictures."

In places, the floor was covered with what appeared to be whitish-yellow petrified honey. These were solidified pools of calcite mineral that had seeped or dripped into the passageway over the centuries. Finally they came to a place where the ceiling of the passage sloped down sharply. Beneath it, the floor had been carved into a flight of five steep stair-steps heading down. These appeared to have been flooded by a smooth waterfall of solid calcite that promised to make further descent quite treacherous. From below the dropped ceiling Mark could make out the lower portion of a huge stone door. Its lower edge was flooded and sealed by a solidified pool of mineral.

"That's as far as we go today," announced Mark.

"So behind that door is Prince Yaroslaw's Library?" asked Victor. It was more a statement than a question.

Mark took a pair of flash photographs of each worker.

"Now, Mark," said Serhiy, "you can stand before those stairs, and I'll take a picture of you. Be careful. Don't step back."

Serhiy crouched down low to take Mark's picture before the stone gate. Two blinding flashes screened from human eyes that which they revealed to the camera.

"Let's head back, gentlemen, before the batteries in our flashlights die out," said Serhiy.

11

THE GROUP OF PEOPLE IN ROOM 401 of the Hotel Dnipro were anxiously waiting for something. Most just milled around. Mark nervously paced the room like an expectant father. By the window Yarko, Serhiy, Father Onufriy, and two bishops viewed the cityscape. Professor Verbytsky sat calmly on the edge of his bed. The bishops were both dressed in civilian clothes. Ksenia, on guard duty, hovered by the door to the apartment with a Kalashnikov hanging from her shoulder.

"Okay, Mark, tell us again," said Professor Verbytsky. "To what degree has the bottom of the stone gate to the Library been sealed in calcite deposit?"

"Not much, maybe ten centimetres or so. You'll see when the pictures get back."

"We'll be able to chip it away in a couple of hours," said Serhiy.

"Just don't damage the stone gate," cautioned Professor Verbytsky, "The door itself is an archaeological treasure."

The conversation was interrupted by a knock on the door. Ksenia opened it to the chain stop and issued the usual challenge, "Slava!"

"Yaroslava," came the answer.

Ksenia opened the door for her brother.

Vlodko dropped a paper packet on the bed. "The pictures are ready. I confess that I've looked at them already."

Professor Verbytsky slit the package open and began viewing the photo enlargements one by one. He examined each photo himself, and then dropped it on the bed for the others to see.

"Not the best likeness, Serhiy," quipped the professor. "Not only did you forget to shave, but it seems that you forgot to wash."

Serhiy rose to the bait. "But, but the tunnel ceiling had just collapsed on us!"

The general laughter on viewing this first photo made further remarks impossible. Professor Verbytsky would drop photo after photo on his bed, and each was then passed from hand to hand accompanied by the general buzz of excited conversation.

But on seeing the last photograph, the professor sat up straight and pronounced the patriotic salute "*Slava Ukrayini.*"

"*Heroyam Slava,*" answered Ksenia reflexively.

This photo now lay on the bed. It was the one of Mark that Serhiy had taken while crouching to get a better angle at the Library entrance area. Behind Mark was a blindingly white reflection off the stone gate. It had the unmistakable shape of a trident, Ukraine's national coat of arms.

"Pure gold," whispered the professor, recovering his dispassionate scientific composure. "Anything else would have tarnished."

Yarko found it funny to watch old men like the three bishops furtively cross themselves, lie down on the shuttle, and close their eyes tightly to get whisked into a metre-wide tunnel on a three-minute trip to the rat's-tail passage. He knew that Serhiy and the miners had worked for several hours on enhancements to their transportation system. Some thirty light bulbs spaced at regular intervals lit the length of the tunnel. Another two dozen were about to be installed in the passage. Some inventive miner had taped an MP3 player with a variety of musical recordings to the front of the shuttle. A short ladder was installed at the intersection of their tunnel and the rat's-tail passage. Simultaneously, a ladder-like system was being constructed at the gate to the Library to deal with the smooth calcite-encased steps. And finally, one miner was still carefully chipping away at the calcite at the bottom of the stone gate.

Yarko followed the three bishops into the tunnel. He kept his eyes open the whole trip. Once he arrived at the rat's-tail passage at the end of the bored tunnel, he found that Serhiy was holding everyone, waiting to collect the complete group before escorting them to the Library entrance. Yarko realized that this group represented all the major stakeholders of Operation Slava. Three churches, a nationalist organization, two youth organizations, as well as the NTSh, the Scholarly Society of Taras Shevchenko, were all represented. This hurried visit was mostly political in nature. The stakeholders had to be shown at the first opportunity that their investment was not in vain. Additional funds were desperately needed by Operation Slava.

"So who's left to come, Yarko," asked Serhiy

"Only Father Onufriy was behind me. After that we can get going. The turnaround time seems to be about six minutes. That means we can only move ten people per hour."

"Yes, that does seem a bit slow."

"We need to be able to put two people in the tunnel at one time to cut the turnaround time in half. Since the tunnel is too tight to pass, we either attach a second shuttle as a trailer, or we make a wide spot like a transfer room at the halfway point and run two shuttles—one from the ops room end and the other from the rat's tail."

"I like that second idea the best," said Serhiy. "Being able to stand up at the transfer spot would also be more comfortable for our visitors."

"Yes, and most of our scientists would be over fifty."

By this time the shuttle arrived with Father Onufriy aboard.

"You can get religion in a hurry in that tunnel of yours," quipped Onufriy. "I can't imagine what it was like without lights."

"Okay, gentlemen, follow me," commanded Serhiy. "The lighting is not yet installed, so use your flashlights and follow my lead. This walk will be straightforward except for one spot in the middle that Mark has barricaded as off limits until properly examined."

"And what's there?" asked Father Onufriy.

"There is an old pointy helmet and a leather quiver, and a few other things."

"Dating back to 1240 A.D., I would think," said Onufriy.

Serhiy nodded. "The year Batu Khan took Kyiv. December 6th, I believe."

It took several minutes to reach the stone gate. Mark had been working with Victor and Taras, two of the other miners. "The gate is moving," he said. "We chipped enough away to get it to open about twenty centimetres. A little bit more and some skinny guy can squeeze through."

Each of the visitors took turns shining their flashlights into the room trying to have a peek. Flashlights were ineffective for that. They were, however, plenty effective to examine the immense golden trident on the stone gate.

"That alone was worth the trouble," said one of the bishops.

As the lead archaeologist of the project, it was now Professor Verbytsky's turn to speak. "For today, I think it will be good enough to let one young man squeeze through with a camera while we shine the halogen work light through the door opening. He should fire off as many photographs as possible in all directions. We can then piece together a general idea of what we have in there. I suggest that the honour should go to Yaroslaw. He is the discoverer of this underground location of The Library of Prince Yaroslaw the Wise."

"And he is the only Yaroslaw among us," said Serhiy. "But before you go in there, dear Yarko, please put this on. Consider it a donation from the Fourteenth Mine of the Name of Lenin. It is a portable gas analyzer that you wear around your neck. Anything bad and it lets out a loud squeal. Think of it as our electronic canary. If it squeals, you hold your breath and scram out of there. Got it?"

"Got it," said Yarko. "Now I understand why Professor Verbytsky is sending me in first. He certainly didn't get his title by being a fool."

The professor smiled. "Go with God … and be careful."

The gate opened outward, which is why the calcite-chipping job was taking so long. With no actual handle, it took three men gripping the gates edge by their fingernails to swing it through twenty-five centimetres. Yarko squeezed through. The miners aimed their work light through this crack, knowing full well that it would illuminate only a sliver of the wall on the left. Yarko lit his own flashlight, and using his digital camera's rapid-fire feature, he began almost mechanically scanning the room with it. The room was huge. The wall on his left had been whitewashed and painted in frescoes of several figures. Before him and also to the right were rows and rows of stacks of books.

Yarko stepped forward. There was a clang under his feet. Lying there was a helmet of the Mongol style. He had just aimed his camera down at it when his electronic canary began squealing. Yarko held his breath and backed up, continuing to sweep the camera as if it were a machine gun. Encouraged by the clamour outside, Yarko squeezed his way past the gate. Serhiy motioned everyone to run from the gate. Victor pressed the gate shut then ran off to catch up with the rest of the crowd.

"Okay, stop. Let's stop now," shouted Serhiy, holding his arms out wide. "That is enough for now. Let me check Yarko's instrument. Let's have a look at it, Yarko."

Serhiy scrolled through the digital readout. "Not a problem, gentlemen. Nothing unexpected. It's just a low concentration level of oxygen. That will be enough exploration for us for one day. Back to the tunnel. Walk and don't run in the dark."

"For me, that is actually good news," said Professor Verbytsky.

"How so?" asked Mark.

"The lack of oxygen ensures that our material will be well preserved. And if it's dry, all the better."

"Well, to go back we'll need oxygen bottles," said Serhiy.

"To continue work we'll need serious ventilation," Professor Verbytsky observed.

"I can try pressurizing the room," said Serhiy. "If it won't hold pressure then there may be just enough leakage to allow me to ventilate by simply blowing air in. Worse comes to worse, we just work every second day or so."

"We need to discuss this over beer," said the professor. "Everyone is invited to my room at seven. And Yarko, you get to a printer and make me huge blow-ups of all your shots."

"Someone get me a bundle of hryvnias, then. I have fifty-six shots. It may be better for me to make regular-sized pictures but have access to a big computer screen."

"Okay, my laptop will do," said Professor Verbytsky.

A dozen people filled Room 401, the professor's suite. Photographs were being passed from hand to hand, while Professor Verbytsky viewed these same shots on his laptop.

"We certainly have a pile of books here," commented Father Onufriy. "I see rows of tables piled high with them."

Vlodko pointed. "Look here—the remains of a body on the ground. There's chainmail and leggings, along with a sword, but I see no helmet or skull."

"Severed, I imagine," said Ksenia.

Professor Verbytsky nodded. "A Rus' soldier no doubt, judging by the mail and sword. Definitely not Mongolian."

"There was a battle here," concluded Vlodko.

The professor motioned to his computer screen. "There's some other weird things here. For example, here I see some very large pots or cauldrons. What those things would be doing in a library, I just can't imagine. And look here: there are some tall vase-like objects against the far wall. They may be amphorae of some sort."

"And these?" asked Mark.

"Ah yes, rolls of parchment or vellum, I would imagine. A library like this would also be a scriptorium, a place where books were copied. This writing material was typically made of sheepskin ... Kind of explains why sheep farming and Western culture went hand in hand!"

Mark chuckled. "Poor lambs. They gave their life to support the propagation of knowledge. Heck, I hate mutton anyway. I vote for clay tablets."

"Not quite as portable, Mark," said Professor Verbytsky.

Father Onufriy held up a photograph. "Well aren't these things here clay tablets?"

"Let's see, just a minute." The professor scrolled through to the same picture on his computer, and tapped a key a couple of times to enlarge it. "No ... I would say they were wooden tablets. That was the preferred writing surface in pre-Christian times in Ukraine. That and birch bark. And the writing used a totally different alphabet. It was called *Cherty I Rezy*."

"Translates as Strokes and Notches," Yarko explained to Mark.

"You can say that the adoption of Christianity along with a Greek-based alphabet erased centuries of indigenous culture and knowledge," continued the professor. "After a while, nobody could read the old stuff any more."

"Well I'm of the opinion that it was, in fact, the Byzantine influence that allowed Rus' culture to flower," argued Father Onufriy, displeased that Christianity was being cast as a destroyer.

"I could easily argue against that," said Professor Verbytsky. "A unified Rus' state with its own culture existed only under princes who were born pagan. The last one was Yaroslaw, son of Volodymyr the Great. Yaroslaw was ten when his father married the Greek princess and brought Christianity to Rus'. I suspect Yaroslaw hated his father for rejecting his mother in this manner."

"I know the story," Yarko said. He was getting bored by the esoteric nature of the discussion. "Prince Volodymyr died while preparing to go to battle against his son, Yaroslaw."

Serhiy had been quietly looking at pictures and doodling on a pad. "Hate to spoil your fun," he broke in, "but the matter of oxygen and ventilation is foremost. I estimate the cave as some thirty by fifty metres and about ten metres high. So before we go back in, we will need about ten standard tanks of compressed oxygen. Then we will need a half-kilometre of large-diameter tubing and an air pump or high-capacity fan. Even then we may have to limit work to half a dozen people every second day."

Vlodko shook his head. "We have no funds for that. I may be able to beg, borrow, and steal the oxygen and that's about it. That gives us what, a day or two in the library?"

"I'll talk to the church leaders," said Father Onufriy, "although that well is also running dry."

"Should I try our politicians?" asked Ksenia.

"Careful," cautioned Vlodko. "Most of those characters would sell their own mothers. They'd have us brokered to the highest bidder in a week. Definitely not Yushchenko; he's just too weak."

Ksenia looked at her brother. "So that leaves Tymoshenko, does it?"

Vlodko let out a long whistle. "Now there's a gamble! Yulia's tough, she's not in Kuchma's pocket, and she has a few million squirrelled away. But she's also wanted by Interpol. She is in the process of a post-Soviet conversion, but she's still far from a Ukrainian epiphany. She's slowly getting her head around what it means to be Ukrainian. So before we go to her I must check with The Saint."

"So then, Vlodko," said Serhiy, "you have all day tomorrow to get oxygen. My boys will work on infrastructure like lights, power, and phone. The day after tomorrow I'll let about six people in. After that, we will see what we can do."

12

YARKO SLEPT IN. This was to be the first full day of actual exploration in the Library. He felt that it was very much his library, so he felt quite embarrassed that others could possibly be exploring it before him. He skipped breakfast and headed straight for the elevator. He was alone. A certain pair of buttons pushed simultaneously placed the elevator in express mode, locking it out from the general public. Another pair sent it down to the sub-basement.

The doors opened. Across from the elevator stood Vlodko, leaning against the hallway wall. He casually swung his AK-74 in the direction of the opening door while pressing the remains of his morning cigarette to his lips with his left. He blew a smoke ring in Yarko's direction. "*Servus*, Yarko. So how's my sleeping beauty?"

"I slept in." Yarko was in no mood for lengthy explanations.

"You don't say! And here we thought you were practising motorcycle stunts in your room. We could hear your snoring all the way down the hall."

"I was tired" What Yarko wasn't about to explain was why. Free time had been such a rare commodity in the last few months that an opportunity to spend a full day with Ksenia could not be missed.

Sharing a bottle of pink Crimean champagne to accompany the room-service dinner was a luxury that he felt that he had well deserved.

"Your tunnel is full of very wise men right now," Vlodko continued. "I doubt that they need your company just now. In any case, our friend Serhiy has the place lit up like an operating room."

Yarko ignored Vlodko's comments and dragged his feet towards the doors of the tunnelling ops room, mumbling "...fucking hole in the wall gang..." to himself in English as the twin steel doors closed behind him.

His brother was in the ops room already. Mark greeted Yarko with an excited torrent of words accompanied by much waving of arms.

"Hell, get me a damned coffee first," said Yarko. "I don't understand a word you are saying. Just get me on that motorized garage creeper, and I'll see it all for myself."

Yarko pushed a button on the bare rock wall surface to send the shuttle scurrying his way. In the meantime, he poured himself the dregs of lukewarm coffee from a coffee urn that had cycled to auto-shutoff long before he awoke. He threw it back like bitter medicine.

Fully lit, the rat's-tail passage had taken on a fairy-tale appearance. Walking towards the Library, Yarko could spot, from time to time, some curious scribbling on the rocks. Thousand-year-old graffiti was talking back at him. Yes, there were people here once, people really much like him. Looking at the ceiling of the passage, Yarko saw a black-and-ochre stampede of long-horned cattle, and in another place, the outline of a mammoth wounded by two spears. Closer to the stone gate of the Library he noted the outline of a most majestic elk pictured in a position of repose, with his legs tucked under. Antlers nearly as long as the animal's back bore a half-dozen artfully curled prongs.

"The mighty elk," came the voice of Professor Verbytsky from one of the few shadows on the passage walls that escaped Serhiy's zealous electrification effort. "The elk is the ruler of the liso-steppe, the forest-prairie borderland that proved so hospitable to early man. The artwork is some ten thousand years old. But it's interesting that around 500 B.C. this same elk became a favourite totem of the Scythians. They too drew the elk in such a sitting position. And so, here the ruler of the forest-prairie lands rests in majestic repose. It is curious too that in one version of the Runic alphabet, the letter 'z' was in the shape of a trident—it was the symbol algiz, or Elk the Protector. So that's just one more explanation of the symbolism behind the Ukrainian trident. Maybe the trident represented the Protector-Elk. The elk is a denizen of the forest-steppe, not of the vast plains of Eurasia. So I see this as one more proof that Scythians were autochthonous and not wandering Asian nomads. I could argue that one with Herodotus."

"Who's been dead for 2,400 years," quipped Yarko, who felt that the professor's imagination was stretching a bit too far. "And mysticism does not mix well with science."

"Actually it does, young man. It's part of anthropology, and that ties directly to my specialty, archaeology. But enough! Follow me. There is much more."

They walked to the stone gate with the golden trident. Serhiy's enthusiasm in lighting this area caused the trident to throw several reflections of itself across both walls and visitors alike, like some overzealous stamping on a passport.

"There is so much to see," continued Professor Verbytsky as they slipped past the half-opened Trident Gate. He was comfortably slipping into his university lecture mode. "There are books in here written in many languages. For example, we have Church Slavonic, Arabic, Greek, and Latin. However, we have some jewels of much rarer languages. On those wooden shingles we have *Cherty I Rezy*, the earliest Slavic writing. And here we have Runic writing, the earliest of Germanic writing.

"Now look at the walls. The wall to the left of the Trident Gate, the western wall, has been whitewashed and has a remarkable fresco of Rus' princes and warriors. That one there, I believe, must be Prince Yaroslaw. As has since become traditional, he is pictured holding a sword and a book. The book would represent Ruska Pravda, the codex of law, or maybe it symbolizes the fact that he established this Library. But he was certainly not the first one in this cave. Look behind you at the southern wall. The wall with the Trident Gate has what appears to be a map. It's a map of Eurasia. Look, here's the Black Sea, the Caspian, and the Aral. I believe it was created by the Cimmerians, and then edited some time later by the Scythians. They decorated the existing Cimmerian map with drawings of their favourite totems. See the Stag by the Black Sea, The Panther by the Caspian, and the Griffon far east of the Aral. I interpret these as totems of the main tribes, or maybe of their ruling families."

"Sorry, but I can't recognize the map," said Yarko.

"Ah, sorry, I didn't explain. North is at the bottom, south is at the top. See the sun is pictured high on the wall. When looking at this wall you are facing south. Now imagine pushing the wall down. The top would fall to the south, the left is east and the bottom, at your feet, is north. Now you see that the Stag is below an upside down Black Sea?"

"Yes, I get it now. Sure changes your perspective, doesn't it."

"Now follow me to the north wall." The professor wasn't missing a beat. "Here we have what looks like an anteroom. Look inside and you will see the remains of a ladder. This, I believe, was the normal entrance to the library. Above this would have been the wooden building, the Scriptorium, I would assume. Notice the huge rocks littering the bottom of this anteroom. If you look up, way, way up, you will see that this entrance has been purposefully blocked off by a huge boulder that has sealed this secret tightly for eight hundred years."

The professor gave Yarko time to examine this entrance before continuing. "Now the east wall is less interesting, although I believe I can make out the outline drawing of a huge bull with long horns. That's an aurox, I believe. However, we do have a mystery. And that is these huge ceramic cauldrons placed around this room. There are eight of them. And all eight are half-full of honey. Yes, nice golden, liquid honey—some five thousand litres of the stuff. Now go figure."

"Well I have an idea," said Yarko. "I remember learning that honey is hygroscopic. Maybe they used it to reduce or at least control the humidity in this room."

"That's it! You're a genius, Yarko. That explains the total lack of mould or mildew, and the excellent state of all the material here."

"Now how about these other ceramic containers?" Yarko motioned with his arm. "The tall slender ones against the north wall? They seem to be sealed."

"I've been meaning to have a closer look at them myself. Don't rush, let me brush the dust off them."

Professor Verbytsky pulled what looked like a wide paintbrush from his back pocket and began brushing the grey dust off one of the slim amphora. A yellow clay surface was revealed. On it was some lettering in black.

"Can't read it," said Yarko, "but it somehow looks familiar."

"Hebrew."

"Yahweh!"

Operation Slava needed to acquire a new partner. Having no expertise in Hebrew, there was an obvious need to include Jewish expertise. There was an equally pressing need for additional funds. Everyone knew that including new participants in the conspiracy would be a delicate matter. First, one had to interest them in the significance of the find, and then convince them to buy into the project in both the financial and scientific sense. Finally, one had to maintain absolute secrecy. Professor Verbytsky was convinced that the amphorae contained scrolls. He insisted that a rabbi representing the Jewish community should be present at the opening of the first container.

A bargain was struck with the chief rabbi of Kyiv that would cover added operational costs, including ventilation, and the doubling of the tunnel shuttle capacity by adding a mid-tunnel station and the second shuttle. Scientific work was delayed while Serhiy and his team worked on these upgrades. The next full day's work in the Library, including participation by the rabbi, was scheduled for October 27. By coincidence, this was the day that Ukrainian government authorities had designated for the celebration of the anniversary of the "liberation" of Kyiv by the Red Army in the Second World War. On this day, President Putin of Russia was taking part in the celebrations at the invitation of prime minister and presidential candidate Victor Yanukovich.

13

YARKO WAS QUITE LATE arriving at the hotel restaurant for breakfast. He had been viewing the preparations for the commemoration of the Soviet liberation of Kyiv. As if on cue, the sun had disappeared. Today, dull grey clouds covered the skies. They threatened rain, but never quite made good on their ominous promise. The presence of Russian tanks on Khreshchatyk Street just four days before the first round of presidential elections was disconcerting, even though these were merely restored Second World War vintage vehicles. Both sides of the street were lined with police. Security was tight. News media had been reporting that Vladimir Putin had brought his own security team, including snipers. These were to be stationed on rooftops.

Various military units, some dressed in Second World War-era uniforms, were gathering at the South end of Khreshchatyk, preparing
for the march-past planned for later that day. Banners and posters
glorifying the Russian Red Army added to the strangeness of it all.

Compounding the strange mix in the city was the arrival during the week of international election observers. Yarko's father had
arrived the day before, and just now he was attending some all-day
orientation meeting. Yarko had even arranged for a late dinner that
evening with his dad.

So it was no surprise that the restaurant was full for breakfast.
After some delay, Yarko was given a small table for two in the corner.
He ordered coffee, scrambled eggs, and sausages as well as the mandatory glass of cherry juice. As he waited for his meal to arrive, he
became aware that a young lad in his mid-teens was watching him.
Noticing that Yarko had become aware of him, the young man got up
and approached Yarko's table.

"Are you Mister Yaroslaff," the lad asked, speaking with a Polish
accent.

"And who needs to know?" Yarko was taken aback by the fact that
the stranger knew his name. His hand fruitlessly searched his pant
pockets for his PSM. But Yarko had followed Vlodko's instructions
and left the gun, which Ksenia had returned to him, in his room this
day. With so much nervous security in the city these days, Vlodko
made it very clear that no risks were to be taken.

The lad sat himself across from Yarko. "Call me Yuzio," he
replied.

Yarko stared at the stranger. He was slim and rather short for a
teenager. Yarko could not help thinking that he had seen him before.
He was frustrated. During the past few months there were several
other times that he thought he had seen someone before but couldn't
recognize them. For no reason at all just now, the phrase "sheep in
wolves clothing" crept into his consciousness. He remembered the

smiling border trooper of well over a year ago at the Lviv airport. Suddenly it dawned on him that the smiley trooper was none other than Petro! Petro was the guardian angel that Yarko had met at the Bohdan Khmelnytsky statue weeks ago on the day that they had learned of Yushchenko's poisoning. Involuntarily, Yarko's eyes lit up with a spark of recognition. He was feeling quite self-satisfied at having made that connection.

Baffled, Yuzio completely misread the expression on Yarko's face. "So you remember me?"

"No I don't," Yarko said. "At least I don't think I do. Oh dammit! Yes I do! I do remember you! You're the bloody bastard who tried to steal my bike by Saint George's Cathedral last year. Right after the explosion."

"Shh, quiet, Yarek," Yuzio whispered. "I'm no thief, and I'm not as young as you think. I'm twenty-three years old ... Now listen. I work for an intelligence service."

"What? You, a spy?" Involuntarily Yarko reached again for the non-existent PSM. "Who the hell for?"

"Quiet, Yarek, keep it down. People could hear us ... I work for—well—I kind of work for the Vatican."

Yarko choked back a sputtering laugh. Lowering his head he allowed a sarcastic smile to crease his face while waiting for more clarification.

"And I know about Operation Slava," said Yuzio.

Blood drained from Yarko's face. His eyes widened.

"And what's more, the Russian FSB knows too." After a measured moment of silence, Yuzio continued. "That's right, the FSB knows that you guys have found the Library of Prince Yaroslaw."

"So how the hell did they find out?"

Yuzio kept his voice low. "You've got a traitor—maybe two, but one for sure. He's a priest in the Greek-Catholic Church. He's been an agent of the Moscow Patriarchate for decades. His code name is

Seraphim, but no one knows who he really is. The Vatican has been trying to catch him for many years. He's been my personal assignment for the last two. Anyway, what's more important, the Russians have been drilling their own tunnel—starting from the Metro subway."

The mention of the Metro brought back a memory of several weeks ago. He remembered the barricaded entrance to the Metro. He recalled the team of workers and their leader. He remembered the bushy white eyebrows. Dammit, he had seen them before.

"Father Ivan!" exclaimed Yarko.

"What?" The Vatican spy was baffled.

"Father Ivan, that bastard. Father Ivan from Saint George's Cathedral in Lviv! That's where I saw the boss of those subway workers before!"

"What subway workers? When did you see them?"

"Early September, the same day they announced that Yushchenko had been poisoned. They closed the subway entrance. They were starting to bring in heavy equipment. And the workers' leader was Father Ivan."

"So it's nearly six weeks," Yuzio calculated. "They must be almost done. Then that explains it!"

"Explains what?"

"The special team. Among Putin's security service is a group that has nothing to do with security. They are special ops types, more like an extraction team. They arrived yesterday, so today must be the big day. They will hit the Library cave today!"

"Christ! We've got no weapons down in the tunnels!" exclaimed Yarko. "I've got work to do. Sorry buddy, but I'm outta here."

"Go with God. And don't you worry about Father Ivan. He's mine." Yuzio drew his left index finger across his throat.

Yarko commandeered the elevator and sent it to the sub-basement. As he stepped out, he saw Vlodko and another armed guard serving sentry duty. Serhiy was sitting on the floor chewing on a dark-rye-bread sandwich. Serhiy had been working all night putting the finishing touches on the tunnel upgrades. Today was the day that the three leaders of Ukrainian Christian churches were being joined by the Rabbi of Kyiv.

Yarko feverishly explained to Vlodko that Operation Slava was not very secret any more and that the Library itself was under immediate threat of attack.

Vlodko pulled out his cell phone and gave someone a lengthy series of instructions. Meanwhile, Yarko opened the weapon storage closet and grabbed the most convenient weapon. This happened to be a short-barrelled, folding-stock AKS-74U grease gun. He picked out two additional magazines. After finishing his call, Vlodko selected an AKS-74U too, but he also grabbed a pair of Fort pistols along with a strange-looking optical device.

"Just in case," Vlodko said, noting the puzzled look on Yarko's face. "An American Barr and Stroud thermal imager. We acquired it for safety reasons, you know, for looking for survivors in rubble."

Serhiy made a face, but continued looking through the arsenal in the weapons closet. "Aha, found it!" He beamed as if he had found his favourite truck in the toy box. "An AGS-30 grenade-thrower. I used the 17 on my helicopter in Afghanistan. This newer one is lighter and can be carried by one man."

"Careful, my friend," said Vlodko. "That's not a close-quarters weapon!"

"It's not, but since you're not stocking any hand grenades today, I couldn't think of a better way to seal off a tunnel."

While these two were discussing the merits of a hand-held cannon, the soles of Yarko's running shoes had long disappeared into the tunnel.

"If you pull hand over hand on the guide-ropes you can cut your trip time in half," Serhiy yelled into the tunnel opening.

14

MARK HAD BEEN WORKING in the Library cave for two hours already. He had been assigned to help the rabbi. The seven amphorae with the Hebrew markings stood along the north wall of the room, next to the alcove that opened into the vertical entrance shaft. The amphorae had been closed with stoppers and sealed with bees wax. This meant that Mark had to open each one with the help of a hair dryer on a long extension cord. He was working on his third ceramic vessel. The first two had contained papyrus scrolls with Hebrew writing. He could gauge their significance by the tears that had welled up in the rabbi's eyes. So far no translation was being offered.

By the western wall of the room, nicknamed Yaroslaw's wall for the fresco of the prince, stood long tables covered with parchment rolls. Under these tables were even more parchment rolls, which lay side by side in two or three layers. All of these were covered by a millennium's worth of dust. As there was no writing on this parchment, it was concluded that this must have been a material preparation or work area. The south wall, with the Trident Gate near its western end, was the one with the map and various totems; thus it became nicknamed the Cimmerian wall. Most of the actual Library was filled with row after row of long tables, all stacked with books higher than a man could reach. Here and there one could find other writing media—stone or clay tablets, wooden shingles, rolls of birch bark, and, not surprisingly, rolls of parchment or vellum with writing of every sort. At this early stage of exploration, all this material was being catalogued and codified, primarily by language and script.

While he performed the tedious task of heating and softening the wax to open the amphorae, Mark had time to observe the work going on throughout the Library. The Bishop of the Autocephalous Orthodox Church was leafing through an early Bible written in the

Glagolycia script of saints Cyril and Methodius. Professor Verbytsky was investigating what he believed was a Bible written on wooden shingles in the long-forgotten *Cherty I Rezy* script. Each of them had excitedly announced his individual find. Near him, hidden behind mountains of books in the middle of the room, the Greek-Catholic Bishop was silently poring over a scroll of particularly weathered parchment.

"Unbelievable, simply unbelievable," announced his disembodied voice from behind a stack of books. "I am looking at a map. On this map I can recognize the outlines of Greenland, and the north-eastern coast of North America, where Canada is today. It just cannot be anything else. And what's more, there is Cyrillic writing on this map."

Mark also watched while two young archaeologists, students of Professor Verbytsky, struggled with a large chest that had been standing under a table by the Cimmerian wall. In the light, Mark could see that the chest was made of bronze, or sheathed in bronze. The two archaeologists manoeuvred the heavy box to a position where they could open its lid. The lid had been locked by what appeared to be a steel ring or chain-link. This had sufficiently rusted away that its remains could be easily snapped.

Mark's attention then drifted to Yaroslaw's wall and the hundreds of dust-covered rolls of parchment arranged on and under the tables. He knew that each such roll was the skin of a single sheep. Hundreds of such skins were needed to produce a single book.

"Poor little lambs," he thought aloud. "They had to give their lives for the vagaries of human culture." In his imagination, the dusty rolls under the table were turning into fluffy little lambs that lay sleeping peacefully all snuggled side by side. Mark allowed himself to enjoy this bucolic fantasy, finding a moment of rest for himself. The lambs were breathing rhythmically in their sleep, shoving their neighbours with each such movement. Mark smiled while watching as one after another the little sheep reacted to these shoves with even stronger shoves in reply.

Silly sheep, thought Mark, as he watched the whole herd of sheep wake to this mutual shoving and roll out from beneath the table.

The ring of the telephone by the Trident Gate woke Mark from his reverie. To his amazement he realized that the rolls of parchment under the table really were moving and rolling about. A blackened face emerged from among these rolls, followed immediately by the trademark underslung gun barrel of a Kalashnikov automatic. As the phone rang a second time Mark watched the bright white cruciform flash and heard the dry staccato chatter as the intruder opened fire.

The rabbi, who had been standing closest to the intruder, slumped to the ground. Mark jumped back and dove headlong into the alcove in the north wall, chased by the snap of bullet impacts along the rock face. He reached for the knife he had strapped to his belt. A second volley of automatic fire followed the first. Mark saw the group of archaeologists at the Cimmerian wall cowering behind the lid of the chest that they had just managed to open. From within the open chest, the light of one of Serhiy's array of lamps reflected the yellow fire of an emperor's ransom of Scythian gold. A third volley of 5.45-mm rounds hammered along the lid of the chest, drowning out the third and final ring of the phone.

In a moment of insanity, Mark flung his knife at the intruder, who was now standing upright, then scampered between the stacks of books towards the Tryzub Gate. Two more blackened faces were crawling out from among the parchment rolls. The first intruder doubled over, but the second and third sent fresh bursts of fire in Mark's general direction. Mark felt a sharp burning in his back.

Suddenly, from the Trident Gate in the Cimmerian wall, came an answering chatter of automatic weapons fire. Yarko had just arrived, having ran the whole distance of the rat's-tail passage. Dark splatters on the latest two intruders' chests testified to the volley's accuracy. Yarko slapped a new magazine into his AKS. But a second later, from under the parchment roll table, came a fresh volley as two additional intruders emerged. Yarko made a headlong dive to his right towards the open treasure chest. He had felt nothing, but a red stain was spreading from above his belt. Yarko had now joined the two terrified archaeologists hiding behind the open lid of the chest. He could see Mark lying spread-eagled as flat as a shadow less than two metres away. Another volley of rounds hammering along the open lid served as more than enough argument to convince Yarko to keep his head down. Voices speaking Russian confirmed that the fourth and fifth intruder had been joined by a sixth.

After several seconds of silence all three Russians opened fire towards the Trident Gate. Yarko realized that it had to be either Vlodko or Serhiy who had become their new target. Holding his short-barrelled AKS-74U well beyond the cover of the chest, Yarko sent an un-aimed volley in the general direction of the parchment roll table. Repeated hammering on the lid of the chest confirmed that his distraction worked.

Now, from the rat's-tail passage just beyond the open Trident Gate, came a distinct *kafoomp*, followed by an ear-shattering explosion by Yaroslaw's wall. Having acquired his target by the bright muzzle flashes, Serhiy had fired a single plum-sized round of his AGS-30 at the feet of one of the three Russians. The exploding round shredded these intruders, along with the bodies of Yarko's two victims and several dozen rolls of dusty parchment.

Serhiy stepped into the Library cave and casually walked to the area by Yaroslaw's wall where the intruders had stood. In the floor under the parchment roll table was the opening to the intruders' tunnel. Serhiy looked into the opening. "They were good. Straight as an arrow." He pointed his cannon into the hole and fired. The characteristic *kafoomp* of the AGS-30 was followed by the rattle of the shell ricocheting off the sides of the tunnel.

There was silence while Serhiy peeked at his watch and walked back towards the Trident Gate. At that moment a breathless Vlodko burst into the cave.

"*Servus*, Vlodko," said Serhiy. He raised his right hand while looking at his watch. "Wait here for a moment ... Twenty one, twenty two, twenty three, twenty four, twenty five, twenty six—"

Blam! The sound of an explosion was followed by a spectacular belch of rock-dust from the tunnel opening. To everyone's amazement this was followed by a two-metre-wide smoke ring that travelled diagonally upwards from the hole.

Vlodko pointed at the magazine on Serhiy's AGS-30. "Still a twenty-seven-second self-destruct on those?"

"Count on it. It's like clockwork." Serhiy peered into the tunnel opening. "Poor buggers. Anyone at the other end had just enough time to get curious and stick his head in the tunnel."

Mark had gotten to his feet and walked up to Vlodko by the Trident Gate. Yarko was groaning in new-found pain from behind the treasure chest. The acrid smell of gunsmoke filled the cave.

Suddenly, from somewhere at the far eastern end of the Library cave came the sound of a short burst of automatic gunfire, followed by some cursing in Russian. The first intruder, despite his knife wound, had snuck along the northern wall, and having reached the east wall he unexpectedly met up with two of the bishops who had managed to escape the firefight.

"Hostage situation," said Vlodko in his matter-of-fact policeman's voice. To Serhiy he whispered, "Cut the lights."

Serhiy spun through the Trident Gate and reached for the switch by the gate. Vlodko raised his Barr and Stroud thermal imager to his eyes.

The Library cave went black. This was not the kind of darkness that one would normally experience. This was the absolutely solid absence of any form of radiation. It felt as thick and oppressive as an ocean of tar. A second stream of unintelligible Russian swearing emanated from the east end of the cave.

Mark barely sensed the cat-like footsteps and the slightest disturbance of air current as Vlodko floated past him like a wraith. Now there was complete silence, except for the sound of one's breathing.

Blam! The sound of a single gunshot echoed like thunder off the walls of the cave.

"It's over," came Vlodko's voice from the east wall. "You can turn on the lights, Serhiy. His worship is wounded." He was referring to one of the bishops.

"And the rabbi, and Yarko, and me," added Mark.

Vlodko jogged·back to the Trident Gate and dialled a number on the telephone on the wall. Cell phones were ineffective at this depth. That was the reason for the hard-wired phone on the wall by the gate. Vlodko talked briefly on the phone. Then he dialled another number and gave some more instructions. Serhiy had two stretchers that he kept in the rat's-tail passage as a safety precaution. These he hurriedly dragged into the Library cave.

"So that's four wounded, right?" asked Vlodko. "We have to hurry, and no idle chit-chat with the police, understood? We don't need any government involvement right now. Certainly not with Putin right above our heads." Vlodko pointed straight up. "Okay, now listen up. First we take the rabbi and the bishop to the fifth floor. That's where the ambulance service will find them. Then we have to get Yarko and Mark across the street to the park. That's where the ambulance will pick them up. As usual, this being Ukraine, the attackers of these four victims will not be found. We're used to that. For now, leave the dead Russians here. I'll be taking care of that."

15

AFTER A LONG TWO WEEKS IN THE HOSPITAL, they finally allowed Yarko to go free. Vlodko had handled all the paperwork, and now accompanied the young man as he left the premises. On the street, Ksenia and Petro awaited them, standing by a shiny BMW 530.

Yarko climbed into the car. "So who won the lottery?" he asked.

"No lottery," said Ksenia. "The Bishop of the Kyiv Patriarchate lent it to us."

"I recognize the driver. That's my guardian angel in the uniform of Ukraine's Border troops."

"I'm Petro," the driver introduced himself. "Petro Pidhayniy. Anyway, if I'm supposed to be your guardian angel, then I guess I failed. Them Muscovites just keep putting holes in you. Every year you come to visit us and each time you manage to shed blood for dear Ukraine. That just can't be a healthy habit."

There was no need to remind Yarko about his wound. He was very uncomfortable sitting in the car. There was a clear tube exiting the lower part of his abdomen, ending in a clear sac taped to his thigh. He had to sit diagonally, keeping his leg straight. It had been a complicated operation. The risk was not so much the perforation of an intestine or two, but the high risk of developing an infection in the abdominal cavity.

"So how are the other wounded?" asked Yarko. "All I know is that my brother is okay. My dad saw me last week and told me that."

Vlodko answered. "Yeah, your brother is fine. They kept him in the clinic for less than an hour. The bugger is all muscle and bone. The bullet bounced off his scapula. Things are somewhat worse for the rabbi. They perforated his lungs in three places. He could have drowned in his own blood. He also has a plastic tube in him, Yarko, except it works a little differently from yours. Whenever it gets hard for him to breathe he opens a valve to lower the air pressure in his chest cavity. He's being let out of hospital today. Now the situation with the Bishop of the Autocephalous Church is somewhat worse still. He was hit in the lower back. His legs are paralyzed. He'll be in a wheelchair for the rest of his life."

"Listen, Yarko," said Ksenia, "our project is still secret. We have not gone public yet. That is why you need to understand the little legend that we have created. Now pay attention. You and Mark were in the park. Some idiot shot at you from a distance. You never had a chance to see him. That much you know already. Now listen, the bishop and the rabbi were both shot on the fifth floor of the hotel. You see, the Conference for Unification of the Churches was nearing the end of their deliberations and had invited the Rabbi of Kyiv as an observer. This was kind of a gracious ecumenical act, you see. Now just as the bishop was leading the rabbi along the corridor to a meeting room, an unknown gunman jumped out of the elevator and opened fire. There was only one attacker. It just so happens that both the bishop and the rabbi were shot by the same gun. The bullet that hit Mark was deflected, and the one that hit you was a through and through. Your exit wound is just below your kidney. So your bullet is gone too. "

Yarko nodded. "I get it. That means that our nervous gunman, after shooting the bishop and rabbi, runs into the park, and thinking that we saw him, he shoots us too."

"Exactly," said Vlodko. "And in time, the militsya will come to just that conclusion. Now it's interesting that they have already found the body of that gunman, along with his infamous gun. Somewhere in the Chernihiv district. Too bad I shot him in the head. His skull blew apart like a melon. Identification will be impossible."

"Now why did you say somewhere in Chernihiv district, dear brother," teased Ksenia. "You could have been more precise. You could have said in the town of Konotop. That wouldn't be, by any chance, a symbolic gesture, would it?"

Yarko remembered his history. Konotop was the location of a major victory by Ukrainian kozaks over Russian forces in the seventeenth century.

Vlodko smiled. "Too bad that identification won't be possible. He's likely a member of a Russian special service, but which one? And who was it that sent them? If it were a simple criminal operation, then it's over. But you see, our Operation Slava could attract various Muscovite interests. For example, you have the Moscow Patriarchate, you have Zhirinovsky and his Liberal Democratic Party, you have their Academy of Science, you have General Husak, you have the FSB, the GRU, and finally you have their whole damn government."

"The usual suspects," chuckled Yarko.

"I would pick the first two in your list," said Ksenia.

"And my guess," said Petro, "is all of the above suspects, in concert."

"I respect the opinion of a Border guard," said Vlodko. "That would be his specialty."

Yarko sighed. "That means it's not over, then."

"Far from it. This was amateur hour compared to what's coming."

"Vlodko, don't forget to tell Yarko about the Jews," reminded Ksenia.

"I was just getting to that. All in good time. And now is just about the right time to explain to Yarko about our new allies."

Yarko frowned. "I don't understand. What allies?"

"Much has happened in the past weeks," said Vlodko. "For one, we've had the first round of presidential elections, and Yushchenko leads Yanukovich."

"Despite a ton of falsification, coercion, and the administrative resource," added Ksenia.

Vlodko nodded. "But we've also had the journalists' revolt. They have all pledged to report news honestly without toeing the government line."

"No more *temnyks*," said Ksenia.

Yarko chuckled. "'Administrative resource' means something like home-field advantage for the government's candidate. I got to see my share of that in the hospital. This hospital was a polling station. Patients got wheeled to the polling booth, the administrator told them who to vote for, some orderly would help make the X marks, and, bingo, the administrative apparatus delivered the appropriate vote count just like magic."

"That's the least of it," said Vlodko. "The Internet-based newspaper *Ukrayinska Pravda* reports that Heorgiy Kirpa, the minister of transport, diverted money that was meant for bridge building and gave it to the Yanukovich campaign. He also donated the use of railway cars to ship Yanukovich voters from the east to western regions so they could vote twice using the infamous 'detachable stub' method of vote rigging. But it seems that for candidate Yanukovich even that was not enough. Possibly Kirpa refused to do the same during the second round of elections, because I hear that Yanukovich punched him in the face and knocked a couple of teeth out. Today Heorgiy Kirpa is registered in the same hospital that you just left.

"But back to our main topic. We've had conversations with members of the Jewish community. As a result, we have a delegation from Jerusalem. Among them we have two rabbis and two scientists, as well as a group of, shall we say, specialists. These would be specialists from the Mossad. Most are here under the guise of international election observers. As you can imagine, at first we didn't want such specialists. But experience teaches that whether we invite them or not, such specialists will be here anyway. I figured it would be better for us to have them where we can see them, and to have them cooperate on a friendly basis, rather than to have to keep looking over our shoulders. What's more, I'm sure that they could teach us a thing or two. The organization could use that. To make a long story short, our guests have been here for two days.

"Officially," continued Vlodko, "the rabbis are here to ascertain the circumstances around the wounding of the Kyiv rabbi. Of course, they are also here to give moral support to the Conference for Unification. Funny isn't it? One rabbi is Orthodox and the other is Reformed. Anyway, another advantage to us is that the presence of such distinguished foreign guests affects the attitude of the Kyiv militsya to the Conference, and that keeps them off our case. The Orthodox Church of the Moscow Patriarchate is the largest church in Kyiv, so they have been trying to undermine the Conference in every way."

Petro now took up the briefing. "There is now a different risk, if I'm right about the whole government apparatus of the Russian Federation being behind it. Since they weren't able to seize the Library riches by a secret assault, they will try it much more directly. First, Putin will call President Kuchma and tell him that there is something going on under his very feet in Kyiv that he doesn't have a clue about. Then he will explain that Great Russia will protect the treasures of her culture from those snotty-nosed Ukrainian peasants and that certain steps have to be taken, and so on. Otherwise the gas pipeline gets shut off in mid-winter. That's all."

"No wonder you're a Border trooper!" exclaimed Vlodko. "Did they teach you superpower politics in school, Petro?"

"Nope, but I've seen similar situations with my own eyes. You know, weapon transfers, weapon exports, ownership of strategic objects, and so on."

"But in any case," Vlodko said, "it is much better with our Jewish friends with us. Their presence here keeps the Russian emperor in check. If anyone should even try something we'll publicize everything about Operation Slava in the world press. Then no one would be able to take it from us."

"If so," said Yarko, "then we have to prepare material for the press. The Internet could spread our news to the farthest corner of the world in an instant. We're going to have to start work on a website."

Vlodko nodded. "You're right. We'll talk to Professor Verbytsky and Father Onufriy. This seems to be an ideal task for some English-speaking cripple who can't go through the tunnel. I'm thinking of, well, gee, someone just like you."

"In that case," said Yarko, "that poor invalid would need a helper, somebody who's really good at writing in Ukrainian—say, someone like Ksenia." Yarko hoped to create some pleasant surroundings for this next assignment.

"And maybe you're right again—except I'm not leaving you alone with my sister. I think you will need a third co-worker—say, someone that could write in Hebrew. That way the website would be tri-lingual."

Darn, thought Yarko. It's check and mate for my plans.

The computer work had been proceeding slowly for several days. The content of the website, named Yaroslaw's Treasure, was painstakingly being put together, article by article, picture by picture.

Moishe Friedman was about Yarko's age. His tanned face betrayed his Mediterranean origins. Dark eyes flashed from under a shock of brown hair with the youthful enthusiasm of a patriot of his people. He was searching here in Kyiv for the same thing that Yarko was looking for. They were both searching for the shadows of their ancestors. Moishe was looking for long-lost branches of the tree of his nation. Yarko was searching for the very roots of his.

Yarko liked the erect military manner of his newfound friend. Their common language proved to be English. Yarko nicknamed him "Freddy."

"You know, Freddy," he began teasingly, "I figure that you're a spy from the Mossad."

"Listen, Jerry," said Moishe-Freddy, "if I were from the Mossad, you wouldn't see me, and you wouldn't even hear me."

"Not hearing you—now that would be a true pleasure. In any case, your accent betrays you. I can tell that you come from the capital city of Israel. I'm just not sure which one, Brooklyn or Miami?"

"To be honest, I have, in fact, been to Brooklyn," confirmed Freddy.

"Now why am I not surprised?"

"Why don't you stick your nose back in your laptop and get some work done, Jerry."

"He's got a point there," said Ksenia, picking up on the sense of Freddy's jab. "I'm almost finished my section, but where are you? I even had time to visit mom in Lviv and vote in the run-off election. And I'm still ahead of you."

"That's not fair," Yarko complained. "All the information comes to us in Ukrainian, so you don't have to translate. But I've got to translate every word into English. Look at all the dictionaries in front of me."

"You need so many dictionaries because you don't know either language," teased Ksenia. "You are bilingually illiterate."

"Oh shaddup. Leave me alone. It's much more fun talking to Freddy-the-spy over here." Yarko lifted the collar of his shirt and spoke into the button. "Freddy, Freddy, can you hear me?"

Both Freddy and Ksenia cracked up laughing.

The introductory paragraph was about the actual Library. Obviously the Library was not created by Yaroslaw the Wise. It had existed for centuries, even millennia, before the time of the Rus' princes. The Cimmerian, southern wall of the Library cave had to have been originally painted before the eighth century B.C. Although he could not decipher it, Professor Verbytsky said that some of the writing on stone or clay plates appeared to be Phoenician. In fact, in order to work with these, they had recently invited Professor Stoyko from America, who was expected to arrive the next week. The northern wall had traces of writing that the professor claimed looked like Hittite. The outline of a long-horned hump-backed aurox bull could just be made out on the eastern wall, hidden under centuries of soot from countless candles and torches. It was very clear that the Library cave had been a repository of knowledge and cultural artifacts for over two millennia.

Professor Verbytsky speculated that this could have been a temple for shamans and priests from as far back as Neolithic times. It had become a repository of plunder and trophies of trade as well as for a mountain of autochthonous cultural riches. It could take a decade of painstaking work by a dozen experts to reveal all the secrets that were preserved in the Library cave.

Yarko was finally finishing up his first article, sorting through a gigabyte of photographic files, and selecting those that would best enhance this opening chapter. He felt that he had become the hub of Operation Slava. Information about all the discoveries in the cave came to him. The exception was the work of the Jewish scientists. That information came to Moishe first, who translated it into English for Yarko to include for his portion of the planned website. Yarko had to translate these items into Ukrainian for Ksenia's Ukrainian section.

The amphorae with the papyrus scrolls had arrived in Kyiv during the time of the Khazar Empire. For a time, Kyiv had been a vassal of this mysterious empire. This empire's state religion was Judaism and its ruling class was mostly Jewish. It ruled over a territory that would rival that of Charlemagne. Kyiv marked the westernmost limit of its rule. But the scrolls themselves were much older than that. They had once breathed the hot winds of the Babylonian desert.

This work in the sixth-floor computer centre of Operation Slava was interrupted by the arrival of Father Onufriy. Covered with dust from the Library cave, he appeared quite out of place standing in the hallway of the ritzy Hotel Dnipro. He was holding a manuscript in his hands. Not big enough to be considered a book, it was more like a parchment notebook of sorts.

"Here is the handwriting of the young Prince Yaroslaw," announced the priest. "You won't believe it. As a young man, he lived in his duchy of Novhorod and was constantly in contact with Swedish and Norse traders, known to us as Varangians, or Vikings. One of his friends was a trader and a courtier of King Olaf of Norway, by the name of Leif Erikson. Not only did Yaroslaw know Leif, but he also financed his sailing adventures. What's even more unbelievable are these notes. They were taken while Yaroslaw accompanied Leif on his voyage of discovery to North America. Yaroslaw would have been a lad of twenty-two when they sailed to the east coast of Canada. You know that map that you saw, the one showing the coast of North America? Well, that was likely the work of the young prince!"

Yarko froze with his hands still poised over the laptop's keyboard. Ksenia's fingers too stopped their staccato tapping. Moishe, not understanding Ukrainian, gave his partners a quizzical look.

"What? What happened?" he asked.

"It turns out," said Yarko, translating into English, "that Yaroslaw the Wise accompanied Leif Erikson on his voyage to North America. We have his notes. We have the map."

The renewed moment of stunned silence at this incredible discovery was interrupted suddenly when Vlodko burst through the unlocked door. He looked grim. "We're under guard," he announced. "There is a bunch of security police types guarding all the exits from the hotel. There is someone clumsily trying to hide the fact that he is taking pictures of everyone that goes in and out of the hotel. They speak Russian without a trace of a Ukrainian accent. PORA reports that they are Russian Black Sea Fleet commandos dressed as a Crimean detachment of the Ukrainian Ministry of the Interior troops. From now on, only priests and nuns can go in and out of the hotel. Get it?

There's something about to happen. I'm putting every able body on guard duty in the sub-basement round the clock. I'm trying to get a hold of The Saint. We'll need a busload of Interior Ministry troops that may still be loyal to him. They would need to arrive here at a moment's notice if things get hot in this hotel."

Without saying a word, Ksenia turned on the TV and selected Channel 5. She put the volume on mute. Moishe walked to the wall by the window and scanned the sidewalk by the entrance through the slits of the vertical venetian blinds. A half-dozen men in black were forming a cordon around the main entrance doorway.

"There is even worse news," continued Vlodko. "This hotel is being bought by a consortium headed by an oligarch called Ihor Bakay. He is definitely from the Dark Side. Yuriy Liakh's Ukrainian Credit Bank is fronting the money. If the deal goes through as planned next week, then there will be a new management team running this place—and we won't be able to play our little game any more. I'm sorry, but we will have to wind down all work in the Library and concentrate on building a false wall of cinder blocks behind the double steel doors. We'll have a functioning electric panel on that wall, circuit breakers and all. Everything will get sealed and closed off. Serhiy will set explosives just in case."

Ksenia cranked up the volume as the evening news came on. *"The CEC is expected to announce the winner of the presidential run-off election later tonight. Although exit polling is showing that Victor Yushchenko has won by a handy margin, it is widely rumoured that, in fact, Victor Yanukovich will be announced as the winner.*

"A large crowd is forming outside the Central Election Committee offices, waving the orange banners of Yushchenko's campaign. It is reported that Yulia Tymoshenko was seen entering the premises of the CEC earlier this afternoon. Several activists from PORA have been seen setting up tents in the Maidan Nezalezhnosti.

"Victor Yushchenko has refused to call for mass demonstrations. In

contrast, Yulia Tymoshenko, his political ally, has been actively encouraging voters to picket the CEC *in order to protect their vote.*

"*A squadron of helmeted riot police has circled the entrance to the Presidential Administration Building. Barricades of metal grates are being put into place.*"

Ksenia turned down the volume as a commercial came on.

"I guess I never did get a chance to tap Yulia Tymoshenko for some financial support," mused Yarko.

"And I guess you never will," said Vlodko. "She'll be way too busy now ... although one of her big financial supporters is a Jewish chap who was involved in getting us our team of new allies from abroad. I'm sure there's a few bucks of his in our coffers already."

Ksenia cranked up the volume on the TV again.

"*In a related story, Channel 5 has had a phone call today from the Borispil Airport control tower. Apparently a flight of two Russian military transport aircraft was refused permission to land. Our caller reported that as a Ukrainian citizen he could not allow the unauthorized landing of foreign military aircraft at a Ukrainian airport.*

"*Since the time of that phone call there has been an unconfirmed rumour that two large Russian aircraft did, in fact, land at Borispil, although they may have stopped in a far corner of the facility and have not approached the terminal.*

"*It is widely rumoured that President Kuchma has no confidence in the personal loyalty of Ukrainian police and Interior troops, believing that if ordered to shoot they may not actually open fire at crowds of demonstrators. For that reason it is expected that President Kuchma may ask for Russian Special Forces to provide protection around the Presidential Administration Building.*

"*As of this moment we are unable to verify that the air traffic controller who had phoned this story to the station today has now been fired.*

"*In a story broadcast by news service* UNIAN, *it was reported this morning that President Kuchma has fired Defence Minister Yevhen*

Kyrylovych Marchuk. It is further reported that the now former minister has checked himself into a hospital with an undisclosed illness.

"*President Putin of Russia has sent a note of congratulations to Victor Yanukovich on the occasion of his win in the presidential run-off elections. It is notable that the Central Election Committee has not yet officially announced the results...*"

A commercial break interrupted the string of news stories. Ksenia again turned down the volume.

"I have another piece of news," added Father Onufriy, who had been listening in silence. "A priest found Father Ivan from Saint George's Cathedral in Lviv dead in his room in that church. He hadn't been showing up at the Conference for the last few days. We knew he had gone back to Lviv to vote. But he never made it back. The inside scoop is apparent suicide. Strange one, at that. Apparently he cut his jugular vein with a letter opener. But please, everyone, it is better if no one talks about that. The Catholic Church may want to give him a Christian burial anyway, so if you please, no talk about suicide, understand?"

Yarko remembered his brief conversation with little Yuzio of the Vatican. He remembered Yuzio's parting words: "Go with God..." and the hand gesture that was one stroke short of a sign of the cross.

Ksenia turned the volume up as the news came back on.

"*... press conference by Russia's prosecutor general.*

"'*I am pleased to report that agents of the FSB have cracked a major drug-trafficking ring. Raw opium was being shipped from Iraq to airfields in Ukraine by officers of Ukrainian forces currently stationed there in support of the NATO military occupation. This material was being transported by nationalist members of Ukrainian clergy, including those of the Greek-Catholic faith as well as those of the schismatic Orthodox rite of the so-called Kyiv Patriarchate. A laboratory in a Kyiv hotel was set up to produce crack heroin and hashish, which was then distributed on the Russian and Ukrainian markets.'*

"*When asked for comment, Patriarch Aleksey of all Russia said, and I quote: 'God must be served in the union of the one Orthodox Church and that a breach of this union leads to greater and greater sin.'*

"*In Ukraine, Minister of the Interior Smeshko had no comment when asked whether a joint Ukrainian-Russian operation was being planned in order to bust the drug ring.*

"*And now for The World of Sport after the commercial break…*"

"It's beginning," said Vlodko as Ksenia muted the TV again. "They have the cover story. They are moving in the troops. It's only a matter of time."

"We'll have enough to open a website after tomorrow," said Ksenia, shutting off the TV and returning to her computer.

"Opening the website prematurely is a last resort," said Vlodko. "We'll do that only if the enemy seizes the tunnel. In fact, I would prefer a booby-trap bomb in the tunnel to going public. Only problem is, Serhiy can't move in fresh supplies any more. And we have no industrial explosives on site. As you know, this place is being guarded. We are being watched."

16

YARKO, KSENIA, AND MOISHE had been working feverishly all morning. The Leif Erikson chapter of the website was being prepared. However, now the work had slowed down quite noticeably.

The Central Election Committee had just announced their results of the run-off election for president. They had declared Yanukovich the winner over Yushchenko in a close result. This was contrary to the estimates of exit polls. The results indicated a near one hundred per cent voter turnout in the east, and in fact many eastern districts showed over one hundred per cent voter turnout. Election observers reported massive violations of voting procedures as well as outright fraud. Yushchenko had now joined Yulia Tymoshenko in calling for mass demonstrations.

The TV monopolized all of Yarko and Ksenia's attention. Moishe stood at the window watching as the nucleus of a few thousand demonstrators on Maidan Nezalezhnosti grew by additional tens of thousands. Traffic on the Khreshchatyk had ground to a halt. A grandstand like those used at outdoor rock concerts was nearing completion. Yellow-and-black headbands and T-shirts marked the PORA activists who controlled the crowd. They worked with military discipline, preventing clashes with police. Additional police arrived by busloads, but they too were trying hard to avoid confrontation.

"Well look at that," remarked Moishe. "We have two charter buses unloading demonstrators. That must be the first big wave from outside Kyiv."

Yarko pulled himself away from the Channel 5 reports to look out the window. "Looks like a sea of orange flags out there!"

"And here comes another chartered bus. They're letting them park right in front of our hotel."

"I don't think those are demonstrators," said Yarko, seeing the first passengers to disembark. "Black uniforms and black bowling ball helmets—that's riot police back where I come from."

By now Ksenia had joined the two at the window. "There's no shoulder patches at all on those boys," she observed. "This can mean nothing but trouble."

The first two to disembark walked over to the cordon of six black-suited troopers who had been performing sentry duty in front of the hotel entrance, and began a conversation with the apparent leader.

"Look at the third guy getting off the bus," said Moishe. "Riot police, my ass. That's Kevlar body armour he's wearing. And that's an AKS-74U short-barrel close-combat automatic. Those guys are Russian speznaz commandos!"

"They keep talking and looking at the hotel," said Ksenia. "You are right. Those are no riot cops, that's the Russian assault team that Vlodko has been expecting. Probably the guys from the two Russian planes that landed at Borispil."

Ksenia grabbed a phone and dialled her brother down in the sub-basement. "Answer, you fool … Hello Vlodko. We've got one busload of black-suited troops that has just arrived in front of the hotel. Body armour and Kalashnikov AKS-74U semi-automatics. These guys mean business. This would be a good time for your friend The Saint to send us a busload or two of his loyal Interior Troops. Okay. Okay. My PORA friends? I'll try. Bye."

"Christ," exclaimed Ksenia as she feverishly dialled a number on her cell. "Vlodko figures there's another busload or two of these buggers. He wants PORA to stop those buses before they get here. Come on, answer. Answer, you fools!" Ksenia lowered her voice to a conspiratorial whisper and spent a minute or two talking on her cell. When she finished the call, she turned to Yarko. "So who does Vlodko have down there with him?"

"Well, there's Mark and Serhiy, and two other miners. That's it."

"Against say sixty, plus another two dozen Black Sea Fleet commandos," calculated Ksenia. "I don't like those odds. Your friend The Saint better come through."

"Well, I'm going down to the lobby to see what I can do," said Moishe. He reached into his laptop carrying case and pulled out a pistol. "Not much against body armour, but up close and personal this can still do the job."

"You bastard!" exclaimed Yarko, realizing that Moishe had understood the whole conversation. "You know Ukrainian and have been leading us on all this time! All the translating I had to do!"

"Just a bit," said Moishe in Ukrainian. "Grandparents left Lviv, some years before the war. We just kept the language up, along with Yiddish and Hebrew. You just never know when it will be useful."

"Glad you're on our side. I'll get my PSM, then I'll join you."

"No way, Yarko," said Ksenia. "You're in no shape. They pulled the tube out of you barely two days ago. You haven't healed yet. Stay here and keep Vlodko informed of all movements outside by cellphone. That's the most important. We need eyes and ears up here. Give me the key to your room. I'll borrow your gun. Then I'll put on my nun's habit and go to the lobby too. If The Saint's boys arrive, they'll need me as a guide to help with our tricky elevator controls."

Moishe nodded. "Good thinking, Ksenia. And we can slow the boys in black by sending both elevators back up to the top floor."

Yarko reluctantly handed Ksenia his room key and walked over to the window. The suite door closed. He heard an elevator moving up its shaft, and the quiet ding that signalled its arrival.

The troops in black were getting out of the bus, putting on their helmets, and making last-minute adjustments to their Kevlar armour. The black helmets were spherical with a protruding neck-guard at the back. A hinged clear polycarbonate visor afforded facial protection. It was easy to see why, with the visor lowered, such troops were derisively called "cosmonauts" in Ukrainian slang. The troops formed two rows. The original six Black Sea Fleet commandos were now joined by those that had been watching other exits. Yarko dialled Vlodko.

"Vlodko, we have no additional busloads, thank God," Yarko began. "So the count is eighteen of our original Black Sea Fleet friends and fifty-two speznaz from the bus. They're getting ready to enter the hotel. Armament is mostly AKS-74U folding-stock short-barrel automatics with some full-sized 74s with RPGS."

Mark had just finished moving the last of the munitions cases to the tunnelling ops room behind the twin steel doors. He opened it and unwrapped three spare magazines for his AKS-74U. Two fit in his back pockets, the third he jammed awkwardly into his front pocket. The two remaining miners from the original tunnelling team were likewise stocking up. Serhiy was checking over his AGS-30. Vlodko was on his cellphone.

"So far just one busload of the bastards," said Vlodko, relaying the information he was getting. A full-sized AK-74 hung from his right shoulder.

"Safe to say there is only one way in for them," said Serhiy, sighting his weapon down the long hallway.

The sub-basement of the Hotel Dnipro was a long hallway, with a wide hall at either end, which created a long dumbell-shaped open space. The elevator was located in the middle of this hallway. Opposite it were several doors to equipment and storage rooms. The staircase, and thus the only entrance available to intruders, was at the far end of the hallway. Most of the hall, including the doors to the tunnelling ops room, was shielded by the corner of the hallway wall from any direct gunfire originating near the staircase. Vlodko had ordered that a barricade be built of all loose objects to offer additional protection from, say, a grenade rolled down the hallway.

"What are you doing?" Mark asked Serhiy, who was looking down the hallway from various vantages.

"Ever play billiards?"

"A little, but I don't play well."

"Well, I learned to play in the Soviet army... Look, I plan to stay behind the corner of the wall, and bounce one of my plums off the hallway wall at a shallow angle just that side of the elevator door. It should ricochet into the far wall by the staircase doors. The more difficult shot would be two banks into the corner pocket. What I mean by that is hitting the hallway wall just before the elevator door, deflecting to the opposite wall, bouncing off it and popping it through an open door into the staircase."

Vlodko was listening too. "Tell me Serhiy, does the safety still prevent detonation before thirty metres travel?"

"Yes it does."

"And is the self-destruct at twenty-seven seconds?" He eyed the huge AGS-30 that Serhiy was sighting in.

"Still at twenty-seven seconds," replied Serhiy

"Okay, the sub-basement is over sixty metres long, I guess you have my blessing." Vlodko turned so that everyone could hear him. "Now pay attention. When Serhiy fires his grenades, if any one of them fails to explode on impact, you count to twenty-seven before showing your face in the hallway. If not detonated on impact, these babies explode twenty-seven seconds after firing."

Turning back to the Afghan war veteran, Vlodko asked, "Listen, Serhiy, can our intruders do the same billiard trick with their RPGs?"

"Not with any kind of accuracy. The result is totally random. The RPG is a rocket, not a projectile."

"One more thing, Serhiy," added Vlodko. "Make yourself a comfortable nest in the barricade and take careful aim referencing the red Exit sign. Once any serious shooting starts, I'm cutting electrical power to the building. I have jacketed rounds for my AK-74, and in any case, I'll aim for their visors." The Barr and Stroud thermal imager was hanging around Vlodko's neck.

Mark looked around the hall for screens that could show the location of any ventilation shafts. There were two of them. One was near the ceiling and the other down near the ground. "Inlet and outlet," he said to himself. Both had already been covered over with cardboard duct-taped to the wall. Vlodko had thought of everything.

Vlodko called for attention again. "One more thing, everyone. Once we hear any kind of noise by the locked staircase doors, I want everyone out of line of sight. Note that we have moved the convex mirror away from the elevators. It's now on the wall over here, aligned with the hallway. No shooting until either Serhiy or I give the order. We want as many intruders as possible to be trapped in the opposite hall when Serhiy fires his damned cannon. Oh, and don't forget, this bucket contains wet cloths, in case of tear gas."

Vlodko's cellphone rang. He answered it and listened for a few seconds. "Okay, thanks," he said. "Now watch for any sign of The Saint's Interior Ministry boys. I expect they'll be wearing the speckled black-blue-white urban camouflage. Call me immediately. In the meantime, don't be surprised if the power goes out."

Vlodka set his cellphone to vibrate, put it in his shirt pocket, and buttoned it down. "Silence everyone," he ordered. "It's beginning."

17

THE SILENCE IN THE SUB-BASEMENT was interrupted only by the click-clack of the cocking of Kalashnikov automatics. Serhiy braced his AGS-30 and pulled the T-handle, much like a rope-start lawnmower. The floors were way too thick for him to hear any footsteps in the basement above, but Mark could imagine the movements of the intruders. They would spread out over the lobby floor, then take both the staircase and the two elevators to the first basement. From there they would attempt some form of reconnaissance. The locked doors at the bottom of the staircase to the sub-basement would be frustrating.

Vlodko placed one finger over his lips and motioned towards the covered-over ventilation screen. Mark heard a barely perceptible scratching behind the cardboard. Vlodko explained the source by placing his closed fists over his eyes in binocular fashion. This was some sort of camera or fibre-optic viewing device that had been snaked through the ventilation ducts. Mark knew that a similar device would be inserted under the staircase doors. There would still be nothing for the intruders to see.

The silence was broken by a strange hiss from down the hallway. All eyes were on the convex mirror. Sparks in the area of the distant doorknob told them that a pyrotechnical charge, probably thermite, was being used to break through the locked door. Their image reduced to a miniature in the convex mirror, the twin doors of the stairway entrance slowly opened. For a moment nothing happened. Then, like black ants, four or five intruders scurried across towards the wall opposite the stairway and disappeared from view. This group was followed by another half-dozen, then another and another. After a minute or so, a group of four began making their way up the hallway, hugging the walls for cover.

Serhiy glanced at Vlodko. Vlodko blinked his eyes, signalling agreement. Serhiy aimed at the hallway wall while remaining out of sight. *Kafoomp! Blam!* And *kafoomp* again. He fired two rounds. The explosion echoed throughout the sub-basement. An AK-74 came sliding up the hallway towards them. The shockwave from the blast behind them had knocked the four advancing intruders flat on their faces. Vlodko leaned into the hallway and fired four short bursts, aiming carefully between each one.

"They were knocked down, but still dangerous," Vlodko said as he ducked back behind the corner of the wall, "and the ones at the far end are blown to bits."

All eyes turned to the convex mirror behind them again. There was another movement of black ants from the staircase doors. Two RPG rounds shrieked up the hallway, exploding against the wall with the mirror. A scythe of shrapnel, concrete, and fine glass particles slashed across the hall. A miner standing behind Mark screamed. Mark looked. Half of the poor chap's body looked like he had been dragged over coarse sandpaper. Serhiy was knocked flat, face down.

"Lights out!" ordered Vlodko.

Mark saw that neither miner behind him looked capable of even hearing the order. He scampered to the power distribution panel behind the open twin steel doors.

Blam! The second of Serhiy's AGS-30 rounds self-destructed somewhere just in front of the open doors of the staircase. Serhiy picked himself up. He repositioned himself and took aim for his planned two banks in the corner pocket billiard shot. Mark pulled down on the power supply switch handle. Total blackness enveloped the sub-basement. The background noise of all the machinery that keeps a hotel operating stopped. The only sound was the occasional falling of loosened plaster and the groaning of the two miners. *Kafoomp! Blam!* Serhiy fired another round. It took a rising trajectory, deflected twice, and flew past the open entry doors, detonating against the staircase wall. The red Exit sign above the entrance to the staircase now dangled at an odd angle.

"I've got the thermal imager," said Vlodko. "I'm going down the hallway. I'll signal when it's safe. Then we're going to fight our way up the staircase, Serhiy."

"Meanwhile I'll find an AKS for the close-up work," said Serhiy.

"I'll signal with my flip-up cellphone," explained Vlodko. "One light flash means it's okay to advance. Two flashes means Mark turns the power back on because help has arrived."

Somewhere in the darkness Mark heard the whine of a starter motor. It was an emergency generator starting up. The engine caught and ran, but the sub-basement remained black.

"Got it," said Mark. "Two flashes of your phone's screen means power on." Mark moved out beyond the barricade to have a better view of the crooked Exit sign and the invisible figure scampering towards it.

Yarko was restless. He was watching the activity outside the hotel, hoping to see a bus filled with Interior troops. Instead he saw a gaggle of dump trucks filled with sand. This was some kind of police tactic to protect strategic buildings from the crowd of demonstrators. The crowd had now grown beyond anything that Yarko had ever experienced. Channel 5 was reporting over 100,000 demonstrators. Official government estimates placed the number at only half that. Yarko believed Channel 5.

Police vehicles and marching cohorts of uniformed police were moving up and down the roads past the Dnipro Hotel. The crowd was making the movement of normal traffic along the Khreshchatyk impossible. But Yarko could only think of the battle that was no doubt beginning far below him.

Channel 5 was showing the steel lattice grandstand that had been completed in front of the Maidan Nezalezhnosti, Independence Square. The last adjustments were being made to the sound system. Tall lattice towers supported oversized speakers. Back in Canada, all this would signal a rock concert. In Ukraine, these were the tools of revolution. Yarko watched as the TV showed someone ascending this podium. Suddenly the screen went black, shrinking to a rapidly fading point of light. All lights were out, but outside nothing seemed to have changed. Yarko thought of his brother Mark and of Vlodko in the sub-basement.

"That's Vlodko and his Barr and Stroud thermal imager," Yarko said out loud, a smile creasing his face. He stepped back to the window. He hid himself behind one edge of it, then behind the other as he scanned left and right. Directly below were three black-suited figures who continued to patrol the area in front of the hotel entrance.

Finally a bus drove up, parking in typical Kyiv style right on the wide sidewalk. It stopped just out of Yarko's view. The black uniformed guards did not appear too concerned at the arrival of still more police. Today Kyiv was a city under siege and police were everywhere. Straining to see below, Yarko noted the speckled black-blue-white camo of the newcomers. There was a short conversation with the three in black uniforms, and then it became clear that the three were being disarmed and arrested. They were marched into the bus by two of the speckled chaps. Yarko picked up his cellphone and dialled Vlodko. The Saint had come through, and not a moment too soon.

Yarko watched through the window for a moment longer. A navy blue Ford Mondeo bounced onto the sidewalk right in front of the hotel entrance. From it emerged a tall man in a dark uniform. Yarko saw the bald spot for just a moment before an officer's cap quickly covered it up. It was The Saint himself.

The lights came on. The TV sputtered to reveal another vitamin commercial. Seeing that there was nothing more for him to do on the top floor of this hotel, Yarko decided to get closer to the action. He took the stairs so as not to interfere with the elevators that The Saint's boys would need. Every stitch in his abdomen screamed in protest with each step of the five flights of stairs.

Yarko stepped out into the hotel lobby. A handful of troops in speckled camo seemed to have everything well in hand. A dozen men in black had been disarmed, and herded into a corner. Zap-straps served as makeshift handcuffs. The tall man in dress uniform spotted Yarko and smiled at him.

"Greetings, Mr. Yuriy," said Yarko, feeling awkward addressing this military officer by name.

Yuriy winked. "It's General Yuriy for today." His cellphone rang and he hurriedly answered it.

"Come with me. We'll take the elevator," said The Saint.

Yarko nodded in agreement and joined him in the elevator. They found Ksenia, dressed in her nun's habit, already waiting there.

"To the first basement level, please," The Saint said to her in a rather self-satisfied manner.

On exiting the elevator, Yarko could clearly see the reason for The Saint's display of confidence. Two dozen men in black were disarmed and were being processed by the troops in speckled camo. All armour was stripped off. Belts were removed, and hands were being zap-strapped behind their backs. Lying scattered on the right side of the hall were bodies of four more such troops. Vlodko and Serhiy were both sitting on the floor, leaning against the far wall by the staircase that led to the sub-basement. They looked exhausted. They were not in a talkative mood. The Saint left Yarko and joined his troops. Ksenia ran to her brother.

It was Moishe Friedman who welcomed Yarko. On seeing Yarko, Moishe left the group of speckled troops and walked over to greet him at the elevator. "It's over."

"Thank God," said Yarko. "So Freddy, how did the battle go?"

"Well, it turns out that Vlodko and Serhiy and the rest of the boys handled the fight in the sub-basement quite well all on their own. Up here, with Ksenia's help, we coordinated a two-pronged assault from both the staircase and the elevators. With their attention focused on battling Vlodko and Serhiy at the staircase to the sub-basement, we were able to surprise them. We only had to fire a couple of shots and all their hands went up. Personally, I think that they had orders not to engage any uniformed Ukrainian forces. Politics, you know."

"Any casualties?" asked Yarko, clearly thinking about Mark.

Moishe read Yarko's mind. "Mark is okay. The two others have shrapnel wounds."

"Could have been a lot worse."

"In any case, I'm sorry but I have to go. I have my orders," continued Moishe. "In case anything even smells like an incident, I have to make myself scarce. The sunrise should find me in Tel Aviv."

"So suddenly?"

"No goodbyes, just L'Chaim," said Moishe as he shook Yarko's hand.

"Next year in Jerusalem, Freddy?"

Moishe laughed. "I hope not. You're way too much trouble. Anyway, I'll help myself out. I'll take the stairs."

As Moishe walked away, The Saint finished what he was doing and walked back to Yarko. "Talented young man," he commented looking in Moishe's direction as he disappeared up the staircase to the lobby.

"Mossad," said Yarko as casually as he could, himself looking at the empty staircase.

"We know," said The Saint.

"So what's going to happen to all your prisoners?"

"Good question. They are foreign nationals. Any publicity will cause an international scandal. It will also force you guys to make Operation Slava public and I don't sense that you are ready for that."

"Ukraine isn't ready for that—not with this falsified election results business."

"I'll talk to their ranking officer," General Yuriy said. "I propose getting them train tickets to just across the border, say to Starodub. Maybe I'll ask Transport Minister Kirpa to arrange for suitable security. It's time the minister and I had a heart-to-heart talk. It may be time for him to switch sides."

"What do you mean switch sides?" asked Yarko.

Yuriy lowered his voice. "Kirpa has been diverting ministry funds to the Yanukovich campaign via Liakh's Ukrainian Credit Bank. And he's been transporting for free all those gangs of travelling voters so they could cast their votes twice. If there is a recount, or if the run-off election is declared void, then George Kirpa ends up on the wrong side of history. He's not really a bad guy; he just didn't realize that things simply won't be done that way any more. I think having to transport a bunch of disarmed Russian speznaz back to Russia will help his thought process."

"If the missing teeth haven't already," Yarko added with a smile.

"You heard that too, did you?" General Yuriy choked back a laugh.

"My lads have indeed confirmed that Internet news report. Kirpa was in fact hospitalized with knocked out teeth and a groin injury. The hospital staff quotes him as saying that Yanukovich punched and kicked him during an argument."

The Saint turned to his troops. "Gentlemen, we will keep these Russian lads here until nightfall. We will take them out of here in our bus at night. Alpha company will be on guard and escort duty. The rest of you will be on cleanup—I hear that the sub-basement is a mess. And one more thing, boys, no personal trophies—strip and collect only the military equipment. Watches and rings stay on the bodies. Are there any questions?"

"We have no body bags, Mr. General," said one of the speckled troops.

"We'll organize some plastic garbage bags and duct tape," said the general. He turned to Vlodko. "Vlodko, can you take care of those logistics?"

"As ordered," came Vlodko's tired voice from the far end of the room. Ksenia left her brother's side and ran up the staircase to the lobby level.

"Now," said the general, "how the hell do we ship three dozen bodies out of here without anyone noticing?"

"I have an idea," said Yarko. "The police are moving dump trucks full of sand all over the place. It's some kind of anti-riot measure."

"Perfect, just perfect, especially if we can rig a compartment under the sand. Like a false bottom. I think two trucks should do. This is a job for Fedora. Excuse me for a minute, Yaroslaw."

The general stepped into the open elevator, which was still locked in service mode. He pulled out his cell and made first one long phone call, then followed it by another.

The smells of the firefight below wafted out of the elevator shaft. Inadvertently, Yarko rubbed his nose. Strangely, there was the distinct smell of gunfire residue on his right hand.

When he finished talking, The Saint walked over to the prisoners. The elevator doors closed and the empty elevator dropped to the sub-basement.

"Tovaryshi," General Yuriy asked in Russian, "who is the ranking officer here? And, may I have a word."

General Yuriy then had a private conversation with the speznaz officer.

"So what was that all about?" asked Yarko, forgetting to mind his own business.

"Professional courtesy. I asked him if they wanted the bodies of their fallen comrades shipped back to Russia or should they be made to vanish without a trace. I won't tell you his answer. The one way, there will be total silence about this after midnight tonight. The other way, you will probably hear a news report of a terrible ambush in Chechnya. You know, flag-draped coffins and all that." The general winked.

Yarko heard the elevator doors open behind him. He turned to see two stretchers being carried in the elevator. His brother Mark was accompanying the four stretcher-bearers in speckled camo.

General Yuriy looked at the wounded miners. "Ambulance to the hotel lobby, pronto," he commanded. "We've had a terrible industrial accident."

He then turned to Yarko. "No questions will be asked. Our doctors are used to this sort of thing, right, Yarko?"

Yarko smiled, remembering his own recent stay at the hospital.

Mark got off the elevator, leaving the four Interior Ministry troops to take the wounded up to the lobby. Mark was trembling uncontrollably. Yarko hugged Mark, squeezing him in silence for a long time. Vlodko and Serhiy joined the group standing by the elevator doors.

"Well, Vlodko," began the general, "shall you take me downstairs and make your report?"

"You guys go. I'm not going down there," said Mark. "It's a mess."

"With all respect, Mr. General," Serhiy said, "it's a case of counting the boots and dividing by two."

"Grenades?"

"AGS-30."

"In close quarters?" asked the general in disbelief.

"Sixty metres wall to wall down the full length of the hallway."

"Cholera!"

18

"SO WHEN IS THE DEAL GOING THROUGH?" asked the Bishop of the Autocephalous Orthodox Church, sitting uncomfortably in his wheelchair.

All the stakeholders in Operation Slava were meeting on the sixth floor of the Hotel Dnipro to hear the security status report from Vlodko. The TV set was turned on, but with its volume reduced to a whisper so that it would not interfere. The Orange Revolution had now been going on for over a week. Those at this meeting had front-row seats at what was surely the greatest show on earth. There were new developments every hour. If news reports on the TV were not enough, there was the bird's eye view of a quarter of a million demonstrators just below the room's window. Those present at this stakeholders meeting included three Ukrainian prelates, two Israeli rabbis, and Professor Verbytsky representing the NTSh, the Scholarly Society of Taras Shevchenko. They were prepared for bad news, but Vlodko still found it hard to deliver it.

"To the best of our knowledge," began Vlodko, "the ownership transfer of the Hotel Dnipro is to be completed on December 4. On that day, a consortium fronted by Ihor Bakay will have controlling interest of the hotel. I need not tell you whose interests that group represents. The moneyman behind this purchase is none other than the Moscow criminal mastermind Mad Max Kurochkin. In any case, they have already selected their new hotel management team, which means all of the arrangements that we have put together are gone out the window. That includes the personnel manager and maintenance staff. The elevator control panel will have to return to normal. All traces of unusual activity in the sub-basement will have to be cleaned up. This has been greatly complicated by battle damage from the incident that I described earlier. We cannot possibly complete this work in three days. We are down to a half-dozen able-bodied men. We also need to discuss what kind—"

"We seem to have some kind of breaking news," interrupted Ksenia. "I see Yevhen Marchuk's face on the tube."

"...*In connection with the helicopter crash in Turkey last month, President Leonid Kuchma has ordered the arrest of the former minister of defence, General Yevhen Marchuk. It was widely known that General Marchuk had been hospitalized ever since his firing two weeks ago. However when we contacted the hospital today we were told that the general had checked himself out last night. His whereabouts at this time are unknown.*

"*The president of Poland, Alexander Kwasniewsky, is expected to land at Borispil Airport within the hour. He will be joining the president of Lithuania, Valdas Adamkus, and the president of Georgia, Michael Saakashvili, at an emergency meeting of the Presidential...*"

"Okay, we can turn it down now," said Yarko. "Let's get back to business."

Vlodko resumed his briefing. "As I was saying about security measures for the future after we shut down our Operation Slava, first, we can seal off access to the tunnel with a cinder block false wall, or we can make the same wall with a secret door. Next, we can booby-trap the tunnel with explosives. Finally, we can install audio and video monitoring devices, even an alarm to warn of unauthorized access."

"How about shipping the scrolls to Israel?" asked the Orthodox rabbi in Russian.

"You know Ukraine's laws about exporting historic artifacts. And the scrolls are too big for a diplomatic pouch. Everyone in and around the embassy will know all about them."

"Then why not go public, and open the website and all that?" asked the Reformed rabbi.

"The risk is that with the current make-up of Ukraine's government, they will not resist any pressure from Russia. Your scrolls will end up in the Hermitage with the rest of their plunder. Our stuff too. And the Scythian gold will end up as jewellery on every whore in Moscow." Realizing that his last statement might have been somewhat insensitive, given his audience, Vlodko quickly added, "My apologies for my policeman's mouth."

"No offence taken," said the Greek-Catholic bishop. "Your colourful expression may be much closer to the truth than we think."

"We've got photographs of most of the contents?" asked the Reformed rabbi.

"Much, but not all," said Vlodko. "Four out of seven scrolls. A cataloguing of books, including one Torah. Photographs of inscriptions and maps."

"Okay, but once an Orange government is elected we can go back in, right?" This from the Orthodox bishop of the Kyiv Patriarchate.

"Maybe. But our fear is that both the current president, Kuchma, and the usual Russian agents of influence will keep a firm grip on things. Then there still is the matter of the ownership of this hotel. We know there is both money laundering and a large unsecured loan from Yuriy Liakh's Ukrainian Credit Bank involved in this hotel purchase deal. But to try to get the transaction declared null and void—now that is another matter."

"The courts for one," said Professor Verbytsky, "are all bought and paid for."

"Yulia Tymoshenko would do it," said Ksenia, "if she were prime minister."

"Yes, she would try," Vlodko agreed. "But she'd be on a short leash. And we know that Yushchenko does not have the backbone for it."

"So what you are saying," said the Reformed rabbi, "is that even if the Orange Revolution succeeds, crooked oligarchs and foreign agents will still be running your country?"

"We will know that for sure after such a government is formed— simply by seeing who the president appoints as prosecutor general. It may just be the cop in me talking, but to sweep clean one needs a good new broom. In any case, let's proceed and take a simple vote. Cinder block wall with no secret door so we can save time? Unanimous. Explosive booby-trap? Five to one—passed. Silent alarm? Unanimous. Video and audio monitoring? Unanimous. Thank you, gentlemen. Time for us to go to work."

There was now a television set up in the sub-basement hall where the remaining members of Operation Slava were busy covering up all traces of the tunnelling operations as well as the battle damage. News and events unfolding around the Orange Revolution were happening so fast that Vlodko was forced to agree to this apparent luxury. The TV set was silent, but Ksenia got to wear a headset while she painted the walls. She could then alert the crew of any breaking news. It was December 3.

"Here it comes. It's a special news report," announced Ksenia. "I'm turning up the volume."

"*... Channel 5 has just received this report. Yuriy Liakh, director of the Ukrainian Credit Bank, is dead. His body was discovered this evening in his bank office with a mortal wound to the neck. Initial reports term this death an apparent suicide. The instrument of his death appears to* *have been a letter opener. We will be bringing you additional details as they become available.*

"Today, Channel 5 has received videotape from a private citizen showing Russian speznaz troops, dressed in black, travelling by train in the Chernihiv province heading for the border. No armaments were seen on their persons. When asked, these men offered no explanation for their presence in Ukraine.

"And now for international news: We repeat the following report that was made public earlier today by the Kremlin. The Ministry of Defence of the Russian Federation has announced that a convoy of Russian troops suffered heavy casualties in an ambush by some two hundred Chechen bandits in the hills south of Grozny. The ambush occurred on the road between Duba-Yurt and Sovyetskoye. It is believed that this attack was engineered by Shamir Basrayev, the warlord that has claimed responsibility for the tragedy in Beslan where more than 300 children lost their lives. The enemy has suffered heavy casualties and our troops are in hot pursuit of the criminals. Thirty-seven defenders of the Fatherland were returned to Moscow today to receive a hero's burial. Minister of Defence, General..."

Ksenia turned down the volume. Vlodko held his breath.

"Yuzio!" Yarko muttered under his breath. Cold beads of sweat formed on his forehead.

"That answers the question about the bodies," commented Serhiy.

"The big question is," said Vlodko, "with Liakh's death, does this mean that we have a reprieve for Operation Slava? Otherwise we would need to be finished by midnight tonight, or at the latest no later than 4 a.m."

"Another three days work for the six of us, and you expect it to be completed in seven hours?" asked Father Onufriy. "It's not going to happen."

"We've been working fourteen hours today already," said Serhiy.

"Let's assume that a miracle has happened and go to bed. We meet for breakfast at 7 a.m. and see what news we hear."

"So we are hoping that the takeover of the hotel is cancelled or at least delayed, are we?" asked Mark.

"We are," said Vlodko. "And yes, we are going to bed."

"Good night, all," said Father Onufriy.

The death of Yuriy Liakh gave the team members plenty of time to seal up their operation. The takeover of the hotel was not cancelled but was postponed until some time in the New Year. On the evening of December 6, 2004, Operation Slava was formally suspended. Local handling of audio and video monitoring as well as the alarm in the tunnelling ops room was left to a confidant of The Saint known by the code-name Fedora. Vlodko left Kyiv to resume his police duties in Lviv on December 7. Father Onufriy drove back with him. Serhiy collected his last paycheque in American dollars and returned to Yenakiyevo, a suburb of Donetsk in the Donbas region of Ukraine. Mark, Yarko, and Ksenia stayed in Kyiv, camping in tents in the snows of the Ukrainian winter on the Maidan Nezalezhnosti. They joined the nearly 100,000 campers and another 150,000 commuting demonstrators who pledged to remain there until final victory.

19

ON DECEMBER 3, 2004, the Supreme Court declared the announced results of the November 21 run-off election as fraudulent and invalid. Oleksander Moroz, the old Communist Party leader who had repainted himself as a Socialist, rammed through changes to the Constitution that would eventually rob the president of half of his powers. The Parliament of Ukraine ordered the members of the Central Election Committee replaced in a packaged vote along with these constitutional changes. In a way, Moroz stole any presidential electoral victory even before there could be a victory.

On December 4, the new CEC scheduled a repeat of the presidential run-off election for December 26.

On December 9, Svyatoslav Piskun, a crony in the previous regime, was reappointed prosecutor general, in an apparent deal between President Kuchma and Victor Yushchenko.

On December 24, Yarko, Mark, and Ksenia took the train to Lviv. Ksenia needed to be there to vote.

On December 26, an undersea earthquake created a tsunami that killed thousands from the islands of Indonesia all the way to India. That same day Ukraine had the cleanest and fairest presidential election in its history. Exit polls showed that Victor Yushchenko was the clear winner of the presidential elections.

On December 27, at 5:40 p.m., Transportation Minister Heorgiy Kirpa's body was found in the bathroom of his home in Bortnychi. The death was officially pronounced a suicide. The cause of death was a bullet that entered his right temple and exited the left, embedding itself in the bathroom wall. The instrument of his death was a Makarov PSM 5.45-mm pistol. The recently re-appointed prosecutor general, Svyatoslav Piskun, personally visited the scene.

On December 30, France, Iceland, and Luxembourg sent notes of congratulations to Victor Yushchenko for winning the presidential elections.

On January 10, 2005, the Central Election Committee, having rejected all further appeals from as far back as December 30, 2004, as frivolous, officially declared Victor Yushchenko the winner of the presidential elections with a margin of 51.99 per cent to 44.2 per cent of votes cast.

On January 23, President Victor Yushchenko was inaugurated.

On February 4, Yulia Tymoshenko was appointed and confirmed as prime minister. The Ministers of the Cabinet were selected from all parties represented in the pro-Yushchenko "Orange" block. Prosecutor General Svyatoslav Piskun, recently reappointed by the previous president, remained in his position.

On March 2, Prosecutor General Svyatoslav Piskun held a press conference regarding his ongoing investigation into the murder of Internet journalist Georgiy Gongadze.

20

"IT'S NICE, KSENIA, that neither of us have any lectures on Wednesday afternoon," said Yarko.

"Don't get any ideas! My mother will be home any minute."

"I wasn't thinking about that—you have a one-track mind. I meant we have a chance to talk, you know."

"You want to talk, then talk." Ksenia tried to hide her smile.

"Well, it was your idea that I try a semester at the Lviv University."

"Not that you had much choice. You missed registration for the spring semester in Vancouver."

"Burnaby. Simon Fraser University is in Burnaby. Anyway, something is up."

Ksenia couldn't resist. "You mean in the Biblical sense or the political one?"

"I said you've got a one-track mind! Anyway, all last week the news was full of nothing but the Gongadze murder affair. Interviews with his widow, interviews with his mother, and yesterday the president announced on TV that the case is just about solved. So now today the prosecutor general announces a press conference."

"It's bullshit," said Ksenia.

"What's bullshit?"

"The whole solving-the-murder business. Lard-ass Piskun was appointed prosecutor general for the very reason that he is an expert at *not* solving cases. He is an expert screw-up. He's there to make sure nothing sticks to Kuchma. And he's there to avoid stirring up any scandal, whether national or international."

"International—that's kind of what Saint George said."

"So what exactly did he say?"

"It's a long sad business," said Yarko, "but basically everybody on the inside knows it was a Russian spezoperazia."

"You mean the whole business of discrediting the Ukrainian president, and sucking him into Russia's orbit?"

"Pretty much what the *Zakryta Zona* program on Channel 5 implied."

"Well, now it's Putin who has had his pants pulled down and his ass kicked in public." Ksenia was referring to the wild and woolly Ukrainian presidential elections. "He certainly bet on the wrong horse."

"Exactly," said Yarko. "Kuchma got him to bet on the only jackass in the horserace. And the one spezoperazia is a direct result of the other."

"Damn, we're missing the Piskun press conference," said Ksenia, not quite picking up on the implication of Yarko's last statement. She fiddled with the TV "On" switch.

"We don't want to miss Ukraine's very own Sherlock Holmes in person!" said Yarko.

"*... Gongadze was strangled. Those that forced him into that car intended to kill him. They were executing a criminal order, and the prosecutor general is aware of who gave this order. After the killers discovered that Gongadze was alone, they sent a car belonging to the intelligence service and on the way to the designated place three members of the militsya beat him in the car. All those that executed this* order were residents of Kyiv. After the murder, the body was doused in gasoline and set afire."

"What was the motive for this killing?"

"You will have to wait a while. The prosecutor general's office is not ready to provide answers to that question."

"How did the prosecutor general's office determine the details of his killing and of his reburial?"

"These conclusions were made based on biological as well as botanical examination."

"Was Georgiy Gongadze killed the day he disappeared?"

"We now know that because of some reluctance on the part of the executioners themselves, the murder did not occur on September 15, 2000 as originally planned. We have two of them under arrest and the third was released but is not allowed to leave town. General Pukach is a subject of an international manhunt."

"Will you be arresting or questioning anyone else?"

"The investigation of who gave the order is not complete. This coming Friday, General Yuriy Kravchenko will be giving evidence at the prosecutor general's office. General Kravchenko was minister of the interior at the time of the Gongadze murder."

"When do you expect to question General Kravchenko?"

"As usual we will begin work at ten in the morning."

"Do you know the whereabouts of General Yuriy Kravchenko? Is he in Ukraine?"

"Yes we do. And yes he is in the country."

"Have you arrested Mykola Astion?"

"No. Major General Mykola Astion has not been arrested."

"Do you have evidence that General Kravchenko ordered the murder of Gongadze?"

"We do not discuss what evidence we have or don't have with the press. That can jeopardize the investigation. Thank you, that will be all for today."

A file photograph of General Yuriy Kravchenko was displayed on the TV screen.

"To summarize, General Yuriy Kravchenko has been summoned for questioning in connection with the Georgiy Gongadze case to the prosecutor general's office for 10 a.m. on Friday, March 4..."

Yarko looked at the photograph on the TV—a handsome officer in a spectacular black uniform with silver trim. "That's The Saint! My friend Yuriy—Saint George!"

"So you never knew who The Saint really was?" asked Ksenia incredulously.

"No. It was a big secret as far as I was concerned. And the only time anyone else saw him in Kyiv was at the end of the battle under the hotel. Only Vlodko and I knew that the officer present there was The Saint."

"Well, I'm sure Vlodko knew exactly who The Saint was. He's been in the militsya long enough to know his former boss. He is the organization's highest-placed mole, if you wish. A true Ukrainian patriot, he's been play-acting the role of an unconscionable KGB-ist for several years now. That's how he got to be the minister of the interior and then the minister of revenue. He could have made president."

For half an hour the two sat in silence. Each of them was lost in thought.

"Bringing him in for questioning is a provocation," Yarko said finally. "And what's this about announcing it to the world two days before? People will think The Saint had something to do with the murder."

"Dirty game, that," Ksenia said. "I wonder if Piskun will listen when Yuriy Kravchenko tells him who really was behind the murder."

"He'll listen; he just isn't allowed to hear."

"In any case, I wonder how they will keep his testimony off the front page?"

"They won't," came Vlodko's voice from the vestibule. "This is his chance to let the whole truth out. International incident be damned. Yulia Tymoshenko won't be afraid to kick some Muscovite ass, even if Yushchenko may be."

"International relations are the president's prerogative," Ksenia reminded her brother, "and Tymoshenko just cares for herself."

"Both Victor Yushchenko and Yulia Tymoshenko are popular on the world arena today," said Yarko.

"It's a chance to end the charade once and for all," said Vlodko. "In fact, I should get my Boychyshyn file together for The Saint."

"You mean so as to show an unending string of political killings ordered by the Kremlin?"

"Exactly. I like your angle, Yarko."

"Then phone him and get things going."

"Can't. I tried from my cell. The line is busy."

"Well, after this broadcast, his fax will be busy, and his e-mail server will crash. In fact," said Yarko, "in these days of easy communication he'll be cut off just by the sheer volume of it all."

"I tried Fedora," added Vlodko, predicting Yarko's next thought. "Constantly busy too. In any case, I'll have to deliver the files in person."

"So hop on a plane!"

"Not on a policeman's salary. And the Operation Slava funds are depleted to zero. No, I'll get the files ready and head for the train station tonight. You can join me if you wish, Yarko. I'll certainly enjoy your company."

"I'll start packing. So where will we be staying?"

"I'll call Professor Verbytsky. I'm sure his phone still works."

21

"He's been shot!"

Two strong arms were shaking him awake. Yarko couldn't comprehend what he was hearing. It was a cold March morning in Ukraine's capital.

"What? What? Who's been shot?" muttered Yarko sleepily, barely able to mouth the words in Ukrainian. It's all a dream, he thought; I'm still good for a half-hour's sleep.

"Kravchenko! Yuriy Kravchenko!" yelled the tall figure above him. "For God's sake, it's The Saint. The Saint is dead!"

Yarko sat bolt upright, feeling the blood drain from his head, momentarily darkening the silhouetted figure of his friend.

"How, Vlodko? How?" Yarko's voice cracked in a pleading tone.

"Fedora just called me. He's on the scene. He's in Yuriy's garage. There's blood all over. He says he no longer has a face!" This time it was Vlodko's voice that cracked. Tears streamed down his cheeks. Gathering his composure, he continued. "Get dressed, Yarko. I know where his house is."

Yarko was finally able to compose a rational thought. "How do we get there? You have no car in Kyiv."

"Cholera! You're right. I better call a taxi, pronto."

A half hour later, Yarko and Vlodko were in the back of a Czech Skoda of unknowable vintage and dubious state of repair.

"Forty dollars," the driver demanded as he ground the transmission into first.

"Blyaa," cursed Vlodko with the ubiquitous Russian expletive. "I'll give you one hundred hryvnias, max. Only once you get us there through this fucking snow. And no bargaining, I'm a cop!" Vlodko's Russian was accented but very clear to the taxi driver.

"Zapadynets?" asked the driver, recognizing the strong Ukrainian accent that marked a Ukrainian from the less Russified western provinces.

"East and West together!" replied Vlodko, quoting a chant from the Independence Square demonstrations of the recent Orange Revolution. "Now shut up and drive."

The snow was crisp. It crunched and creaked under the tires of the Skoda. The bright sun rising in the bluest of azure skies caused Yarko to squint. He had forgotten to bring his shades. Vlodko was wearing his polarized lenses. He was hanging on to a large briefcase as if it were chained to his left arm.

Minutes later they found themselves in a very exclusive part of Kyiv. This was an area filled with detached, single-family homes, something still rare in Ukraine. Many were gated and hidden behind tall snow-covered hedgerows. Soon they came upon the expected police barricade. The driver stopped. Vlodko got out to talk to one of the officers. There was a heated discussion accompanied by much gesticulation. Vlodko walked back and leaned into the open passenger side window.

"Yarko, you get out and stay with me." He turned to the driver. "Here's your hundred hryvnias. You can't help us any further. The gebnia won't let you through." Vlodko used the derogatory slang for state police, spitting into the snow for emphasis.

The driver's eyes widened. "Dyakuyu!" he thanked Vlodko in Ukrainian.

"We have to wait here," Vlodko explained to Yarko as the Skoda drove away. "We have to wait for Fedora to escort us through to the scene of the crime. It's still over a block from here."

Yarko pointed at Vlodko's briefcase. "Still hanging on to the file?"

"Quiet. It's safest with me," Vlodko replied in a conspiratorial tone. "You know that I had hoped to add the Boychyshyn murder to The Saint's testimony about the Gongadze case. Looks like none of that will happen now."

A half-dozen SBU state security police were manning the make-shift barricade of two Daewoo patrol cars and the usual yellow tape. Farther up the snowy road, a dozen more black-coated cops were milling around. A dark blue Daewoo was moving towards Yarko and Vlodko. Still farther away, a large black SUV was backing out of a driveway. Two very large and very black Mercedes sedans stood at the side of the road near the SUV. White clouds of exhaust wafted behind each car. Yarko was frozen. He was shivering and hungry. The tension was eating his guts.

The dark blue Daewoo pulled up to them. The driver's window was down.

"Fedora?" Vlodko greeted the driver tentatively through the window. Fedora was a code name, a nom-de-guerre of sorts. In fact, he was a highly placed police official.

"Hello, Vlodko."

"Can we go to the scene?"

"Not much use now. It's all fucked up. They're taking the body out as we speak."

Vlodka put two and two together. "The black SUV?"

"The black SUV."

"Do you know these guys?" asked Vlodko, clearly worried that the scene had been compromised.

"Not all of them. That's the fucking prosecutor general's department's car."

"Did you see Piskun?"

Fedora shook his head. "No. I wouldn't expect him to be here so early. But his boys are here, that's for sure."

"Can't you do anything?"

Fedora sighed. "I took pictures. I have digital pictures of the crime scene before those idiots started moving things."

"Can we go there?"

"Yes... and I presume this is Yaroslaw."

"My apologies, for not introducing you," said Vlodko. "Yes this is the one who started everything. This is Yarko, the crazy Canadian; Yarko, this is Fedora."

"The man with the finger on the button?"

Fedora cracked a conspiratorial smile. "In a manner of speaking. Now get in, both of you, before you freeze to death."

Yarko did not have to be invited twice. The clear window glass testified to the output of the car's heater.

The large black SUV passed them going the other way as they drove to the crime scene. Both Fedora and Vlodko doffed their black sheep's-fur hats as the Mercedes Gelandewagen passed by; Yarko bowed his head. No one could speak. Silent tears rolled down their faces.

Fedora stopped across from the victim's house. The garage doors were wide open. The three of them passed past four cops as they walked silently up the snowy driveway. It had now been trampled by a hundred pairs of boots. This garage was even messier than his father's back in Vancouver, thought Yarko.

Fedora shook his head. "What a mess. They've moved everything. The chair was here, not there. The gun is gone. He was shot sitting in this chair, you know."

"Did I just hear one of the cops talk about a suicide note?" Vlodko asked.

Fedora looked grim. "So the cover-up begins! It couldn't have been suicide. It just couldn't. Two shots to the head! Explain that!"

"If you have the pictures," said Yarko, "then let's get the hell out of here and post them on the Internet. E-mail them somewhere. Anywhere."

"Yarko's right," said Vlodko. "They will start making up some kind of fiction unless they know that the pics are out there."

"The truth is out there," said Yarko to himself, picking up on Vlodko's words.

Fedora reached for his cellphone. "My house is five minutes away. I'll tell Oksana to make breakfast."

Fedora insisted that they eat before they viewed anything on the computer screen. Nobody could taste their breakfast. Their minds were on this morning's grisly event. The little Minolta was busy downloading two hundred megs of jpeg files while they ate.

"Before we even begin," said Vlodko, "e-mail any reporters you know, the Maidan website, copy everyone. Send them all your headshots. They won't be able to make one wound out of two if the pictures are out there."

"I know a chap at *Without Censorship,* the crime magazine," said Fedora.

"That's a start."

Fedora pushed back his chair. "Let me do the e-mail now, while you guys finish breakfast." He left the table and walked to his study.

Vlodka raised his voice. "Is it true that all the mafia types have left the country?"

"There was a veritable exodus after Yushchenko's election," came Fedora's voice from the adjoining room, "and after Tymoshenko was confirmed as prime minister, all those who were still hanging around Kyiv ran for Moscow."

"How about Mad Max—the new owner of the Dnipro Hotel?"

"No news about him leaving. They say Max Kurochkin is rather hands-on in his new business acquisition. He's probably living in that hotel."

"Any construction work in the sub-basement?"

"Don't know. Our news sources have dried up. But the sensors are still quiet."

Yarko rose from the table. "I'm finished," he said. Turning to Oksana, Fedora's wife, he added, "Thank you for the delicious meal."

The last bit was a chivalrous white lie. He had tasted nothing. A stack of water-soaked cardboard would have done just as well. He hurried into Fedora's study.

Fedora began scrolling from picture to picture. All three of them crowded around the computer screen. Oksana, who was quite used to her husband's police work, ignored the men and busied herself washing dishes.

"How many of the damn things did you take?" asked Vlodko.

"A hundred or so. A hundred and nine, to be exact."

"Let's focus on the cause of death. The method, if you will. Show us the head shots first."

Picture after gory picture scrolled on the screen. Yarko gasped, revolted by the grisliness of the images. "What happened to his face?"

Fedora pointed. "Here, under his chin, do you see the hole?"

"Yes." Yarko was trying hard to hold down his breakfast.

"That is the non-fatal wound. Under the chin and up and to the left, shattering the upper jaw and part of his nose. There is nothing left to hold the bone with his upper teeth. It's just hanging by the skin of his upper lip. That's why it looks like the beginning of an elephant's trunk growing out of his face."

"A hell of a way to cure sinus troubles" muttered Vlodko. He was now as cool as the Siberian winters of his youth. If there was any true emotion, Vlodko had it well buried under his icy exterior.

Fedora made a face at Vlodko's attempt at gallows humour. He pointed again. "The fatal shot is this one: into the right temple and out the left. Almost at perfect right angles to the fore-aft plane."

Vlodko leaned closer to the computer screen. "Hold this shot of the entry wound."

"You're the police detective," said Fedora. "So what do you see?"

"Something peculiar. Yarko, do you see it?"

Yarko knew that this wasn't a real test in forensic skills, but in any case, he prided himself in his keen intellect. "The blood pattern," he said. "The trickles change direction. Down then forward. You said he was shot sitting in a chair, didn't you, *Pane* Fedora?"

"He was found sitting upright, with his head tilted to the left and down."

"So the head position is consistent with the final leg of these blood trickles, but the first leg is straight down, indicating that the head was held straight up and down after the gunshot."

"The head was held," agreed Fedora.

"A termination with extreme prejudice, would be your English expression," Vlodko said to Yarko. "They held his head upright by his hair, then blew a slug into his right temple."

"And they had to hold the head up because of the first wound, the one that almost blew his face off," added Fedora. He sounded professionally clinical and detached even though he was dealing with the death of his best friend.

"Desperation," said Vlodko.

"Desperation!" Yarko remembered the desperation he felt anticipating his own death at Saint George's Cathedral the previous year. "That explains the odd location of the first wound!"

Vlodko frowned. "It is odd. Nobody commits suicide shooting himself under the chin. The trajectory angle is quite weird. It's actually up, left, and forward. And it's awkward as hell if that were an execution, too. So explain it, Yarko."

"They tie him to the chair. They try to make him write a suicide note, or they try to get some information out of him. Whatever. When that is over they tie his hands behind the chair."

"So there had to be two or more killers."

"Yes, two at least. They put the barrel of the pistol in his mouth."

"Typical of a Russian mafia hit: you get to eat the barrel of the gun that kills you," commented Fedora.

"But The Saint was strong and healthy—a super-cop," Yarko argued. "Isn't that right, Vlodko? He wouldn't go down without a fight."

"Yes, go on."

"They put the gun barrel in his mouth, then, just before they pull the trigger, he throws his head and himself backwards, probably chair and all. And the gun goes off just as Yuriy has thrown his head back. Another millisecond and the shot would have missed altogether."

"But what would that gain him?" asked Fedora. "Another ten seconds of life. He had no chance. Not against two."

"You're right, but even that ten seconds is a victory. And it destroys any attempt to call it a suicide. It makes things messy."

"And messy they certainly are," said Fedora.

Vlodka picked up on Yarko's reasoning. "So, now the second guy picks the wounded Kravchenko up; he gets all pissed off, so he holds his head by the hair and blows a bullet into his temple."

"One gun or two?" asked Fedora.

"Could have been either," said Vlodko, "but for the suicide theory to hold they must officially make it one."

Fedora scrolled through a dozen more pictures. "Here's the gun. Nicely placed under the chair, with the barrel resting on the crossbar between the chair-legs pointing backward and upward."

"Dear God!" exclaimed Vlodko. "They were not even trying to make it look like a suicide. Any professional investigating the scene would immediately know ..." His voice trailed off.

Oksana entered the room carrying a tray with three coffees, cooked in the Armenian manner. "Did you hear the news?" she asked innocently. "General Yuriy Kravchenko has committed suicide. Didn't they say he didn't want to testify before Piskun's Gongadze Commission?"

"The hell he didn't," said Fedora. "This was his best chance to publicly expose those who ordered Georgiy Gongadze's killing. It would have caused an international incident."

"Now, now, my friend," said Vlodko, pretending to chide. "You know how we don't want any international incidents. They can lock you up for that. You know, the charge of re-awakening inter-ethnic hatred and all that."

"So did you e-mail the pictures?" asked Yarko.

Fedora clicked onto the Outlook icon. "Yes I did. Here it is in Sent Items, and the Outbox is empty."

"Can you send it to my computer in Vancouver?"

"Will do." Fedora and busied himself with the mouse. "Shit!" he exclaimed.

"What?"

"The fucking Internet is down."

Vlodka was not the least bit surprised. "It is, is it? Trouble with the server, I'll bet. Let's hope your previous e-mails made it. Just don't let any repairmen in here to fix your computer."

"Better still, I'll unplug the cable, and start burning copies on disks. I'm sure I'll be visited by more than one black Mercedes in the next few days."

Fedora bent to unhook a cable. "So where goes Operation Slava now?" he asked as he jiggled the connector.

"I will phone you in a few days," said Vlodko. "In the meantime, you might as well take us to the train station tonight. There's nothing more I can do here."

Yarko was exhausted. He was lying on a bunk in a sleeping compartment, known as an eS-Ve, of the overnight train to Ternopil. After taking all night to cover some 500 kilometres, it would still take another half-day to reach Lviv. Vlodko was snoring in the bunk across from him. The upper bunks were empty, giving them some privacy. Yarko was sure that Vlodko's status as a police officer may have had some influence on this bit of luck.

Yarko could not sleep on the train. He hadn't slept on the way to Kyiv either. The condition of the tracks was certainly not conducive to slumber. Every few hundred metres, one rail or the other, recently lifted by a frost heave, would tilt the train a dozen degrees either side of vertical, making the trip seem like a ride on a cheap roller coaster. With each violent lurch, Yarko would involuntarily shoot out an arm to grab at a tiller that wasn't there. He was remembering the times when he had experienced the most restful sleep. These were invariably in the family sailboat, standing at anchor in some secluded bay of British Columbia's Sunshine Coast, being rocked gently by the wavelets of a quiet sea. The last time was nearly three years ago. The memories of sailing the waters of the Georgia Strait calmed his jittery nerves sufficiently to allow him to fall into a fitful sleep.

22

ON FRIDAY, MARCH 4, 2005, AT 7:15 A.M., General Yuriy Kravchenko's bloody body was found in his garage. There were two gunshot wounds to the head. The first bullet entered the soft tissue under the jaw, exiting just below his left nostril, breaking off the upper mandible with all the front teeth. The second bullet entered the right temple, exiting the left. The body was seated on a wooden chair with the torso slumped to the left. The instrument of his death was a Beretta 9-mm pistol. It was found lying under the chair with its barrel resting on a lateral crossbar between the legs of the chair, pointing up and towards the back. The body was wearing blue track pants and a black cloth jacket with a hood. There was no blood spatter on the victim's right hand. There was no blood spatter on the pants. There was a blood smear on the slide of the Berretta. The blood trickles on the right side of the face ran in a downward direction then turned through nearly ninety degrees and ran forwards towards his lips. The General's dog had just been taken for a walk and had been left unattended in the snow outside the garage. A note was found, allegedly beneath the victim's underclothing. It read:

My dear ones. I am not guilty of anything. Forgive me, I have become a victim if the intrigues of President Kuchma and his environment. I leave you with a clean conscience, farewell.

This death was immediately termed a suicide, and the case was closed as such. It is officially classed as a suicide to this day.

Epilogue

LVIV, UKRAINE
March 2005

On Monday, March 7, Vlodko Ohorodnyk visited the Metropolitan of the Ukrainian Greek-Catholic Church in Saint George's Cathedral in Lviv. From there he contacted all key members of Operation Slava. The project needed to be permanently closed, and protocol called for a democratic vote of the operation's members. They needed to act quickly. He called the meeting for Thursday, March 10, at the cathedral. The death of General Kravchenko was a message written in a language that could be read very clearly by those for whom it was intended. It was a declaration, informing anyone that may dare to think otherwise, of who was still boss in Ukraine.

At the March 10 meeting, it was agreed that there was no hope of continuing any work through the tunnel from the Dnipro Hotel. It was also agreed that it was almost certain the Russian mafia who now owned the hotel would discover the tunnel. Serhiy, who was attending the meeting as the technical expert, explained in detail that if the explosives were detonated, the tunnel could be rendered permanently unusable. It would then become safer and cheaper to drill a new tunnel than to try to reopen the original. This would result in an ultimate Mexican standoff between those in Operation Slava and the Russian side. Three months of tunnelling by one side could not occur without its discovery by the other. Serhiy ended his presentation with, "I created the tunnel, and I must now order its destruction."

Yarko found the meeting depressing. The thought that the Library would be buried again—for who knew how long—frustrated and saddened him. Still, the meeting had given everyone an excuse to reconnect, and he was thrilled that he had a chance to see his old friends Serhiy and Moishe "Freddy" Friedman again.

The meeting had run through the lunch hour, so everyone was hungry when it finished.

"So do you have anything to eat in this town?" asked Serhiy.

"How about the Café Pid Levom, where I used to work," suggested Ksenia. "That's were Yarko and I met almost two years ago."

Yarko smiled at the memory. "And we haven't been back there since then."

"As long as there's something kosher," said Moishe.

"They used to serve the world's best latkes. I'm sure that hasn't changed," Ksenia assured him.

"Okay. We'll take my rented car."

"Nothing but first class for our friends from the Mossad," said Yarko.

Moishe took a friendly swipe at Yarko, ruffling his hair. "You ride in the trunk."

"I'm taking my blue Lada," said Vlodko. "Father Onufriy can ride with me."

"What do you mean *your* blue Lada?" teased Yarko, who always claimed the trophy car as his by right.

"For that you ride in my trunk too."

It was well after lunchtime, and the café was nearly empty. Since the tables were too small for six, Vlodko and Father Onufriy sat at a table adjoining the one for Yarko and the rest. The long-legged waitress who served them was dressed in a black mini-dress with a white apron. She was definitely to Moishe's liking. He had trouble staying focused on the menu.

"No more of that!" ordered Ksenia, seeing that Yarko too had taken his eyes off the menu.

"So whatever happened to your old waitressing outfit?" asked Yarko with a grin.

"And no more of that!" Ksenia took a swipe at Yarko's hair.

Serhiy grinned. "So, speaking of no more of that, when are you two getting married?"

Moishe burst out laughing, and Ksenia turned red as a beet. Vlodko and Father Onufriy both cocked an ear Yarko's way while pretending to read the menu.

"Well, it's not very formal yet," stammered Yarko, "but, I think, maybe—maybe this summer."

Ksenia laughed. "Not formal! You haven't even proposed yet! Is this your idea of a proposal?"

"Well, I was going to ask your mother first. Call me crazy, but I like to follow the tradition." Yarko was now totally off balance, and digging himself deeper into trouble.

Ksenia continued laughing. "Ask my mother? I would think one should at least have a ring, shouldn't one?"

"I agree." Yarko reached into his pocket and pulled out a tiny velvet box. "And, yes, I bought a ring in Kyiv." He knelt on one knee. Ksenia sat in stunned silence.

"Dammit!" said Moishe. "I think I'm a witness to an engagement. L'Chaim!"

Ksenia recovered enough to stand, pick Yarko up off his knee, and crush him with a kiss that wasn't ever going to end.

Vlodko motioned to the waitress for a bottle.

"I told you I prefer weddings to funerals," quipped Father Onufriy. "So you finally listened to me."

What followed was the most joyous meal in Yarko's life. Beef rouladen stuffed with sauerkraut, onions and wild mushrooms may have been the most exotic item on the menu, but it was Ksenia that he feasted his eyes on. All afternoon he shared with her the unending sequence of champagne, cognac, and horilka that Vlodko kept ordering from his neighbouring table.

Moishe was enjoying his rouladen over latkes in a fusion meal that covered at least three countries and a century of history. His eyes never missed a chance to catch a glimpse of the waitress, but ever the professional, his ears were catching snippets of Vlodko's discussion of business matters with Father Onufriy.

"…fingerprints matched," Vlodko said to the priest in a lowered voice.

"Will he be charged?"

"Not for murder, but he will be charged with something else."

"So he'll just leave the country; he knows we can't extradite him," whispered Onufriy.

"That's where the organization comes in."

"In Russia?" Onufriy asked incredulously.

"Sybir," answered Vlodko in Russian, pointedly enunciating the soft *r* like a breath of icy wind.

It was an hour later when Serhiy had to interrupt desert. "I'm afraid that I have to excuse myself, but I've got a train to catch."

"Stay here. I'll give you a ride to the station," said Moishe. "What time does it leave?"

"It leaves at 5:35."

"So you can stay a little longer. Finish the liqueurs."

"Thanks, that's very kind of you."

"It seems you're not quite yourself today. And I don't think it's just regrets over the fate of your tunnel."

"It's just the tunnel."

"You know I can tell these things," continued Moishe.

"I noticed that too," added Yarko. "All through the meeting you had the look of someone who is saying just a little less than he knows."

"Naw, it's just my life in Yenakievo. You know. The usual mining town blues."

Sensing that Serhiy did not want to be pressed further, Yarko turned to Moishe. "Speaking of secrets, you seem a little distracted too, Freddy. It's not another secret Mossad mission, is it?"

"No. As I told you before, if you can see me or hear me, I can't possibly be Mossad."

There were a lot of broad smiles around the table.

"Okay, okay, you guys win: I'm on a secret mission," admitted Moishe. "Of sorts."

"Oi!" said Yarko. "Should I bring out the Kevlar vests now, or can it wait?"

"You sure you're not Jewish, Yarko? You sound just like my mother."

Yarko drained his Chartreuse Vert. "Oww! A little below the belt, Freddy."

"No. You remember how I told you that my grandparents came from Lviv? They emigrated just before the war. Well, I figured that since I don't fly back to Tel Aviv until Monday, I may as well see if I can find the old place. It's in a suburb called Zamarstyniv."

"It begins again!" exclaimed Ksenia. "And if your grandparents buried something in the basement of the old place before leaving town, you get to pick up the cheque."

Moishe pretended not to hear Ksenia. Being the driver of the group he had stuck with Coca Cola all afternoon. He now knocked back the remains in his glass as he stared across the room at the leggy waitress. She lowered her gaze and blushed demurely.

"Cheque please," he said.

On Friday, March 11, Vlodko phoned Fedora in Kyiv. He gave the order to detonate the booby-trap explosives in the tunnel.

"Code word: Flaming Vengeance," he said into the phone.

Glossary

Batiar. Hoodlum.

Borispil. The town where the Kyiv civilian airport is located, on the left (eastern) bank of the Dnipro River.

Butterbrod. Sandwich, in Russian and the eastern vernacular. Called a Kanapka in the west.

Cherty I Rezy. Literally "Strokes and Notches," the earliest (pre-Christian) Slavic alphabet characterized by rectilinear letters, some of which survive to this day in the so-called Cyrillic alphabet.

Dazhboh. The Sun God, the greatest of the gods.

Desyatynna Church. The Church of the Tithes, built by Volodymyr the Great financed by donations of one-tenth of the income of the faithful. Historically the site of the last stand of Kyiv's defenders, after the Dytynets was breached at the Sofiyski Gates.

Donetsk/Donbas. Donetsk, formerly Yuzivka, is the capital of the Donbas coal-mining region in Eastern Ukraine. Located in the areas ethnically cleansed during the Holodomor Famine-Genocide of 1932–33 and repopulated by Russian migrant workers, it is now largely Russian-speaking. Today the people who live there feel loyalty to local bosses or leaders rather than to any nation-state.

Dytynets. Citadel, literally the "Children's Place," the fortification within a fortification providing the last defensive line. In the city of Kyiv after its expansion by Yaroslaw, the inner fortification was the older "City of Volodymyr." Kyiv's Jewish quarter, the Desyatynna Church, and all the oldest structures were within the Dytynets.

Dzhura. Page, a servant of a knight or warrior.

Gachi. Slang for men's underpants.

Halychany. Residents of Halychyna, the province of Western Ukraine. This territory is also known as Galicia in Polish or German.

Heroyam Slava. Hail the Heroes, the reply to the greeting "Slava Ukrayini."

Holodomor. The term, meaning extermination by starvation, refers to the Famine-Genocide of 1932–1933 that killed 7 million Ukrainians in 16 months. This ended a period of Ukrainian national awakening in the Ukrainian SSR and consolidated Russian rule. The death rate is equivalent to five 9/11 terrorist attacks daily for all 16 months.

Horilka. Ukrainian for Vodka, literally "firewater."

Hryvnia. Unit of currency in Ukraine. In 2004 it traded at about 5.4 UAH to the U.S. dollar.

Idu na Vy. Literally "I go on You." This was a challenge and warning to enemies by Prince Svyatoslav at the start of a campaign.

Ihumen. The head of a monastery (from the Greek *hegumen*).

Iskorosten'. The 10th-century fort of the Derevliany tribe that was razed by Princess Olga in revenge for the killing of her husband. Today it is the town of Korosten' some 80 kilometres west of Chornobyl'.

Ivan Franko. Ivan Franko (1856–1916) was a poet, writer, social and literary critic, journalist, economist, and political activist. He was a political radical, and a founder of the socialist movement in western Ukraine. In addition to his own literary work, he also translated the works of William Shakespeare, Lord Byron, Pedro Calderón de la Barca, Dante, Victor Hugo, Adam Mickiewicz, Goethe, and Schiller into Ukrainian.

Kalyna. Viburnum, also known as the high bush cranberry. A flowering shrub that produces clusters of red berries, it is unofficially the national plant of Ukraine.

KGB-sty. KaGeBeesty is the vernacular for members of the Soviet KGB state police. Also referred to as GeBeesty or collectively as Gebnia. Singular form is KGB-ist.

Kobzar. Minstrel. The title of Taras Shevchenko's collection of poetry.

Kopiyka. The smallest unit of Ukrainian currency, equivalent to the penny. Worth less than a fifth of an American cent at the time.

Kozaks. These were frontiersmen/warriors of the steppe (prairie) that lived in the no-mans land beyond the Dnipro rapids. They were independent freemen, composed of escaped serfs, disgruntled noblemen, even foreigners from distant lands, who served as a bulwark against Ottoman Empire slave-trade raids. In many ways, they were to the empty steppes what Pirates were to the Caribbean. The spelling Cossack (from Circassian) usually refers to the Russian Imperial shock troops of the later 19th and 20th centuries.

Lviviak. Slang for a resident of Lviv. Properly it's Lvivian.

Lyadski Vorota. The Lyadski gate. Understood to mean the boardwalk gate, as the entry road went through a swamp. This was the location of the Mongols breach of Kyiv's defences. The defensive factor of the swamp and moat was negated by the unusually cold early winter of 1240.

Marshrootka. Small city bus, usually privately operated. From the French *marche-route*.

Muscovy. The historical name for today's Russia. Only after the conquest of Ukrainian (Rus') lands in the 18th century did the name Rossia (Greek for Rus') come into use. Western cartographers continued to label this northern state Muscovy, or even Tartary (recognizing that it represented a regime-change of Ghengis Khan's Empire more so than a different state). They applied the latinized designation Russia to the lands of Rus' proper—today's Ukraine. The usage change renaming Muscovy as Russia came gradually in the 19th century, creating confusion and a discontinuity in customary practice. Ukrainians continued to use the term Muscovy (Moskovshchyna) in reference to their northern neighbour well into the 20th century.

OMON. Russian initials for Special Purpose Police Squad. Since 1979 the USSR had such units in every city or territory. They were often called upon for riot control.

One and Indivisible. A term for the Russian Empire, as in "The One and Indivisible Russia."

Oseledets. A scalp lock on an otherwise shaved head. The popular coiffure of Ukrainian kozaks, its use dates back to the mid-10th century per Greek descriptions of Prince Svyatoslav.

Otrok. An young apprentice of the warrior's art.

OUN(b)/UPA. The Organization of Ukrainian Nationalists (Bandera wing)/Ukrainian Insurgent Army is the political organization and the military formation that fought for Ukrainian independence prior to, during and after the Second World War. At various times it fought against forces of Poland, Hungary, Germany, Russia, Communist Poland, and Communist Czechoslovakia. CIA and MI6 attempts to assist the UPA were sabotaged by the Soviet mole Kim Philby who, ironically, was directly involved in these operations.

Pan. Lord. Modern usage is equivalent to mister. *Pane* is the vocative case used when addressing a person. Panstvo refers to a group of Lords (or Mr. and Mrs.).

Perun. The Thunder God. Equivalent to Thor of Norse mythology.

PORA. A civic youth organization in Ukraine espousing non-violent resistance and advocating increased national democracy, in opposition to the authoritarian governing style of Ukraine's then-president Leonid Kuchma. Espousing the non-violent methodology advocated in the Albert Einstein Institute's "From Dictatorship to Democracy," they marshalled the protests of a nation and the demonstrations by hundreds of thousands. The organization had no formal leadership structure. It was united by an idea, not a hierarchy.

Porok. Trebuchet, a large mobile catapult capable of launching boulders at fortifications.

Pysaniy Kamin. Pysaniy is an adjective meaning "written," or "drawn" (as in a pysanka Easter egg). Kamin is a rock. There is a pysanyj kamin in one of the mountain passes of the Carpathian Mountains. It is a rock face with petroglyphs.

Ratush. Also known as Ratusha, the historic name for Lviv's city hall and tower. From the German word rathaus and Polish ratusz.

Rukh. Rukh meaning "movement," or Natsional'ny Rukh, meaning National Movement was the name of the political party formed in 1989 during Gorbachev's "glasnost'" period. Its aim was the political revival of the Ukrainian nation. They took 25 per cent of the seats in parliament in 1990, then steered the Communist majority into declaring Independence in 1991. They remained a potent political force in Ukraine until 1999, although they were never in power. The head of its secretariat at the time, Mykhaylo Boychyshyn, disappeared January

15, 1994. In 1999, at a time that a split in the party threatened to reduce its significance, there was a move to reunify these Ukrainian patriotic forces around the
presidential candidacy of Vyacheslav Chornovil. Chornovil died on the night of
April 22, 1999, when the Toyota he was riding in crashed into a Kamaz tractor-
trailer that was blocking all lanes while allegedly making a U-turn on the main
road from Kyiv to Borispil.

Rus'. Rus' (commonly Latinized as Ruthenia) refers to both the local princedom around Kyiv (roughly within a 200-kilometre radius), and the vast political state ruled from Kyiv from the 10th to the 13th century. Later, the south
and western territories of historical Rus' became incorporated into the Grand
Duchy of Lithuania, Rus' and Samogitia. The Grand Duchy was dominated by
Rus', as it was populated mainly by Rus', its nobles were of Rus' origin, and
Ruthenian is the sole language of most surviving official documents prior to
1697. The territories in The Grand Duchy of Lithuania were named: Belorussia
(White Ruthenia or Belarus); Chernaya Rus' (Black Ruthenia), in the northwest
part of modern Belarus; and Chervonaya Rus' (Red Ruthenia—Halychyna and
today's Right Bank Ukraine). The naming followed the practice predominant in
Eurasia of assigning colours to directions: Black for North, White for West, Red
for South, and Blue for East. Poland called this area the "Ruthenian Voivodship."
The residents of these lands called themselves Rusyny, Ruthenians.

Rynok. Literally "market," it was the name of the cobblestone street square that
surrounded Lviv's Ratush city hall.

SBU. Literally the Ukrainian Security Service, this is the Ukrainian State Police
formed from the Ukrainian KGB of Soviet times.

Servus. An idiomatic Western Ukrainian greeting, from the Latin *servus* meaning servant. It is used in the sense of "your humble servant."

Shimano. Brand name of modern derailleur-type bicycle gear-shifting mecha-
nisms and other components.

Shlyak by trafyv. May one have a stroke, a western Ukrainian epithet. Also
Shlyak tebe travyw, may you have a stroke. From the German Schlag getroffen.

Slava Ukrayini. Glory to Ukraine, a greeting popularized by the OUN. The required reply being Heroyam Slava, or Hail the Heroes.

Slovo o Polku Ihorya. The Tale of Ihor's Campaign, an epic poem written in the 12th century about a campaign that ended in defeat.

Sotnyk. Centurion, an officer leading a hundred or more men (but less than a thousand).

Steppes. The treeless plains of Ukraine that continue eastward through southern Russia and Kazakhstan.

Sturmey-Archer. Brand name of the 3-speed in-hub bicycle gearset that was replaced by the modern derailleur design.

Suka. Bitch.

Sybir. Siberia in both Ukrainian and Russian, although the pronounciation is a little different.

Temnyk. A Theme Guide, government instructions to the media as to the spin and emphasis to place on news events. It was during the 2004 elections that the media revolted against this practice. In mediaeval times a temnyk was a military leader of ten thousand or more men, a "tma," equivalent to a division.

Topir. Battle Axe.

Tysiac'kiy. An officer leading a thousand or more men.

Ukrainian Autocephalous Orthodox Church. In 1921 a Synod in Kyiv created the Ukrainian Autocephalous Orthodox Church (UAOC). The UAOC was at that point independent of all other churches. It obtained its autocephalous status a few years later, in 1924, when the Patriarch of Constantinople, Gregory VII, issued a tomos re-establishing the Kievan Rus'-Ukrainian Metropolitan diocese as an Autocephalous Church. The UAOC in Ukraine was liquidated by the Soviets with the assistance of the Patriarchate of Moscow. Any UAOC hierarchs or clergy who remained in Ukraine and refused to join the Russian Church were executed or sent to concentration camps.

Ukrainian Greek-Catholic Church. The church formed in the late 16th century when part of the existing Orthodox Churches in Ukraine accepted the leadership of the Roman Pope. Also referred to as Byzantine-rite, these churches retained all the Orthodox traditions, including a married priesthood. This church was persecuted and banned in the USSR.

Ukrainian Orthodox Church—Kyiv Patriarchy. Formed in August 1989, when the parish of the Church of Sts. Peter and Paul in Lviv announced its breach with the Russian Orthodox Church under the Patriarch of Moscow. In June 1990, Metropolitan Mstyslav was elected as the church's head under the title of the Patriarch of Kiev and All Rus'—Ukraine. Patriarch Mstyslav was the last surviving hierarch of the founders of Ukrainian Autocephalous Orthodox Church. He was enthroned in November at St. Sophia Cathedral. Patriarch Mstyslav (Skrypnyk) died in June 1993 and was succeeded in October by Patriarch Volodymyr (Romaniuk). Patriarch Volodymyr (Romaniuk) died in July 1995. His funeral near St. Sophia Cathedral in Kyiv was marked by a clash between the funeral procession and law enforcement forces. The current head of the Church, Patriarch Filaret (Mykhaylo Denysenko), was enthroned in October 1995.

Ukrainian Orthodox Church—Moscow Patriarchy. The UOC-MP has the allegiance of religious communities mostly in the central, eastern, and southern regions of Ukraine. The UOC-MP officially views other Orthodox churches of Ukraine to be canonically invalid "schismatic nationalist organizations." Its puppet status was reaffirmed during the Orange Revolution when it blatantly backed the pro-Russian candidate, Yanukovich, contrary to all principles of separation of church and state.

Voyevoda. A military leader, of almost any rank.

Zakryta Zona. Literally "Closed Zone," an investigative journalism TV program on Channel 5 hosted by Vladimir Aryev. It provided in-depth coverage of major crimes and the shenanigans of the presidential elections, including secret service telephone recordings.

Zdorov. Literally "healthy," in the sense of be healthy; a common greeting.

Zdrastvuy. Russian for Good-bye. Literally "stay healthy."

Zoloti Vorota. The Golden Gate, the main gate into Kyiv at its southwest sector.

Credits

A NUMBER OF PEOPLE have contributed to the creation of this book. I express my genuine gratitude to:

My wife, Luba, for first suggesting that I channel my feeling of frustrated obligation into writing, and then for putting up with the late hours and the mood swings that seem to be an integral part it.

My son Adrian, for lending his talents as an actor and student of literature to the thankless task of critic and advisor. He is the only one who, after reading a fresh sixteen-page chapter, could convince me to leave eight pages on the floor.

George Foty, Associate Professor of Slavic Studies, University of Saskatchewan, for encouraging me with the words, "this needs to be published," not once, but twice; and then serving as an energetic pre-editor with results that allowed the manuscript to pass muster before the actual publisher.

Grant MacEwen College Foundation for the Anna Pidruchney Award for New Writers 2002, recognizing the fruit of my Ukrainian-language effort enough for me to seriously consider pursuing publication in Ukraine.

Vasyl Vanchura of Dzhura Publishing in Ternopil, Ukraine, for being the one to allow me to make the jump from writer to author. In his opinion I had also jumped from author to harbinger of revolution. I had described in that book events that actually transpired a year after its publication.

Professor Mykola Riabchuk, for appraising my early product a tad higher than deserved; but most importantly for sharing his home with me during the adventure that was my election observer mission to Ukraine. I thank his son and daughter for letting me be witness to the unchained energy of young revolutionaries.

Paulette MacQuarrie and all those others who encouraged me to write this novel in English, at a time when I stubbornly refused to even start.

Dominic Farrell, my editor with Blue Butterfly Books, who managed to navigate between the twin reefs of writer's ego and foreign subject matter, forcing some sense of readability and story structure onto the raw product. My wife insists, as a result of his editorial sensitivity to the sequencing of love scenes, that I take lessons in romance from Dominic.

Gary Long, in charge of layout and design of *Yaroslaw's Treasure* at Blue Butterfly Books, for showing that the art and craft of book-making still endures as the high calling of skilled perfectionists.

Dr. J. Patrick Boyer, Q.C., president of Blue Butterfly Books, for seeing what this novel could be, at a time when it was yet to be. Patrick gave me much more than encouragement, he gave me back the pride that one swiftly loses when peddling one's work past gatekeepers of conformity. But most of all I thank Patrick for the investment of his time and resources in publishing this book.

President Victor Yushchenko of Ukraine for suffering all that he did in championing the Orange Revolution; for wearing the scars of poisoning on his face, but not on his soul; for championing democratic rule of law to people accustomed to neither law nor democracy, and for being the true public face of his post-genocidal nation.

Myroslav Petriw

BORN JUNE 5, 1950, in Munich to post-war immigrant refugees, Myroslav Petriw came to Canada from Germany with his parents the following year and grew up in Toronto a Canadian citizen. Known to acquaintances as "Myron," he became a product of Toronto's vibrant ethnic community and, attending Saturday school, emerged fluent in Ukrainian.

Graduating from University of Toronto in mechanical engineering, he began his career with Ford of Canada. Cars were more than his livelihood, however. As a young man Myron's instinct for sports found him racing formula cars at Mount Tremblant-St. Jovite in Quebec and at Watkins Glen, New York. After moving to British Columbia, he added sailing to his sports repertoire. He is also an avid mountain biker, cross-country skier, and kayaker.

Myron and his wife, Luba, have raised three sons, the eldest of whom he coached to the Canadian autoslalom class championship in 2005. Today they are grandparents.

In 2004 Myron volunteered as an election observer from Canada's Ukrainian community for the October 31 first-round of presidential elections in Ukraine, serving as one of four observers in the city of Kharkiv in the "russified" eastern part of the country. When he chose to monitor voting in the poverty-stricken Moskovsky Raion, he could observe first-hand what James Mace called "a post-genocidal society." At the time, he recalls, people feared that staged incidents could cause the election to be declared invalid, leaving the incumbent president in power. Patrolling this territory, he identified breaches of the election law but drew them to the attention of the authorities, resulting in them being promptly corrected.

Following this first election, Petriw visited Ternopil and Lviv, as well as the capital city of Kyiv, talking there with Ukraine's youth and a number of the intellectuals of the democracy movement. Doing so, he was able to gauge the build-up of energy, months before it exploded into the Orange Revolution.

With that experience, and after taking early retirement, he applied his efforts to complete the object of his passions, this novel *Yaroslaw's Treasure*.

At a December 6, 2008, "National Leaders" ceremony in Edmonton, Myron Petriw was awarded the Taras Shevchenko Medal by Canadian Ukrainian Congress for his "outstanding leadership in community development." It is the highest honour that can be paid to a citizen by Canada's Ukrainian community, having previously been awarded to prime ministers John Diefenbaker and Brian Mulroney for their leadership in Canadian-Ukrainian relations.

Interview with the Author

 When did you begin writing for publication?

MYROSLAV PETRIW: This is a question with two separate answers. I started writing the Ukrainian novel *Skarb Yaroslava* in 1995. That novel was completed in 2001 and published in Ukraine in 2003. I began writing this English-language book, *Yaroslaw's Treasure*, in late 2006.

 Both are historically rooted works. How did your interest in Ukrainian history first develop?

PETRIW: I was exposed to stories from Ukrainian history from early childhood. As a child of the post-war emigration, I found that the most basic existential questions had their answers in history. The very fact that I lived in Canada and not Ukraine had its roots in history. I thoroughly enjoyed the study of history during the Saturday high-school-level Ukrainian courses I took for four years. It was at that time that my initial interest became a real passion.

 The plot for Yaroslaw's Treasure *is unusually intriguing. What caused you to connect earlier Ukrainian history with the recent turbulent events of the Orange Revolution?*

PETRIW: Again I need to return to my Ukrainian novel, which was written and published well before the Orange Revolution. I knew it was a story that needed to be retold in English, but in the meantime the Orange Revolution had changed history, making the original story obsolete. So then I began studying how I could weave the original story of secret archeological digs into the actual events of the Orange Revolution.

 What did your studies tell you about that?

PETRIW: Very little if anything had been published in English that dealt with the Orange Revolution. I discovered a vacuum just begging to be filled.

 So this is not revisionist history, but revision of a novel to incorporate history.

PETRIW: Yes, I found that I could take many of the mysteries and loose ends of the Orange Revolution and tie them directly to the story of the search for Prince Yaroslaw's fabulous Library. Serendipitously, the result works on many levels. By neatly tying up these loose ends the fiction becomes very believable. The fact that General Yuriy Kravchenko and Mad Max Kurochkin were both bidding on the same Dnipro Hotel and were both killed under unresolved circumstances lends credence to much of the fictional story. The fact that

Independence Square (Maidan Nezalezhnosti), the epicentre of the Orange Revolution, stands on the same bit of real estate as the Lyadski Gates through which the Mongols broke Kyiv's defences in 1240 A.D., ties those two political events metaphysically, raising the tale of the loss and rediscovery of the Library to an even higher plane. A post-genocidal nation's search for self must naturally include a search for its history, thus the quest for the Lost Library becomes an allegory for the Orange Revolution.

 So Yarloslaw's Treasure *is substantially different from your earlier Ukrainian novel, plus it was written in English, right?*

PETRIW: Correct on both counts. It is surprising how history rewrites itself, never mind a book.

On that score, you convey a great deal of fascinating information about early Ukrainian history in Yaroslaw's Treasure, *not to mention all of the rich detail about events during the Orange Revolution. How did you manage to keep the political and historical information from getting in the way of the story?*

PETRIW: The story came first. But being a story about history, setting it against the background of current history was only natural. What is more, the events in Ukraine prove that fact is often stranger than fiction. I am convinced that very few readers could categorize all the events depicted in this novel correctly as fact or fantasy.

Did you cut out a lot that you might have liked to include?

PETRIW: I did not. I had the good fortune to work with a Blue Butterfly editor who allowed me the freedom to express what needed to be said, while holding me to the discipline of brevity. A large pile of adverbs bit the dust, but none of the story.

What is your greatest satisfaction as a writer?

PETRIW: I think a writer has to satisfy himself before he can hope to satisfy others. The fact that even after having proofread the story a hundred times, I still catch myself engrossed in it provides great satisfaction. But I think the greatest satisfaction is yet to come. It will happen when someone who is completely unfamiliar with Eastern Europe, finds himself or herself reading the story just for the pleasure of reading a tale well told.

Yaroslaw's Treasure is a work of historical fiction, but readers will no doubt recognize some places, events, and personalities.

PETRIW: Yes, places are real, the history is accurate, and the Orange Revolution took place. Public figures, some still living, are portrayed in both real and fictitious circumstances, while others are merely referred to in statements by the fictional characters who populate the story.

When it comes to works of fiction, which *Yaroslaw's Treasure* definitely is, readers understand that the story is larger than its facts. It is about the human condition. Whether reading books or watching movies, people are very sophisticated about understanding this, and in recognizing the blurred line between fact and fiction.

So the types of disclaimers printed in novels and shown at the end of movies, "No resemblance to anyone living or dead, etcetera," are not necessary?

PETRIW: Does anyone take them seriously? In fact, for this to be historical fiction and not just plain fiction, such resemblance is absolutely necessary. I like Blue Butterfly's approach "Think Free … Be Free!"

The "factual" parts, then, are intermingled with your creative writing?

PETRIW: Exactly. Documentable deeds need to be present in an historical novel, to establish both a realistic setting and believability for the story. That's what separates historical fiction from fiction of other types.

How did you achieve this in Yaroslaw's Treasure?

PETRIW: Many instances in this novel include direct translations of actual statements and news reports of the period. Others are purely my fictitious inventions. It's the blending of both that maintains the sense of realism required in historical fiction.

Of course, given the era in which the story is set, statements by public figures and reports by the controlled news media are themselves likely to contain distortions and fictions. As stated early on in this novel, it's "Alice in Wonderland"—all is not as it seems.

Does the same apply to the characterization of public figures in your book?

PETRIW: Certain episodes and personalities in *Yaroslaw's Treasure* will be instantly recognizable to anyone who follows current events in Ukraine, because the story reflects what has been reported in news reports, documentaries, and exposés at the time. Oddly enough though, compared to some accusations made in the media about some of these characters, I may have inadvertently cleaned up somewhat one or two very tarnished reputations!

Is that an issue for a writer, whether inadvertent or intentional, altering a reader's perception of a real person?

PETRIW: The big challenge for any writer is ultimately to pin such insects, be they wasps or butterflies, to a board and label them. However, these public figures are much more complex as individuals than news reports, editorials, tape recordings, and television sound bites ever reflect. In this novel, I've tried to bring that across. Even choosing on which end of the good-guy/bad-guy spectrum to pin a living individual can become problematic, as it must be interwoven into the higher purpose of telling a good tale.

Initial reaction to Yaroslaw's Treasure *has been extremely positive because of the way you engage readers. Is this what you expected?*

PETRIW: It is what I had hoped. It is what I was attempting to do in crafting this story. But it would be very presumptuous of me to say that this is what I expected.

Readers connect with this story. Can you shed light on what is happening?

PETRIW: The protagonist, Yarko, represents the average reader. He begins outside the story, even outside the country where the story takes place. He is sucked into the whirlwind of history quite involuntarily. Often it is the situation that dictates his actions. He is rarely fully in control of the events around him, yet he is never just a mere bystander. Similarly I had hoped that the reader would get carried away by the current of the story, coming out of it unscathed, but in a different place.

Your novel makes clear that, for a very long time, the relationship between Ukraine and Russia has not been a happy one. While most outsiders might be aware of this in a general way, Yaroslaw's Treasure *portrays some of the more horrid details. Do you foresee a time when the relationship between Ukraine and Russia will improve?*

PETRIW: I will not even attempt to foresee the future. What I can say unequivocally is that the relationship between Ukraine and Russia-the-empire will always be problematic. On the other hand, the relationship between Ukraine and Muscovy-the-nation-state could be quite neighbourly. I think that exactly the same thing can be said about Russia's relationship with many other neighbours, ranging from Georgia to Estonia, Latvia, Lithuania, and even Poland.

In fact today's Polish-Ukrainian relationship is proof of what I'm saying. The historic relationship between Ukrainians and Poland-the-empire had been one of hostility and mutual "ethnic engineering," while today's relationship between the two nation-states is the very epitome of neighbourliness and friendship.

Is there any hope, do you believe, for Ukrainian-Russian relations to normalize?

PETRIW: The pre-conditions for this normalization were given in my previous answer. Now your question becomes whether there can be a Muscovite identity that does not rely on conquest and expansion for its source of self-respect. Regrettably, today all those who could give voice to such a self-identity are being killed. What is more, the worship of past brutes of imperialism is being revived. The short-term answer to your question is negative.

If someone asked you about your single most important message in this book, what would you answer?

PETRIW: I never visualized this book as something that carried a single message. I saw it more as a cleverly crafted menu, something to tease a reader's taste buds. For some it would waken a taste for Ukraine's history, for others an interest in its archaeology, for still others it could pique a taste for the language. For many it should create a new awareness of the existence of a Ukrainian political entity on the European continent. For those who find their roots in the Ukrainian nation, I hope to reawaken their sense of pride.

 Do you envisage Yaroslaw's Treasure *as a feature film?*

PETRIW: Yes. The film has been playing in my head for a dozen years. I would love to see it transferred to the silver screen.

What's in a name? Graphemes and Phonemes

Debate Erupts over "v" versus "w"

BEHIND EVERY BOOK lurks a special story or two. Blue Butterfly likes to share these with readers interested in back-story issues. Whereas *translation* is the art of finding the right words and phrases to accurately yet creatively convey in a different language an author's meaning and moods, *transliteration* involves the construction, or spelling, of foreign words themselves.

One reader of the manuscript, political and cultural activist Myroslava Oleksiuk, who publishes the world's largest bilingual (English and Ukrainian) Internet newsletter, *ePOSHTA*, took exception to the original spelling of many Ukrainian words in the book.

This resulted in a spirited debate over "v" versus "w". The author had originally transliterated Ukrainian words phonetically, noting that the Ukrainian letter "B" is pronounced as either a "v" or a "w" depending on where it stands in a word. Ms. Oleksiuk pointed out that formal transliteration tables show that the Ukrainian "B" is to be transliterated always as a "v", even when it is pronounced as "w". The author's own name as spelled in English reflects this very conflict. "Myróslav" is formally correct but phonetically deficient, while "Petriw" is phonetically correct but contravenes transliteration rules.

A compromise was reached in that the transliteration rules are followed throughout except for the titular character's name. Yaroslaw is the English spelling, as well as the correct Ukrainian pronounciation, of the name of a Canadian on whom the story character is based.

Readers interested in more of the details of this linguistic debate can go to the *Yaroslaw's Treasure* pages at the Blue Butterfly Books website—bluebutterflybooks.ca.

About this Book

ON A VISIT TO UKRAINE to retrieve a family heirloom secretly buried by his grandfather during the Second World War, Yaroslaw, a Ukrainian-Canadian university student, stumbles into a world full of spies and secret organizations, peril and political intrigue.

His discovery of the hidden cache yields clues to the location of a fabled lost treasure—the greatest in all Europe. Working against time, Yaroslaw and a small band of accomplices struggle to uncover and save a nation's heritage, operating in secret to prevent the corrupt leaders of the government—and the Russians—from stealing it.

Yaroslaw's Treasure is a thrilling suspense story set against the gripping drama of the Orange Revolution, the 2004 popular uprising that saw hundreds of thousands of people take to the streets in Ukraine to overthrow a corrupt government and reinforce democracy in a land long occupied by repressive and foreign regimes.

Rich with history, romance, politics, and danger, *Yaroslaw's Treasure* superbly captures the wonders and horrors of Ukraine's past, swirls through the treacherous currents of its present politics, all the while providing entertainment as a first-rate thriller.